RESTING

WITCH

FACE

RESTING

WITCH

FACE

JULIETTE CROSS

UNION
SQUARE
& CO.

NEW YORK

UNION
SQUARE
& CO.

NEW YORK

Edited by Corinne DeMaagd and Krysten Kruse
Cover design by Jenny Zemanek
Cover images by Shutterstock.com: Dancake (cauldron); Incomible (mask); javarman (ombre); kosmofish (fangs); Kate Macate (ribbon); Mid0ri (mystic symbols, stars); Nimaxs (flourishes); Panuwach (crown)

For my husband,
who continually shows me in all the little things
and in so many ways what true love is.

Content Warning

Please note that there are instances of torture and blood/gore in this book.

PROLOGUE

Twelve Years Earlier . . .

~JULES~

"Give me what I want." The dark command seeped into my skin from Ruben's questing lips.

A gasp tore from my throat when he shifted me higher up the wall and stroked inside at a deeper angle. Like last time, he wasn't pounding me into oblivion with ruthless thrusts, but stroking me tortuously slow, like a vampire who knew how to wreak havoc on a woman's body and psyche with hypnotizing, drugging pleasure.

Heaven help me. We'd crossed the line to lovers on Tuesday. I could hardly imagine my mental state after weeks, months . . . years of falling deeper under his spell. I wasn't the witch here; he was. He didn't know how far I'd fallen because I refused to tell him. I was out-of-my-mind obsessed, and the realization was both immensely wonderful and intensely terrifying.

This was so dangerous, but when I was in his arms, I couldn't even force myself to care.

Gripping his bare shoulders, I tipped my head back against the wall, arched my neck for him as semi-sane moans poured up my throat and echoed off his high-ceilinged living room. Though I was in the perfect submissive pose, completely naked, offering my throat to a vampire while he fucked me sweetly against the wall, he wouldn't bite me. I'd forbidden him to do it.

Still . . . that less-than-lucid part of me wished he would, wished he'd take the choice away and give me his ultimate pleasure.

Since when did I yearn to be violated in such a way? The fleeting desire nearly jerked me from my current state of ecstasy. But then he dipped his head lower and stroked a fang across my taut nipple, ripping a cry from me as my climax raced closer.

"Give it to me, Juliana," he grated against my breast before sucking the tip to a painful sting. "You know I need it," he whispered up my throat. "Need to feel your sweet, sweet cunt clamping around my cock, choking me like you can't live without it."

"Oh God! I'm coming, I'm coming!" I curled my nails into the flexed muscle of his shoulders, my heels digging into the backs of his bare thighs.

His hand at my throat scooped around and fisted in my short hair, jerking my head down to look at him as he crushed me against the wall, still thrusting with all the feral carnality and rolling sensuality of a true, centuries-old vampire.

"Let me see those eyes," he murmured against my mouth, his own shining pure silver in the semi-dark. A frenzied predator

2

intent on his prey, his powerful magic electrified the air. "Yes, my darling," he rumbled deep and beastly. "Squeeze me tight, just like that." His liquid silver eyes slid closed. "Like I'm meant to come for you alone, come inside you alone."

I leaned forward, his fist tightening in my hair, but he let my mouth inch closer till I could whisper against his jaw, "Like you're mine." Then I nipped him with blunt teeth.

He grunted, then pounded me fiercely—*finally*—four times before pinning me to the wall and groaning out his orgasm, his hand at my thigh squeezing painfully. I'd smile later at the bruises. His climax sparked a second fluttering of my own.

I whimpered as I went limp in his arms, my forehead falling to the crook of his neck and shoulder. He didn't move for nearly a minute, panting and holding me close. Then he wrapped both arms around my back, still buried deep, and carried me to his camel-colored sectional sofa. Laying on top of me, he cupped my cheeks, fingers edging into my hair, holding my gaze with that intense expression that made me nervous and giddy at the same time.

No one had ever looked at me the way Ruben Dubois did. He saw past my solemn mask and cool exterior to the warmest, brightest heart of me. When he looked at me like this, I was left feeling raw and vulnerable and lost. I think he knew it, which was why he also seemed to know when to lighten the mood.

"I hadn't intended to seduce you and fuck you against my wall when I asked you over for dinner."

I laughed, combing a disheveled lock back off his forehead, loving that his usually perfect hair looked sex-mussed because of me. "Yes, you did."

His smile widened, canines sharp, as he watched my mouth, seemingly mesmerized by that part of my face at the moment. "All right. Perhaps I did. But I'd planned on feeding you first."

"I'm not sure you can reach the kitchen from this position." I wiggled my hips, reminding him that he was still planted inside me.

His still-silver eyes finally flickered up to mine. He skimmed his lips across my mouth, then moaned into a deeper kiss. When I trailed the back of my heel up his bare calf to his thigh, he groaned, then lifted off me and to his feet. I gasped at him leaving my body so suddenly.

"Give a girl some warning." I laughed.

His gaze smoldered as he stared down at me, goose bumps had risen on my skin from the cool air. He unfolded a soft-knit blanket from the end of the sofa and draped it over me. Then he tucked me in like a burrito and leaned over to give me a quick kiss on the lips.

"Don't move."

"If I don't, I might make a mess on your sofa."

He rolled his eyes. "I'll buy another one."

He slipped on his boxers from where they'd been tossed in his hurried attempt to get naked and inside me and then headed to the kitchen. I popped up with the blanket around me and walked to the bathroom. I wasn't going to ruin his rather expensive sofa.

After taking care of business and cleaning up, I stared at myself in the mirror, nude except for the blanket draped over my shoulders like a shawl.

I barely recognized myself. Pale skin flushed and marked from Ruben's rough kisses, gray eyes glistening with dark sensuality that rarely sparked there, expression softened from being well-used and deeply pleasured. The sight of me was again that paradox of something wonderful and frightening.

I shivered as I remembered what had gotten me from standing in a fury on his doorstep to being naked and fucked mercilessly minutes later.

Sighing, I washed my hands and pulled the blanket around my shoulders. When I opened the door, Ruben stood there, still in only his boxers and holding a glass of red wine. Fully dressed, the man was heartbreakingly beautiful. Without his clothes, he was devastating. Too fine and perfect.

"Thank you." I took the glass as he watched me.

"You don't believe me."

He knew exactly where my thoughts had gone and what had put the somber expression back on my face.

"I do believe you, Ruben."

Ever watchful and examining, he didn't move to pull me into his arms and comfort me. But he did take my hand. "Come. Let's talk." Then he led me to the kitchen.

I took a seat at his marble island that was bigger than our dining table at the Savoie home and held my blanket closed with one hand, sipping wine with the other.

"You don't have to cook for me to impress me," I told him lightly.

He tossed a charming smile over his shoulder, his fangs gone now, then went back to chopping peppers. "I want you to know I'm fully capable in the kitchen and I'm not dating you for your culinary skills." He tossed the peppers and onions in a pan with butter. "Back to Beverly."

The mere mention of her name had my gut tightening with nausea. I was insanely jealous of a woman who he'd never even slept with.

"Why did you think I was sleeping with her?"

I had no reason to be embarrassed except for my assumptions, but still a flush of heat crawled up my neck.

"I went by the Nightjar looking for you today." The Nightjar was the new vampire den he'd just recently opened behind his rare bookstore. "Gabriel said you were in your office and to go on back. But as I approached your door, Beverly stepped out, and she was . . ." I paused, feeling sick at the thought of it. "Buttoning up her blouse. And she looked . . . guilty of something."

Ruben didn't sigh or throw a fit of temper. It wasn't his style. Still, there was an elevated charge in the air, his magic percolating with anger when he moved the skillet off the stove and turned to me. He leaned on the island on his forearms so his face was level with mine.

"Beverly is threatened by you."

"But you said y'all were never an item."

"We weren't," he said emphatically. "If you don't believe me, you can get your sister Clara over here and she can do her lie-detector thing. I know Auras are the best at detecting truth from lies."

I shook my head. "That's not necessary. But why would she see me as a threat?"

He blinked heavily before going on. "I knew her when I lived in New York. She hung at the vampire den I frequented, and one night"—he paused, brow pinching with what might have been regret—"I did drink from her."

My own blood ran cold at the thought of Ruben's mouth on Beverly's slender, beautiful throat. But then again, he had to drink from someone. Vampires often drank secondhand for convenience but asking him to never drink directly from the vein again was like condemning him to a life of cold, bland soup. I couldn't be that selfish. Still . . .

He detected my change in demeanor at once because he slid his hands closer to take the one I had on the counter beside my wineglass. I wanted to be petty and jerk my hand free, but I kept still.

"There was no sexual exchange, but I knew afterward it was a mistake. A terrible one."

He frowned guiltily. He didn't even have to say it, so I did for him.

"Your toxin seduced her."

Vampires release a toxin when they bite to numb the sting but also to give the host pleasure. It's one of the reasons many humans, and apparently other vampires, offer themselves as blood-hosts. It's said that the older the vampire, the more potent and addicting his or her bite. I could only imagine what Ruben's felt like since he was over three hundred years old.

"Worse, I'm afraid." He clenched his jaw. "She became fang-spelled."

I flinched. Becoming fang-spelled, developing what is also called fang mania—formally known as vampire toxin psychosis— was a disorder that occurred when a vampire fed from another magical being and the blood-host became sick with a kind of lust hysteria for the vampire. The victim would forgo food and sleep and become a danger to their vampire host, wanting only one thing. The bite and the toxin at any cost.

Over the centuries, no one knew what caused it or how to prevent it once it had happened. It never happened to humans, only other supernaturals, which was why vampires preferred human blood-hosts. It was theorized that some magical signatures should simply never be crossed through blood, and that dangerous crossing is what caused the mania. It was a magical sickness no one could quite explain.

The victim could be cured by a witch healer, but they were warned to never play blood-host to another vampire ever again.

"I hired a very competent witch healer to treat and care for her for several weeks," he said softly. "I, of course, told her she could never be my host again and apologized for the entire mess."

"But it wasn't your fault. Vampires can't know who will contract the mania."

"Still, I felt responsible. She was fixated on me even after she was healed," he confessed with obvious discomfort. "But soon after, I was offered the position here in New Orleans."

That was just three months ago.

"Beverly followed you here?"

My gut turned at the thought that perhaps fang mania couldn't be healed completely.

"Last week, she showed up at Nightjar, begging me for a job, having lost her apartment in New York when she was indisposed because of the sickness. I felt some responsibility toward her, so I offered her a job." He laced his fingers with mine. "What you saw today was her attempt to lure me in as more than her employer. I was working at my desk when she came into my office, and when I turned, I found her unbuttoning her blouse. I

told her that she could get out, pack her things, and leave immediately." His frown deepened. "Then she cried and begged me to
stay, swearing it would never happen again."

There was truth in every word and every line of his sincere expression.

"But if her presence makes you uncomfortable, I will send
her away. Say the word, and it's done."

"You'd fire her and kick her out on the streets if I told you to?"

"You have no idea what I'd do for you."

His expression shifted to something dangerous and feral.

"I don't want the woman jobless and homeless."

"I could find her a job somewhere else."

What did it say about me that I couldn't stand the presence of
a blonde bombshell who happened to be desperately in love with
my boyfriend? What did it say that I'd consider throwing her out
on the streets to appease my vanity and ease my insecurity?

"No. Don't do that."

Our elbows were propped on the island, hands linked like we
were going to arm wrestle. I smiled and tugged our joined hands
closer to me, pressing a kiss to the back of his. His sapphire eyes
rolled silver again, gaze darkening in a millisecond.

"I'd do anything you asked," he whispered hoarsely. "*Anything.*"

And that was what I was worried about.

The desperate longing I glimpsed in Beverly's eyes today had
nearly eaten me alive with jealousy, but now only made me sick
with pity. I recognized that longing within myself.

This frenzied yearning I had for Ruben hadn't been quenched
by finally giving in to our desires. It was growing stronger,

rolling like an avalanche, and I was afraid I'd be crushed beneath its powerful force before this was over.

During sex, he liked to scrape his canines but he never broke the skin. He wanted to bite me. I've seen it in the rolling silver of his eyes. And I wanted him to bite me too. The compulsion was frighteningly potent, demanding that I bend my neck back and let him drink his fill. If I begged him, he'd do it. He just told me he'd do anything for me.

Ruben pulled our clasped hands to him and placed a kiss on the back of mine, mimicking me. With a wink, he turned back to the stove.

"Now, for a gourmet dinner."

Smiling, I spun on my stool and crossed my bare legs, my blanket sliding wider. "And what is the main course of this gourmet meal?"

"Omelet?"

I let out a throaty laugh. "An omelet is what all people cook when they can't cook much else."

I was still laughing when he tossed the spatula back on the counter and attacked me, hugging me tight, running a large hand up one thigh and kissing my neck.

"So an omelet isn't going to impress my fancy chef girlfriend?" He nipped my earlobe.

"I'm already impressed." Then I opened my arms and blanket as well as my thighs so I could envelop him in the warmth against me.

A desperate groan rumbled in his chest as he wrapped his arms around my waist beneath the blanket, his hands flattening on my back and pressing me close.

"You're too tempting. I'll never get this dinner cooked."

"Then call the Italian place on the corner for takeout and carry me back to your sofa."

He pressed a smiling kiss to my mouth, eyes glittering with joy. "This is why I'm dating you. You're the smartest person I know."

"Because I know where to order good takeout?"

"Because your priorities are set properly."

I yelped as he scooped me off the stool.

"Takeout shouldn't be long, and I'll just nibble on you till it gets here."

"This is why I'm dating you," I told him, grinning with the sheer bliss bubbling inside me. "You know exactly how to make efficient use of your time."

When he took me to the sofa, I forgot all about the incident with Beverly and those feelings of dread that threatened to take this all away from me. For now.

CHAPTER 1

~JULES~

The mandap we carried had an ivory silk and lace canopy, tiny crystals dangling on the underside, each twinkling bright with Aura magic. Clara's doing. My sisters and I carried the four wooden posts of the mandap with Isadora walking beneath it up the wide aisle of Ruben's garden. The twins, Clara and Violet, carried one pole together with Evie to their right, Livvy was on the back left, and I was on the back right.

Devraj and Isadora had opted for an intimate and private wedding in Ruben's garden. The reception would be under a large tent on the other side of his pool. Considering his home was in the posh upper Garden District with a high castle-like privacy fence and vampire guards to boot, we weren't worried about anyone crashing our supernatural wedding.

Classical Indian music filled the garden as we escorted Isadora to her groom. She glowed with beauty and love, her gaze fixed forward on Devraj.

She was dressed in a wedding lehenga, a two-piece gown in red velvet and silk and embroidered with gold beading and crystals. She looked stunning. We sisters each wore a less ornamented silk lehenga in different colors. Clara's was a subdued pink, Violet in lavender, Evie in sapphire, Livvy in darkest crimson, and I wore champagne gold.

It was Isadora's wish that the ceremony reflect more of Devraj's culture than our own Western one. She'd said that he'd been forced to give up so much of his homeland and had lost his mother so many years ago that she wanted to surround him with everything he loved the day they became husband and wife. In the family room one night while we were planning the wedding, I'd heard her whisper to him, "Maybe your mother will be watching and will be proud to see you married under a canopy."

He'd simply hauled her into his lap, gripped her nape to pull her closer, and whispered something I couldn't hear. All I know is it made Isadora wrap her arms around his neck and bury her face in his hair, and they'd remained just like that for a long, long time. So long that the wedding planning ended and the rest of us disappeared to give them privacy. That picture of them kept coming back to me, two lovers content to simply hold one another in silence, letting love soak through them in quiet contentment.

Their love was palpable, especially today as we made our way up the torch-lit aisle, the few rows of white chairs on both sides filled with our family and close friends. JJ and Charlie, Tia and her boyfriend Marcus, the whole Cauldron crew, and the vampires who worked with Dev and Ruben. Next to the vampires sat Sean, Tom, and Lindsey from Empress Ink. Our two cousins,

Drew and Cole, and their business partner and best friend, Travis, from Lafayette sat on the bride's side behind my parents.

Mom and Dad sat in the second row with Aunt Beryl, each of them holding one of Mateo and Evie's triplets. But it was my grandmother Maybelle who made me smile the most. She was cooing to Diego, who was propped over my dad's shoulder. Diego kept giggling as he played with the giant pearly beads of her necklace, trying to stuff them in his mouth. That baby tried to eat everything.

Maybelle loved pretty dresses, jewelry, and accessories. She had invaded our home like a whirlwind two weeks ago and needed half my closet for all of her fancy clothes. I'm surprised she hadn't worn a lehenga.

My sisters' partners Nico, Mateo, and Gareth stood along the front as groomsmen as well as Henry Blackwater. At the center stood Devraj and immediately to his left was his best man, Ruben.

Feeling eyes on all of us as we walked up the aisle, and a particular set on me, I stared at my hands holding the pole. Isadora had hired a Hindu witch named Nilika to paint our hands with traditional Mehndi. The red-orange dye wove a stunning and intricate design of flowers, patterns, and even moons and stars on the backs of our hands, fingers, and up our wrists.

Nilika was a hex-breaker, which meant she was also good at casting spells. She'd told us that she'd cast spells of blessings, good fortune, and joy into our henna tattoos as she'd painted them on. And I did indeed feel her tranquil magic tingling on my skin, casting a balm of peace and serenity over all of us as we guided our sister and gave her away to Devraj Kumar.

Devraj had eyes only for his bride, dressed in the traditional sherwani. His long jacket was embroidered in the same vibrant reds and golds of Isadora's gown. The groomsmen wore sherwani as well, but I refused to even glance their way, or my eyes would betray me and find the one I was avoiding.

By the time we reached Devraj, he was beaming. We lifted the canopy even higher as we walked our poles over the both of them to set them in the holders.

For some idiotic reason, I hadn't thought that the pole I held would go into the holder right next to Ruben. When I maneuvered into place and set the pole in its holder, I felt his heavy gaze and even heavier aura more than before.

To be fair, in the last few weeks since we'd been working together on our campaign to bring the werewolves into the High Guild Coven, as well as planning this wedding, I'd noticed that the boundaries I'd set years ago were starting to erode. Not only that, they were being crossed. Not specifically by him. He wasn't doing anything but being . . . Ruben.

It was me. And the devastatingly powerful pull he still had on me had me gulping nervously. The walls I'd erected and the distance I'd kept over the years had been enough to contain my fixation and keep those feelings at bay.

But now, as he stood merely a foot behind me, definitely watching me, my entire body shook with a tremor of warning. Like the silent flash of lightning in a distant sky, a storm approached.

After the canopy was in place, the bridesmaids and the groomsmen all took our stances outside the canopy in rows on either side. Though the temptation to glance his way was maddening, I kept my eyes on Isadora and Devraj.

The priest led them in their vows and prayers to bless their union. I didn't hear a word, but I watched the sheer bliss emanating from my sister as she spoke quiet words of devotion to Devraj. Her skin began to glow with magic as she apparently was pulling in energy from the night, letting it flow through her as she tied herself to her beloved.

The same happened with Devraj, his eyes glowing silver as he spoke his vows to my sister. Isadora beamed even brighter as Devraj clasped the traditional mangalsutra necklace around her neck, a Hindu tradition that represented their lifelong bond to one another. The gold ropelike necklace was dotted down the front with emeralds that led to a unique floral design at the center surrounding a larger emerald. He whispered more words of love in her ear as she turned to face him, her fingers gently caressing the necklace.

This moment. It was one of many I cherished for my sisters. My sweet family. Being the eldest always felt so hard—and came with sacrifices they'd never know, sacrifices I didn't want to burden them with—but I was more than willing to make them. To take the weight of responsibility so we had moments like this. So they found the joy they deserved.

Still, it didn't mean I couldn't find happiness of my own. A partner of my own. I'd tried, but no one compared to the vampire overlord dripping with power and charisma who'd I'd endeavored not to notice staring at me across the canopy. Maybe I should try again. Seeing the utter joy between Isadora and Devraj made me want to find my someone. One who wouldn't erase my will altogether and endanger my family and community.

When the priest said his final blessing and Devraj swept his bride into his arms for a kiss—a decidedly Western tradition—everyone erupted in applause and cheers. I did, too, laughing with a lump in my throat until my attention slipped, and I looked at Ruben.

Big mistake.

I'd been so intent on not looking at him that it was only then that I realized his long, embroidered jacket matched my champagne-colored one. The other groomsmen had all apparently decided to match the bridesmaids. But this detail, probably agreed upon by Isadora, had escaped me until this very moment.

The fact that we'd all been paired off by partner—or future partner for Clara, because you'd have to be blind not to see where things were headed with Henry Blackwater—stunned me still for a second. Because I was paired off with my *ex*-partner.

Then again, the way he was looking at me right now didn't feel very ex. He hadn't looked at me quite like that in years.

And good heavens, the way the torchlight gilded his physique in that jacket, the contours of his perfectly symmetrical face, his chiseled jawline, and his golden hair, simply wasn't fair.

How was I to go on this long business trip abroad and resist him at every turn?

Of course I could. I was Jules Savoie, renowned ice queen and serious-as-fuck Enforcer of New Orleans. Surely I could withstand the slight temptation of being in constant proximity to a beautiful vampire.

All of us bridesmaids and groomsmen followed the happy couple, Devraj carrying Isadora in his arms, back down the aisle and across the Greek architectural courtyard that wound in a wide arc around Ruben's Greek mosaic-tiled pool. The rest of the guests followed noisily after us toward the reception tent.

This was where the ceremony turned much more Western. Gareth had hired the DJ from his club as a gift to the couple.

"Wait, Dev!" Isadora squealed as he set her on her feet, took her hand, and tried to pull her onto the dance floor. "Pictures."

"Oh, right." He laughed and let her tug him back to the part of Ruben's courtyard that was set up with lights for the photographer.

I admired the Greek sculptures in between the Italian cypress trees that bordered the terrace area as we passed next to the pool. One sculpture of Hades carrying away Persephone particularly drew my attention, but before I could inch closer to get a better look, I felt a hand at the small of my back.

"Pictures, Jules."

Ruben's voice in that low register close to my ear brought up memories I didn't need to be remembering. I jumped and quickened my pace across the rounded terrace steps to where the photographer, Jackson, a werewolf Livvy knew and hired for us, was positioning everyone.

"Perfect," he said as my sisters stood in front of their boyfriends.

Except for Clara, who was facing Henry and whispering something up to his scowling face. Whatever she had said made his frown disappear, and she turned to stand in front of him to line up perfectly with the rest of the wedding party. Except for me and Ruben.

"I'll need the best man and maid of honor over here on this side of the bride and groom."

"After you," said Ruben, smirking at my side.

I took my place beside Isadora, who wouldn't stop whispering and laughing with Devraj, as was natural for newlyweds. Ruben took his place slightly behind and to the left of me.

Jackson looked through his lens. "Ruben, just a little closer to Jules there." I felt his heat at my left shoulder. "Yeah, like one inch closer. Just like that. And if you can put your right hand on her right hip."

Good lord, I was going to kill this photographer.

The weight of his hand found my hip, and I bit back the whimper that nearly escaped my mouth.

This was ridiculous!

It was lust. Plain and simple. Oh, yeah, Livvy's damn grim was standing too close. I glared at him over Livvy's shoulder. When he saw me, his brows went up in surprise but then lit with wicked humor.

This wasn't fucking funny.

I just hadn't prepared myself for all of the emotions today. And to be bombarded with that grim's aura while Ruben was practically on top of me . . .

My brain did a quick rewind to a night many years ago when he was on top of me, whispering in my ear all the things he planned to do to me.

Snap.

"Okay," said Jackson, "I think that about—"

"We're done?" I belted out with a little too much aggression. "Great! I'll go see if Maybelle needs anything."

I zipped off the terrace steps and beelined, like my ass was on fire, back to the tent where the party was picking up speed.

Finally out of the heady orbit of Ruben, and that grim exacerbating everything, I inhaled a deep breath of non-vampy air and headed for the bar.

"There she is," crooned my cousin Drew, pulling me into a side hug and handing me a glass of red wine.

"Were you waiting for me?" I arched a brow at him while I downed half the glass.

He grinned wider. Drew was an Influencer like Livvy. He also happened to be handsome as sin and a natural-born charmer. His brother, Cole, a Seer like Violet, was the exact opposite, dark and broody and propping up the bar while glaring at the guests.

"Not waiting, but I could tell from here that you needed a drink."

"That obvious?"

"Let me guess. A certain vampire rubbing you wrong?"

"No." Lies. "It's just been a long day and lots of preparation, and I leave town in two days for heaven knows how long and—"

"Easy, Jules." Drew leaned back and grabbed another glass of wine, taking my now empty one, because yes, I'd downed it all in a matter of minutes. Or maybe like a minute and a half. Not quite *minutes* plural.

"Thank you." I turned back toward the reception just as Isadora and Devraj made their way under the tent, followed by the rest of the wedding party at a leisurely pace, not the breakneck, someone-save-me pace that I'd set. They all started to mingle with family and friends.

Mateo and Evie immediately went up and relieved Mom and Dad. My grandmother no longer had Diego. No telling where that rascal had gotten himself.

"Say, who's the dark-haired beauty Travis is talking to?" Drew asked, gesturing across the candlelit tables to the dance floor.

Shaking my head, I replied, "Her name is Nilika. She did our henna tattoos for the wedding. She and Isadora became fast friends when they met a few weeks ago, and Is invited her."

Watching Travis with his telltale devilish grin, I knew all the charming words he was currently using to woo Nilika into his bed later tonight. I was about to go warn her, but then Cole suddenly shoved off the bar and marched over to them. With a few quiet words, he gestured toward my mom and dad, currently talking to Aunt Beryl. Travis nodded and wandered toward them, leaving Cole smiling down at Nilika.

I burst out laughing. "Did he just steal Travis's date?"

Drew shook his head. "Happens all the time. Those two have a nonstop competitive streak when it comes to women. In a few minutes, Travis will realize Cole just sent him on a fool's errand and come retaliate."

The wine calmed my nerves, and I hid a smile as I watched Maybelle swishing in our direction. My grandmother, who was close to four hundred years old and looked like a very healthy, vivacious woman in her fifties, was what most men would call a femme fatale. When our grandfather died a hundred years ago, she said she'd never marry again and decided to sow her wild oats.

Apparently she has been in every country around the world since she's been traveling for decades now. Currently, she had one of Ruben's men, Sal, who had to be at least two centuries younger than her, following her to the bar.

"Was he really that terrible?" Sal asked as my grandmother sidled up right beside me.

"I'm telling you, dear boy, your grandfather was the worst rake I'd ever met. Even after I'd demoted him as overlord of the region, he was still slobbering at my doorstep. I had to actually cast a guarding spell around the damn house."

I snickered into my glass. A guarding spell was basically a supernatural restraining order. When someone violated and came too close, they'd get a zap not unlike a cattle prod.

Sal seemed both disheartened and fascinated by this news, probably in shock that his grandfather had turned into a slavering dog over a woman.

"Don't feel bad," I told Sal, patting him on the arm. "Maybelle simply has a way about her. Men can't help but make fools of themselves over her. Right, Maw Maybelle?" I teased.

She gave me a sharp look. "Watch your tongue, sweetheart."

She preferred for us to call her Maybelle. Clara was the only one who could get away with calling her Maw Maybelle without that hard look she'd just given me.

"I can believe it," added Sal with a smile, his handsome, dark features even more attractive by candlelight. He leaned closer to me to whisper conspiratorially. "Do you think I have a chance, Jules? Maybe you can put in a good word."

"I have little to no influence over my grandmother."

"That's a load of drivel," said Maybelle, her elegant green gown accentuating her full bust, small waist, and rounded hips. Livvy had certainly gotten her figure from Maybelle. I'd only managed to get the hips. "You have my undying devotion," she said, pinching my chin, then turning to the bar and giving Drew a hug.

Sal leaned in closer, his voice low, amber-brown eyes fixed on mine. I was suddenly reminded why this Italian man was so dangerously seductive. He had the look of both an innocent angel and a wicked devil as he said sweetly, "If I was really lucky, maybe the granddaughter would give me a chance."

I stared at him in shock for a second, but before I could reply, the air around me stirred with a crackle of magic.

"If you'd like to die a slow, painful death," said the vampire who'd suddenly stepped into our circle, "then why don't you finish that conversation?"

Sal flinched at the sound of his sire's furious warning, but he merely bowed—to Ruben first and then to me—and excused himself with a guilty smile.

"Is that a common practice of yours? Threatening death to your subordinates?" I sipped my wine, feeling suddenly calmer than I did earlier in his presence.

Ruben's demeanor had shifted only slightly from before. The grave hunter was now more agitated, his cool facade cracked by the pinched lines on his forehead.

"Sal should know better."

"What does that mean?"

Okay, the small frown morphed into a death glare. "Are you being serious?"

"We aren't dating, Ruben. We haven't dated for many years now. What does it matter? Sal can ask if there's a chance."

"*No.* He can't." He took the tumbler of bourbon from the bar that had been poured for him and swigged the entire glass. Then his snapping sapphire eyes turned on me again. "Wait a minute. Are you saying you'd give him a chance?"

There was a menacing threat in that question that gave me a moment's hesitation.

"No, I wouldn't. But that's beside the point."

"I don't see how."

I snorted indelicately. "You can't tell your employees who they can and can't date."

"The hell I can. When it comes to you." His gaze glinted silver, then skated over my throat and bodice before returning to my face. His voice was a dark rumble when he said, "I'd bury him in a shallow grave if he even tried."

For a second, I simply blinked. I'd never heard him sound so possessive, not even when we were actually together. Something was shifting. Time to lighten the mood.

"I wonder . . ." I tapped my chin thoughtfully, mockingly.

"What? You wonder what, Juliana?" he snapped impatiently.

He was suddenly too close, but I didn't back away. I wasn't going to be cowed by Ruben, no matter what state of dampness my panties were currently in.

"So you have a strict no fraternization policy among employees?"

"It's a good one to keep, yes."

"And have you always kept it?"

He crowded me against the bar. "Except when I dated my boss once upon a time. I'd break every rule for her."

Oh, hell. That wasn't where I was going with this. And where had that come from?

The corner of his mouth curled in the most seductive manner imaginable.

"I wasn't talking about us," I snapped back. "I was talking about Beverly. I wonder if you finally ended up letting her have what she wanted. After all, we stopped dating years ago, and you've kept her around. Surely, you let her scratch that itch she'd wanted so badly."

What a mistake to drink two glasses of wine in under ten minutes and let my loose tongue take over. I'd all but admitted I still had jealous feelings about Beverly. Even if I'd tried to keep my voice light and playful, it was so obvious. And you can only be jealous over something, or in this case *someone*, you covet.

I expected him to laugh or for that wicked smile to spread wider across his beautiful face, but the exact opposite occurred. His eyes widened in shock—and hurt. He looked as if I'd slapped him, and I found myself wanting to apologize. But I wasn't even sure what for. I'd only asked a simple question. Then he gave me the answer.

Tipping his head down to me, piercing me with a razor-sharp gaze, he whispered, "If that's what you believe, then you know nothing at all. You don't know me at all."

I swallowed hard while he continued to torture me with that sorrowful, agonizing look. But then it turned to fury.

"And what about Carter?" he asked with malicious venom.

I flinched, a roll of nausea turning my stomach at the memory. I looked down, guilt and shame permeating me for something I should've felt zero guilt or shame about. We were broken up, *long* broken up when I dated Carter. We weren't dating now, so what the hell was going on? And the memory of Carter immediately traced my thoughts back to the night of the twins' birthday party when I'd gotten into an argument with Ruben about a rogue vampire and then later that evening received a picture text that had turned my world upside down.

The music abruptly died, and the DJ called through the sound system, "Would the wedding party please report to the dance floor? Time for the bride and groom and the bridesmaids and groomsmen to kick off the first dance."

Ruben stepped back, washing away the stricken expression that had gutted me a minute earlier, and then held out his arm. "Shall we?" he asked rather stiffly.

I didn't say a word, but I took his arm and let him lead me to the dance floor.

CHAPTER 2

~RUBEN~

FOR TWELVE YEARS, JULES HAS BEEN REMOTE, PROFESSIONAL, AND impersonal in all of our conversations. Even when her eyes betrayed her, like tonight when she looked at me beside the altar, she never let on that her thoughts were anything but indifferent where I was concerned.

And the first time she questioned me about something unrelated to business, it was about fucking Beverly. She actually believed that I'd drink from her or fuck her after I knew the mere idea of it had hurt her when we were together?

But then, she had no idea, did she? No idea the pain it would cause *me* to do something like that.

I nearly lost my mind when she'd let that human Erik into her home about a year after we broke up. Thankfully, he hadn't stayed long enough for me to take drastic measures. Jules was practical and she wouldn't entangle herself emotionally with someone she'd outlive by several hundred years, so I figured he wasn't worth worrying about. Thankfully, whatever had happened between them was short-lived. He'd never entered her house again after that one night.

It was that fucking warlock Carter she'd dated briefly that nearly undid me altogether. When Gareth reported to me that she'd gone home with him and stayed all night, it was the first time I'd contemplated murder. The first time I'd also considered finding a cold, dark crypt in the ground to while away a few decades. But she let him go soon after, and I was saved from destroying another life in cold blood. Or destroying my own.

"All packed?" I asked her casually, pushing the pain of her earlier question out of my voice.

"Yes."

"Of course." I smiled, realizing I knew her better than she realized. "You've been packed since this past Monday, haven't you?"

She gave me one of those narrow-eyed looks that went straight to my cock. I wonder if she had any idea what her defiance and fury did to me. Likely not, or she wouldn't still be glaring at me with murderous intent.

"I like to be prepared." Her hand slid down to the ball of my shoulder, and though the touch was light, I could still imagine what it felt like with no clothes between us. A faint marking was still there after all these years, waiting for her to rediscover the paths she'd mapped over my skin.

"Yes, I know." My hand on her waist was mostly on the material of her gown's skirt, but my thumb and forefinger rested on bare skin.

I had loved and hated these lehengas alternately throughout the night. The first second I saw her from the altar, carrying the canopy with her sisters, the Aura magic from the dangling crystals glowing on the fair skin of her face, neckline, arms, and midriff, I was forced to lock my knees so they wouldn't buckle or I wouldn't do something suicidal like snatch her and trace away to my bedroom with her.

My fangs had elongated instantly, my throat had gone dry, and that fierce sensation of rabid need nearly slayed me on the spot.

Obsessed, stupefied, besotted. None of them quite measured up to the truth, to the emotion that had wrapped an iron fist around my heart at the sight of her tonight. I wasn't sure there had been a word yet created that could define what I felt for Juliana. The worst part of all is she had no idea.

Or perhaps, some idea. Her pulse picked up speed when my thumb brushed against her lower rib cage, skin on skin. It was beyond intoxicating, but also agony, the feel of her in my arms. And not truly the way I wanted.

The wedding party song "Movement" by Hozier kept our dance in a slow, intimate circle, very much like the rest of the bridesmaids and groomsmen, the bride and groom. But it meant more to me because it was an excuse to hold the woman who belonged to me and who'd rejected me twelve years ago.

I caught Devraj's glance over Isadora's shoulder, his expression one of compassion and knowing. As my best friend for centuries, he was the one I'd confessed to the moment I had met Jules. He understood her significance in my life, and he'd also been the only one to understand the depth of her loss when she had ended it.

"So," she cut into my whirling thoughts, "the plan is still the same? You and I will travel to Houston, then fly to Salem where your men will join us? And from there, we'll fly straight to London?"

"That's the plan."

My gaze glided back to the bar where Sal, Gabriel, and Roland had gathered, laughing together about something. Correction, Sal and Roland were laughing, not Gabriel. My business-focused right-hand man rarely laughed about anything.

Sal. What the ever-loving fuck was he thinking by hitting on Jules? The man truly wished to die before his hundredth birthday.

"What's wrong?" asked Jules.

I hadn't realized my grip had grown too hard, my fingertips curling into the flesh of her hip. I loosened my hold.

"Your mother will stand in as Enforcer while you're away?"

I already knew this, but I needed to get my mind off the fact that one of my men apparently had a death wish. If he thought because I hadn't shown any outright interest in Juliana for over a decade that I'd given up and had moved on, I'd have to set things fucking straight.

"Yes. Mom and Dad will stay and help out here. Don't worry. I've taken care of everything."

I wasn't worried. I'd also enlisted Gareth and Henry to ensure the Savoie family and my coven were safe while we were away.

As the song ended, the DJ announced, "And now we'll have the bride and her father and the groom and Mrs. Savoie dance."

We broke away as Jules' parents stepped onto the dance floor. Devraj's tearful smile at Serena Savoie stepping in for his own mother who died centuries ago was lovely beyond words. Devraj deserved the family he never had.

"I need to"—Jules gestured toward Aunt Beryl and Tia, and her boyfriend Marcus who were holding the triplets—"go check on the babies."

I relished the idea that pretty damn soon, she wouldn't be able to run away from me at all. I let her go and turned abruptly, then headed toward the trio at the bar. I reminded myself to calm down and do this delicately. Yes, they were my employees, but they were also like brothers to me. All three of them had worked under me in New York and moved here to my new coven in New Orleans when I'd been promoted. Gabriel and I had been friends even longer from our younger days in England. They were also now friends of Devraj and guests at the wedding, so I couldn't tear Sal a new asshole like I wanted to.

Even while I kept my expression cool and aloof, they must've sensed the rage radiating around me. Gabriel stood straight from where he'd been leaning against the bar, frowning and checking for danger around the room. Roland and Sal were slower to alert at my approach, probably because they'd already drank too much.

"What's wrong?" asked Gabriel when I stopped into their circle.

I took another moment to calm myself before I spoke, but that only seemed to heighten the unease in all three of them.

"I wanted to address something so that it is quite clear before we go on this trip abroad. Juliana is under my protection." They waited while I paused yet again to get my temper under control. "Let me rephrase. I expect you all to give her the utmost respect and look out for her safety at all times, especially when we are in England. But know this . . . she is *mine* to protect." My voice had dropped several octaves, my canines had extended, and I knew that my eyes shone silver. I pinned each of them with my feral intent, hanging last on Sal. "Do you fucking understand?" I asked with eerie steadiness.

"Yes, sire," came all three of their immediate responses.

"Good." I smiled, fangs still sharp, as I clapped Sal on the back. "Enjoy your evening then."

I roamed away, not in the mood for socializing anymore. Finding a corner with a glass of Macallan on ice, I watched.

Gareth, Livvy, Violet, and Nico spent most of the night carrying on with the Savoie cousins and friend from Lafayette. Henry left early, much to Clara's obvious disappointment. After she watched him skulk away—as was his style—she spent the rest of the evening playing with the triplets. After Evie and Mateo danced several more times together, they left with the babies.

Juliana played hostess, going from one group to the next, making sure no one needed anything. Though it was Isadora's wedding, it was Juliana's nature to take care of everyone. The thought of her acting as hostess at a party in my backyard had me wondering what it would be like if she took on the role here permanently. A blaze of flame licked through my body at the thought.

"Brooding and sulking in a corner on the happiest night of my life, eh?" Devraj stepped up to me, having changed into black slacks and a white button-down.

I noticed Isadora had changed into a simple cream-colored dress. They were getting ready to slip away to the Monteleone for the night. Tomorrow, they'd fly to the south of France for their honeymoon.

Smiling, I held up my glass. "Congratulations, my friend. You deserve all the happiness."

He clinked the glass of bourbon he held in his own. "So do you, Ruben. You deserve it as much as I do."

He turned and we both looked at Jules telling Isadora something while they held hands. It was an obviously tender moment between sisters.

We watched them while Devraj spoke quietly to me. "It's about time you did something about that, isn't it? You've put the hunt off long enough."

"A decade isn't so long for vampires as old as we are."

"It's been twelve, my friend. And twelve years is an eternity for anyone living as a monk."

It was true that twelve years seemed like a blink in time when you'd been born in the early 1600s. But these past years without her had been an acute kind of agony. Only being close to her had kept me true to my word.

"She needed space." More than space. *I can't trust you.* "I gave it to her. Being near her has been enough."

"Is it still enough?"

Devraj turned to face me, but my gaze wouldn't leave Juliana.

"You can't let it go any longer," he murmured, an edge of pity in his tone. Then he squeezed my shoulder and walked toward Isadora, who was just then looking around for him.

Those still at the reception wandered toward the garden gate. I followed at a steady pace, watching Juliana pass out sparkler sticks to everyone she passed. The entire party was overflowing with joy, completely enraptured by the blissful magic of the night.

Meanwhile, my mood had taken a decided turn, not toward melancholy, but on a different path altogether. My mind began to retreat from the world around me, mulling over what Devraj had said. He was right.

Dev's Lamborghini was parked in my circular drive, waiting for their departure. Juliana and Clara ushered everyone into place, creating a border to send off the newlyweds. Candles were being passed to light the tips of the sparklers. The photographer, Jackson, was already in place near Dev's car, ready to capture the moment.

"Here they come!" shouted Clara.

But as the cheers erupted and my best friend and his bride made their way through the archway of sparklers, my gaze was fixed on Juliana directly across from me, the sparks in the air caressing her face with light. As Devraj and Isadora passed, her focus fell to me. And stayed there.

Even as everyone rushed to the car and yelled and waved goodbye, she remained still, ensnared by my gaze. I wasn't using glamour. I wouldn't do that to her.

The two of us didn't move for a moment. I wanted nothing more than to soak in the dawning awareness sliding across her delicate facial features that something had changed between us. I was no longer going to play nice and give her space. I was done waiting for her to realize she could trust me. As her only lover. As her partner in life. As her devoted mate.

It was time to erase the space between us and hunt her, woo her, worship her the way she was meant to be as my one and only.

When I finally moved and stalked across the open walkway, her eyes widened. Her heart rate tripled, and my canines extended on instinct, my beast detecting the quickened pulse of our most coveted prey.

She didn't back away when I finally stood well within her personal space. Nor did she flinch when I leaned down, my mouth close to her ear, her heavenly scent filling my veins with hope.

"Time's up, Juliana," I whispered, grazing my lip against the top shell of her ear.

She gasped and jumped but still didn't step back. I raised my head and pinned her with a look I knew told her my intent. I wanted her aware and ready for what was coming. She didn't ask me what I meant because she knew.

When her heart rate sped up even faster and the hypnotic scent of her desire warmed the air between us, I knew I was right. It was finally time to make Juliana Savoie mine.

CHAPTER 3

~JULES~

I POURED THE TWO CUPS OF CRAWFISH TAILS INTO THE PAN OF SIZZLING butter, added the green onions, and stirred, humming to the song "Prologue" by my favorite singer Loreena McKennitt. Stirring so that the crawfish and onions didn't stick, I picked up my glass of wine and sipped, gloriously happy to have the house to myself for one night.

Mom and Dad had taken everyone, including Maw Maybelle, out to dinner and then to see the Christmas lights in City Park. I begged off since I was still packing for the trip and, quite frankly, because the idea of having an empty house to myself for one night sounded like nothing short of heaven.

"All right, baby. We'll see you later tonight," Mom had said with a wink, knowing me well enough to realize I needed the quiet time.

Alone time was rare for me even though I got up every morning at five a.m. I spent the first several hours of every day going through emails and managing coven business. If I had to handle any problem in person, I'd get my sous-chef, Mitch, to handle the Cauldron for the day. Most small kitchens didn't employ a sous-chef, but Mitch had to sometimes handle the kitchen for the entire day, so it was necessary to have him on staff for those days I didn't even get to enter my kitchen. But most days, coven business could wait till after hours.

Around ten a.m., I'd head to the Cauldron and start prep for the day. My line cooks and Mitch would already be at work, and I'd spend the rest of my day in the kitchen, which I loved. But again, it was still work and often stressful. If there was no coven business after hours that day, then I'd go over inventory and receipts with JJ or Isadora. And by the time I got home, my sisters would be milling around the house, needing one thing or another. Nowadays, there were three more tiny supernaturals who needed lots of attention.

I adored my niece and nephews, and I loved having Mateo and Evie in the house with their young family, but sometimes, I just wanted some space and peaceful silence. Like now. So I could finally unwind and have a chat with Z, our very old black cat, about what was on my mind.

Right now, there was only one thing on my mind. Or rather, one vampire.

I took the half dozen crawfish tails I'd set aside and turned to Z—his affectionate nickname, short for Zombie Cat—who was still curled on the cushioned stool where I'd put him.

"Here you go, Z." I set the crawfish tails on the napkin in front of him. He blinked his orange eyes slowly at me, then started eating his first one.

"We both get treats tonight, don't we?"

Setting my wine down, I opened the half-and-half on the counter and poured a generous amount into the pan. My mouth watered at the smell of my crawfish macaroni and cheese coming together.

"No telling what kind of food I'll be eating in London, Z, but I can tell you they won't have this."

I didn't even try to pretend that I wasn't cooking my favorite comfort food because I did, indeed, need comfort.

Time's up, Juliana.

Ruben's deep, velvet-smooth voice rang in my mind, like it had a thousand times since he'd said those words to me last night at the reception.

There was no mistaking what he'd meant. Twelve years ago when I broke up with him, he'd told me he'd let me go. He'd also told me I'd regret it. He'd stayed away from me for a long time. Then when he didn't come near me except for coven business or to talk to me for professional reasons in the next months, I figured he'd accepted our status as colleagues only and . . . friends.

But we weren't friends. We couldn't be. There was no going back to something so mild and basic after what we'd been together for those few blazing months. Even when I tried to pretend that it never happened, not even telling my sisters the extent of our relationship, the memories still haunted me.

I'd wake up in a panic, even years later, after dreaming of him—tangled limbs, sweat-soaked sheets, bruising grips, and pounding flesh. It would feel so real for that split second before I fully awoke that I'd choke back a sob when reality washed over me.

But the softer, sweeter dreams were the worst, cradling me in such tenderness that my heart broke—again—the second I opened my eyes and realized they weren't real. Not anymore. Even now, the distant memories of what we once had were seared into my mind as if they'd been engraved there with painful precision.

Still, it had been the right choice. It had been my *only* choice.

So why now, when he had looked at me the way he did at the reception, as if he was calculating all the ways he'd devour me bite by slow bite, when he'd said those words as if he'd simply been biding his sweet time to come after me again, did the thought both thrill and terrify me? Thrilling because the mere hint of being the full focus of Ruben's attention, to be the object of his desire again, was beyond beguiling. But terrifying because . . . well, because I didn't want to resist him anymore. I wanted him. His words had shocked me because I hadn't realized he was still interested after all this time.

After receiving that anonymous text at Violet's and Clara's birthday two years ago, I was sure he'd finally moved on. Strange, too, because we'd started to talk more again, and I'd even wondered if we might mend some of what we'd broken. But after we'd argued that day about how to handle a particular rogue vampire in New Orleans, someone else—the one who'd sent that text—wanted to remind me that vampires couldn't ignore their nature. They had to feed. And when Ruben fed . . .

The picture that had been texted to me, which I'd deleted after getting wildly drunk that night, flickered to mind. Ruben on a red velvet sofa, a petite brunette sitting on his lap. He had one hand at her nape, tilting her head back, teeth in her throat, his other hand clenched mid-thigh on her leg. It was the woman's expression that still haunted me the most. Half-lidded eyes, mouth open in ecstasy as she, obviously, was crying out in pleasure. The photograph seemed to capture the perfect prelude to a night of mind-blowing sex.

What they did after the feeding wasn't my business. We weren't together anymore, but it had eviscerated me all the same. As if someone had taken a dull knife and carved out my heart, that picture had reminded me why we couldn't be together.

I was a possessive bitch, and I'd never abide him drinking from others if we were together again. The experience of being bitten was intensely sexual, regardless if there was sex or not during the drinking. Or so I was told.

"Besides, Z," I told him over my shoulder as I always did when I could be alone like this, "I could never let him drink from me." Frowning, I turned to Z, who was eating his last crawfish tail. *"Could I?"*

As usual, Z had no answer. He was a terrific listener, though.

"No, definitely not," I emphasized as I poured in a cup of Colby Jack cheese and stirred. My brain was already spiraling down places and paths and delicious trails it should never, ever go. "I could never do that even if we did date again. The risk hasn't changed."

Then why did the risk feel so much less?

Probably because I was confident in my station now. Still, that didn't mean it was safe to let Ruben bite me and drink my blood.

"But it's kind of unfair if you ask me. One of the greatest advantages of having a vampire boyfriend or girlfriend is experiencing the pleasure of their bite."

I poured in the cup of cheddar cheese next and stirred, adding a little more half-and-half as it thickened.

"Not that he's my boyfriend or even wants to be," I corrected myself, glancing back at my silent friend. "I mean, I'm not an idiot.

Please don't think that, Z." I shrugged a shoulder. "He just said time was up, which could mean anything really. Like, *time's up, let's stop being so formal and professional together and be real friends.*"

I sprinkled in the crispy bacon pieces I'd precooked, mulling that over. The heat in his feral gaze, the rough aggression in his voice, the not-so-subtle brush of his lips against my ear.

"No." I poured in more half-and-half, needing extra creamy and cheesy mac tonight. "I'm pretty sure that's not what that look meant."

My neck and cheeks flushed with heat, remembering how easily he could make me come undone. I didn't think time apart would change the fact that Ruben knew how to use his hands, his mouth, among other divine parts of his body. If he was coming for me, then . . . "Z, I think I'm in big trouble."

Blowing out a breath, I sprinkled a few dashes of Bon CaCa Cajun seasoning into my crawfish mac and cheese, then tasted it. "Mm. Perfect."

After moving it off the burner and turning off the stove, I spooned a giant heap into a pasta bowl. Then I pulled the other stool next to Z and sat next to him, my wine on the counter. Blowing on a spoonful, I ate the creamy, melty deliciousness, already feeling better.

Z blinked up at me, his tail twitching.

"Yes, I know I can't just eat my feelings and hope all my problems go away." I ate another bite. "Not that I want this problem to go away." Heart tripping faster, I shook my head at myself. "No, Z. I'm pretty sure I'm ready for this problem to be up front and in my face."

Z meowed, a creaky sound from his old vocal cords.

"Yes, I know. Finally, right?"

It was kind of a shock to me too. But I think I was actually ready for Ruben Dubois. Again.

~RUBEN~

"So Simon from Lafayette will run the Green Light?" Gabriel asked, sliding a glass of Scotch whiskey over the bar to me where we were currently sitting in the Green Light. "What about your tech businesses?"

"Gareth Blackwater will handle it."

I owned a few apps in addition to my vampire den and the bookstore. My employees for the app businesses all worked remotely, and they'd been given instructions to go to Gareth while I was out of town. I was an investor in several other vampire dens in the city, but they were all owned by other vampires.

"And Simon will manage any vampire problems as well."

Simon was the overlord of the Lafayette region and agreed to step away from his own region to fill in for me while I was gone. His second could handle the smaller region, whereas not many could manage the larger area of New Orleans and surrounding cities that I ruled over. Simon and I weren't friends, but we'd met often enough over the years at Guild Summits that I knew I could trust him.

"And when Devraj gets back from his honeymoon," added Gabriel, taking a sip of his own Scotch, "he'll take over for Simon?"

I shook my head, not touching my drink, my mind so distracted. "No. He and Isadora will be staying in the south of France for at least two months."

I'd teased him about taking his honeymoon for so long, but he'd reminded me that on my own honeymoon, I'd likely take my *pretty little wife* far away from the world for much longer. I hadn't argued if I was ever able to take Jules to wife, then he was absolutely fucking right. I'd take her far away. And they'd be lucky if we ever came back as far as I was concerned.

"And the bookstore?" Gabriel leaned his elbows on the bar top.

"I'm closing the bookstore while we're gone."

"Beverly couldn't handle it?"

My muscles tensed at the mention of her name. "No," I ground out.

Gabriel frowned but said nothing because there was a sudden spike of my magical signature in the room. It flared with anger as a warning that my temper was up. I recalled the conversation with Jules at the wedding.

She thought I'd been fucking Beverly? After I knew how she felt about her? I'd only let Beverly keep her job because Jules had insisted she didn't want her fired. But sure enough, Jules had believed I'd kept her around so I could *scratch that itch.*

If she only fucking knew.

As if conjured by telepathy, Beverly clip-clopped into the room from the long corridor that connected the bookstore to the Green Light. Her blonde hair and makeup were impeccable, complementing the tight version of a 1940s red dress that fit her Marilyn Monroe–like figure to perfection. I narrowed my gaze as she approached the bar.

Beverly always dressed in similar attire. She likely thought this was my favorite era since I dressed in a contemporary version of custom-made suits from the 1940s and because I often listened to music of that era to wind down. It's what I liked to have playing in the bookstore for customers in our lounge area. It had always circled in the back of my mind that she was imitating my likes, probably in some effort to become more appealing to me. She probably thought draping herself in this bygone era would somehow attract my attention.

What she, nor anyone else, realized was that the forties had no true appeal other than being stylish and sophisticated. It was the 1920s decor of my bookstore and club that reflected where my heart lay. But Beverly would never know that or understand. I suppose no one would.

Not until I told *her*.

The mere thought of Jules hammered home what must be done.

"Beverly."

"Yes, sire." She beamed as she approached, swaying her hips to the best of her ability, stopping a foot in front of my stool. "What can I do for you?"

Yet again, I took note of the intentional curve of her lips and sensual look in her eyes, something I'd ignored for far too long.

"I need you to go back to the bookstore and pack all of your belongings. This is your last day."

As expected, she gasped dramatically, tears immediately springing to her eyes. "What!"

"Do not raise your voice with me," I warned.

"But, sire, I don't understand."

"It's easy. You're fired. That means you'll leave this job and find one elsewhere."

Yes, I was being a cynical dick, but I'd put up with her flirtation for far too long, ignoring it like it didn't matter. Apparently, it did, because the woman I wanted most in the world thought I had some sort of relationship with Beverly. And that, I couldn't have. I wanted zero obstacles between me and Jules moving forward.

"But I've always served you well." She was openly weeping now. She reached out as if to touch my arm.

"Don't you dare."

She jerked her hand back, looking stung.

"I'm sorry I didn't do this sooner because, apparently, you've been under the delusion that there might one day be some chance for us. Let me be clear." I stood from the stool. "There never will be nor would there ever have been."

She sobbed openly, trails of black mascara running down her face. "But where will I go? What will I do?"

"Beverly, this is a job. Not even a career. There are thousands of covens to find a home in. But I can't have you in mine any longer."

She opened her mouth to protest again, but I was done with her.

"Gabriel, escort Beverly to the bookstore to gather her things and then to her car. And collect her store keys as well."

"That's it? After all we've been through!" she screamed with more venom now.

I took a menacing step closer, which had her stepping back, mascara-smeared eyes widening. Gabriel was already standing in front of the bar, waiting for her to leave, his expression tight and grave. Ready to defend me, I'm sure, should this become violent.

"If you bare your fangs at me, Beverly, you will regret it."

Fortunately, she wasn't stupid.

"We have never *been through* anything," I clarified for her. "I took pity on you and gave you a job when you begged for one. If there was ever anything other than sire and vampire or boss and employee, it was in your own deluded brain. Now, *leave*. I'll have your final check deposited in your account this week."

I gave a tight nod to Gabriel, who immediately took Beverly by the arm and led her back down the corridor, her sobbing cries echoing in the hall as they went.

The sight of her leaving, for good, suddenly buoyed my mood. I gulped down the Scotch and strode for the door, a lightness in my step.

One more day, and I'd be on the road with Juliana.

CHAPTER 4

~JULES~

As always, Clara stood outside the witch's wheel for the invocation of our ceremony. Today, she'd forgone her floral tiara and Harry Potter wand, settling for something more serious. She wore a blue-gray shawl she'd sewn just for me. She wanted to enmesh all of her Aura energy from the witch's round tonight into the threads, then she'd give it to me to take on my trip.

"For extra protection," she'd said with a bit of a dimpled frown this morning.

It was sweet of her to worry about me. That was typically my job. Even Violet had grown quiet and somber tonight.

"Don't start without me," called Maybelle as she opened the wrought iron gate that separated our little, secret garden we kept private just for this.

Mom followed right behind her. "Like you'd let them get far without you, Mother."

Maybelle was already dressed for bed, which meant she was wearing a red silk kimono robe over some sort of gossamer-like nightgown beneath.

"Have a seat right there, Maw Maybelle." Clara pointed out a cushioned seat at the top corner of our chalked wheel in front of the written word Samhain.

Violet sat at the top of the wheel above Yule on the wheel. Mom sat in Isadora's place by Imbolg. Livvy was in her spot by Lughnasa. I was already settled cross-legged in the lower right side of the wheel beneath Beltane, having just lit the white pillar candles. The crescent of the new moon hung high over us in a clear night sky.

"Where's Evie?" I asked.

"She's taking a nap. She and Mateo just got all three down."

I wanted to argue that she needed this round more than anyone, but I'd also seen how utterly exhausted she'd been since the birth of Diego, Joaquin, and Celine. She probably needed a good night's sleep more than anything else.

"How do you girls do your rounds as a group?" asked my grandmother.

"Like we've always done them, Mother," Mom said sarcastically.

"Don't get snippy, Serena."

"Well, we can't all be world travelers, recharging magical energy with whatever hot warlock happens to offer his services." Mom didn't say it with venom but rather teasingly.

"Mom and Maw, that's enough," said Clara in a much more serious manner than was her norm. "This is about Jules, and we need to focus all of our magical energy on her."

"And her protection," added Violet soberly.

That had the hairs on the back of my neck rising. When I frowned in her direction to ask a question, Violet shook her head with a cryptic, "Later."

Then Clara began our round as always.

"Sisters—for we are all sisters in the round—our attention should be on Spirit's protective hand tonight. Close your eyes and let's begin."

Before I closed my eyes, Clara's skin had already begun to glow white with her Aura magic. She projected a great deal in the round, feeding off our emotions as we linked our magic as one.

"Mother Moon, Goddess Earth." Clara's voice shivered into an otherworldly timbre. Then she spoke her rhyming invocation. It was always a rhyme. "Hear our plea for witchy energy. We ask for your guiding hand to keep our sister safe in a foreign land."

"Well done, Clarabelle," said my grandmother, using her nickname.

Clara's rhyming invocations weren't necessary to begin our witch rounds. Nothing was needed to be said at all, but it made Clara happy, so it had become tradition when I'd taken over the witch's rounds after Mom and Dad had retired to Switzerland.

Thinking about that time of my life when I struggled with taking over as Enforcer of New Orleans twisted something deep. Especially after what Ruben had said before he left me standing there like a slack-jawed idiot at the reception.

Time's up, Juliana.

A shiver ran through me at the memory of the fierce intensity in his voice when he'd said it.

"Jules," cooed Clara in that silvery, ethereal voice, "stop fretting and focus on the round."

Exhaling a heavy sigh, I turned my attention to the magic beginning to work and move in our circle, sliding in warm tendrils around us.

Mom mumbled, "Spinners' threads can pull too tight." She was already deep into the magical realm. We often said strange things in the round.

I smiled and let myself slip away to that place too. Like sliding and floating on the surface of a pool, my body felt light, immersed in the humming energy of my sisters, my mother, my grandmother. Three generations of witch magic merged in the round, gathering strength with each passing second.

Before I fell deep, I heard Violet whisper, "Stones are old, stones are cold, but blood is colder."

Then I was in the deep dark of my inner self where my power pulsed thick and heavy. Oftentimes, I saw nothing at all while here, simply existed on this other plane, basking in the strength Spirit gave me. I let the waves of energy wash over me.

But then a square of golden light pulled my mind closer. The square grew larger until I was standing in a doorway, looking in on a strange scene, a bizarre dream.

Whirling couples in black tuxedos, gowns, and masquerade masks danced in a dizzying blur to eerie music. A small orchestra performed the music on a stage. The maestro was covered in head-to-toe black, his face fully cloaked, his long dark hair swaying as he swooped his arms, weaving his baton in the air to the creepy, carnival-like melody.

My focus shifted to the dance floor where the couples waltzed in twirling loops in perfect harmony, never noticing me at all. Ruben was there, also wearing a full black tuxedo, the mask only covering half his face, bringing my attention to his beautiful mouth. He did nothing but watch me.

Then a flicker of white caught my eye. Dodging through the couples was a familiar, pixie-like girl in a gossamer gown. Her pointed ears and worldly eyes in the deepest shade of purple found me through the crowd. She smiled and dodged away. It was the Goddess, or Spirit, one of the forms she liked to portray when she came to me in this vision realm.

"Follow me," she called over her shoulder, her voice a blend of child, mother, and crone.

But it was Ruben who followed her first.

"Wait!" I called after them, pushing through the masked couples still whirling on as if they didn't even see me.

She ran to the far wall of books and touched her finger to a thin golden spine. A door swung open, then she disappeared into the darkness. Ruben stood at the threshold and turned to me. He held out his hand and smiled. I reached out and took his hand, then he pulled me with him into the black.

When I stepped through, he'd vanished. So had the pixie. I stood in a wild forest, a stirring of leaves drawing my gaze to the old oak tree next to me where thick green vines snaked up and around the trunk, seeming to strangle it. I stepped toward a glow of flickering light. In a clearing, there was a cauldron hanging over a blazing fire.

No one was around, but it was obviously set there by someone. Then the voice called to me. I walked to the fire and peered into the cauldron, the brew inside swirling with a menacing hiss. Then I heard the voice again. It was Violet.

"Stones are old, stones are cold, but blood is colder."

I snapped awake out of the trance, blinking away the vision as I stared at the candles. They'd burned low enough for me to know we'd been in the round for at least an hour.

Mom and Maybelle were already awake and murmuring to each other. Violet was, too, frowning directly at me.

"Was that you?" I asked.

"What do you mean?"

"Did you send me the message about the stones?"

Her frown deepened. "No, I don't think so. Or if I did, it was subconsciously."

Clara and Livvy roused, both smiling with the fresh energy pulsing through them. I felt it too, like usual. There was always a bit of a high after doing the witch's round, but that wasn't foremost in my mind. I stood and helped Violet to her feet.

"Before we went under, I heard you say something about old stones. Then in the vision world, you said it to me again, speaking from a cauldron."

Violet snorted. "Really? I don't remember saying anything about stones."

Biting my bottom lip, I then asked, "What did you dream about?"

Her brow raised. "Uh, Nico. Duh."

"But what was happening?"

"It was pretty X-rated, but fine. He had me on my hands and knees in a barn. I don't know why a barn, but—"

"Never mind." I waved her off.

Sometimes what we saw in our minds during the round was nothing more than dreams or fantasies. But oftentimes, they were visions. Premonitions. What I experienced was definitely a premonition.

"What's going on?" Clara asked, placing an arm around my waist and pouring her happy spell into me.

I gave her a smile, for she always seemed to worry about me the most. "It's fine, Clara. I just had a strange vision that I don't understand."

"Sometimes clarity comes later," Violet explained. "My Seer visions hardly ever show me anything that I can decipher at first. But something may come to you later to help you out." Violet tilted her head, the purple-dyed ends of her long blonde hair sliding over a shoulder. "Did you sense danger?"

"No." I paused, remembering the vines strangling a tree. "Not really. But it wasn't exactly a good vision."

Violet gave me an assuring nod. "Keep your psychic eye open. It will likely come to you soon enough."

Violet was our Seer, who could call upon her innate gift whenever she liked. But the rest of us had only degrees of psychic ability. It came and went as quickly as the breeze.

"Let's go make some hot cocoa and warm up those turtle brownies Clara made," said my grandmother, shuffling out of the gate in her silk slippers. "These rounds always give me the munchies."

"Oh yes, I second that," agreed Livvy, wrapping an arm around Mom as they followed Maw into the kitchen.

Clara picked up the candles, blowing them out one by one, then followed.

As the others filed out, I asked Violet, "What did you need to tell me *later?*"

She crossed her arms, bunching up the oversize hoodie she wore. Must be Nico's. "I had a flashing premonition earlier. When I returned that constellation book to your library, I touched the chair you always sit in to read." She paused, glancing toward the chalked witch's wheel.

"And? What was it?"

"A sculpture of a woman with a hooded cloak veiling her face. The sculpture stood in a field, surrounded by woods."

"Weird."

"My visions are always weird, but that wasn't even the creepiest part. There were vines wrapping around her like they were alive, like they were trying to strangle her. Or keep her anchored to the ground."

Vines again? That *was* strange. What did it mean?

"You think the premonition was of me?"

"Yes. That I know for sure." She stepped closer and squeezed my shoulder, saying softer, "Maybe you shouldn't go on this trip."

I huffed out a breath. "And give up the campaign to get the werewolves a seat on the High Witch Guild where they belong? Not a chance." I linked my arm with hers and guided her toward the house. "Besides, like you said, these visions aren't always what they seem. The vines could mean anything. It could mean connection, strength, the tying of the werewolves into the Guild."

"Or strangulation and suffocation and death."

"Don't be so morbid, Violet. Did you see death?"

She was quiet before finally shaking her head. "No. Not yours anyway."

"What does that mean, not mine? You saw someone else's?" Panic flooded me, my pulse speeding wildly.

"I didn't see death at all. The statue was probably you, but I didn't sense death."

"The statue may not even represent a person. A hooded figure. It could be the host of witches in the Guild or it could represent witchcraft or magic itself."

"Or it could be you."

I laughed because Violet always narrowed in on the worst-case scenario when she had visions these days. Ever since she didn't see her own imminent kidnapping, which resulted in no harm to her, and the attack on Livvy, which resulted in great harm to her attacker and emotional distress to Livvy, Violet had been hypervigilant where her visions were concerned. And always thinking the worst.

"Okay, Vi, if I see vines on my trip, I'll run."

"Don't make fun."

She jerked on my arm as we crossed the courtyard to the back patio door. I smiled at the birdhouse that was a mini Swiss chalet that Dad had made and brought back to us.

"If you sense anything dangerous at all," continued Violet, "you tell Ruben. I plan to tell him about this vision, too, just to be on the safe side."

The mention of his name shot a double dose of adrenaline through my blood, and I was reminded that I'd be spending the next several weeks, maybe two months, in his daily company. My pulse hammered so hard I felt it in my throat.

"If that makes you happier, then go ahead," I finally said as I opened the door to the smell of chocolate and the sound of feminine laughter coming from the kitchen.

"I thought you were going to argue and tell me not to tell him."

"Whatever makes you more comfortable, I'm totally fine with."

"It's not about that, Jules. It's about taking care of you." She pulled me to a stop to face her before we entered the kitchen. "You're always taking care of us, of everyone else, but sometimes, someone needs to watch over you."

A pinprick of emotion stung my eyes because I knew it was true. I'd always been watching out for them. It was my duty and responsibility as the eldest sister and as the Enforcer of New Orleans. I never minded or regretted that. Well, maybe I did once. But I'd made the right decision then.

After what Ruben said to me last night, I understood I'd be given that choice again. And the blood coursing hot through my veins told me I might be making a different choice altogether this time. Rather than fear it, and though I was unsure, I still found myself eager for tomorrow.

I combed a brush through my wet hair, staring at my open suitcase and wondering if there was anything I was forgetting, even though I'd made a list two weeks ago and had been pre-packing ever since.

Trying not to work myself into a fit of anxiety about this trip, I meandered down the hallway. Evie and Mateo's bedroom door was slightly ajar, but only Evie was sound asleep in their bed. Down the hallway, the babies' nursery door was open. Mateo was in his boxers and a T-shirt, rocking Diego with one foot while the wildest of his little brood sucked on a bottle. Then I heard the little grunts coming from Celine's crib.

"I'll get her," I whispered.

Mateo smiled and nodded sleepily. "Thank you."

Cuddling the soft, sweet-smelling bundle in her pink quilt that Clara had made her, I slung a burp cloth over my left shoulder and made my way downstairs.

"Someone's hungry?" I cooed as she chewed on her fist, eyes crinkling with delight. "You're such a sweet girl."

She smiled bigger, her almond-shaped eyes tiny slits of green like her mother's.

"You're going to be a little heartbreaker, aren't you?" I whispered as I walked through the living room. "And your daddy is going to have to beat up all the boys."

"He probably will," said Mom, grinning as she walked in from the darkened kitchen with a bottle in hand. "I knew she'd be up soon, so I went ahead and made a bottle."

"You know their routine already too?" I took a seat on the sofa.

Mom sat next to me and handed over the bottle. "If Celine hears either of her brothers up, then she's up."

"That's the truth." I tucked her close and slipped the nipple in her mouth. She went right to work, kneading my pajama top in her fist, her eyes sliding closed while she fed.

Mom propped her arm along the back of the sofa behind me and placed a hand on Celine, patting gently. We both watched her in silence for several minutes, listening to her make sweet baby sounds.

"So you're all packed?" Mom asked. "You ready?"

Smiling, I glanced up at her very maternal expression. She was checking in on me without asking the direct questions.

"I'm ready."

"And"—she paused, her voice even—"how do you feel about traveling and working so closely with Ruben?"

What an excellent question. "There is no one emotion I feel at one particular time, Mom. I'm feeling *all* the feelings all of the time."

"And by all, you mean . . . all?"

Swallowing hard, I held her gaze, wanting her to understand something quite clearly. "When you warned me back then, Mom, you were right. I couldn't trust him." *I never took you for a coward.* His accusation back then still stung. "I was untried, and there were reasons I couldn't let myself continue in that relationship."

After handing my mom the bottle, I lifted Celine to my shoulder and softly patted her back.

Mom shifted to angle sideways, facing me. "Another woman?"

I shook my head. "No."

I almost wish it had been. It might've been easier to get over him. But had I ever truly gotten over him? I'd been able to block him out and focus on business and suffer in silence, yes. But that wasn't getting over someone. If I had, then his promise—his warning—at the wedding reception wouldn't be playing on repeat in my head, taunting me like a siren's song.

"That's good," Mom added softly. "Did you fear what happened to your aunt Penelope might happen to you?"

When Ruben and I had first started dating, Mom had told me the story of my aunt Penelope, her sister, who'd been seduced by a vampire overlord named Broderick. Once he'd gotten his fangs in her neck, he'd used her power as a Siphon—or Enforcer—for himself. Mom had told me the story not because she thought Ruben was like that vampire who'd abused my aunt but simply to remind me that Siphons held unparalleled power, which came with a heavier burden of responsibility.

"No," I finally answered. "Not really. It was a number of things." And one in particular that I still didn't want to consider but had kept me well away from these thoughts and the possibility of what-if with Ruben for the past twelve years.

"And . . . do those number of things still add up to the same conclusion as before?"

When I tucked Celine back into my arms, put the bottle into her mouth and looked up, Mom was smiling.

"Is there something you want to say, Mom?"

She reached out with the arm that had been resting on the sofa back and tucked the damp strands of my hair behind my ear. She hadn't done that in so long, I couldn't even recall the last particular time. But the memory of it, of that maternal touch, given softly and with the knowing look in her eyes, made my heart pinch. She was the only one who could make me feel so vulnerable and small and loved with a single touch. Well, not the only one.

"Ruben Dubois has established himself as vampire overlord here. He seems content in his place."

"I know, Mom, I—"

She stopped me with a wave of her hand in the air. Not by magic, just simply a motherly shush move. I stayed quiet.

"As I said, he knows his place. And you have grown into your own power. You have full control as Enforcer of New Orleans. I keep tabs on you, you know, and everyone says that my daughter can hold her own against anyone and she leads this region with honor, and force when necessary." Her hand fell to rest on Celine's belly, brushing the back of mine where I held the bottle. "I couldn't be prouder of the witch and the leader you've grown into."

"Then why do you look so sad?" A hard lump had lodged in my throat.

"Because I'm afraid I might've been too harsh during your transition. It might be my fault that you're still . . ."

"Still single?" I huffed a sort of laugh.

"No. And yes. But I meant that you're still so unhappy."

I tried to swallow around the lump that had grown, my throat dry, my eyes stinging with tears I would *not* shed. I would not.

Mom brushed a thumb gently over the back of my hand. "All of the things I told you were meant to protect you, but perhaps I was wrong."

"You weren't, Mom. It wasn't just you." It was *me*. And him. So much of him. "Why are you pushing this anyway?" I whispered down at Celine since my throat was raspy with emotion.

"From what I've seen, there's something different in Ruben's gaze now. He's more tempered than he was when he first moved here and when you were going through the transition of power."

"Are you saying that you think Ruben's tame?" I smiled at the ridiculous thought.

When she laughed, my tension eased, the knot in my throat melting away. "I seriously doubt that, sweetheart. But before, he seemed to be driven by an earnest ambition."

"I know." I remembered.

"People change, Jules. And he's changed." She stood and leaned over, pressing a kiss to the crown of my head. "There's always a catalyst for change in a man as independent and strong as one like Ruben Dubois." She lifted my chin with her fingers. "I bet

I know what's taming his beast. Or rather, who." She patted my cheek and left the living room, walking toward the den that we'd made into a guest bedroom while her and Dad were here.

I sat for a long time as Celine slept in my arms, mulling over what Mom had said. Ruben was by no means tame, but he was different than when he'd first arrived. I tried to recall one moment when he'd overstepped since that last time, but there hadn't been one. As a matter of fact, he'd made himself so scarce for a while that I thought he'd left town altogether.

He hadn't. He'd put all of his focus on building his businesses, especially his vampire den, which he'd renamed the Green Light. I wondered why he had changed the name. Perhaps telling me in some symbolic way that vampire-kind didn't need to hide their nature like a dirty secret, giving the *green light,* as they said, to drink blood to their fill.

I'd never said they couldn't or shouldn't, but perhaps I'd implied something along those lines in my rejection of him. Either way, I never had the courage to ask him about the name change, and he'd never bothered to offer up the information. He'd stayed out of my way—as I'd asked—for a very long time.

The past two years had brought us together more, with the curse on Mateo, the blood trafficking ring we'd worked on, the werewolf pack coming to town, and with what had happened to Livvy. And now, the campaign to gain werewolves a seat in the High Witch Guild would throw us together for the weeks to come. Heightened anticipation and a touch of anxiety hummed in my veins.

I stood from the sofa, holding Celine securely in my arms, and then headed upstairs, knowing I needed to at least try to get some sleep. Stepping into the nursery, I smiled at the sight of Mateo, head tilted back and out cold. Sprawled with legs and arms splayed wide was Diego, confident and secure in a deep sleep in his father's arms. He already looked so much like Mateo with those dark curls. He'd be a lady-killer one of these days.

The thought of our growing family and the future filled me with both joy and sad unease. What would my own future look like as my sisters started families of their own? Would I ever only be the doting, spinster aunt? And whose fault would that be if I was?

After tucking Celine in her crib, I did the same with Diego, and then I roused Mateo. "You can go get in bed," I whispered.

He murmured something inaudible and shuffled back to his bedroom, while I followed him out. Knowing the baby monitor was set up in Mom's room for the night to give Evie and Mateo a break, I reached in to pull their door shut. I couldn't help but watch Mateo curl an arm around Evie's waist and pull her spoon-fashion into the crook of his body. She sighed happily and snuggled back against him. I shut the door quietly, a pinprick of longing squeezing my heart.

CHAPTER 5

~RUBEN~

"Are you cold?" I asked but turned down the AC anyway.

Jules had her arms crossed over her chest as if she were trying to keep warm. "I'm fine." She added with a tight smile, "Always a little colder than everyone else."

"I remember."

She glanced my way, probably thinking I referred to her personality, but I remembered how often she liked to be snuggled in a sweater or blanket. Without looking at her, I felt around the back seat until I found my suit jacket and then placed it across her lap.

"That's okay," she started to protest.

"You're cold. You packed all your sweaters in your suitcase obviously." I glanced at her blue dress, simple and professional, and made of a thin material. "Just use my jacket till we get there."

When I thought she might argue again, she didn't. Instead, she opened up the jacket, facing her, and draped it over her upper body and lap. My jacket practically swallowed her entirely, and my body's reaction was rather unexpected. I'm not sure how or why, but the simple action of her being covered in an article of my clothing had my dick hardening in my dress pants.

"Are you hungry?" I asked to find something to talk about since we'd been mostly silent the past two hours on the road.

"No." I felt her gaze on me. "Are you?"

Now my dick was fully hard, no half-measures about it. I knew Jules wasn't offering her own throat. If she ever did, I'd likely lose my fucking mind with desire. I'm not sure I could ever trust myself near her perfect, slender throat, but because I knew her better than she understood, I knew exactly what that question was about.

"No, I fed last night. I should be good for a month or two."

She turned her gaze out the window, a flush of pink crawling up her neck. If I were cruel, I'd let her think what she was thinking. She was already stewing over my declaration at the wedding reception. Likely, she was wondering when the hell I was going to make my move and what that would entail.

I was a patient hunter. I'd waited this fucking long, so I was going to do this right. No spooking my prey. No sudden movements to let her get away. I'd wait in the underbrush, let her get comfortable with my presence and my intent, let her circle and draw closer by small degrees. It would be a slow, deliberate seduction so that once she was within my reach, she'd be ready for me.

But no matter if my tactics might appear merciless to her in the near future, I wasn't going to let her imagine all kinds of nefarious bullshit that she could use as ammunition to reject me. It was time to set some things straight, even if by slow degrees.

"Damon is capable of letting me feed longer than most," I said evenly. "I should be good for quite a while now."

As suspected, her head snapped in my direction. I kept my expression smooth, eyes on the road as we crossed Texas, growing closer to Houston.

"Damon? You feed . . . from men?"

"Why wouldn't I?" I refused to give in to the temptation to look at her and soak in her surprise. "I don't fuck my blood-hosts. For me, there is no sexual exchange."

No matter what women claimed on the iBite app, a matchmaker for vampires and blood-hosts, I didn't touch them sexually when I drank from them. If they happened to find pleasure, it was out of my control. I was aware my toxin gave pleasure. For Damon, it apparently felt more like a drugging high rather than an orgasmic one.

I'd recently chosen Damon as my preferred blood-host because there were no mixed signals. Oftentimes, women thought I chose them as a prelude to a relationship. It could become awkward and annoying. Since Damon was heterosexual, I knew there would be no chance of him misconstruing this as a ploy to get him into bed. Ours was a mutually beneficial exchange. He received the strength and youth-giving properties of my toxin, and I was well fed for weeks, sometimes even two months at a time.

"I wasn't aware you used male blood-hosts."

"Now you are."

"You've been using them often?"

"More and more recently. Damon has been my only blood-host for a little over a year now."

She went silent, watching me curiously, that brilliant brain of hers whirling with all kinds of thoughts.

"Go ahead," I told her, "ask me."

"Ask you what?"

I smiled, meeting her gaze. "Why do I solely choose a male blood-host? I'll tell you." A surge of gratification washed over me. Finally, I could address this nonsense. "Because I was told about a year and a half ago that a certain witch got up onstage at her sisters' birthday celebration, performed an inebriated rendition of Alanis Morissette's 'You Oughta Know,' then was put soundly to bed by her sister who happened to see a text on the drunk sister's phone of me feeding on another woman."

All right, so maybe I wasn't going to move at a snail's pace. Not when it came to shit like this. I wasn't going to sabotage my chances and throw it all out there at once, but it was time to clear the air about this.

I relished the slack-jawed shock on her face.

"Isadora *told* you?" she practically hissed.

"As if your sister would betray your confidence." I scoffed. "It was Devraj."

She bristled, but I was getting exactly what I wanted because she snapped, "Did you know who sent it?"

"No. I tried to discover who it was, but by the time I did, the burner phone they'd used had long been trashed. Gareth couldn't find who it was."

"Probably Beverly."

Beverly knew her place and that if she crossed me, there would be severe consequences. "It wasn't her. And while we're on the topic of Beverly, I fired her."

Her eyes widened in surprise. "You did?" She blinked swiftly a few times, a nervous tell. "When?"

"The day before we left on this trip."

"Oh. You didn't have to—"

"She means nothing to me. And you mean everything, so yes, I fired her. She's out of the picture. So if it was her, she's gone now and won't get in between us again."

My blood pumped hard and fast through my veins, still furious at whoever had betrayed me in such a way. And for what reason? I suppose the only one with motive would've been Beverly, but I still didn't believe she had the balls to do something like that, knowing my wrath if I ever found out.

"It doesn't matter." Her voice dipped solemnly. "You can feed on whomever you like. We aren't together."

Pushing past that last gutting sentence, I stated succinctly, "It hurt you—seeing me feed from another woman—so I stopped."

I was thankful she hadn't realized the peculiar resemblance that young woman had to Jules. I remembered that night in particular because I'd been carousing with my men and a few business partner vampires from out of town. They'd invited their long-term blood-hosts and girlfriends, in addition to a beautiful brunette I'd just met, back behind the red velvet curtain in my club, an exclusive after-hours party.

While the rest of them fucked their blood-hosts that night on the chaise lounges, the sofas, and up against the walls, I hadn't. I recalled looking into the young woman's jade-green eyes after drinking from her. They were entirely the wrong shade, the wrong shape. I'd left the party and had a driver take me back to my house where the paintings I'd commissioned taunted me. The echoes of a throaty laughter and gray eyes followed me into a hellish sleep.

"But, Ruben, we weren't—" Jules stopped suddenly, turning to the window again.

The speeding of her heartbeat thrummed in the air, the pulsing sensation so delicious I could taste her heady emotions filling the space between us. My fingers tightened on the steering wheel so that I wouldn't do something reckless like jerk the car off the highway and kiss her sweet mouth. She wasn't ready yet, but she was close. So fucking close. I knew it on instinct. Still, I refused to do anything too fast that would set me off-course. I had one and only one endgame in sight, and I'd die before I did anything to jeopardize reaching it. Before I finally reached her.

"I know, darling," I said softly, my voice a rough rasp as Shawn James crooned "Like a Stone" on the radio, the melancholy melody hitting home a little too closely. "You said it already. We weren't together. You'd broken up with me. But I'd never broken up with you."

I had continued to behave as if she were still mine. All these long years.

She pulled the jacket up higher around her neck, tucking her nose beneath the collar. She closed her eyes, shutting me out.

That is also fine, Juliana.

She could go silent and not respond. It made no difference. Because the reality was that she hadn't once rejected my obvious intent to pursue her again. She hadn't even rejected my rather frank words just now. And at this moment, I could hear the speeding of her pulse and her deep inhale of my scent from the collar of my jacket draped over her.

It was perfectly fine if she took her time getting used to what was happening, only so long that she understood I wasn't backing down or playing nice anymore. I'd given her space—twelve years of it. That was goddamn long enough.

≷❧

We walked across the parking garage adjacent to the skyscraper that held the headquarters of the Southern Regional High Guild Coven. Jules had remained quiet the entire rest of the drive, only finally muttering a "thank you" when she had handed over my jacket and stepped out of the car.

We took the elevator—again in silence—up to the thirty-first floor where Clarissa's office was and where we were expected to present our campaign to the High Witch Guild of our southern region, which included the ruling vampires, witches, and warlocks of her region. Grims held a seat at the council but never voiced their opinions or participated in voting. They merely observed.

Of course, after recent events with the trial of that heinous piece of shit, Richard Davis, it became radically clear that Gareth Blackwater was the most powerful supernatural being I'd ever known. After the trial, Jules had asked Gareth in my presence if he wanted to claim rights as head of New Orleans. As the strongest in magic, it was his right.

He'd quickly declined and had even shivered in revulsion. It hadn't escaped my notice that Jules had smiled and replied, "I completely understand." It made me wonder how heavy the crown was. I knew it was heavy enough as overlord of the vampires of our region, and her responsibility was even greater.

I let her step out of the elevator ahead of me into a spacious reception area with a wall of windows overlooking downtown Houston. The receptionist looked up and smiled.

"Hello, Ms. Savoie and Mr. Dubois."

"Hi, Aimee." Jules greeted her warmly. "Is Clarissa ready for us?"

"Not quite yet. I believe we're waiting on one more arrival. If you'll please have a seat in the lobby area, I'll take you back as soon as they're ready."

"Of course. Thank you."

We both took a seat on a sofa in front of a coffee table. We'd left around 6 a.m. from New Orleans to arrive for our 11:30 appointment. The offices were indistinct from any other corporate building, nothing distinguishing it as supernatural. Aimee was, in fact, human, giving off no magical signature at all.

"I emailed Clarissa the presentation files with the data," Jules said softly, her legs crossed, fingers clasped tightly around her bouncing knee.

"I knew that you would," I said reassuringly. "We know Clarissa supports us. No need to be nervous."

She gave me a tight smile. Then she glanced past me, going completely still. I turned my body to the distinct buzz of a powerful warlock entering the lobby and met the gaze of a tall, russet-haired man with a pointed chin and weasel-like eyes. He didn't even glance my way, his focus on Jules. A possessive darkness bloomed inside my chest.

He gave her a haughty look and a dismissive nod. "Ms. Savoie. It's been a long time."

Juliana's posture was perfectly square, her expression as serene as ever when she replied, "It has, Mr. Gentry. Good to see you."

He grunted. "We'll see." Then he marched down the hall without even looking in my direction.

I counted to ten before I opened my mouth because my instincts were to bury my fist down that prick's throat. I had no idea why he treated Jules with such disdain, but I could barely think past the rage that had swept over me.

"It's all right," said Jules softly, laying two fingers lightly on the knuckles of my left hand.

I glanced down to see I was gripping my own knee with white-knuckled intensity.

"He's nobody to get angry over."

My gaze lingered on her delicate fingers atop my hand before I finally looked up. She jerked them away.

"Who the fuck was that?" I managed to ask, barely above a whisper.

I was controlling the level of my voice because the fury was too close to the surface. If I loosened the leash, I'd be roaring.

Jules kept her storm-gray eyes on me as she said calmly, "His name is Geoff Gentry. He's a Siphon like me." Clearing her throat, she glanced away. "He acts as Enforcer over the region of Mississippi. But a while back . . . he had his eyes on New Orleans."

"What happened?"

Her knee started bouncing again. "He called me out on an issue that had gone all the way up to Clarissa. It was a dispute between a warlock and a witch. I assured Clarissa I was handling it, and I thought I was. But I'd read the warlock wrong and trusted him enough to heed my warning and back down. Next thing I know, the witch was found unconscious from a black magic spell and the warlock had fled the city." She kept her gaze on the hallway.

"Needless to say, my inept ability in taking control resulted in a badly wounded witch who never fully recovered and a criminal warlock escaping without punishment. And Geoffrey Gentry used my mistake as proof that I was too weak to rule a region as big and rife with wild supernaturals as New Orleans."

Her knee was still bouncing. I reached over and set my hand on it, trying to calm her with a similar gesture she'd just given me. Her head swiveled back to me, a sad vulnerability swimming in the cool gray of her eyes.

"Clarissa, apparently, had faith in you," I reminded her.

She dipped her chin but made no comment.

"And you've proven your strength, haven't you?"

"I have."

"So don't worry about that fuckstick Gentry."

A small throaty laugh escaped her before she bit it back, her eyes dancing with glee. It was a sound I'd nearly forgotten, one I hadn't heard in all the time since we'd broken up. Those few months we'd spent together were the happiest of my life, her laughter one of the sounds that brought me the greatest joy. Equal only to the sound of her screaming my name as she came on my cock. She'd become so serious in her position as Siphon that I began to wonder if I'd ever hear her laugh again.

Swimming in the sweet slant of her eyes, I admitted, "I've missed that sound."

The small smile on her face vanished altogether, her gaze dropping to where I still had my hand on her knee. I pulled back, clasping my fingers together loosely in my lap, realizing something about her story.

"When did that happen? With Gentry?"

She didn't answer at first and certainly didn't look my way when she said, "In the beginning of my transition. Right after Mom and Dad moved to Switzerland."

Of course. Another man of power questioning her. My gut tightened, and I wanted to march into the conference room and pummel that fucker Gentry until he was bloody. But then, I couldn't blame him for what had happened between me and Jules. That had been my fault . . . and hers.

"Ms. Savoie? Mr. Dubois?" Aimee now stood in front of us. "If you'll come with me, they're all ready."

Jules popped up and followed her before I did, likely trying to escape any more of my questions. Aimee paused at the corner of the corridor, gesturing to an open door across from us that led into a large conference room with ten seated around the table—the heads of covens from all regions, from here in Houston to Florida.

There were seven more regions in the US—west of Houston to Southern California, northern California to the Pacific Northwestern states, the Midwest, excluding Chicago, which was a region by itself, from Pennsylvania down to North Carolina, New York City and, lastly, the rest of New York State and those above it. That last one was our next stop when we flew out tomorrow to Boston, then took a car to Salem.

"Welcome, Jules and Ruben," said Clarissa, standing at the head of the table and coming to meet us. She shook both our hands, then gestured toward the two empty seats on the opposite end where she was sitting. "Please take a seat and we'll get started. I'll go around the room and introduce everyone, Ruben, since you may not know everyone."

I knew everyone already. All that I needed to know anyway. Their names, addresses, spouses if any, hobbies, habits—good and bad—who they fucked, where they drank, partied, and/or lay down their heads at night. It might sound morbid and perhaps it was but after spending enough time with Gareth as an employee and now as a friend, I'd become well aware the importance and power of information.

"Of course." I nodded politely to Clarissa and kept my expression polite as she went around the room.

"This is Dr. Derek Sullivan, head of Baton Rouge and north Louisiana."

And total asshole. The warlock had dated and hurt Juliana's sister once.

"Very nice to meet you, Mr. Dubois." He rose and bowed over the table at me in a deferential gesture. Probably because he knew any bad report would get back to Evie and her husband, Mateo—also known as Alpha—which might result in a maiming or injury.

I nodded, then Clarissa went on down the table, introducing Ms. Ramirez, a voluptuous Hispanic woman with beautiful eyes and a deadly smile as head of Florida. There was a vampire named Titus who ruled all of Alabama, not one Siphon warlock or witch in the state. He wore a cream-colored suit, custom-tailored—I should know since all of mine were as well—which contrasted with his dark skin, giving him an attractive yet powerful look. We vampires were all vain creatures. His eyes glinted with silver when he gave me a welcoming smile.

It didn't surprise me that there was an entire state without a Siphon, also called Enforcer, like Jules. They were rare. We'd be traveling tomorrow into mostly vampire territory again. Salem was known for its witches, but vampires ruled the territory now. During the colonial period, the scars that the Puritans had left behind when they burned sisters of witchcraft had carried through time. Still, to this day, not many witches or warlocks chose to live within that region. That was why an old vampire named Declan still ruled there as Head of the Guild. It was a different place, a different perspective, one I'd need to prepare Jules for.

I welcomed each new introduction with a polite nod until we finally came to Mr. Fuck-face.

"And, finally, this is Mr. Gentry, Enforcer of Mississippi."

When his arrogant gaze met mine, I didn't smile or nod or show any signs of respect at all. He didn't deserve it. He actually deserved to have his intestines spilled onto the conference room floor, but that might be an overreaction on my part. Still, I let my mind wander to how delightful his screams would sound as I strangled him with his own guts.

"Ruben." Juliana's voice broke through my straying, homicidal thoughts. "Let's get started, shall we."

I took a seat next to her, corralling my malicious desires. That was what most people—supernaturals included—didn't realize about vampires. Our foremost instinct in this world was to draw blood. That could come through violence or through more sensual means. But when confronted with an enemy—and anyone who'd tried to harm Jules was a fucking enemy—they deserved to be punished in the most painful way. That's what my instincts were telling me at the moment.

Unlike werewolves and grims whose beasts dwelled deep within them, vampires simply *were* the monsters in the dark.

But what was worse, our monsters wore the mask of seductive beauty. Better to lure our prey closer so we could catch them. It was a macabre truth that few realized.

"Now that we're all acquainted, Jules, you may begin with your proposal, the Werewolf Coven Position. I previously sent the information to all Guild members. However, we wanted to hear the formal proposal from you directly, of course. The remote next to you is connected to your presentation." Clarissa gestured toward the interior wall where a screen already showed the first slide of our presentation.

Dragging my thoughts back to the task at hand, and not on murdering fuckstick warlocks who irritated me just for breathing and existing, I let my attention slide to Jules, who was now standing next to the presentation screen. I already knew what was on the slides. I'd much rather watch her.

"As you are aware, in my preliminary report," she began, "history has blatantly left the werewolves outside of our High Guild. They've never been offered a seat at the table. The only reason has been because of their history of violence and, quite frankly, our own history of bigotry."

She flipped to the next slide, which showed the data of violent incidents across the globe, separated by supernatural race. Gareth had been quite happy to hand over this information. Where he got it, I didn't ask, but I was well aware that Obsidian Corporation was one of the hubs of grim intel, owned and run by his uncle, Silas Blackwater. He also happened to be the father of Henry and Sean Blackwater. They were estranged from their father, and perhaps so was Gareth from his uncle, but he'd still been able to acquire what we needed, nonetheless.

"As you can see from the data, the difference in violent crime among supernaturals has leveled out over the years, although werewolves still outpace the other three races. There seems to be a decline in werewolf violence in England, Scotland, and Ireland in the past decade."

"That's most likely because they fled to safer grounds," interjected Titus in his husky, silken voice, leaning back in a relaxed posture in his chair. "I have brethren there who state that the werewolves aren't welcome in the UK."

"Specifically England," I added. Juliana's attention swiveled to me when I went on. "I can't speak for Ireland or Scotland, but England's High Guild has never tolerated the Lycan."

"My father has never relayed that to me," said Clarissa, bristling somewhat since her father Perry Baxter was in charge of London.

Offering her a deferential smile, I added, "London is the exception. But the outlying parts of the country have never accepted those they see as interlopers or troublemakers, so Titus may be right about why we see less violence in werewolves in England. There simply may not be a large population of them left there."

Clarissa's expression was pensive. "Where does your intel come from?"

"My parents live in London. They have many connections in our world throughout England."

I felt Jules staring at me. I'd mentioned my parents once when we were dating, only that I'd wanted her to meet them one day. But that never happened before we broke up.

Clarissa's attention turned back to the screen. "Please continue, Jules."

"As you'll see, there's been a sharp decline in werewolf violence in the past year. Specifically in the United States and Canada."

"Where did you get this information? Can we even trust these numbers?" Geoffrey sneered at the screen. He had no idea how close to a bloody beating he was.

"The data has been verified," said Clarissa. I'd connected her with Gareth and a high-ranking grim at Obsidian Corp to be sure there was no question about our data.

"As I was saying," Jules continued, "the data clearly shows that the violence isn't as lopsided as it used to be. Especially in the last year."

"What's changed in the last year?" Ms. Ramirez asked in her sultry yet authoritative voice.

Jules clicked again, revealing a picture of her sister Violet in front of Empress Ink, her arms around Nico on one side and Shane on the other. The rest of the Blood Moon pack stood on either side, smiling at the camera.

"This is my sister Violet and the Blood Moon pack. She used an old magic on them that—"

"Old?" questioned Geoffrey. "You mean black magic? Your sister dabbles in the forbidden arts?"

"Why don't you keep your mouth closed until it's time for questions." My threat, because it was definitely a threat, rolled out of my mouth in a deep, rumbling timbre, my fangs descended.

Geoffrey's thin face paled as he realized his rude, cutting remarks were irritating the oldest supernatural in the room. He might be an Enforcer with the ability to null magical powers, but I could easily trace faster than he could blink and rip out his throat before he'd even thought of it. He held my gaze, beady eyes wide with shock and a touch of fear. The vampire Titus simply smiled from his reclining position, apparently enjoying the display.

"As I was saying," Jules went on calmly, her gaze flicking to mine in appreciation, "Violet discovered the ability to embed spells into ink and tattoo it into the skin as a permanent charm to help supernaturals with their magic. Or I should say, she rediscovered it because this practice was used by druids and witches centuries ago. My sister also discovered the correct spell to aid werewolves in controlling their inner beasts. For every werewolf descended from Capitán Ortega, the original Lycan curse instilled the need to let the beast out. And as we know, this can happen spontaneously and against the werewolf's will in times of distress, anger, or when the wolf feels threatened."

"And you're sure it actually works?" asked the older witch with a benevolent face in charge of Arkansas.

"We are positive," said Jules.

"And I can second her findings," added Clarissa.

Jules looked back to the graph of data, pointing to the dramatic decline in violence in werewolves in the US and Canada.

"My sister has been training other witches to spell tattoo ink like she does, which is why we've seen the spread across the United States and Canada. Our proposition today is twofold. One, we propose to create an organization of witches to teach this practice across the globe to benefit all werewolves. My sister Violet has volunteered to be on the board of this organization. And secondly, we propose to open a seat on the High Guild for werewolves. Their exclusion is against their civil rights to be a part of our supernatural community. They deserve a voice, and the refusal of this is nothing more than blatant prejudice." Her eyes brightened with both passion and empathy. "Please know I accuse no one here. I am aware that I've been a part of this blindness, never seeing this as a problem that needed to be addressed, but now that I'm aware, I can't allow the exclusion of werewolves at our table to continue."

She stopped and seemed to be at the conclusion, but she didn't sit down.

"Thank you, Ms. Savoie. We appreciate your presentation."

Before Clarissa could go on, Jules said, "There is one more issue I'd like to bring to our table."

Clarissa clasped her hands, shifting forward in her seat, seemingly curious and unaware of another issue. I wasn't aware of one either. Jules's gaze glimpsed in my direction before she addressed the guild again.

"There is the matter of the name the High Witch Guild. I realize in its inception, the guilds of each region were organized by witches and warlocks. Shortly after, vampires and grims were given seats at each regional guild."

I knew where she was going, and I could hardly suppress my pride in this woman. The High Witch Guilds across the world were the regional coven leaders of all supernaturals in the area. The leaders of an area were run by either a witch or warlock Enforcer or the most powerful vampire, typically the eldest, of the region.

"And though there are covens only for individual supernaturals, such as for vampires, witches, and grims—even packs for wolves—the High Witch Guild has professed its purpose to unite and uphold the laws for all supernaturals. However, the name has never changed. It seems only natural to me that if our guilds are comprised of all supernaturals, then the name should reflect that."

There was a moment of uncomfortable silence around the table, though I couldn't suppress a smile. Neither could Titus, it seemed. The witches and warlocks have forever held the position that they were in charge of keeping the order among magical kind. And so the name of the High Witch Guild has reflected that in a rather oppressive way. No one that I know of has argued this point till now.

With that, Jules took her seat next to me. There wasn't a hair out of place, a tremor in her voice, or a wrinkle in her perfect, pale skin. Serene and calm, she awaited their verdict, but I couldn't tear my eyes off her.

She was the same woman I'd met and fallen in love with years ago, but she was also different—more confident and self-assured than the woman I knew then. Though we'd worked alongside one another all this time, I wanted to know more of the woman she was now. She stared down the table, regal and magnificent and utterly bewitching.

Clarissa stood at the other end of the conference table, her expression blank but for the twinkle in her eyes. "Thank you, Ms. Savoie. Is there a name you'd like to propose instead?"

Still holding her passive veneer, she said, "Simply the High Coven Guild would seem to suffice, since it is the highest office of all united supernatural covens."

She didn't even falter, which had me smiling again, because the vote to include werewolves hadn't even been decided. She was hammering home the need to welcome the werewolves to our table.

"Again," Clarissa continued, "thank you both, Ms. Savoie and Mr. Dubois. You've given us three very important issues to discuss and consider. If you will both please step outside into the lobby, we will vote on your proposal."

I followed Jules, who went straight to the wall of windows overlooking the city. It was early afternoon, and the light gilded her with a soft touch. Tucking my hands in my pants pockets, I sauntered over and leaned my shoulder against the glass so I could face her.

She looked up at me, the flicker of that unsure, vulnerable younger woman appearing on her face. She didn't ask me what I thought or how I thought she did. She wouldn't ask me, but I wanted to give her an answer anyway.

"You were wonderful."

She closed her eyes for a brief two seconds, and a shift washed over her expression. Relief and joy. She smiled up at me. "I'm not sure I'd go that far. I merely stated the truth."

I shook my head, absorbing the astounding beauty of her— her brilliance, her grace, her poise, her cool conviction—as she told every one of us that we were essentially lazy and ignorant for ignoring the fact that we'd been unfairly excluding the werewolves all this time.

"You," I repeated, lifting a hand to sweep her straight dark hair behind an ear, letting my fingers absorb the silk of her skin, "were wonderful."

Her expression shifted yet again. She pressed her full lips together, letting me see a glimpse of longing in those beautiful eyes before she blinked it away.

"Jules," called Clarissa, rushing across the lobby toward us in a fast clip, beaming from ear to ear. We turned together and stepped forward as Clarissa wove around the furniture to reach us near the windows. She wrapped a hand around Jules's upper arm. "You won. On all counts!"

Jules let out a laugh and exhaled a heavy breath she'd obviously been holding. "Really?"

"Truly." Clarissa leaned in and whispered, "Not even Gentry dared to vote against." Then she winked at me and tapped me on the arm. "Well done putting him in his place, Dubois."

"My pleasure." Because indeed, it had been.

"We are officially now the first to be called the High Coven Guild instead of the High Witch Guild. Funny that I never even noticed our own name was exclusionary."

"We can all become complacent and accepting of what's handed down to us," said Jules. "But just because something has always been done one way doesn't mean that it's right."

"Well said." Clarissa winked. "So now, you're clear here. I'll be leaving for LA with Aimee tomorrow. I'll also be adding in the suggestion of the name change. That'll be a guild by guild decision."

"Are you sure you don't mind taking care of all the other guilds here?"

She waved a hand with a dismissive sound. "They'll be easy votes. I know it. You've got the hardest one anyway, which is why I leave it to you." She glanced at me. "And you, Dubois. I'm expecting you to exert some of your influence over Declan. He can be a hard one."

"I'll do my best," I promised. I had my own doubts about where Declan would stand on these issues, but I'd wanted to get a victory in the bag before I told Jules.

The other guild members walked into the lobby and toward the elevators. Titus gave me a nod and a smile, seeming to approve of our campaign wholeheartedly.

"Thank you for everything," said Jules, leaning in for a hug.

Clarissa had been a good friend to Jules's mother and had done well in mentoring Jules as the new and youngest Enforcer in New Orleans. She had been in her thirties when she took over for her mother, but even now in her forties, she was considered to be a very young witch to hold such power.

"You're welcome. You're doing great work here," she said, pulling out of the hug and squeezing her once more before letting go. "Both of you are. But beware when you're abroad. That will be the tough part."

"I know," I answered before Jules could.

She frowned up at me in question, but I simply shook Clarissa's hand.

"Thank you for your support."

"Of course. My father will help you in England. He's a good strategist and knows all the influential players."

"We'll rely on his help," I assured her.

I guided Jules toward the elevators once all the guild members had gone. I didn't want to spend any time alone with Gentry on the elevator because I didn't want to sour the mood by getting blood on my Italian Canali suit.

I smiled to myself as I hit the button for the garage, pleased that I'd arranged something special for Jules. She deserved it after what she'd just done not simply for werewolves, but for vampires and grims as well. Interesting that no one had questioned the passively oppressive title of our guilds. Not in the modern age anyhow. Except Jules.

"What's that mysterious look about?" she asked, a lightness I liked very much back in her voice.

"I have a surprise for you."

CHAPTER 6

~JULES~

"WHAT'S THE SURPRISE?"

Ruben kept his eyes on the road as we headed farther away from the business district, which is where our hotel was.

"It wouldn't be a surprise if I told you, now would it?"

Facing the window, I bit my lip to keep myself from smiling too wide. A giddy sensation filled me at the thought of Ruben planning a surprise. We hadn't even discussed his declaration at the wedding reception. That he intended to . . . what? Date me? Seduce me? Either way, apparently I wasn't entirely adverse to the idea because my entire body lit up like a firecracker when he told me he had a surprise for me.

Even though my mental walls were slowly crumbling, we hadn't gone over all the reasons we'd broken up in the first place. I suppose I was ignoring that *little* conversation because I was afraid of what it might lead to. Besides my own likely meltdown of emotion, which was something that made me want to vomit just thinking about it, there was the possibility that the conversation might reveal truths that would keep us from moving forward.

And I was pretty sure that the well of bursting excitement inside my body, sending adrenaline coursing through my veins, was indeed a sign of my willingness—eagerness, even—to move forward. With Ruben.

Rather than focus on the circus of emotions having a party inside me, I focused on the highway, realizing we were leaving Houston. "Okay, how far is this surprise?"

"Not too far. Are you really hungry? We can stop and get a quick bite on the way."

I actually shivered at his nonchalant suggestion of *getting a quick bite*. Against my will, my attention went to his mouth. *Why* did he have to have such a pretty mouth? And *why* was I remembering how well he could use it? Then his lips curled upward, reminding me I was staring and he'd noticed.

"Not even a little hint?" I asked playfully.

There was a moment of shock on his face that I was actually flirting. Flirting with fire, that is, because I was still unsure, but also crazy excited that this might be happening. Again. And this time, I felt more prepared. I wouldn't be blindsided by my obsession. My gaze dropped to his mouth again. At least, I hoped I wouldn't be blindsided.

I forced myself to stare out the window as we finally exited the highway into an unpopulated area. "Where in the world are you taking me?"

He reached into his inside jacket pocket and pulled out a black silk scarf and then handed it over to me. "I'm going to need you to put this on over your eyes."

My heart exploded into overdrive, panicked and thrilled at the same time. "What is this, Ruben? Not some kinky . . . ?"

His expression was downright devilish. "Some kinky what?"

I wasn't going to voice what I was thinking because my brain couldn't even process thoughts of a sex dungeon, black silk, and Ruben in charge.

He waved the scarf at me and laughed. "Put it on and tie it tight. I promise I have nothing salacious in mind."

As I tied the scarf around my eyes, I heard him add in a low rumble, "Not today anyway."

I pretended not to hear him, tending to my scarf, which rendered me completely blind.

Huh. This was new. I didn't hesitate at all to make myself vulnerable in Ruben's presence. Because I trusted him. Why did that realization hit me so hard?

Because you didn't before.

Clasping my hands together in my lap, I waited. I felt us slowing onto bumpier terrain and gravel. I heard the distant voices of people, then a car door opening and closing somewhere to my right. Ruben put his car into park.

"Stay right there and don't peek."

I did, getting more jittery by the second. I had no idea what was going on. He opened his door, and there was a rustling sound as he removed his jacket, then tossed it in the back seat. For someone who prided himself on his many custom-made clothes, he handled them with little care.

He closed his door, and then a few seconds later, my door opened. He took me by the hand and guided me out. He kept hold of my right hand in his right hand and wrapped his left around my waist to steer me toward the sound of people. Lots of people, talking excitedly, some laughing.

"Ruben, I can't stand it anymore."

He pulled me to a stop, and I felt him shift behind me, the heat of him at my back sending a wave of heat through my entire body. He untied the scarf and removed it. I blinked a few times, staring up at a big sign over a large gate leading into a walled structure.

"The Texas Renaissance Festival?" I read it aloud as a question because I couldn't believe Ruben would bring me to something like this. It was so not his style.

He stood at my side, having taken off his vest and cuff links, his shirt sleeves rolled up, looking about as casual as I'd ever seen him. Besides when I'd seen him naked.

He stared up at the sign, arms crossed, seemingly very proud of himself. "It's Highland Fling weekend. Apparently, they do themes, but that's not why I wanted to bring you here. Guess who is their special folk band for this weekend?"

"I have no idea," I said, still stupefied and staring at the sophisticated, debonair vampire overlord of New Orleans, smiling like a schoolboy outside of a themed Renaissance festival.

He beamed down at me. "Loreena McKennitt."

"*What?* My favorite singer?" My heart jolted.

"Indeed."

He pressed a hand at the small of my back to get me moving toward the gate as he pulled two tickets from his back pocket. He'd been planning this for a while.

"How did you possibly know she'd be here?"

He arched a brow as if he thought that a foolish question.

"She should be playing this afternoon, but I'll bet you're hungry. Let's go find some meat on a stick, shall we?" He looked down and waggled his eyebrows suggestively.

The laughter belted up my throat as I soaked in this boyish charm that I hadn't seen in so, so long. His smile softened, but his gaze remained intense.

"I can't believe I'm going to actually see her."

She was a Canadian singer and songwriter with Celtic and Middle Eastern influences. And she was getting older, so I didn't think she traveled for concerts anymore.

My sisters always teased me about my eclectic taste in music that leaned toward German and Celtic folk bands more than anything else. Well, I also adored the Hu, a Mongolian folk metal band, which was probably the most conventional of my favorites. I suppose that wasn't saying much.

Ruben passed our tickets to one of the gatekeepers and took my hand, tugging me alongside him into a jostling crowd. Warmth washed through me at that single touch. He pulled me closer when three men dressed in full barbarian garb marched by. Once we were inside and in the open lanes beyond the crowds at the gate where people fanned out in different directions, I glanced down at where he held my hand. He noticed and dropped it with a friendly smile. A small pang of loss stung me, but I smiled and we walked on.

Feeling a little awkward because this felt very much like a first date, or actually our second first date, I took in my surroundings. Excited to finally see the Texas Renaissance Festival with my own eyes, I knew that the permanent village was built with Elizabethan-style shop fronts and theaters even though it was open only a few months a year. Violet and Livvy had come a few times and told me all about it, always wanting me to tear myself away from work to come.

"I've always wanted to come here, but just never seemed to have the time."

Ruben laced his fingers with mine, his hand swallowing my smaller one entirely, gazing down at me with dizzying adoration. "I'm glad I brought you then. I'd like to be the one at your side when you do all the things you've always wanted to do."

Rather than comment because my throat had become suddenly bone-dry, I gave him a small smile. He was making lifelong affirmations, and I wasn't there yet. Not even close. I was currently just at that first-date feeling of excitement and possibility. No matter that we'd already kissed and licked and fucked each other senseless. This was the beginning of starting over, and I needed to go at that pace to see if this was truly as right as it felt.

"Look, how about that place? Captain's Galley." He pointed with his free hand. "Not exactly fancy enough for a chef, but it'll make your stomach stop growling."

"My stomach isn't growling." Which of course, it immediately made me a liar and rumbled.

He laughed. "Come on. Let's get you fed."

I got sausage on a stick and fried mushrooms. Ruben got the turkey leg and peasant potato fries. We found a table in the open where we could watch the people walk by.

"Why are you eating anything?" I asked. "This isn't your regular fare."

Vampires ate regular food, but it was blood that gave them the sustenance they needed and the power to their magic. Ruben enjoyed only fine dining. When we were together before, I almost questioned if he was dating me for my culinary skills. Outside the Michelin-star restaurants of New Orleans, I'd only seen him eat my meals.

"But I need to get the full experience, don't I?"

Then he bit into his giant turkey leg, looking utterly ridiculous. Because the sight of this ultrarefined man slumming it at a ren faire and eating a turkey leg roasted by the fry cooks at Captain's Galley was completely hilarious, I laughed loudly. He shook his head and put his turkey leg down and grabbed a few fries.

"What?" I asked.

"Nothing at all. I'm just enjoying that sound."

"Stop, Ruben. You're making me self-conscious. It's not like I've become a curmudgeon. I laugh."

"Not around me." He didn't say it accusingly, but it hurt all the same.

I picked up my sausage on a stick. "I know," I said softly, then added, "This is nice."

Us is what I meant. Being in each other's company without the tension of . . . everything.

I bit into my sausage and then licked my lips. Smoky, spicy, and juicy. "Mmm. Not bad, Captain's Galley."

When I glanced up, he was frozen with his gaze on my mouth. Oh boy. I remembered that look. My body reacted with a tumble of my stomach and a tingling between my legs.

"So." I took a sip of my water, needing a distraction. "What should we do until Loreena performs?"

He refocused on his food. "I thought we could go see the joust."

"That sounds good."

We finished our meal quietly, watching the fairgoers, and then I picked up our plates to go throw them away.

"No." He stood and took them from me. "I've got it."

I was so used to doing the cooking, cleaning, and picking up after others. It had become second nature as the oldest sister and then as the owner and chef at the Cauldron. I was used to being in charge, but I was also used to taking care of everything and everyone else.

Don't get me wrong. My sisters always helped and chipped in, but I was the one who always led the charge in everything, even in the smallest of chores like clearing the table after dinner. It was my instinct to do it now, but Ruben's little gesture of taking over made me feel . . . quite good actually.

I used a hand sanitizer on the bar along the wall, then Ruben joined me.

"Shall we?" He gestured to the path on the right. "The map showed the jousting arena was this way."

The lane leading to the arena was crowded, and people suddenly started laughing and clapping, some turning around. I was short and couldn't see over the heads of the crowd to see what had caught their attention behind them.

Ruben put both hands on my waist and guided me off to the left, then pulled me to a stop. Two jesters came jogging up the lane while juggling, one with balls, the other with batons. The crowd clapped as they did some acrobatics while maintaining their balls and batons in the air.

I clapped, too, but Ruben didn't. His hands remained firmly on my waist, his long fingers and broad palms seeping through the thin fabric of my dress to my skin. While the jugglers did some silly antics, juggling their objects between them, grabbing a hat from off a man's head and tossing it into their little show, my focus was entirely on the vampire standing at my back.

He stroked his thumb along my hip where he lightly held on to me. My breathing quickened, my body luxuriating in his slight touch. It felt familiar and new at the same time. I was sure he was testing the waters, to see if I might reject him. I didn't want to. Not even a little, even though I still wasn't sure if this was the wisest course. And yet, it felt so right.

A roar of applause went up as the jugglers took their bows and skipped off, the crowd resuming their wandering. Ruben dropped his hands, then touched me lightly on the back, pointing over a blacksmith shop where I could see the tops of banners waving. "The arena is right over there." His voice was husky and warm.

When I glanced up at him, I didn't miss the glint of silver.

We walked on, passing another small gathering around men in kilts tossing logs. The Highland games were apparently underway. But we kept moving to the jousting arena.

There were a couple hundred people in the stands when we found a spot.

"Look, the king and queen and courtiers are watching." I pointed to the actors on a dais behind the arena facing us.

They were dressed in Tudor fashion, and the actor playing the king was portly and red-bearded, very much like King Henry VIII. The queen looked perfect in a green frothy dress with lots of flounces, her courtiers in various shades of pastel around her.

Ruben looked across at the royal gathering. "You know, I was born about a hundred years after that king, but the costumes match fairly well."

Even though I knew this, I was still gobsmacked. It always hit me hard. "I still forget you were born so long ago."

"Still spry for my years, darling," he teased. "Don't worry. I can still handle a young one like you."

Oh, I knew he could.

Squirming uncomfortably, I ignored the smirk on his face as the green knight and black knight rode out to the jousting ring. The red, blue, white, and gold knights remained outside the gate of the arena but could be seen holding their banner flags.

"Who are you going for?" I asked.

"The black knight. No doubt."

"The black? Isn't he supposed to be the villain?"

"Depends on how you look at it."

"What do you mean?"

"Well, the villain doesn't see himself as the villain. He sees himself as misunderstood. The world is stacked against him and has no compassion for his cause."

Looking curiously up at him while he watched the knights fly down the line with their jousting spears ready, I wondered. "Do you see yourself as a villain, Ruben?"

He chuckled. His elbows were braced on his knees, set wide apart. He turned his head and leaned closer, speaking a little more intimately. "Not usually, no. But there are times I could be. I feel like I have been." He mapped my face with his sapphire gaze as if he were memorizing it, as if he hadn't stared at me so many times just like this over the years. "Sometimes, I regret being the villain."

"You're not the villain," I assured him.

But that was all I could manage to say under the weight of his hopeful gaze, wanting more from me in that moment.

"Sometimes, I was," he corrected.

The crash of shields and spears and roars from the crowd went up, bringing our focus back to the arena. The green knight had been dismounted. The black knight tossed his spear aside and grabbed his banner flag from a squire and circled the ring. I clapped to the cheers and boos of the crowd as the green knight was helped from the arena field and the blue knight entered through the gate.

Ruben leaned in close, his biceps brushing my shoulder. "Who are you rooting for?"

Still clapping, I smiled down at the arena as a flourish of the dark banner caused an uproar as its owner did a victory lap. "The black knight."

CHAPTER 7

~RUBEN~

WE'D WALKED THE ENTIRE FESTIVAL, HAVING STOPPED AT THE BLACKSMITH shop to observe them forging a sword, seen the belly dancers perform, and watched the birds of prey show, but nothing, not one fantastic thing today, compared to the joust. To hearing Jules tell me she was rooting for the villain after I professed to feeling like one sometimes.

I often wondered if I'd handled myself differently the day we broke up, we'd still be together. But I knew that it would've only prolonged the inevitable. The truth was, she couldn't trust me—some of those reasons outside of my control—and when she told me so, I behaved badly. A simple apology wouldn't have corrected it because we were both in different places. She couldn't change who she was and where she was in that pivotal time in her life, and I couldn't see past my own desires and rage and hurt to see if we could mend it.

Giving her time had been the right thing because I had needed the space too. To figure out exactly where I went wrong and how to alter the outcome in the future. I worried about how to prove that this time was different as we strolled past a flower and jewelry boutique on our way to the stage where Loreena McKennitt would be performing.

Something caught my eye. I touched her arm and pointed over by a pub. "The stage is right there." I'd memorized the map of this place in the past month when I knew I'd be taking her here. "Will you go find us some seats? I need to make a quick stop."

She gave me that serene smile. "Sure." Then walked on toward the stage.

Forcing myself not to stand there and ogle her as she walked away, I bought what I'd wanted and sauntered over to meet her.

By now, the sun had set, and the stars were high in the clear night sky. The lanes were lit with torchlight. I kept my gift behind my back and found her sitting on the outside of a bench toward the back. That was Jules. Never wanting to bring attention to herself, always trying to sit toward the back or blend into the landscape.

What she didn't understand was that there was no way for her to blend in. I'd been refraining myself from punching random men all fucking day long. While Juliana always played it cool, it was her small smiles that gave her an air of mystery. Her gray eyes were wide and stunning, adding to her mystique. Her flawless skin and petite body with generous curves made a man's fingers itch.

Hence, the reason I'd been doing my best to be a gentleman and not maim or kill the many men eye-fucking her when she hadn't even noticed. At the moment, some burly guy dressed in a kilt was sitting next to her and rambling on about something.

She nodded politely, but I caught her glancing around. A wave of relief came over her when she saw me coming.

"Excuse me." I cut off whatever the highlander was saying and took her hand.

She came easily enough as I tugged her away from the lights and chatter of people who were finding seats for the concert.

"Relieved to see me?" I asked.

"Yes."

"It's your own fault."

"How is it my fault?" she protested.

I took her by the shoulders and turned her to face the glass window of the pub. "Because you're so fucking beautiful. They can't help themselves." She tensed under my hands, staring at my reflection by the torchlight, saying nothing. I added gently, "I have something for you. Close your eyes."

She obeyed my soft command and, again, I felt an overwhelming sense of both power and arousal rush through me. I knew this was part of my vampiric magic, warning me of my need for her to submit and yield to me. These submissive traits were not ones she wore on a regular basis. But I'd seen her portray them in the moments I'd needed them once before, and I hoped she would be able to give some of that back to me this time.

Right now, all I wanted was for her to wear my gift. I lifted the coronet of flowers and placed them on her head, then put my hands on her delicate shoulders. I leaned down. "Open."

She opened her eyes, then her lips quirked up. "A crown of flowers?"

"Not really your style, I know," I murmured close to her ear, holding her gaze in the reflection. "But there's something you should know that I'm not sure you understand. Or that you ever have."

"What's that?" she asked, a little breathless.

I never dropped her gaze in the glass, voice rumbling deep. "You've always been my queen, Juliana. You always will be."

Her shoulders stiffened under my hands, but I held her for a moment longer, letting it all sink in. Once, she didn't believe that I could or would be ruled by her. Over time, I'd proven her wrong. I'd shown her on countless occasions that I could stand down and take her orders. But I was speaking also of a more intimate meaning of the term *queen.*

Her eyes widened in the reflection. Then the strumming of music began onstage behind us. I let her turn, noticing something I hadn't before about one of the flowers in the crown.

"A red camellia." I smirked at the pinprick in my chest. "How appropriate."

"Why's that?"

"Come on." I ignored the question and nudged her toward the stage, finding us a spot in the back where I knew she'd be comfortable. Just not too close to the flirty highlander.

It was true that a Renaissance fair wasn't my kind of an outing. If it hadn't been for Juliana's love of the singer currently starting her opening song onstage, I would have lived another three hundred years without attending one. The truth was, the century or two after I was born wasn't fantastic. The general lack of hygiene was enough of a disaster, not to mention the lack of plumbing, medicine, and a decent tailor.

The twentieth century was much more improved, and the twenty-first even better. I loved a world speeding along in technology and progression at the pace I desired. All that being said, there was no place on earth I'd rather be right now than right here.

Her beatific expression gilded by torchlight, her lips faintly moving to the words of Loreena. The softness in her eyes and mouth, no tension whatsoever. And with that crown of flowers, which was shockingly still on her head, I was completely beguiled. Entranced.

A few couples stood to dance in the aisles to the softer ballad Loreena began to sing, her haunting melody filling the night with an ethereal ambiance.

"Surprised she's not a witch," I murmured softly.

Juliana's eyes crinkled with a smile when she looked at me. "I've often wondered the same with a voice like that."

I stood and held out a hand. "Dance with me."

She stared at my hand, then finally placed hers in mine and let me lead her to the shadows behind the audience facing the stage. She was tentative but not unreceptive. And when she stepped into my arms, allowing me to pull her close, I felt like the black knight himself, relishing my victory.

Her pulse fluttered in her throat, thrumming in the air and against my chest where I pressed her to mine. It was a siren song to my blood, and I couldn't keep my fangs from descending. To have her in my arms, looking up at me with a soft sweetness, it slayed me to the heart.

I didn't want to ruin the moment, but the compulsion to confess my thoughts was too much. "Shall we speak of this now?"

She hadn't once questioned my motives, which meant she well understood them. She also hadn't protested, so that meant she was on board. Or, at least, that's what I wanted to verify.

"Should we?" She swallowed nervously. "Speak of this now?"

"Where's my brave girl?" My timbre was low and caressing.

"Hiding," she admitted freely. Her attention was on my throat for a few seconds, then she lifted her gaze again. "Can't we just pretend for now?"

"Pretend that this is our actual first date? That we don't have a past? That we haven't hurt each other and denied what we've both wanted for years?"

She didn't answer, her gray eyes widening, her small hands tightening on my shoulder. I dipped my head lower, face inches from her own.

"That I don't know what it feels like to have your tongue in my mouth, to have my own in your cunt?"

Her eyes slipped closed, but I wasn't done.

"To have you squeezing my cock when you come and scream my name?" I pressed my lips to her forehead, my words whispered and soft as they continued to pour with burning aggression. "Should I pretend that I haven't wanted all day long to push you to the ground, mount you on all fours, and fuck you like an animal? So I can be inside the only woman who was ever meant for me. Till you remember what we've both been missing and have been for twelve long fucking years."

"*Stop.*" She tensed and pulled away till our bodies weren't touching, but her hand remained on my shoulder, her other still in my own.

"You don't have to tell me what we've lost," she snapped, eyes shimmering pools by the torchlight. "I'm well aware."

"Are you? What about that fuck-toy Erik you were with?"

"I never slept with him," she hissed back. "And that was ten years ago anyway."

Time made no goddamn difference when it came to this.

"And Carter? What about him?" Fury flooded my veins at the thought of her with him.

"That"—she glanced away guiltily—"that was a mistake."

"You're fucking right it was a mistake."

Her gray eyes met mine, and it was no mistake there were tears shimmering there. "We were broken up," she argued.

I clenched and locked my jaws to keep from screaming my rage, my own fangs cutting into the inside of my bottom lip.

"Besides," she scoffed, the sweetness of the moment now long gone, "are you going to stand here and make me feel ashamed like you haven't slept with countless women since our breakup?"

She stared up at me accusingly, but I didn't bat an eye. Didn't say a fucking word. I was too afraid of what would come out of my mouth. I couldn't ruin this before it had actually gotten started, even while liquid fury poured through my veins.

"Ruben." She stared, questioningly, searchingly. We'd stopped dancing, but I didn't look away for a second. "You're not serious. You've been—? I mean, you're not saying you haven't—?"

I wrapped the hand that was at the small of her back around her waist, drawing her into my body. Mouth agape and eyes widening, she let me pull her closer till her breasts pressed against my chest.

"There is one thing you cannot ever do again," I growled, trying to rein in my temper, "and that is question my loyalty. There has been no one since you. And never will be again. *No one.*"

Her expression shifted from shock to horror. "But we'd broken up," she whispered, panic seeping into her gaze.

"That makes no difference to my hardened heart. Or my fucking immortal soul."

She did push out of my arms this time, and I let her go. Shaking her head as if to deny what I was telling her, or perhaps regretting some decisions she'd made, she then walked back through the shadows to the bench in the back row.

After I took several deep breaths, calming myself, I sauntered over and sat next to her. We listened to several more songs, but before Loreena was finished, Jules leaned toward me.

"I'm ready to go."

"Don't you want to wait till she's finished?"

She shook her head, refusing to look at me, her expression tight.

Fucking hell. I'd ruined the whole night for her. I should've waited and brought this up tomorrow. This wasn't what I intended.

"Please," she whispered, still avoiding my gaze.

Fuck. What had I done?

I stood and waited for her, walking close but not too close, touching her only when others ventured into our path so I could steer her safely out of the way.

In the car, we rode in silence. Again. But this time, it wasn't with nervous excitement but, rather, sad regrets. Yes, I wanted to punish her for taking a lover, if even for a short span of time, because I hadn't let a woman touch me intimately since she had.

She was the only woman with the right. And I was the only man who had the right to touch her. Yet, she had let another into her bed, into her body, and I couldn't pretend that the jagged shrapnel it left in my heart didn't still twist and make me bleed.

It was my own fucking fault. I wanted to be noble, to obey her wishes, and telling her that she was my true mate—my soul mate, my blood-mate—would've terrified her even more and sent her running even farther from me.

So here we were, weighted with remorse and sorrow and shame . . . and burning, body-trembling longing. The mixture was a potent concoction of paralysis, keeping us from moving forward.

That was why she wanted to pretend earlier like our wonderful day was simply a first date. She was always smarter than I was. I should've listened and pretended too.

I parked at the hotel and carried both our luggage. She didn't fight me on it at all, carrying her leather laptop bag herself.

Once checked in, we rode in the elevator to the fifth floor, our rooms next door to each other of course. I waited for her to unlock her door and turn to take her bag from me.

"I'm sorry," I told her bluntly. "I wanted today to be wonderful."

She let out a sad laugh and then *finally* looked at me, for Christ's sake. Relief drained through my body at the softness in her eyes even if the sorrow still lingered.

"It was a wonderful day." She took her floral crown off her head, smiling down at it, fingering the red camellia. "Truly, Ruben. You were—" She cleared her throat as it broke with emotion. "You were wonderful."

Then she turned and shut the door.

My heart ached at the bittersweetness of the moment, at the tortuous look on her face as well as the kindness in her eyes. She was beating herself up for taking a lover when I never had. That wasn't what I wanted. Not truly. Even though some part of me needed her to feel regret.

"Good night, Juliana," I whispered to the closed door before walking away to my own separate suite.

I showered in the dark, able to see perfectly without the light, preferring the darkness tonight. Then I lay down in my bed and stared up at the ceiling.

Her shower was on. I could hear the droplets of water hitting the tile, but it was the other noise that caught my attention and pricked my ears. The distinct sound of her retching in the toilet with sobbing cries in between. For the first time, I damned my own heightened senses, wishing I didn't have to hear and feel her heartbreaking sobs through the walls.

I rolled to my side and closed my eyes, willing myself to *not* go to her, to *not* comfort her. Even while my gut hollowed out at the sound of her heaving and weeping, sick with remorse, I lay there, her grief a dark balm to my bruised soul. Like a cool, black shroud spreading over me, I mourned what we'd lost. In silence. And alone.

Unsure how much time had passed, I felt the slightest twinge of relief when I heard the toilet flush. Then I noted her bare feet padding across the bathroom, the few steps from the toilet to the shower. There was only silence except for a hiccup of air every few seconds as she continued to weep under the water. Even while I heard her washing her body, a small whimper or hiccup would escape, the tears obviously still coming.

I swallowed the heavy emotion threatening to force me out of bed and send me next door. Instead, I rolled onto my back and listened to every sound: the faucet turning off, the towel dragging over her body, a brush being used then set down on the bathroom counter, the slide of clothes against her skin, the light switch turning off, and finally her tucking herself into bed.

The last sound I heard was of her deep exhale as she settled onto her pillow. Only then did I let myself relax, still staring at the ceiling, at nothing. She was right next door, yet still a million miles away. I'd lay alone in bed hundreds of nights before this, wishing she were still mine, longing for the time when I could have a day like today with her. A new start.

It *had* been wonderful, she was right. But the ghosts of the past crept back in all the same, still haunting us both. And we hadn't even tackled the biggest issue of all, the one that had torn us apart in the first place.

But there was no fucking going back. Closing my eyes, I told my lonely heart to keep beating, as I had so many, many nights before. She'd be ours again soon enough. She had to be.

CHAPTER 8

~JULES~

"Here, I've got it." Ruben took my suitcase and put it in the back of the rental.

We'd landed in Boston, the closest airport to Salem, and were taking the short drive along the coast of the Massachusetts Bay. I'd grabbed a cardigan out of my suitcase before he loaded it since the temperature was much colder here, in the lower fifties.

Ruben had opted for casual today in black chinos and a cream cable-knit sweater. He looked like a goddamn Ralph Lauren advertisement. All he needed was a horse and a polo mallet and a cloud of mist to curl possessively around his body.

Once belted in, I pulled my comfy cardigan around me and crossed my arms. As Ruben pulled out onto the highway, I asked, "It's a thirty-minute drive?"

"Thirty or forty. We'll take a private jet from the small airport outside of Salem to London."

"Private jet? Declan's?"

Ruben kept his eyes on the road. "Mine."

I balked. "Since when did you buy a private jet?"

And since when could he afford one? I mean, yes, Ruben was wealthy, quite wealthy from his many side businesses in technology and apps and his own vampire den as well as being an investor in many other clubs and dens around New Orleans. Not to mention his rare bookstore, where collectors paid top dollar to acquire some of his oldest and most antiquated finds.

"I hadn't realized business was doing *that* well."

"Yes, well, I've been very business-focused the past several years."

I guess he had been. "I've been focused on business, too, but the Cauldron isn't bringing in private jet money."

He smiled. "Different businesses accrue different kinds of wealth."

"And what have I been accruing? Regulars and recipes?"

"Friends and family. That investment brings more happiness than private jets."

He looked a little forlorn as he stared at the road ahead.

"My sisters were happy to hear that we were successful in Houston, by the way. I texted them the good news this morning."

"Tell them to keep their good witchy mojo coming our way. Houston was the easy round."

"I will." I agreed with a smile though he was focused forward.

I turned toward the window and stared out at the bay in the distance, coming in and out of view between houses and trees dotting the landscape as we rolled along the scenic route to Salem. He was right, of course. I thought about all the Sunday dinners that included not only my sisters and their significant others but also our staff at the Cauldron. We were family.

I'd never invited Ruben, but I'd often wondered what he was doing as I sat there at the end of the table of a huge meal I knew he'd have enjoyed. He didn't have any family in New Orleans. He had his vampire brothers and Devraj since he moved to town, and from what I understood, there was now a guys' game night at his place. Still, I often wished I'd have invited him, even if as a platonic friend.

Ha! What a joke. That was why I never had, and I knew it. There would never be anything platonic about our relationship, especially not now after last night.

Still gazing at the scenery, I bit my lip at the memory of yesterday. The glorious bliss of being with Ruben had raced back like we'd never broken up at all. It was so heavenly that I had never wanted it to end. I certainly hadn't wanted to shatter the whole day with confronting the haunting ghosts of our past relationship, all the regrets and wrongs. But Ruben had. I'd wanted to pretend everything was perfect for a little while longer. He didn't. And so that nightmare of hellish truth came spilling out between us.

He'd never taken another lover? Not in twelve fucking years?! It was unfathomable. For a vampire anyway. They were notoriously lusty and sexual. According to legend and lore, there were many who wouldn't even drink blood without fucking at the same time.

Vampires. Their blood ran hot, their appetites hotter.

Yet Ruben had deprived himself for all that time. I had not. I doubt telling him it had only been the one time would help matters. Or that I'd vomited and cried in the bathroom afterward.

I'd truly tried with Carter, and I hadn't let on to Ruben how viscerally repulsive sex had been with him. It had nothing to do with his skills, not that it would've been possible for me to come when my mind was panicking, trying to force my body to enjoy the experience. All the while, I was waiting for him to hurry up and finish so I could escape to the bathroom.

I'd even stayed with Carter for another three weeks, trying to make myself fall in love yet avoiding sex with him like the plague. When I'd realized it was no use, that my heart and brain weren't on board, I'd returned my focus to work. Just like Ruben, apparently.

I glanced at him, that familiar melting sensation pooling inside me at the sight. He was beyond beautiful, this man. I'd always known this, but I hadn't allowed myself to yearn for him like I was right now for such a very long time. I had called last night short, not for anything he had said or done, but for the grief of not having him in my life the way I'd once wanted and for having slept with another to try to rid myself of his memory. It was a crime, a sin I couldn't wash away, so I needed to be alone.

I was working myself up to an apology when the car suddenly jerked and shuddered, the dashboard blinking on and off. Ruben had his arm out and across the console, a palm pressed to my stomach, even though I was wearing a seatbelt.

"What happened?" I asked.

He frowned as he pulled over to the side of the road. "I'm not sure."

As soon as he pulled to a stop, the car died. He tried to turn it over, but it didn't start.

"Fuck," he grumbled. "This isn't good."

"What do you think it could be?" I wasn't good with vehicle problems.

"Could be alternator issues or a malfunctioning ignition switch or sensors. None of it's good." He glanced behind us, the road mostly empty and no buildings anywhere near. Then he searched something on his phone.

"Calling the rental company?"

He nodded right before he said, "Hi, yeah. This is Ruben Dubois. Your rental just died on us in the middle of nowhere. Must be the alternator or malfunctioning sensors or something, but you'll need a mechanic to be sure." There was a pause, then he looked at me while he listened. He finally said, "That's fine, but be quick." Then he hung up.

"Well?" I asked.

"They'll have a new car first thing in the morning, and they're sending a tow truck out now."

"Wait. We can't get another car now?"

"Not a car left." He checked his expensive watch. I never knew the brand names, but I knew they cost money. "It's just after five now. We passed a bed-and-breakfast a few miles back. I'll message them where to deliver the car."

"But . . . seriously? We're just stranded?"

He finally turned to me. "I'm here, Juliana. I'll protect you."

The way he said it and the wicked gleam in his eyes made me shiver.

"I'm not worried about that, but Declan's coven is expecting us tonight."

Ruben started texting at supernatural speed, his fingers flying so fast it was unnerving. And I was a damn witch.

"He knows we'll be there in the morning now."

"You could get us there," I suggested.

"Definitely." He spread his arm along the back of my head-rest, crowding me with his divine perfection. "But it would be difficult to trace as a vampire with you and all of the luggage in my arms. I'm good, darling, but I'm not sure I'm that good." His simmering gaze was giving me all the melty vibes again.

Clearing my throat, I glanced out the window at the water on the bay, a dark sheet now at twilight. "That's true."

"And we wouldn't want any humans detecting us. Besides, I'm not sure it would be advisable to trace that long with you. It's disorienting."

"I remember," I told him, then bit back a smile.

"You mean that day at City Park? You said it didn't bother you."

"Ruben, I was totally lying to you so you wouldn't feel bad." His face was all shock and awe.

I laughed. "You traced me from your house all the way to NOMA. And I'd never had a vampire carry me before."

"And never will again," he stated emphatically.

Ignoring his possessive tone, I added, "Anyway, I didn't want to hurt your feelings. And the date went well, didn't it?"

His sapphire eyes glistened with a metallic edge. "It was lovely." He leaned closer, his fingertips brushing the top of my head. Whether in a caress or an accident, I felt the barely-there touch all the way to my bones. "To watch your face when you first saw Klimt's *The Kiss* is still one of the memories I cherish the most."

Swallowing hard around the lump in my throat, I confessed softly, "It was one of mine too."

His metallic gaze drifted over my face, falling to my mouth, where it stayed a fraction too long. My pulse escalated in response.

I looked away, unable to handle the suddenly thick air, heavy with tactile memories of that sinful mouth on mine, as well as other places.

I hopped out and leaned against the passenger side, facing the water with my arms crossed at the cool air rolling in. Ruben joined me a minute later, but we waited together in silence.

Fortunately, we didn't have to wait long. A tow truck pulled up quickly with a light tap on his horn. A big man with weathered skin and a friendly face waved as he joined us behind the vehicle.

"Hey there. Name's Pete," said our rescuer. "Let me get the car hooked up, then I'll take you where you want to go."

"How about that bed-and-breakfast back a few miles?" asked Ruben.

"Oh yeah. Willow Beach. It's run by the Willows." He chuckled. "Get it?"

I bit my lip to keep from smiling. Ruben gave me a look.

"Yeah, I can take you there as soon as we take care of your car."

"*Rental* car," Ruben corrected.

I rolled my eyes. Car snob. What was it with vampires and their machismo with cars?

Without further ado, we moved our luggage into the space behind the truck's seat and climbed up for our ride back to the bed-and-breakfast.

Pete told us all about his aunt's pie shop that had the best pies that we had to experience but was unfortunately closed due to her gallbladder surgery. Then he told us about his son, Ethan, getting detention so many times this school year that he was finally expelled last week for dancing on the cafeteria table while doing a TikTok challenge. By the time he'd told us about his rheumatoid arthritis and his wife's need for back surgery, we were pulling onto the long drive toward the bayside bed-and-breakfast.

After we'd gotten out of the truck, Ruben pulled our luggage from behind his cab. "I've got something for you, Pete. It'll help with your ailments."

Ruben opened the pocket of his carry-on messenger bag and pulled out a glass vial with an amber tint.

Pete eyed the vial Ruben held out to him. "We've tried CBD oil and stuff like that. None of it seems to work."

"This one is special. You need to trust me. You and your wife drink two drops each in a glass of tea for a week, and you'll feel better than ever."

"You two pharmaceutical reps?" Pete's brow rose into his shaggy hairline.

I was about to say "no" when Ruben interrupted, "Indeed. We're co-owners of a brand-new medicine. FDA approved. It won't just kill the pain but will rejuvenate the broken-down cells that are causing pain from bone deterioration. I'm positive it will help your arthritis and your wife's back problems."

"Wow." He scratched his head, looking at the inconspicuous vial, not knowing what he was holding. "Thank you very much, Mr. Dubois."

"My pleasure." Ruben shook his hand, then lifted our luggage and walked beside me to the door.

Pete then looked behind us at the large, two-story beach-style house with a wrap-around porch. "Looks like the Willows are having one of their hippie workshops."

We could hear lots of voices on the bay side of the house. A sign on the steps read: *Welcome to a Weekend of Connectivity and Spiritual Growth.*

"Well, good luck to you two." Pete waved and headed back to the tow truck.

I frowned at the sign, but then turned to Ruben, hiking my laptop bag higher. "Ruben," I hissed as we made our way to the large front door, "did you give him your toxin?"

He shrugged. "They needed it. Not only will it give him and his wife relief from pain, it'll extend their lives a decade or two."

I couldn't believe this. "You carry vials of your toxin around with you?"

He stopped at the door while I opened it.

"You may need it, Juliana, and I know you don't want my bite. I collected the toxin just in case."

Two things struck me rather hard. First, he had predicted the possibility of danger ahead, and we needed to discuss that, especially if he thought I might need vampire toxin to help me heal a severe injury. And, secondly, he had the forethought to collect his own venom so that he could give me its healing properties without actually biting me, since that had been an obvious point of contention in our past.

I didn't know what to say or think. I stared at Ruben as he walked past me through the open door I held for him.

"Come along, darling." He gave me that cavalier, lopsided smile that always made me weak-kneed. "Let's find a room and our bed for the night."

Still digesting what I'd just discovered, I followed him to the front desk, which was more of a podium with an antique quill pen and inkpot sitting atop it. The room was nautical and a tad crowded in decor. There were wreaths made of shells and starfish hung on one wall while another wall bore a string of blue and green glass fishing floats tied together with coarse rope. A collection of lighthouses in different sizes was stacked along a long end table, and at least four sea-glass chimes dangled from the back deck, which I could see through the double door.

"Hello, there! May I help you?" A round-faced man as tall as Ruben stepped from a swinging door up to the formal, antique podium.

"Our rental car broke down," said Ruben, "and we have another car being delivered in the morning. We were hoping you had some rooms available tonight."

"Oh." His brow pulled down in concern. "I believe we're full, but let me check to be sure."

Just then a man and woman walked down the wooden staircase, the man wearing swim trunks and the woman in a short cover-up. It was November in Massachusetts. There was no way they were swimming in the bay.

"Isn't it kind of cold for swimming?" I asked as the couple passed through an open lobby and through the double doors onto a back patio.

The round-faced man chuckled. "It is." He gestured to a sign on an easel off to the right. "Our workshop is in full swing, and the Browns are heading to our next session on the back lawn." He frowned, looking in the cubby of the podium. "Mrs. Willow usually handles reservations but she's leading the next session out back. I'll check the book and see if we've got anything available."

There was a book? Indeed, there was. A bible-size one. Who didn't use a digital guest registry these days? The Willows, apparently.

Mr. Willow was babbling about his wife's meticulousness when Ruben nudged me with his elbow and dipped his chin toward the sign on an easel beside the podium.

I looked. Then gasped.

Tantric Sex at Its Best: Learn to Love with Spiritual Growth. And beneath the sign was a bulleted list: *meditate your way to multiple orgasms, find your sensual center through erotic yoga,* and *invite your partner to your sexual plane.*

I froze. Literally, I stopped breathing for at least five seconds before I finally turned to Ruben. Nothing but the devil in his blue eyes and wicked smile.

"Here we are. We actually do have one left. I'd forgotten that our regulars, the Harveys, had to cancel. A shame. Bill is a certified yoga instructor in Boston and was going to lead tomorrow's session, but his husband had to be on-call at the hospital. Good thing Mira agreed to fill in. She's actually a contortionist for the Cirque de Soleil."

While Mr. Willow word-vomited information I didn't need to know about the Harveys or Mira the contortionist, my mind had stuck on a particular part of his dialogue.

"One room?" I croaked.

"Oh yes. We've been booked for weeks. This weekend is our semiannual Lifetime Lovers Retreat." He beamed at the both of us. "You're welcome to join tonight's session if you'd like."

I was struck near dumb.

Ruben casually turned to me, placing a hand on the small of my back. "What do you think, darling? A little connectivity on sexual planes?"

I flinched. Not because I was repulsed by the idea, mind you, but because it was a little too much temptation. It was way too soon for connecting on sexual planes! We'd just ended one perfect date in a bitter fight last night.

However, Ruben was in a terrific mood today. He seemed to be enjoying himself and our predicament. I glared at him while Mr. Willow went on, unaware that I was dying inside.

"The Rose Room is one of our larger suites with a view of the bay. Very lovely."

Thank heavens! A large suite. Space to spread out. I slid him my credit card. "I've got it," I told Ruben, fully expecting him to try to pay. "I can put it on my business account."

"As you wish," he replied while Mr. Willow struggled with the card reader. Apparently, it was something else Mrs. Willow handled on the regular.

"There you go," he said, finally handing over my receipt and smiling back at us.

"Do you have the room key?" I asked since he seemed to have forgotten about that part.

"Oh! Of course." He chuckled and turned and opened a cabinet shaped like an anchor. He plucked one rustic-looking key tied with a red ribbon off an empty row. "If you'll go up the stairs and take a right, it's your last room on the left. Our dining room opens at six. So about"—he glanced at his watch—"an hour from now. We don't have a wide menu, but our chef is excellent. Just let us know when you come to the dining room if you have any preferences or food allergies."

I was nervously observing the small dining room through the open archway, which was filled with two long, rectangular tables. Communal dining. That would be a nightmare for me on a regular day at a regular restaurant. But here, crowded in with tantric sex retreat couples and Ruben, I was afraid I'd have a panic attack before we'd finished appetizers.

"Do you have room service?" asked Ruben, his expression sobering as he watched me.

"Yes, of course," Mr. Willow answered agreeably. "If you'd like privacy alone, that's absolutely fine." He winked. "We want our guests to be as comfortable as possible. If privacy is what you desire, then we shall give it. Just know that you are welcome to join us at any session if you like." His gaze swiveled to Ruben. "The sexual planes session starts after dinner, at nine."

When he gave us a cheeky smile, I was unclear if he thought our rental car breakdown was a ruse in order to crash their tantric sex retreat.

"Thank you, Mr. Willow." I turned and walked away quickly with Ruben and his long strides on my heels.

"Unreal," I muttered.

"Why is that?" Ruben asked as we made it to the landing on the second floor. "That there are couples in the world seeking to connect both spiritually and sexually?"

"That there are couples who are obviously engaging in private activities on the back lawn. And that Mr. Willow thinks, well . . . whatever he's thinking." I quickened my pace, flustered and making no sense. "And thank you for asking about room service."

"I could see the idea of socializing with the Willows' illustrious guests didn't appeal."

"I'm sure they're lovely people," I explained, "but I just . . ."

"Yes, I know."

Of course he did. It wasn't news to Ruben that I was an introvert. I enjoyed socializing with my sisters, family, and friends, but large crowds of strangers, especially this kind of crowd who might be sharing their sexual experiences at the table, would set off my anxiety to an alarming level.

I inserted the key into the door of the last bedroom with the oval gold plaque reading *Rose Room* and opened the door. I had no idea what I was thinking because it hadn't even dawned on me the major differences between a bed-and-breakfast and a hotel—besides the sex-on-the-lawn experiences—until I walked through the bedroom door.

Just one bed. It was a queen-size four-poster bed with a gossamer rose-colored canopy.

I looked at Ruben next to me, who was gazing at the room with extreme delight.

"Did you plan this?" I accused.

His smile curled into wicked lines. "Yes. I planned for our rental car to break down and for our only sleeping arrangements to be at this tiny bed-and-breakfast where their biannual tantric sex workshop was taking place and would knowingly make you uncomfortable."

Okay, fine. This wasn't a conspiracy against me. Unless fate itself was toying with me. I continued to glare at Ruben as if he were solely responsible for this awkward situation.

"You can give me that ice-queen glare all you like. But you forget, darling, I know how hot you burn."

"Stop that," I warned.

"What? Flirting with you? Never."

On a huff of exasperation, I moved farther into the room, hoping for a pull-out sofa. It was a suite, after all. But all that meant was that in addition to the bed, there were two club chairs beside a fireplace and a chaise lounge in red velvet along the farthest wall near the bookshelves. It was obviously an antique and looked narrow and uncomfortable.

"I'm not sleeping on that," said Ruben.

"You wouldn't fit. I'll sleep there."

Ruben made a rough, amused sound in his throat. "Go lay down on it. Let's see how comfortable it is."

Raising my chin at the challenge, I walked over. "Fine." I lay down on my side, cushioning my head on my bent arm. The chaise sloped forward, so I automatically rolled toward my stomach. I caught myself with my free hand. I then realized if I slept here, I'd be struggling not to roll off all night.

Ruben stood there, arms crossed over his chest, looking smug and superior.

Growling, I popped up into a sitting position. "Well, I'm not sleeping with you, Ruben."

"If you're referring to sex, yes, I know. Not yet. But we can be adults and sleep in the same bed."

Ignoring the *not yet* comment, I added, "If we do, then you have to keep your hands to yourself. No touching."

Grinning, he showed me said hands—beautiful and long-fingered—then clasped them behind his back. "I won't have a problem with that, but you might."

"What do you mean?" I folded my arms across my chest.

"If I recall, your ice-cold toes always found their way to my side of the bed."

"I can't help it if I get cold toes. I have poor circulation in my hands and feet. You know that."

"I do. And I'm not the one complaining." He took three steps toward me till he was towering above me, his hands still clasped innocently behind his back. "If you want to put your corpse-like, freezing toes on me all night long, I'll gladly suffer through it."

"Stop teasing me, Ruben."

"Why? It's so much fun."

I stared up at him, thrilled at the thought that we were playing again.

"We can't jump into sex." I made myself very clear. We hadn't even kissed or had the "difficult conversation" yet. I didn't want to rush into sex too soon. The reasons had more to do with me than him.

"Who's jumping? We're simply going to share a bed. People do it all the time without having sex."

The offending object of my ire looked decadent and comfortable and inviting against the far wall, the afternoon light casting an orange hue on the gold coverlet and the rose gossamer forming a private abode for whoever decided to sleep under those covers.

"What are you afraid of exactly?" Ruben asked, his tone solemn now. "Me?"

"No." I shook my head, looking at him.

Me.

"I'm going to take a shower, then we can order dinner." I walked around him to grab my clothes and made my escape into the bathroom, not ready to admit my greatest fear that ended our relationship the first time. A fear that didn't control me anymore, but still lingered like all of those old ghosts we'd yet to banish.

CHAPTER 9

~RUBEN~

I'D THOUGHT I'D BUILT UP A STAMINA AGAINST TORTURE OVER THE YEARS, but listening to Jules shower in the small bathroom of our room for the night was testing my limits. With my heightened vampiric senses, I heard every slide of her hands over her body, every scrub of her hair with her blunt fingertips, every slight gasp as she relaxed under the warm water.

Envisioning these things as I heard them wasn't even close to imagining me in there with her, washing her hair with my own hands, sliding my hands over her lush, silken curves, gliding my fingers along her slit till I found the entrance of her body and stroked deep.

"Christ," I muttered just as there was a soft knock at the door. "Thank fuck."

Room service. Something else to occupy my mind. I'd ordered what I knew Jules would enjoy best, opting for a rare rib eye for myself. I figured she'd be hungry after today. The last time she ate a decent meal was breakfast in the Houston airport. I'd insisted, knowing our flight wouldn't be serving food.

I was kicking myself for not having my pilot pick us up in Houston. I'd paid some of Clarissa's men to drive my car back to New Orleans. I'd wanted that time alone with Jules on the drive to Houston, so I'd left my jet to bring my men to Salem. I'd been trying to eke out as much private time as possible.

I opened the door to find a stout woman in a billowy dress with tiny daisies printed all over. She was carrying a silver-domed serving tray and a bottle of red wine tucked under her arm.

"Dinner for two, Mr. Dubois." She smiled cheerily, her curly hair springing wildly down to her shoulders. "Mrs. Willow at your service."

"Thank you. Let me get that." I quickly took the tray. "That was fast."

She set the bottle of wine on the end table beside the bed, then walked back to the door. She propped both hands on her generous hips, standing just inside the doorway as I set the heavy tray on the small table between the chairs by the fireplace. A cozy blaze crackled in the grate, which I'd started when Jules went to take her shower.

"Oh, Chef Broque does not like his food to get cold. Since you ordered your steak rare, he insisted I hustle it up here." She glanced around, seeming to look for Jules.

I pulled out a hundred and handed it to her. "Please take this for the meal rather than putting it on the credit card used for the room."

She stared at it with a brighter smile than the one she walked in with. "Chef Broque is good, but not that good. I'll get your change for you."

"No, it's fine. Keep it as a tip or donation to Willow Beach."

"Thank you, Mr. Dubois, and I, uh, apologize."

"For what, exactly?" I tucked my hands in my pockets.

"I know you and your friend aren't here for the retreat and, uh, we usually only book retreat-goers on Lifetime Lovers weekends."

"I don't follow, Mrs. Willow. What are you apologizing for?"

She gave me a wink with a cheeky grin, looking very much like her husband. "You'll find out. There's a bottle opener underneath the dome. Have a good night." Then she closed the door behind herself.

I was wondering what that could mean when the bathroom door opened.

Jesus, fuck.

Jules was wearing a matching short-sleeved, gold silk pajama set with pants rather than shorts. Her pajamas weren't meant to be sexy. I suppose if any other man looked at her, they wouldn't see what I did. Hell, if any other man looked at her right now, I'd gouge out his eyes with my thumbs.

Get a fucking hold of yourself.

I had to keep my manner aloof, or she'd start freaking out. Still, I couldn't help but devour every inch of her. From her small, bare feet to her rounded hips, from the tips of her peaked nipples visible beneath the cool silk to the delicate wings of her collarbone, from her flushed, bare face to her damp hair.

She looked so vulnerable and sweet and delicious. I had to tear my gaze away to keep myself from doing something I'd regret. She'd made herself clear on the matter of "jumping into sex." There would never be jumping. Licking, sucking, thrusting, pounding, and long, slick slides, yes. But no jumping.

"The shower's yours if you want it," she said shyly, carrying her dirty clothes back to her open suitcase on the bed.

"Why don't we eat dinner first? Before it gets cold."

"Oh. You ordered for me?"

"Yes."

I braced for her to chastise me for assuming to know what she'd like to eat, for *overstepping*, even in something as small as this.

Instead, she whispered, "Thank you. I'm starving."

Relief loosened the tightness in my chest. "I thought so."

She joined me at the wing chairs beside the fire. I lifted the silver dome off the serving tray. Two wineglasses lay flat next to our dinner plates and silverware.

"Wow, this looks delicious." Her nose crinkled as she sniffed.

"I thought you'd like the pan-roasted halibut with lobster and clam cream sauce."

"Good guess." She smiled as she spread a cloth napkin over her lap and took the plate when I passed it to her. "It smells like heaven."

So did she. I got a whiff of her honeysuckle and hyacinth scent. I wasn't sure what combination of products she used that produced her smell, but it was made distinct by the undercurrent of spice and heat that was her own.

"A rather informal dinner," I observed as I opened the bottle of wine, then poured us both a glass. I sat with my plate of steak and roasted potatoes on my lap and took up my silverware.

"I love it," she said around a bite, her eyes squinting with pleasure.

"The food or the informality? Or the warm fire?" My steak knife melted through the prime piece of meat, the juices bright red. Perfection. "Or the company?" I teased.

She took a bite of her whipped potatoes. "All of the above."

I raised my brow in surprise, which made her laugh before she turned her attention back to her plate.

"I'm glad to see you smile after the day we've had."

"It wasn't all bad." She shrugged a shoulder. "Meeting Pete was rather interesting."

"Mr. Willow was entertaining as well." I savored another bite of meat as we ate in companionable silence for a few minutes.

"I wanted to ask you about the vial of toxin."

I'd been expecting this, and there was no reason to pretend I didn't know what she wanted to ask me. I'd been wanting to have this conversation with her, and now was a good enough time as any.

"You're wanting to know why I would carry toxin that you'd only need if you were severely injured."

"Yes." She continued to eat, taking a bite of lobster and clam.

I ignored the jolt of arousal when her pink tongue flicked over her lip to lick a drop of cream sauce.

"England is different than the United States."

"How do you mean?" she asked, finally setting her plate aside and lifting her wineglass. She curled her legs underneath her and to the side as she tended to do when she was relaxed.

Another flush of warmth bloomed behind my sternum. She was comfortable with *me*. It had been a very long while since we'd relaxed and conversed in this way together.

"Do you mind hearing a bit of a history lesson?" I asked.

"Of course not. You know I love history." She blinked rapidly and sipped her wine, a blush cresting her pale cheeks.

Yes, I knew so many things about her, and vice versa. We were sinking back into that place of connection and familiarity. Rather than comment on it, I went on. "The Saxons, who invaded what is now England in the four hundreds, were actually a coven of brutal vampires, intent on staking out new territory and conquering the new land for their kind. In fact, the seax knife, which the Saxons were known for, was shaped with a slanted, sharpened tip to mimic the shape of a vampire fang."

"Really?" She leaned forward, interest glistening in her gray eyes. "I knew that the covens in England were very old, but I didn't realize they originated elsewhere."

"The first vampires originated in Germanic tribes along the coast of Germany, the Netherlands, and Denmark. But they wanted more land to control, more people to own as their blood-hosts. I'm sure you're aware that in those days, vampires didn't check themselves when drinking. Blood-hosts often died in the arms of their vampire masters."

"I know that the Dark Ages were named as such, predominantly because of the vampires' free rein."

"Precisely. Over time, the guilds were formed with powerful witches and warlocks, and Siphons"—I nodded to her—"whose power outranked the vampires. They were the ones to bring the wilder ones to heel. And then finally vampire overlords became civilized. Many vampire rulers condemned their ancestors' behavior. The European clans fell into line. The last to finally do so were the covens of England, the Anglo-Saxon ancestors."

Her brow wrinkled as she took another sip of wine. "I'm still unsure what this has to do with you thinking I could be in danger."

"To this day, the greatest population of vampires still resides in England. More than anywhere else in the world, including Germany where vampires originated. And though Perry Baxter rules the supernaturals of London, every guild beyond London is ruled by a vampire."

Surprise widened her eyes. "Clarissa said that her father would help us bring the other guilds to our cause. I'd assumed his influence was over guilds with witch and warlock leaders."

Since guilds were ruled by the most powerful supernatural in the region of the guild, it tended to be either a Siphon witch or warlock or a vampire. Though there were some grims more powerful than any of us, like Gareth Blackwater, grims stayed out of supernatural politics, preferring to be observers rather than participants.

"There are no Siphons in any of the regions outside London?" she asked.

"Not a one. What intel I do have claims that Siphons are not welcome and are quickly driven out whenever they move into a guild already ruled by a vampire."

She sank back into the chair, gaze moving to the fire. "And you're afraid that a Siphon coming in to tell them to open a seat for werewolves on their guilds will lead to violence."

Fear spiked in my blood at the thought of her being in danger, but I wasn't going to take any chances and pretend that my ancestral brethren would be kind and welcome her with open arms. I was a descendant of an original line of Anglo-Saxon vampires, just like my second-in-command, Gabriel. The urge to invade, conquer, and dominate ran so very deep.

"I'm unsure what kind of resistance we'll encounter when we get there. But I want to be prepared for every eventuality. Fortunately, Gabriel's brother Edmund is leader of the most powerful coven and largest supernatural guild outside of London. We have that on our side." I couldn't admit to her, because I could barely admit it to myself, that even under my protection, Jules could be harmed. "You embody three things that English overlords might immediately reject."

"And they are?"

"You are a foreigner, an American."

"Strike one." She smiled and sipped her wine.

"You are a Siphon, a threat to their power."

"That one, I understand. And the third?"

I hesitated but couldn't withhold the truth. "You're a woman."

Rather than flush with anger, her head tipped back as she laughed. And laughed. So much so that when she finally calmed down, there were tears in her eyes.

"Are you telling me that vampires are misogynistic, Ruben?" She giggled again as she drank the last of her wine.

Smiling, I poured her another glass. "Not all. But some. I'm glad you find it amusing."

"For a race that claims to be so civilized, it's rather ironic vampires still cling to old prejudices. Like the idea that a woman can't rule."

"Again," I stated emphatically, "not all vampires believe this. I don't believe this." Her mood sobered instantly. She cooled while blood ran hot through my veins. I was obviously speaking of the two of us. "You do realize this, don't you?"

She didn't answer but held my gaze, a grave expression on her face.

"That wasn't rhetorical," I told her. "I'd like to hear your answer."

Her throat worked as she swallowed hard, then finally said softly, "I know, Ruben. I know you don't."

The tension of the moment eased from my limbs. Then I had to add, "Unfortunately, Declan and his clan in Salem are of the same ilk. I wanted to warn you before we got there that he may not be overly receptive."

She nodded. "I can handle him."

Then we fell back into silence, which was why we heard the noises outside our window quite clearly. Soft moans became deeper groans within minutes, and neither of us could pretend we didn't hear it.

"You've got to be kidding me!" Jules said, her cheeks flaming red as she stood with her wine and walked to the window.

I followed and stood behind her. On the back lawn, surrounding the firepit, were several blankets spread in a circle. On the blankets were the many couples connecting on their sexual planes while Mrs. Willow was giving some sort of instruction.

Jules gasped when one man lifted his partner's ass higher, his woman on all fours. Jules stepped back, bumping right into me, then she jumped and hurried back toward the fire. "I can't believe this," she muttered.

"I think I'll take that shower now." My voice was rough and thick.

I snatched a pair of boxers and a T-shirt, knowing I couldn't sleep nude tonight like I preferred. Even the shower spray couldn't drown out the orgasmic moans from my heightened sense of hearing. If it wasn't so unbearable, I'd laugh at the absurdity of the situation. But there was nothing funny about the insane craving of desire pumping through my blood or the painful hardness of my cock.

Taking myself in hand, I stroked, tipping my head back, the shower spray beating against my chest. Visions of me removing Juliana's modest pajamas in front of the fire filled my mind. Then the fantasy unfolded rapidly.

My hand was on her throat as I licked and sucked her neck, her nipples. She'd fall to her knees and take my cock past those plump lips, letting me fuck her sweet mouth till I was near bursting. But then I'd put her on all fours, grasp the nape of her neck, and press her cheek to the rug so her ass was up and presented to me. I'd slide in deep and fuck her senseless, till her cries and pleas for more drew my balls up tight and I'd empty my cum inside her.

I braced a hand on the tiled wall and jerked my cock with near-painful strokes. Jules's submission was forefront in my mind as I came, jetting ropes of cum onto the shower tiles and down the drain. A heavy groan rumbled in my chest, but I bit back the roar I wanted to loose, not wanting to terrify Jules in the next room. This was nothing new. Me jerking myself to fantasies of her. I'd done it hundreds of times, but never had she been in the next room.

Sagging against the cold tile afterward, I panted, continuing to stroke myself softly. I needed that before I climbed into bed with her and the temptation to touch her drove me into madness. My willpower was being tested fully tonight.

I might've acted casual and confident about us sleeping in the same bed like civilized adults, but the truth of the matter wasn't comical at all. I was desperate to touch her, to pull her into the curve of my body and bring her home where she belonged. To slide my cock inside her from behind and love her deep and slow till she was mewling and begging me to come.

Like she used to.

Though her typical demeanor was cool and aloof, I knew what made her cheeks flush with passion, what her cries of ecstasy and desperate pleas, begging to reach her peak, sounded like. I knew what brought her to the edge and pushed her over into erotic bliss.

Me. I did that to her. And I wanted to do it again. So fucking badly.

The fact that she'd agreed to sleep in the same bed without much of a protest was a win. She was almost ready. But I had to make sure to control my cock. I was too close now, and I wasn't going to spook my prey at this point. Which was why when my dick jerked to life again at the thought of curling behind her, I started to stroke myself once more.

One more time, and I could curl into bed with her and refrain from touching her. So I did.

After showering my body, scalding myself with hot water for nearly half an hour, and cleaning away any residue of my masturbation with the detachable showerhead, I dried off and dressed. I took my time shaving in front of the mirror and brushing my teeth until the last of the moans from the tantric sex session had died out altogether.

When I stepped into the bedroom, the fire had burned down to a dim glow. Jules was in bed, facing the other direction. I tucked myself in next to her, relishing her small presence and body heat beside me. Somehow, after a whirlwind of a day, I fell into a pleasant sleep instantly.

CHAPTER 10

~JULES~

THE FIRST THING I NOTICED AS I CAME OUT OF A NICE DREAM ABOUT rocking my niece Celine to sleep was how pleasantly warm I was. When it dawned on me why, I came fully alert and froze.

I had my arm wrapped around Ruben's waist, my body snuggled against his back, the tops of my thighs tucked against the back of his. Though he was so much bigger than me, my body still fit nicely behind him, his warmth seeping through my silk pajamas.

To my horror, I also noticed that my hand wasn't just wrapped around his waist. It was tucked underneath his T-shirt, pressed flat against his chiseled abdomen. I was the one who'd warned him to keep his hands to himself, and here I was clinging to him like a damn koala bear.

After easing myself backward at a turtle's pace, I slid as quietly as I could out of the bed, not wanting him to realize I'd basically groped him in his sleep. I grabbed my clothes from my open suitcase on the floor and disappeared into the bathroom.

Since I'd be meeting Declan and his coven today, I opted for something more formal—black pants, blue silk tank, and a black jacket. After applying some makeup and brushing my hair, I stepped into the bedroom with my toiletry bag to find Ruben back in his usual attire, full custom-tailored suit. Today's was a deep blue, his vest a paler shade that matched his eyes. As I stepped closer, I noted there was a zigzag pattern of tiny skulls.

"Good morning," he said, stepping past me to the bathroom.

"Morning," I mumbled, lifting my suitcase back onto the bed so I could stow away my toiletries and get everything back in order.

I heard him brush his teeth, and when he joined me in the bedroom again, his hair was combed to perfection.

"Did you sleep well?" he asked as he passed behind me.

"I did."

"I thought so."

My pulse raced. "What do you mean by that?" I asked nonchalantly.

"Well, the snoring gave it away."

I snapped up my head to see his mischievous expression on the other side of the bed. "I do not snore."

"You do, actually." He set his shaving kit into his open suitcase on the floor and zipped it shut, then stood to face me again. "But once you rolled over and snuggled against me, cuddling rather close actually, you stopped."

Heat flared straight up my neck and into my cheeks. I couldn't deny what I knew was true. "Sorry about that," I mumbled.

He grinned wider. "I'm not." Then he turned for the door. "I'm going downstairs to meet the rental company rep. I received a text they'll be here in five minutes."

When he left, I exhaled a deep sigh of relief. I needed a few minutes to recover from my embarrassment. Instead of dwelling on my clinginess as a bedmate, I walked back into the bathroom to be sure we didn't leave anything. Then I did a sweep of the room. Ruben had apparently stowed away the remains of dinner outside the door.

I was closing my suitcase when a flash of color caught my eye. My flower crown from the Renaissance festival sat on the windowsill where I'd unpacked it from my laptop bag.

"I almost forgot you," I whispered, lifting it from the windowsill.

There was no way to keep it intact on the long trip ahead of us. It would get crushed and fall apart in my suitcase or even my oversize laptop bag. But I wanted to keep a few flowers from it.

I studied the pretty coronet, the delicate petals drying, the vibrant color fading already. The red camellia wasn't fading, however; it was darkening to a deep crimson.

A red camellia. How appropriate.

I now remembered about the camellia when he gave the crown to me. I set it on the bed and picked up my phone, then googled the symbolism of the red camellia. I'd wondered what he meant at the time, but let it go, more caught up in the moment that he'd thought to buy me such a gift and the words he'd whispered when he'd placed it on my head.

Adrenaline flushed through me when I read the definition. *The red camellia represents devotion, romance, desire, and passion; but most notably it is a symbol of the flame of the giver's heart.*

The flame of his heart? That was how he saw me. Tears pricked my eyes. I once had believed he'd moved on and was seeing other women. I'd convinced myself of this so that I wouldn't think about him over the years. I actually still believed this until yesterday.

But one thing Ruben was not was a liar.

The door suddenly popped open, and I jumped. Ruben glanced at the coronet in my hands, then back at me, his expression remaining blank. "Ready? The car is here."

"Yes. I'm coming. I can get my suitcase," I added as I smoothed my toiletry bag on top of my clothes, making myself look busy.

He took his luggage and my laptop bag, then headed back downstairs.

Once he was gone, I turned back to the window to leave the coronet for our eccentric hosts, but not before I plucked the red camellia from the crown and tucked it in my bag for safekeeping.

"Not what you were expecting?" Ruben asked, amusement in his voice.

"I suppose a Gothic castle with gargoyles would've been too eccentric," I added. "Even for Salem."

Ruben chuckled. "Like most vampires, Declan appreciates opulence and decadence but isn't prone to fit all of the stereotypes."

"I can see that."

The drive through Salem was lovely with the city draped in vibrant red, brown, and gold foliage. It screamed of the glory of autumn, but the ride up to Declan's house turned creepy with naked trees framing the long driveway, cradling the road like giant, bony fingers.

"Now I'm getting more *Dracula* vibes than *Hocus Pocus*."

Ruben smiled. "That would be appropriate, wouldn't it?"

"Yeah, but still. Kind of dramatic, don't you think?"

Ruben smiled as he steered the rental car out of the tunnel of trees and up to the circular drive in front of the three-story mansion. It wasn't the typical Cape Cod–style home for this area, but rather a white Colonial with tall columns and ornate trim that seemed overly ostentatious. There were giant double doors decorated with intricate stained glass. The design was two red roses, one in each door tipping toward the other, both of them bleeding from the petals. The casual observer might not notice and think it simply an abstract work of art, but I knew it was a mark that a vampire lived here.

"Custom-made doors, I see."

"Indeed," said Ruben, eyeing the two men standing on guard beneath the large portico as he pulled our car to a stop.

Ruben traced to my side as I exited the car, his hand at the small of my back.

"Ruben," I whispered, knowing full well that was a proprietary gesture of his. "I'm not sure I want them knowing . . ."

He caught me by the elbow and pulled me to a stop to face him. His voice low, he asked, "Knowing that we're together?"

My pulse leaped at his casual words. "We are?"

"Of course."

"Ruben, it's not that simple. We haven't even gone over"—I gestured my hand in a small circle between us—"everything."

"But it is simple." He eased closer, smiling that devastating smile of his before tucking a piece of my hair behind my ear. The small touch sent a wild thrill through my body. "More to the point, Juliana, it's inevitable."

Then he turned me with a hand at my back and gently ushered me toward the door.

"Mr. Dubois," said the taller of the two vampires with jet-
black hair and eyes near the same color. He looked a bit like a
grim with his coloring, his pale skin seeming more so in the
sunlight. "I am Jarek. You're expected in the parlor."

Lots of personality, this one. Ruben didn't seem surprised,
adopting a somber and grave demeanor rather than the lighthearted, charming one he'd had with me the past few days.

Jarek opened the door for us to enter, then moved ahead and
guided us down a long, white marble corridor like a butler. The
heels of our shoes echoed on the pristine flooring that gleamed
like a mirror in the sunlight pouring through equally crystal-
clear panes from the rooms we passed, which all appeared to be
parlors of some sort. One was a library or a study. The mansion
was built like older homes but didn't appear old with all the
bright and shiny finishings.

There were larger than life-size Grecian statues on pedes-
tals adorning the corridor. All of them nude females and males
with expressions of rapture and obvious bite marks in their
throats.

I bit back a smile as I gave Ruben an *are-you-kidding* look. He
arched his brow, replying with a *behave-yourself* look. I had to
refrain from rolling my eyes. But then . . . no way! I eased closer
to the wall to study the wallpaper. Yes, it was a repeated pattern
of a voluptuous, Raphaelite woman—nude, of course—being
bitten on the throat by a vampire thrusting between her legs.

The over-the-top and salacious furnishings and formality of
the place was ridiculous. But I was in a vampire's world now,

and I'd need to be respectful if I expected to receive respect in return.

Jarek led us into a large room, the mahogany floors glistening beneath Persian carpets in red and gold. The chaise lounges and chairs were all in complementary gold and sapphire brocade. An ornate wrought iron chandelier hung in the center of the lounge area. Sitting upon the largest chair at the head of the room facing the door was an elegant-looking man who appeared to be in his forties or fifties. For a vampire, that could mean he was anywhere from four hundred to six hundred years old.

"Ah, here you are." He sauntered over to us, his observant gaze flicking down my body and then back up in a blink.

His dark brown hair had streaks of silver at the edges as did his trim, well-manicured beard. His eyes were a pale green, unusual and alluring. And he moved with confidence, reeking of sex appeal in his black slacks and gray button-down. In other words, he looked like the perfect vampire overlord. But still nowhere near as good as Ruben.

"You must be Ms. Savoie?"

When I reached out to shake his hand, he lifted my hand up and bowed over it, brushing his lips across my knuckles. Goodness, these old vamps clinging to their antiquated customs always threw me off.

"You may call me Jules. It's a pleasure to meet you, Mr. Gould."

"Please call me Declan, Jules." His voice was a honeyed cadence I was sure had enraptured many who met him. Then he looked to my left and held out a hand to Ruben. "It's been a long time, my friend."

"It has. Very good to see you, Declan."

I heard genuine affection in Ruben's voice. That was one thing I knew about the man standing protectively to my left. He was good at masking his feelings, hiding behind a facade of indifference or coldness, but when he showed emotion of any kind, it was true to the core. So that smile and deep handshake meant that he did admire this vampire, Declan. I was suddenly more interested to know him.

"Good to have you both here, even if it is on business. Please, won't you sit down."

I took a seat on the sofa next to the chair Declan returned to. Ruben took a seat right next to me. And I do mean, right next to me. I wanted to frown at him and give him a subtle nudge over, but there was nothing that would get past a vampire. Subtle or not, they'd take it as some sort of rift between us, even if it was simply me saying calm the hell down with the possessive vibes.

His nearness was a message to Declan and every vampire in the house. *Mine.*

Ruben had apparently decided for the both of us that we were already back together when I hadn't actually said yes yet. I planned to, but I didn't get the chance when he'd made his own declaration during our walk to the front door.

If it wasn't clear enough, Ruben pressed his thighs wider when he sat next to me until they were flush against mine. We were now touching from hip to knee. It was basically the vampire equivalent of pissing a circle around me.

Declan crossed his legs, all casual grace, a beringed hand casually placed on his lap. "No more car trouble, I take it?"

"None. Can one of yours drop it off at the rental place?"

"Of course." He turned toward the open doorway and barely raised his voice. "Jarek."

The vampire appeared at his side, the wind in his wake blowing my hair around my neck. A prickle of unease raised goose bumps on my skin. I wasn't accustomed to being surrounded by so many vampires all by myself. Not that Ruben would allow anything to happen to me. As if to remind me, he leaned even closer, his upper rib cage brushing my shoulder when he threw an arm over the back of the sofa.

"Jarek will handle it as well as bring your luggage to your rooms." Declan then widened his eyes in questioning surprise. "Or should it be a single room?"

"Two rooms will suffice," I added quickly.

"Of course." Declan's smile was only a little unsettling.

"The keys are in the car," Ruben told Jarek, his voice rough with irritation.

Jarek bowed his head—yes, *bowed*—then disappeared again. He might as well have evaporated. He could trace faster than a blink.

"What time will your men arrive?" asked Declan.

Ruben checked the smartwatch he had chosen to wear today. He usually wore one of those outrageously expensive kinds with Roman numerals on the face.

"My pilot will land at about five."

"Perfect. We'll convene our meeting at seven to get the business out of the way, then dinner and cocktails at eight."

Ruben's thigh stiffened slightly next to mine. "We'll be having dinner at a dining table where actual food is served, I presume."

Declan laughed. "Of course. I wouldn't dare insult Jules by having a traditional vampire dinner."

"I appreciate your courtesy, Declan, but I'm curious. What does a traditional vampire dinner entail?"

His small smile seemed sincere, but there was challenge in his eyes when he answered, "Seeing as our preferred fare isn't human food, it's customary to serve vampire dinners in a comfortable parlor or den, thereby offering furniture that would make consumption more comfortable for both vampire and their blood-host."

"I see," I said. "So your dinner plates are actually sofas."

Declan laughed. Ruben didn't, his body all strained tension next to me.

"That is correct, Jules. We will have our blood-hosts join us for dinner at the dining table, then partake of them after the human meal. Normally, we would, of course, serve beverages and hors d'oeuvres to the blood-hosts first anyway."

"Yes, that would be considerate."

Feeling Ruben's gaze on me, I looked at him, taking in his frowning expression. "I wasn't being snarky, Ruben. I was being honest. It is considerate, right?"

Flexing his jaw three times, he finally pried his mouth apart enough to say, "It is. I'm simply surprised at your cavalier compliments about a vampire's monstrous habits."

"Why wouldn't I be?"

He stared, openly in awe.

Then I remembered his words long ago. *I'll go then and not bother you with my monstrous habits.* "Ruben, I never said that you or vampires were monstrous. You did."

"You certainly didn't contradict me."

"Because I needed you to go. Then."

We were locked together, the sour memory trying to resurface fully. Now wasn't the time or the place, but I couldn't ignore it entirely with Ruben's heartbroken look of confusion and agony bearing down on me.

"I never thought that," I added softly. "And I still don't."

"Splendid," Declan broke in. "Then perhaps we'll have cocktails after dinner so that the vampires in the party can enjoy sustenance."

Ruben was about to protest, but I quickly turned to Declan.

"Yes, that would be great. I don't want to intrude and ruin the night with my witchy ways."

Declan laughed again, a melodic, rolling sound. "I am at your service, Jules. Your request for an audience will be honored with all leaders of guild covens within my jurisdiction."

"How many who lead covens in the area are witches or warlocks?"

"Only one, I'm afraid. Warlock. Though Salem is historically known for its witchcraft, many of your kind left the area after the hangings by the Puritans."

"And the vampires moved in," I added genially.

Ruben was no longer giving me that heartsick look that made me want to lose my lunch on Declan's expensive Persian rug. He had that tilted smile to say he knew what I was thinking, that the witches here were pushed out and the vampires happily took control.

"I look forward to meeting him," I added.

"Wonderful. Splendid." Then he stood with a clap of his hands. "You'll likely want to rest until dinner. Dress will be formal."

I sent up a thankful prayer that I'd let Violet and Livvy help me pack. They both had known better than I about what might be needed. One thing they'd both insisted upon was to bring at least two cocktail dresses for formal dining. I was aware that the little black dress and bolero I was currently wearing wouldn't suffice for a dinner at Declan's table.

"Thank you for your hospitality, Declan. It's a pleasure."

He took my hand and clasped it in both of his, a dazzling smile spreading wide. "The pleasure is all mine, I assure you."

He and Ruben nodded, and we were escorted out by Jarek, who had reappeared as if he had read his master's mind. Of course, he just might have.

Jarek led us up a wide, winding, marble staircase to the second floor, down a wing to the left, and stopped at two adjacent doors. "If you need anything before the business meeting at seven, please let me know."

Then he strode back down the hall a few steps before vanishing in vampire speed back down the staircase.

"Was the walking away for my sake?" I asked.

"Yes," said Ruben, hands in his pants pockets as he leaned a shoulder against my doorjamb. "Vampires try not to be too obvious about their differences in front of witches and humans."

"I suppose it makes sense." Of the supernaturals, witches and warlocks were the only ones who didn't have the heightened senses or speed. Of course, some of us witches had superior telekinetic strength. For example, I could throw an eighteen-wheeler down a football field if I wanted to. But I didn't let that strength be known. I suppose it was a courtesy for them to pretend not to be able to move at the speed of light.

"You don't think blood-drinking is monstrous?" he asked silkily, his gaze anything but angry.

Aggressive, yes, but not angry. More like hungry.

"No," I answered honestly.

His eyes drifted away from mine, traveling southward with infinite care, stopping at the base of my throat right where I felt my pulse fluttering.

"Are you ogling my throat, Ruben?"

For seconds, he let his attention linger with a heated caress before trekking his way back up to meet my gaze. It was quite slow, the smile that curled sweetly until it met his eyes that were gleaming with wayward desires.

He stood away from the doorjamb and took my hand in his. He lifted it and bowed in a mockery of what Declan had done earlier. I started to laugh until Ruben stopped before his mouth reached the skin on the back of my hand. He turned my hand over and hovered his lips over the surface of my pulse, inhaling, then let out a soft huff of hot breath. When he brushed his mouth close, it wasn't the dry warmth of his lips I felt but the wet heat of his tongue circling the vein where my pulse thumped. He flicked a few times with the tip before circling slowly again, a familiar tempo of his tongue that I remembered all too well.

I let out a choking sound at the instant reaction my body had to his erotic attention. The wave of a delicious memory, a flush of heat answering his seductive kiss, pooled between my legs. I squeezed my thighs together, knowing full well he'd scent my arousal all the same.

Arousal? Hell, the throbbing had already quickened, readying me for more. For him.

His head still bowed over my wrist, he lifted his eyes to mine, placing a single chaste kiss where he'd just done extremely naughty things to what I now knew was one of my erogenous zones.

"See you at seven, darling," he crooned with velvet-smooth sensuality. Then he stood straight, turned, and marched into his room, closing the door gently behind him.

Zombielike, I walked into my bedroom and shut the door, barely noting the opulence around me. I leaned back against the door and wondered why the hell I'd ever told him I didn't want to jump right into sex. My panties were on fire, and I was on the verge of an orgasm and all he'd done was make out with my wrist.

What would happen when he finally put that tongue where it belonged?

CHAPTER 11

~RUBEN~

MOTHERFUCKING SON OF A BITCH.

How in the hell was I supposed to focus with Jules in that goddamn dress she was wearing? Especially with all the hungry vampires in this house slavering over her like starved dogs.

Like everything she wore, the sapphire dress was modest, but the scooped neckline, spaghetti straps, and fitted material revealed her full curves and delicate bone structure all too clearly. She exuded soft femininity in every way. It was bad enough that I didn't yet have the right to strip her bare behind closed doors, but now I had to sit through an agonizing guild meeting and then dinner while the rest of these assholes imagined doing the same thing I was.

As I escorted her downstairs, she'd kept quiet, as had I. Our desire was mutual. There was no mistake about that. The question was, when would Jules finally relinquish her hold on the past? It was time to put that shit to rest, once and for all. It had no place here. But we had this fucking guild presentation first, and I wasn't feeling nearly as confident about it as the one in Houston.

Declan once had been my mentor, and I respected his guidance when I'd first became overlord of New Orleans. But he clung to the old ways, seeing progression as a departure from tradition. I also knew that his antiquated views about women weren't so different from many of the older echelon of vampires. He liked to pretend he was progressive as an American vampire, but I'd seen the way he'd treated some of his female blood-hosts. Not cruelly, but certainly not as equals.

I was relieved that my three men were here and we had support. I was especially relieved that Sal was keeping his fucking eyes where they belonged and not on Jules as we approached. The three of them stood in a line outside the meeting room, a study on the first floor, since they wouldn't be included in the guild meeting. Only the heads of covens in Declan's district would be here to vote on our cause.

Roland was my main muscle without Devraj here. His clean-shaven head stood taller than all of Declan's guards. Sal was my front man in the social game, keeping eyes and ears open about what was being said among the vampires and even behind closed doors. Gabriel was my second, next to Devraj, in all things. He stood ramrod straight, his aristocratic features and ice-blue eyes marking him as a vampire related to the oldest of families in England.

"Sire," he greeted me with a stiff nod, then an equally quiet, "Ms. Savoie."

"Hello, Gabriel," she replied politely. "I hope all of you had an easy flight from home."

"Kind of hard not to in a private jet," added Sal with a cheeky grin. "Right, Roland?"

Roland had his eyes on the woman who'd just entered from the front door and was making her way down the long marble corridor, her stilettos click-clacking a steady tempo to her long-legged stride. Her floor-length dress was striped in reds and oranges, a pattern that seemed faintly familiar, though I couldn't place it.

She was a vampire, an old one. Declan would only allow an elder female vampire to run one of the covens in his district. She had dark brown skin and intricately braided cornrows reaching down to her hips, high cheekbones and hazel-gold eyes that looked more like a werewolf's than a vampire's. But there was no mistaking her predatory observance of every person in the room, tallying threats, friends, and potential food. It was in a vampire's nature to always be on the hunt for either allies or prey. She entered the study with only a flicker over us several feet away.

"We'd better go in," said Jules at my side.

Strolling into the room, it seemed we were the last to arrive. The five supernaturals in the room were all still standing near the blazing fireplace, not yet seated. There was a long conference table made of cherrywood along the bay of windows and french doors letting in the moonlight.

"Ruben, Jules," called Declan. "Please come and meet our heads of guild."

Jules stepped confidently in front of me. That was another thing I loved about her. She might be the smallest in stature among a group of powerful supernaturals, but she still held herself like the queen she was. Appearances could be quite deceiving among supernaturals. Jules' magical signature buzzed as bright and strong as Declan's or mine, and we were elder vampires, three centuries older than her.

I had to force myself to keep my heartbeat steady rather than get excited about how hot my petite and powerful witch was. The predators in the room would probably assume fear had spiked my pulse, since we were presenting an unpopular and dangerous proposal. I didn't want to jeopardize the cause because I was drooling over Jules. Again.

"This is Cassius Napoli," introduced Declan.

A gray-haired vampire nodded to us both. I remember meeting him when I worked in New York. He was a second to a rather ruthless coven in New Jersey.

"And Zuri Aku."

The regal woman we'd just seen enter gave us a tight nod. Her beaded jewelry caught my eye, specifically the large ornament that hung between her collarbones in the shape of a Maasai shield. I'd worked with a Maasai warrior-turned-vampire in the 1700s, trying to rid Spain of its brutal Inquisition. He'd still carried his Maasai shield with him wherever he went, even though he didn't need that sort of protection as a vampire.

Looking at Zuri, I'd wager she could date her vampire line back to original African ancestry, another continent where the first vampires made their way in search of lands to conquer and rule.

"This is Phillip Abraham," Declan continued. A thin, benevolent-looking vampire who wasn't half as old as me according to his magical signature gave a polite nod and shook our hands. "And Dean Bishop." The only witch in the room besides Jules. He wore an air of entitlement in his upturned chin and superior expression, seeming to measure both Jules and I.

"It's a pleasure to meet you all," Jules said first, her gaze connecting with Dean, who was a Siphon like her.

"Why don't we have a seat and get the meeting started, then we can socialize and enjoy the evening," urged Declan, gesturing toward the long table with three candelabras lit upon it.

Knowing him the way I did, I was aware that he was implying we wouldn't enjoy this meeting. We all adjourned to the table where there was also a folder in front of every seat with the recent data Jules and I had gathered and presented to Clarissa in Houston.

I held out the chair to Declan's left for Jules and took the seat next to her. All eyes swiveled to her.

"Is it safe to presume that all of you had a chance to read the portfolio sent ahead of time?" asked Jules.

Everyone nodded.

"I appreciate you taking the time to review it." Though it was expected, Jules was taking the right approach with gratefulness. "What you have before you now are the numbers on violent incidents among supernaturals over the past century. You'll see the races of supernaturals in the past few decades have remained neck and neck with a marked difference just in the past year."

She went through the same spiel she gave in Houston, noting in particular how the crimes of werewolf violence weren't much different than other supernaturals in the past century. She'd not yet spoken of her sister Violet when Cassius leaned forward.

"The reason these numbers have leveled is because we've kept werewolves mostly outside our communities. Most of their kind live on the outskirts of civilization, keeping to themselves. That's all this is."

He didn't say it with disdain or arrogance but stated it as a fact.

"I have to disagree," said Jules evenly. "If you'll see the data I've provided, it isn't a slight decline but a steep decline for werewolves in the past year. So much so that their numbers of violent crimes are now less than vampires."

Cassius's eyes glinted silver. "And you think you have the answer as to why?"

"Watch your tone," I growled, the rumble of my beast rolling in my chest.

Jules stiffened but didn't look my way. Cassius's mouth pulled up into a sneer.

"I do have the answer," Jules continued, her voice steady. "My sister Violet discovered a way to help werewolves control their beasts with a permanent tattoo charm."

She explained Violet's gift and how she'd apprenticed witches across the US and some from Europe who'd come to New Orleans to learn from her.

"Interesting," said Dean, the fingers of one hand drumming on the closed folder. "I understand your family connection, and from what you said, you've witnessed firsthand the local werewolves behaving themselves, but how can we simply ignore centuries of violence and mayhem caused by their kind? How can we allow a creature at our table whose supernatural abilities were spawned by a curse, not a Spirit-given gift like the rest of us?"

That was unexpected. The warlock was not on our side.

"Are you saying that because their magic came from a curse they don't deserve the same rights we do?" Jules asked.

Dead silence. Cassius looked on the verge of rolling his eyes. Dean kept his grave, dubious expression firm. Zuri and Phillip looked thoughtful, though Zuri seemed about to say something when Declan placed both his arms on the table, clasping his hands together casually.

"I'm a little surprised that you might not see the differences in our kind and theirs," he said to Jules, "considering it was one of your own ancestors who put the curse on the first werewolf and started their line."

"A witch, yes, but she wasn't my ancestor," replied Jules. "Though I value the connection to my sisters and brothers of witchkind, that doesn't mean that I condone the unjust simply because we share kinship in magic." Jules swept her cool gaze around the table.

"Spirit doesn't see it as unjust when she clearly continues the curse through every male werewolf," Cassius interrupted. "If Spirit sees them as a cursed kind, why should we accept them?"

Zuri scoffed. "Spirit didn't curse them, a witch did. It's her fault they are the way they are, not the goddess's."

Cassius opened his mouth to snap back at her, but I couldn't keep silent anymore. "I believe you're missing a key point in your argument, Cassius." It was obvious their mind was made up and they weren't going to change their minds because of what one *female* witch brought to the table.

He arched a brow at me. "Please do go on." His attitude was nothing less than arrogant, but he sat straight from his slouching position as if finally confronting a worthy adversary.

"If Spirit accepted the curse, then she also accepted the werewolves' gift of creativity and artistry. We don't need data to know that they all have a unique innate gift toward creative expression and production."

No one spoke for a moment. Jules was staring at me, but I wouldn't break from Cassius, who was the most openly against us at the table.

"This is true," agreed Zuri. "Your reasoning to keep them out is flawed, Cassius."

Cassius curled his lip at her, but she didn't even bat an eye. If anything, there was a hint of supernatural gold gleaming in her eyes as she stared down Cassius.

Hmm. Interesting.

"So your proposal as stated in the portfolio is to open a seat at our table for these werewolves," said Declan, sounding completely put out. "While your data is interesting, Jules, I don't see anything here that guarantees they won't turn into a beast in a disagreement and rip our heads off at a civilized guild meeting such as this one."

"But I've shown you proof," she argued. "If you'll take a look at the percentages, specifically in North America over the past nine to twelve months, it's a dramatic turn from—"

"It's not a long enough time to prove it's because of your sister's treatment," interrupted Declan, making me want to punch him in the face.

I didn't miss him using the term treatment like the werewolves were diseased.

Declan went on. "We need a longer time to study the results. I realize, to you, this may not seem necessary, but you're so young yourself. We older vampires require a longer time to study to see the proof of the treatment's effectiveness."

Now he wasn't dismissing her because of her sex, but because of her age.

"It's time to vote," said Declan.

"But if you'll—" argued Jules.

"I request a contingency," I stated emphatically, pouring the power of my persuasion into the declaration.

Though this group was all powerful vampires as well as a powerful warlock and witch, my persuasion would stiffen their muscles and force them to feel my request as a demand. The sudden tension thickening the room told me they all felt the pressure I was exerting on them.

A request for contingency simply delayed their vote. It basically froze the proceedings until another larger guild coven was held and cast their vote. It was a way to see what a larger majority felt on a controversial issue, but also delayed a vote from being shot down entirely.

Cassius growled deep in his chest, and Declan clenched his jaw, neither of them liking my use of magic to dominate the room. I didn't give a flying fuck. I couldn't force their will to my own, but I could make them understand that they weren't dealing with powerless weaklings. Jules and I were a force to be reckoned with, and though they may not see her as such yet, I'd make damn sure we didn't lose this war before we'd even gotten started.

"Ruben, you aren't a member of this guild." Cassius glared at me. "You can't request a contingency."

"But I can," interrupted Zuri before her gaze turned to me. "And whose vote is our contingency placed upon?" Her eyes crinkled with amusement.

"The vote of the High Coven Guild of England," I answered. "Once they've voted, we'll ask that you reconvene and settle your own."

"High Coven Guild?" sneered Dean. "What's that?"

I speared him with icy contempt. "Because of Jules, the south-eastern region guild voted and declared they will no longer be called the High Witch Guild as it is now comprised of all supernaturals. And that's how I will refer to all super-natural guilds from this point forward, whether they vote in the new name or not."

"I appreciate the name change," Cassius said almost begrudg-ingly, "but our High Guild isn't comprised of all supernaturals yet, Ruben."

Declan's tension eased at once, a congenial smile returning to his face. And I knew why. He expected England, whose vam-pires outnumbered witches in seats on the High Guild, to vote against the proposal. He expected us to lose in England. And we just might. But we also might not.

"I'll second the contingency then," said Declan. "This guild meeting is hereby closed and will reconvene after the High *Coven* Guild of England votes on the Werewolf Coven Position." Declan stood, his smile widening to his usual amiable charm. "Well then, let us adjourn to the dining room for cocktails and dinner, shall we?" He clapped his hands. "Jarek!"

A hidden door that seemed a part of the wall opened to the left where Jarek stood at the entrance, gesturing for us to move into the adjoining room. Jules stood from her seat quickly and walked through the door past Jarek.

Fuck. She was pissed at me, but I had known where that vote was going, and the only way to save it was to call for a contingency. We all followed into the next room.

Jules had moved quickly across the room and through gossamer drapes onto an open balcony, to which I was grateful after I took a look around.

The blood-hosts for the evening were sipping on wine. A luscious redhead with a vee neckline that dipped to her navel stood beside a well-muscled man wearing dress pants with a belt and no shirt at all. Typical.

"Phillip," the man called to the vampire walking in front of me, the human's eyes lighting up as he strode away from the woman toward his vampire, and likely his lover.

Cassius traced across the room in vampire speed and crushed the redhead against him, sinking his fangs into her throat without so much as a *hello*. She gasped and dropped her champagne glass, which crashed and shattered on the wooden floor, then she moaned, clasping her vampire's shoulders. Jarek was there suddenly, cleaning up the fragments of glass and whisking it away like this was normal.

Of course, this was normal for vampires. So much for decorum and making sure Jules was comfortable among all the bloodsuckers.

"Sorry about that," said Declan, coming up behind me as a beautiful woman with sable hair and wearing a strapless red dress sauntered toward us, eyes on Declan. "I'll tell them to ease up and wait till after the human meal."

"Yes, Declan. That would be more considerate." I gave him a look right before his blood-host wrapped her pale, slender arms around his neck and bared her throat, like she, too, was expecting a bite before the actual meal.

"Ruben, I'd like you to meet Mingzhu." He placed a kiss on her throbbing pulse rather than bite her.

Fucking hell.

"Nice to meet you," I said before marching away.

There were also servers carrying glasses of what I knew was warm blood by the tangy smell in the air. And though hunger actually twisted my stomach at the scent, nothing could tempt me from finding Jules.

Apparently, I wasn't the only one seeking her out. Zuri disappeared beyond the billowy drapes, and I was fast on her heels.

CHAPTER 12

~JULES~

DEEP BREATHS OF THE COOL NIGHT AIR WERE EXACTLY WHAT I NEEDED. After wanting to throttle several vampires and a warlock for being asinine and bigoted and just plain stupid, I needed a moment to myself. But that wasn't meant to be either.

I sensed the presence of another supernatural before I turned to see the tall, statuesque Zuri at my side.

"Thank you for speaking up in there," I told her. "It's obvious your guild members don't agree with my proposal."

"They're idiots," she said plainly.

I nearly laughed when Ruben stepped out onto the open balcony to join us, his gaze searching my expression. I wasn't angry at him. Not really. I was furious at the stupidity being tossed around at that table.

"Good," said Zuri, opening the slim black clutch she held in her hand. "I wanted to speak to both of you before I left, which will be in about three minutes."

"You're not staying for dinner?" I asked.

She huffed out a disgusted sound before procuring what was obviously a business card from her purse, then snapped it shut.

"I never dine with those men. They don't want my company, and I don't want theirs. I hate pretending. I have to do enough of that simply to keep the peace in the guild."

"Am I mistaken, or do I detect in you a blood connection to the werewolf?" asked Ruben.

For the first time, Zuri smiled, revealing a hint of her canines. "Spirit gives you many gifts, vampire."

"And apparently to you."

She laughed, a throaty, pleasant sound. "The blood connection is distant, but yes, my great-grandfather was a werewolf. Because of him, I have connections of my own close to where you're going." She handed her card to me. "Once you get to England, call me. I'm going to speak to a cousin of mine in the Scottish Highlands and see if I can assist you across the pond." She straightened and glanced through the sheer curtains, then back to me. "Trust me, you're going to need help over there."

"Thank you." I looked down at the deep-red card inked with gold. "I'll call you as soon as we get settled in London."

Zuri extended her hand to me, and we shook hands. "It is I who must thank *you*, Ms. Savoie. This is a cause that has been ignored for too long. And though resistance seems strong, please know that there are many who will support you."

Zuri then shook Ruben's hand and leaned closer. "Protect her over there."

"With my life," Ruben assured her, his eyes on me.

Then she vanished beyond the curtains, leaving me alone with Ruben.

Before I could even fully turn to him, he stepped forward, cupping my elbow. "I'm sorry. I know that I shouldn't have taken over in there, but I knew they were going to shut it down. If we delayed with a contingency, at least we'd have another shot. We couldn't take the chance of losing this vote so soon."

It wasn't that I was angry at Ruben or believed he'd tried to take control when I should've been in the lead, but it reminded me of a time when he'd overstepped before. The day I'd broken up with him. The nauseous feeling kept building, sickening me with waves of remorse and sorrow that wanted to surge to the surface.

"It's okay. You were right to throw out the contingency." I paused, licking my lips. "It saved us. I know that."

"But you're still angry."

"Not at you." Then I sighed, placing my hands on the stone banister and looking up at the half-moon. "You were right about one thing. A lot of these old vampires are misogynistic assholes."

"Like I was."

I turned to him. "You weren't, Ruben."

"A little," he amended, his expression tight, his eyes burning.

"You were ambitious. And aggressive."

"That hasn't changed, but I'll never cross that line with you again. I can promise you that."

I could feel the surging memory rising to the top, and I had to finally admit to him what I couldn't back then. "Ruben, I didn't break up with you just because of that."

"You also couldn't trust me." His jaw clamped at repeating the words I'd once said that had severed us apart.

"I know, but it was more than that." Staring up at him, I swallowed hard, the tidal wave coming full force now. "I also couldn't trust myself . . . with you."

In a blink, I was back there, twelve years earlier, racing to the scene I'd been called to.

ॐ

I pulled up into the driveway of the address I was given by Clara, who'd gotten the call. There were two other cars I recognized already there, Ruben's and the other belonged to his man, Gabriel.

I could hear the wailing from where I stood in the driveway. Instantly, I cast a quieting spell, murmuring the charm and flinging my arm in the direction of the front yard and the street. Why Ruben was here, I had no idea, but he should've cast a spell first thing. Any humans wandering up would've heard her and called the city police, and that was a headache I didn't need.

I walked in the open door to find a witch held down by Sal and Roland on the sofa, her eyes glazed with madness and anguish. My stomach churned. I knew what this was immediately.

Ruben and Gabriel stood in the open kitchen behind the sofa, speaking in low tones to another vampire I didn't know, which had to be the victim.

"I can smell him," said the witch on the sofa, writhing like she was in pain. "I need him. Please, won't you bring him to me. Just a little bite, and I can—" Then she arched her back, wailing in agony again.

My blood went cold. She was in the full throes of fang mania, formally known as vampire toxin psychosis. Her eyes rolled wildly, her mind wholly lost to the madness. A chill swept over me, as well as a whispered fear to my psyche—that could be me.

"Sal"—I stepped over to them—"glamorize her right now."

Sal nodded and pressed his hand to the woman's forehead, muttering a few words. The witch went limp. Glamour could act as a sort of sedative.

"Ruben," I called, stepping over to him and the others. "What are you doing here?"

Gabriel stepped back out of the circle. The other vampire whose home we were in wore a frantic, nervous look and was holding a rag over a bleeding wound in his arm. "I called him. I needed help immediately, so I called Overlord Dubois."

I didn't chastise the vampire, but his first call should've been to me, not the vampire overlord. I was the head of this district for all supernatural cases, especially ones including witches. The only reason I knew there had been an incident at all was because Clara got a call from the roommate of the witch currently whimpering on the sofa. The roommate thought she was going to do something desperate and, apparently, was right.

"What happened?" I asked the vampire who was the victim.

"I only fed from her one time, last Friday night." The mania had set in quickly, then. "She's been following me every day. I rejected her, told her she couldn't be my blood-host anymore. Then today, I came home and found her already inside my house. She tried to cut me. She said, 'If you won't feed from me, then I'll take your blood instead.' I managed to lock her in my bathroom and call Ruben."

"You did the right thing." Ruben patted the guy on the shoulder reassuringly.

But it wasn't the right thing. That would've been to call me first. Yet again, my new appointment as ruler of New Orleans was being questioned. I'd already had the overbearing warlock who ran Mississippi throwing doubt on my position because of a bad call I'd made. And because he probably wanted me ruled incompetent so he could take my place. And now I wasn't even trusted enough to be the first on the scene. No, instead, the experienced overlord vampire who was centuries older than me, and who also happened to be my lover, was called first. And, obviously, the vampire under duress saw nothing wrong with it.

"It's all right," Ruben said to me, noticing my obviously upset expression but not understanding the true reason for it. "I've taken care of everything. SPS is on its way."

Supernatural Psychiatric Services was called for only the direst cases of severe magic-induced psychosis. And though necessary, their methods were often extreme and painful in treatment of their patients.

"What do you mean you called SPS? That's not the first call to make."

Ruben frowned. "Look at her, Jules. She's in agony. She needs help. I've seen this before, as you well know, and trust me when I tell you that SPS is her only alternative."

Reminding me that he'd already put one woman in fang-induced mania wasn't what I needed to hear. It only further rattled my nerves and reminded me that I was playing with fire. One bite, and this woman had lost her goddamn mind. What if that happened to me?

Just last night when Ruben was buried deep inside me, his mouth hot at my neck, I nearly blurted out for him to bite me. I'd wanted— no, needed—to feel his teeth sink into my throat. Fortunately, he'd stroked inside me at a different angle and pushed me to my climax where I couldn't think straight, much less form a sentence.

My obsession with this vampire was stealing my will and my wits. I'd lain awake most of the night, agonizing over the fact that I couldn't trust myself with him. I couldn't control my impulses while under his thrall. He made me want to give him everything. Give up everything.

And now, he was overstepping my authority, blatantly so and without a shred of question in what he'd done. Yet one more man stepping over me and discounting my place as head of the New Orleans coven. I wondered if he could ever accept me as above him in the chain of command now that he was bedding me.

"It may be the right call, Ruben, but the point is, it wasn't yours to make."

His frown deepened, and he stilled. "I'm here to help a vampire and witch in need, Jules. Not tiptoe over your delicate sensibilities about who is in charge."

Flames of heat filled my cheeks. No matter that he was speaking in a low voice or that Gabriel had pulled the vampire victim off to the side, his men could hear us quite clearly. Vampire senses were the most heightened of all supernaturals. So his defiance was a blatant signal to the others that he disregarded my authority.

The fact that he said that to me sent off another red flag that he had no idea how precarious my position was. A thirty-one-year-old female Enforcer, the youngest ever to rule New Orleans, was now in charge of supernaturals far older and more experienced and who were expected to obey my will. And here was my own boyfriend dismissing me in front of his men, and he hadn't even realized what he'd done.

"Tell me something, Ruben." My words clipped now. "When did you get the call about this incident?" I waved a hand around the room, silent except for the gasping breaths of the woman suffering on the sofa.

"About an hour ago. Then I came straight here."

"Why didn't you call me?"

"There was no need. I knew I could..."

I held his gaze as it dawned on him what he was admitting. So I finished the sentence for him.

"Because you knew you could handle it on your own. You didn't need me."

He ground his teeth together, warring against the fact that he wasn't a liar, but he also didn't want to admit the truth.

That was when two burly warlocks from SPS walked right into the living room. I left Ruben to go and talk to them. It was too late to call SPS off, but I wouldn't have handled it this way. I would've gotten my sister Isadora to examine her first before going the extreme route.

While I spoke to the two men who handled the witch more gently than I expected, I informed them she shouldn't receive treatment until I'd sent my own healer to examine her. They could at least keep her secure so she wouldn't hurt herself while I tried to correct the course of this situation that Ruben had put in place.

While the SPS men were securing her into their van, Ruben stepped outside and closed the door. I stood, watching the van go, my heart pounding so hard I was afraid I might hyperventilate. Because I knew what was coming. I had no choice.

Ruben sighed heavily. "Look, I should've called you. I just knew how to handle this situation, so what was the point in dragging you into it? I would've told you about it."

He still didn't understand. Because he was a man.

"Let me ask you this," I said, finally turning to face him, my soul screaming at how beautiful he was and knowing what I had to do. "If

Gabriel had handled a rogue vampire without calling you to the scene first, how would you feel?"

He flinched, his sapphire eyes widening in realization.

"Exactly," I told him.

"I wasn't thinking of it like that."

"I know you weren't. And that's the true problem here. And also why this is going to be even harder."

"What are you talking about?"

There was no point in delaying. I always believed in being up front and direct. My gut clenched, threatening to empty its contents. "I don't think we should see each other anymore."

His expression shifted instantly to open panic. "This is ridiculous. It's one incident."

"But it's not, Ruben. Remember the stalking werewolf situation last month?"

"That's because Lewis knows me, and it was his friend's sister who was being stalked. He just thought to call me first." He stepped forward, looming over me now.

"I know. You and your men handled the werewolf on your own, and you never even thought to tell me about it. I found out through Violet, who knew the witch the werewolf was stalking."

At the time, I'd ignored the fact that he'd left me out of the loop because I was falling so hard for him, and I didn't want to face the fact that maybe he didn't respect me in the role I'd fought for and earned. I didn't think him the exact same as Broderick, the vampire who had used my aunt to gain power, but I also wasn't positive Ruben might not use me for gain without realizing it.

The fact that my role as Enforcer was also my family legacy and a position I'd aspired to my entire life had made this transition to power *a dream come true. Especially since I'd learned everything from my mother and trained closely for the past two years when we knew she was planning to retire.*

Except that it hadn't been the dream come true I'd hoped for because of all the problems I'd had since stepping into this position. And the one person who seemed to constantly make me doubt myself and who also seemed to doubt me whether he recognized it or not was Ruben.

"You're not breaking up with me," he stated emphatically. "Over something like this? Are you fucking kidding me?"

"It's not just this."

"Then what is it?" he bellowed, chest heaving.

I had to crane my neck because he was practically on top of me, and I didn't think he realized how aggressive his posture was.

"It's dangerous for you and me."

"Vampires and witches date all the time. Don't give me that shit, Jules."

"Not vampires and Siphons."

We stared without saying a word for a full minute.

He propped his hands on his hips. "I don't get what you're telling me."

"If you bit me, you could take my power as a Siphon. Use it as your own."

"I don't want your fucking power. I want you!"

Tears pricked behind my eyes, but I blinked them away. "Sometimes what we want isn't as important as the consequences of being together. The two of us together is dangerous. And I don't just have myself to think about. There's my family and all the supernaturals of New Orleans."

"I wouldn't do that." He swallowed hard, his anger flaring higher, intermingled with pain.

My breaths came quicker as I tried to keep my composure. "Your bite could also change me," I finally admitted almost in a whisper. "There's a chance I could become her." I pointed at the street where the van had just left.

"That wouldn't happen."

"You don't know that, Ruben! It could. It happened to Beverly."

"I won't bite you, Jules. I fucking swear it."

"I can't take that chance." He had no idea how he tempted me to give up everything.

Then he was on me, pushing me firmly but not painfully into the wall, his hands cradling both sides of my head. A spark of fear bled through my veins, spiking my pulse even higher. I was well aware of his superhuman strength. I gripped his thick wrists, his muscles tight, his fingertips pressing against my skull but not to the point of pain. Still, he could kill me in a blink if he wanted. But I could null his powers too.

"Please don't do this." His eyes blazed with fear and pain and sorrow at once. "I'm begging you," he rasped desperately.

My body locked and my heart plummeted. It would be so easy to give in, to walk into his arms and bend to his will. But then I'd lose my self-respect. Hell, I'd lose myself altogether. And he just didn't get it.

"I can't," I whispered in agony.

He bared his teeth, fangs extended, his eyes now blazing with silver fire, the hurt flipping to fury. "You're going to sit here and tell me that what we have means nothing." He pressed his body closer, forcing my head to tilt upward to look at him.

"Ruben, stop."

"You're going to pretend you didn't love every second I was inside you, fucking this cunt that is mine." He was raging, spitting cruelty *in malicious words.* "You're just going to forget how you begged me to fuck you, over and over again. That you screamed and cried for me."

"Stop, Ruben. Please!" *I clawed my nails into his wrists, digging in painfully.*

He wasn't hurting me with his hold, but he was slicing pieces of me away with his words.

"You're a goddamn liar, sweetheart, if you think you can walk away from me, from us, from what we have, and not bear the bloody fucking bruise forever."

"Ruben." *Tears streamed down my cheeks.*

"I could make you, you know." *His mouth tilted up into a cruel smile, fangs sharp.* "I could have you back in my bed, begging for me, if I wanted. And you know it."

"Stop!" *I screamed, propelling my magic into a jolt of telekinesis that rippled and rocked him backward a step.*

He froze, then suddenly dropped his hands. With a belly-deep roar, he jerked away from me, turned, and punched a wooden column on the porch. The column broke in half, wood splintering outward, barely remaining upright.

Gabriel swung open the door and was outside, Sal and Roland in the doorway. Roland took a step toward me where I still leaned against the wall.

"Get the fuck away from her," *growled Ruben, dominant aggression pouring off him in oppressive, magical waves.* "And get the fuck back inside!" *He pointed with his bloodied hand back toward the house.*

I nodded at them. Sal and Roland returned reluctantly to the house first. Gabriel stared a moment longer, his hard features unreadable, then he left quietly.

Ruben faced away from me, gripping the porch railing, his head bowed between hunched shoulders, panting.

With shaking hands, I pushed off the wall and stood. My insides trembled at the show of violence. Both his and my own. I'd never used my magic in anger. And I'd never seen Ruben behave like this. It was terrifying and one more reminder that I didn't know him well enough to risk everything to be with him.

Curling my hands into fists, I stood at his back, voice strong. "I can't trust you."

His body stiffened before he turned. His expression was hard and unyielding and cold, but his voice shook with emotion when he said, "I didn't take you for a coward."

"You don't know me," I spat, then gestured to the bent column. "And I don't know you."

His eyes narrowed. "Liar."

"Protecting myself, my family, and my people isn't cowardly!"

"Protecting them from me?"

The pain in his low timbre cut me deep, and I wasn't about to point out that he'd just behaved violently and unpredictably. My own voice shook when I said, "You don't understand what it's like for me." I pressed a palm to my heaving chest. "And you don't even seem to care to find out. All you want is what you want."

A woman in a man's world on the cusp of being the youngest Enforcer New Orleans has ever had. On the verge of losing it all if I wasn't careful. The risk of keeping him was too great. "There's so much for me to lose."

"And nothing to gain," he added bitterly. His voice was softer now, but rough with emotion. Painful acceptance.

"It's not like that, Ruben. You're—" I swallowed the solid lump swelling up my throat. "You're a good man." But you could also be the end of me.

"Good?" He huffed out a bitter laugh. "Not good enough, apparently."

"Please don't be like that," I begged him, another tear finally sliding down one cheek.

His gaze found it, followed its path till it hung on the bottom of my jaw. When he reached for me, I flinched. He froze, balling his fists at his sides.

"Ruben," I begged in a whisper. It was all I could manage because this had all gone so wrong. The pain of it was opening an aching chasm even as I stood there. I wished it would swallow me whole so I could disappear. "Please, Ruben. Just let me go."

He could so easily show no mercy on me, whisk me away to his home and prove to me how desperately I needed him in my life. He could play on my obsession. He could ignore my wish and tell me no, that he wasn't letting me go, and risk everything I'd ever wanted. He'd have my body and soul trapped in his clutches, but not my heart. It would break a little more each day when I was forced to realize I'd lost myself in him.

There was a long, dreadful pause as he studied me carefully, as if putting every curve and line of my face to memory. As if he'd never look upon me again. I suppose in a way, as a couple, this was the last time.

"You're going to regret this one day," he said softly, easing closer without touching me.

I already felt the loss and torture of not having his touch. He didn't have to remind me, but he seemed intent on punishing me. On hurting me for pushing him away. And I welcomed the pain.

Then he stepped so close I had to tip my head back to look up at him. Still, he didn't touch me, his eyes blazing a trail over my face.

"You're going to regret this," he repeated. "But I hope you never feel even half the pain I feel right now." His voice broke, his silver-blue eyes glassy with agonizing heartbreak. "But I'll let you go, Juliana. As you wish."

He turned and walked away, but not before I saw a single tear escape and fall down his face.

&

I blinked away the past, realizing a tear had slid free just like that day back then. I wiped it away with the back of my hand and turned to face Ruben. "When we dated, when we broke up, I wasn't the woman I am now."

He said nothing, holding perfectly still, the moonlight gilding his blond hair silver and contouring the sharp angles of his beautiful face.

"There was too much at risk for me then. I needed to make my own way as the Enforcer of New Orleans. Like my mother and grandmother before me. But there were also other things, fears, that kept me from staying with you."

"The fear that my bite would make you go mad."

He didn't say it with sarcasm or pity, but as a fact. Like he'd been waiting to have this conversation a long time and had the facts at his fingertips. Perhaps he had.

"Yes. But it was more than not trusting you either. That was true, but also unfair because"—I swallowed and glanced through the billowy curtains at the others enjoying themselves inside while I was cutting my heart out and laying it on a platter for Ruben—"I was afraid of myself when I was with you."

His brow pursed into a frown. "How so?"

"I'm a little embarrassed." I cleared my throat nervously. "But I was so insanely and incredibly obsessed with you that I hardly recognized myself. I think you knew that then too."

When he told me he could make me take him back that fateful day, he wasn't wrong.

"I feared I'd beg you to bite me. And you would. I know you would've. And that risk of losing myself entirely—either to the vampire toxin psychosis or simply to your allure—terrified me beyond reason. Especially when I was trying to make my way as the leader of a large, powerful community of supernaturals. And at the time, I was already failing at that."

His chest rose and fell faster, his breathing quickening. "I might've bitten you. Back then, had you asked me to," he admitted, which somehow eased the pain of the loss of time. "But I won't now. Not ever." He stepped closer, his body blocking out the moonlight till I was sheltered by his shadow. "I want you, Juliana," he stated clearly, his eyes gunmetal gray and lethally sharp.

A tangible crackle of his magic buzzed in the air, charging the space between us. He didn't move. Didn't say a thing. He tilted his head in that way that put my primal instincts on full red alert. I'd seen a documentary once on predatory jungle cats, and there was this jaguar who froze in the exact same way two seconds before he leaped and captured his prey.

Ruben remained perfectly and preternaturally still as I moved closer, swallowed by his shadow. I slid a hand up his chest, over his jacket, and cupped the back of his nape. When I put pressure on his neck, pulling him down, he finally moved, tilting his head lower.

Eyes open, I brushed my lips over his, feather-soft and whisper-light. A desperate, agonizing sound escaped him a split second before he hauled me against his body and crushed his mouth to mine. I whimpered when he stroked his tongue inside, invading, tasting, devouring, remapping a territory that was once his.

His hands cupped my skull, keeping me at the angle he wanted while I clung to his jacket lapels, stretching onto my toes, desperate to get closer, to kiss harder, to take more.

"Christ . . . fuck," he murmured against my lips before taking my mouth again.

My entire body felt like a line of gunpowder, the spark chasing its way toward an explosive detonation. His full mouth pried mine apart so he could delve inside again and again, his hands coasting down my body, along my waist, then around to cup my ass, where he pressed me against the hard length of his cock. His hands squeezed my ass painfully tight.

I gasped and pulled back, glancing through the billowy drapes, then back at Ruben. Declan and his guests seemed to be having a good time, soft murmuring voices and a woman's laughter echoing through the curtains, while my world had just upended on his balcony.

Ruben frowned and then let me go when I pushed out of his arms, both of us panting. I wasn't about to give Declan and his guild members a show. Bending, I picked up my clutch where I'd dropped it and walked toward the curtains.

"Juliana." His voice was gruff and husky and commanding.

I glanced at him over my shoulder, nearly melting at his scorching gaze. Taking another deep breath, I sauntered back into the room, seeing Declan instantly on my left at a bar where he was talking to his second, Jarek. There was also a lovely Asian woman glued to his side, letting him feed her a strawberry.

"Jules, would you like a cocktail before dinner?" Declan asked politely.

"I'm sorry," I told him, "but I'm going to have to skip dinner. I'm not feeling up to it right now."

I hoped like hell he couldn't scent my arousal because Ruben had set my blood on fire as well as my panties with just one kiss.

"That's too bad," he said, glancing around the room. "Would you like something brought to your room?"

"No. That's fine. I'll see you in the morning. Good night."

He seemed about to try to lure me into a conversation, but I had only one thing on my mind. And it was the man I felt at my back as I walked toward the exit.

As I turned away to walk through the room, that's when I noticed what the rest of the guild was doing. All of them were sprawled on a piece of furniture with their fangs in their blood-hosts' throats. Phillip half lay on top of a beautiful shirtless man on a black velvet sofa with gold trim. Phillip drank from him while he rubbed his palm over the man's jean-covered crotch, the man's head tilted back in obvious ecstasy.

A redhead sat on Cassius's lap while he sucked near the base of her neck, his fingers stroking beneath the skirt of her dress in a steady rhythm. She was moaning the loudest in the room. And Dean, the warlock, was behaving very vampire-like, watching the display from a wing chair. His voyeuristic gaze was on

Cassius and the redhead while his own date sat crossways on his lap, kissing his neck.

Face flaming—from both embarrassment and arousal at the erotic display—I hurried toward the stairs. Walking up the marble staircase, I didn't dare glance back, but I sensed Ruben following and saw him in my peripheral vision as the spiral staircase curled to the second floor. My pulse quickened with each step I took down the carpeted corridor, adrenaline racing through my blood by the time I was at my door. When I reached for the knob, two large, beautiful, long-fingered hands flattened against the door, the heat of him blocking me in.

"Stop," he ordered.

I did, not turning the knob, my head bowed as I waited.

"You can't do that," he rumbled, his warm breath coasting over my bare left shoulder. "You're just going to kiss me and leave?" His chest pressed against my back. "You torturous witch. You can't do this to me."

I had no intentions of toying with him, and I'd fully expected him to follow me. The fact that he still didn't understand that I was as bewitched as he was surprised the hell out of me. I turned in the cage of his arms.

"What do you want?" I asked as evenly as I could while my entire body simmered in flames of need.

"I'll take anything you'll give me." Maddening desire radiated from every part of him. Then he dropped to his knees, his hands gripping my hips. "I'll beg at your feet for a pathetic glance, a simple touch." He coasted his open mouth across my belly, searing me through the thin fabric of my gown. "I'll be your slave. Anything you want, Juliana. Just put me out of my goddamn misery."

Lifting my trembling hands from my sides, I combed my fingers through his hair, his eyes rolling back in his head on a groan. Then I clenched his hair in fists till I knew it stung and shook his head once. His eyes popped open, nothing but black and silver, his canines long and sharp.

"What do you *want?*" I hissed, demanding the full truth from my vampire.

A feral growl that would've frightened any normal, self-preserving person vibrated in the air. The sound merely tightened my nipples and coaxed a pool of warmth between my thighs.

"Your cum and your blood down my *fucking* throat."

Good thing for the sturdy door at my back because, otherwise, I'd have been a pool on the floor. His fingers curled into my hips as if I might try to get away. He watched and waited for my reaction, probably expecting a slap, or at the very least a laugh.

Instead, I reached down to the sides of my thighs and inched the fabric of my gown up till I knew he could see my transparent black-lace panties. His nostrils flared, his gaze laser-focused on the apex of my thighs.

"I can give you the first," I said steadily, easing my dress even higher. "Take what you want, Ruben."

CHAPTER 13

~RUBEN~

THERE WERE NO WORDS FOR THE PRIMAL, SUBTERRANEAN EMOTION blazing a white-hot streak through my body and mind. I had to channel a never-before-used level of control as I eased forward and opened my mouth over the triangle of transparent black lace, sucking her essence into my greedy mouth.

A guttural groan rumbled deep in my belly at the first taste of her, at the intoxicating scent as I inhaled deep. That mewling, erotic cry I hadn't heard her make in so fucking long escaped her parted lips, setting off a series of signals in my brain. To take, to pin her down, to fuck her hard, but I wasn't going to be denied this moment to savor her small submission and sweet cries. Her fingers clawed into my hair, jerking on the iron-fisted hold of my reins she held in her lovely hands.

Fuck yes.

I palmed the back of her left thigh with my right hand and lifted and draped her knee over the curve of my shoulder.

I lapped through the lace, desperate to taste more of her, the growl of my vampire rolling a steady warning for her not to move so that I could feed my need of her without interruption. She seemed to recognize the danger because she kept still except for the subtle rock of her hips.

"Not enough," I hissed, reaching up and tearing her panties off her.

She was beautifully bare to me now as I circled a finger around her swollen clit. She flinched and made that sensual sound again, which had me locking my muscles to keep where I was. I wasn't done here yet. She wasn't going to fucking rush me after all this time and turn me into a mindless animal.

"Better," I mumbled, now able to see the pinkness and wetness of her.

I latched my mouth onto her clit, then stroked a finger into her slick cunt.

Goddamn, so fucking tight.

Her hip thrusts became more erratic, and then she was coming in seconds, her inner walls clamping around my finger. Before she was done, I scooped her into my arms—still moaning through her orgasm—burst into the bedroom door, and kicked it shut.

Latching my mouth to hers, I kissed her deeply, her arms twining around my neck with desperation to get me closer. Good to know I wasn't the only one about to lose my fucking mind with need. I set her on the floor and pulled away, stripping out of my jacket.

She slowly backed away from me, focused on my sharp, aggressive movements as I stripped off my clothes, popping buttons and tearing my own shirt as I went. I was losing the battle with the starving animal inside me. I had to force myself not to pounce on her. I could easily hurt her. She was so small and fragile.

By the time I'd rid myself of my boxer briefs, she had backed herself to the bed. Her pulse thrummed so fast I could taste her excitement, nervousness, and arousal. She called to my beast. A low rumbling purr filled the space between us. Her eyes were wide with desire and a touch of fear, which only made my cock harder.

The room was dark except for a fire burning in the grate across the room. I wanted her to see clearly. I wanted her to see my face, to see me, when I came for her. When I took her. I yanked open the heavy drapes, the moonlight painting her fair skin with a luminescent glow. Perfection. Her gaze dropped down my body as I walked closer and stroked myself to ease some of the pain.

This time, I wouldn't be relieving myself the way I had for over a decade. I'd be right where I belonged when I came tonight.

"Don't move," I commanded.

I stopped right in front of her and tore her dress in half down the middle. She gasped as I tossed the pieces to the floor. I reached beneath her arms and around her and unfastened her strapless bra, dropped it, then leaned down and fastened my mouth on a taut nipple.

"Ah!" She dug her nails into my biceps and shoulder.

I scraped a fang over the tip of her sensitive peak.

"Ruben!" She scraped her nails across my skin.

I flicked the stinging nub with my tongue, then worked on the other one. I caught her around the waist with one arm when her knees buckled and reached down between our bodies to slide my finger through her slickness.

"Juicy for me, as always," I whispered against her breast, sucking a path back up to her throat, my cock urging me to get this foreplay over with and get inside her.

"Always," she whispered breathily. "I can't help it."

"Have you missed me, Juliana?"

"Yes." Panting, her pulse sped again.

"Tell me. Tell me you want my cock in this sweet, tight cunt." I thrust two fingers inside her and stroked in and out with fast pumps.

"Oh God, Ruben!" Her eyes slid closed.

"Tell me now, darling," I murmured in her ear softly while I pumped my fingers at a quick pace, thumping her clit with my thumb on each inward stroke.

"Yes, yes, Ruben. I want you so fucking bad. I want to feel you stretching me and filling me up till it hurts." She licked her lips. "Please fuck me. *Please*," she breathed the last on a hoarse whisper.

After removing my fingers from her body, I fisted my hand in her hair and pulled her head back, arching her neck. She opened her eyes to lust-filled slits.

Dropping my head closer, I licked her bottom lip, wanting to devour her words and consume her will. I wanted—*needed*—her completely and wholly submissive. Especially this first time.

When I lifted my head away, I held her half-dazed gaze. "I'm sorry if this is too rough, but I can't be gentle." My words were steady and even while my control frayed and splintered with remarkable speed. "I'm going to fuck you so hard you likely won't be able to walk tomorrow."

I spoke the words into her skin, sliding my fang along the vein in her throat, scoring the outside of the skin that I yearned to sink into. "I'm going to pump my cum inside you till my scent is all any man, supernatural or human, can smell when you come near."

Her eyes widened, her heartbeat leaping ahead with a small touch of fear. If I had it in me to calm her first, I would, but her edge of alarm only urged my instincts on, and it had been too fucking long to hold myself back one second more.

In less than a second, I'd folded her over the edge of the bed, my hand at the nape of her neck as I pinned her down with my body. Her dark hair fell over her cheek as I whispered in her ear all the depraved, dominant things I'd wanted her to know in my absence.

"This tight pussy of yours is mine." I was aware that my voice was beyond any civilized being, all throaty and carnal. "This fine body, this brilliant mind, this tender soul, it's all fucking mine. And no man will ever touch you again."

Her mouth curled into a smile, her eyes closed as she listened and absorbed my words. Then I spread her thighs wider with my knees and coasted the head of my cock up and down her wet slit, coating myself in her slickness.

Somewhere on the normal plane of my consciousness, I was also aware that she didn't even know the depth of our connection yet and perhaps wasn't prepared for my demands. But there was no way I could pretend for one second longer that she wouldn't always be mine from this moment forward.

She'd let me back in, and I'd kill any man who tried to take her from me now. I'd die myself before I let that happen.

"Say, 'Yes, Ruben.'" My fangs were painfully sharp. I scraped the tips right under her jaw along her neck without breaking the skin, then licked the same path.

Her breath came in panting huffs, strands of her hair blowing with each breath. "Yes, Ruben." She moaned when I sucked on her pulse at the base of her throat. "Please fuck me. Please, please, please."

On a growl, I gripped my cock, lined myself up, and drove inside her.

"Oh! God!" she screamed.

It took five pumps to finally seat myself, my otherworldly growl filling the room, raising gooseflesh on her skin, my magic dominating the space with a vibrating aura. Her fists tightened in the comforter. She whimpered. For a moment, all I could do was hold her down with a hand at her nape and one on her hip while I circled my hips in massaging motions, relishing her tight body stretching around me, remembering me.

"Mine," I whispered around my sharpened canines, my blood burning and mind hazing at the unfathomable pleasure of being so deep inside her. "Fucking *finally*," I ground out.

Then I really started to fuck her.

With long, hard glides, I groaned at the heady sensation of burying myself inside my mate, of the satisfying slap of flesh when my hips met her curvy ass, of the rightness of being inside her, of the sensual moans and whimpers slipping from her mouth. When she tried to crawl farther up the bed as if to get away, I pulled her hair, held her fiercely, and pounded her harder. Faster.

"Ruben! Ohhh!"

Falling forward onto a forearm to hold my weight, I wrapped my other hand around the front of her delicate throat, holding her firmly but gently. "No getting away from me this time, Juliana." Another deep thrust and circle of my hips, then back to stroking out all the way to my tip and driving hard back in. "You're going to take me. Every inch of me. Every single one."

She whimpered again, her eyes closed, her cheeks flushing with pink. "Yes." She reached back with one hand and gripped my hip, curling her nails into my flesh. "So good. Harder."

"Fuck, fuck, fuck."

Her cunt started fluttering around my cock, squeezing so tight my vision hazed at the edges. In less than two seconds, I flipped her back over, dragged her ass to the edge of the bed, locked my elbows under her knees and spread her wide, then drove back in. "Need to see those beautiful eyes when you come on my cock. You know how I always liked that."

One side of her mouth tipped up into a half-smile as she fisted her little hands in my hair. Then her smile slipped, her mouth opening on a long wail.

"Fuck yes, I missed that sound," I growled, watching her as she came apart, feeling her milking my cock, her nails digging into my shoulders now. "You missed me too, didn't you?"

"Yes," she replied in a husky whisper, her sex still fluttering around me.

The primitive need kept driving me on, urging me to take, take, *take* what was mine. What she'd kept from me. Somewhere in my brain, I was concerned I might bruise her too much, but the beast inside me wouldn't relent. He wasn't yet satisfied.

Even while she still pulsed around my cock, I pulled free of her body, grabbed the backs of her thighs and pressed her knees up to her chest so I could lick and suck all her juices.

I growled at the overflow of slickness. "Yeah, you missed me," I whispered against her clit.

She flinched since it was oversensitive now post-orgasm, but I wasn't nearly done. Very lightly, I pricked my fang over her throbbing clit.

"Ruben!" She reached down and got ahold of my hair to try to push me away I'm sure, but I picked her up and threw her over my shoulder.

"What the hell?" she half yelled and half laughed as I carried her over to the fireplace. I knocked a table and sent a vase shattering on the floor as I went, barely managing to lower her to the plush rug with some gentleness.

She stopped laughing when she saw my face and I lowered over her to press a slick kiss to her mouth. When she whimpered with fresh arousal, I broke the kiss, keeping my face close.

"I want you to get on all fours, ass up, and present yourself to me. Submit to me, Juliana."

I'd never made these sorts of demands when we were together before. Of course, I'd never taken a twelve-year hiatus from sex because my mate had denied me. Now I needed her to yield to me exactly as I pleased. She wouldn't give me her blood, but she would give me her body precisely as I demanded it. The vampire who owned my body, heart, and soul required his mate in full bodily surrender.

For a second, I thought she would deny me. My muscles locked, ready to pounce if she tried to get away. She planted a hand on my chest and pushed me up slowly. Then she rolled onto her stomach, lifted up onto her knees, curved her spine so her ass lifted higher, and peered at me over her shoulder, gray eyes soft and alluring and obedient.

"I'm yours, Ruben," she whispered in that sex-hoarse voice.

"Yes, Juliana." I came up behind her, gripped her hip, and sank right inside. "You are."

Her eyes slid closed as she pressed her cheek to the rug. I fell forward, planting both hands on either side of her shoulders, easily covering her entire body. Content now, I thrusted in a slow, even tempo, satisfied that she knew who owned her again.

"So tight and sweet," I whispered down to her.

Her fingers curled around both my wrists. She widened her legs and raised her knees against the rug, welcoming me deeper as I pumped faster. She was so slick again, easing my way farther into her body.

"Making all that honey for me."

"Yes," she murmured in a daze. "All for you, Ruben. Only for you."

With violent force, she ripped my own orgasm from my body. Burying my face in her neck, I sucked on her pulse at the base, making sure not to prick her skin but wanting to leave marks. Though the urge was near painful to sink my teeth in and drink her blood, I wouldn't ever cross a line that would separate her from me. Never again.

She was fucking "*Mine.*" I rumbled the word into her skin, pumping slower but deeper as my cock pulsed inside her.

My orgasm seemed to go on forever, the ecstasy of it lifting me so high I never wanted to come down. Never wanted to leave her beautiful, warm, welcoming body.

I nipped with my lips up her jaw till I found her mouth, but I couldn't kiss her properly this way. After pulling out, I lifted her off the floor and took her to the bed. As soon as we were under the covers, I was on top of her again. Even though I'd just come, I was semihard and sank gently back inside her. She hissed but then smiled when I was settled to the hilt.

I pried her lips apart and sank inside her sweet, warm mouth, stroking softly with my tongue. She dragged a heel up the back of one of my thighs, bending her leg all the way till she reached my ass.

Breaking the kiss, I took in the soft, sated expression on her face that I'd put there. "Someone is still flexible."

She grinned. "I keep in shape. Besides, Devraj knows some great yoga moves."

"You're taking yoga classes from Devraj?" I arched a brow at her.

"Yes. Jealous?"

"Extremely. Stop fucking doing that."

"You're ridiculous. If you hadn't noticed, he's married to my sister, and he's your best friend. There's nothing to be jealous about."

"Besides the fact that he gets to see you in some tiny outfit doing the downward dog."

She laughed, her sex squeezing around my cock.

"Oh fuck. Don't do that." I brushed my nose along hers. "Actually. Do that again."

She tightened her inner muscles, which had the effect I thought it would, my dick already hardening while inside her.

"Juliana." I brushed my mouth against hers.

She clutched one hand in my hair, the other at my nape. "Kiss me, Ruben. Then fuck me again."

"As my queen commands."

CHAPTER 14

~JULES~

I STOOD IN FRONT OF THE BATHROOM MIRROR, A TOWEL WRAPPED AROUND my middle, while I examined myself. There were three—yes, three—hickeys visible above my neckline and two more lower down, one beneath my collarbone, the other above my right breast. I traced one of the marks with my fingertips.

Ruben had always liked to suck on my skin. A vampire thing, I suppose. And since he couldn't mark me with his teeth, he left the next best thing. He was 100 percent leaving visible signs for anyone to see that I was well and truly taken.

Of course, we'd left a few visible signs in the bedroom as well. Between a torn comforter, a broken end table, lamp, and cracked pane of glass, Declan would know we'd either fought to the death in here or we'd fucked like . . . well, like vampires. The windowpane had shattered when I'd tried to get up and go downstairs to find a glass of water after we were cuddling in bed. Ruben wouldn't have it. He'd fucked me against the window, and it had been his palm breaking the pane when he'd pounded it during orgasm. Then he'd gone to get me the water.

Smiling at that, I picked up my brush and was brushing my hair when Ruben walked into the bathroom completely naked and stopped at my back. He took the brush from me and gently continued. Letting my arms fall, I looked at his reflection, how his body was so much larger than mine, the sculpted muscles of his arms flexing as he dragged the brush through my short hair.

Then he stopped, leaned forward, and placed the brush on the counter, his bare chest brushing my shoulders. I shivered. That simple skin-on-skin contact awakened my senses instantly. He combed his fingers through my short, damp hair, watching me in the mirror as he tucked it behind my ears on both sides.

"How are you feeling?" he asked, all seriousness this morning.

"Incredible," I answered quickly, to which he smiled. "And sore."

He nodded, his expression sobering. "I knew you would be. I'm sorry about that."

"If I recall correctly, you said last night that you couldn't help but be rough."

"Oh, I'm not sorry about what and how you got sore. That was inevitable. I'm simply sorry you have to suffer."

"I'm not suffering, Ruben. Not at all."

"I'll try to be gentler, but I have to warn you, I will be on you as often as possible for a while, making up for lost time."

"That's fine by me. And you don't have to be gentle either. I like the rough vampire."

A flare of those sapphire eyes caught me in the mirror, then he went back to looking at my body. His hands coasted along my neck to my shoulders, then down my arms and back up. He seemed in a trance, his warm palms never stopping their slow movements. It was delightful.

"What are you doing?" I teased. "Petting me?"

His expression remained grave, serious. "For so long, I was forbidden from touching you. Now I don't want to stop."

My stomach twisted. I reached back with one hand and gripped his wrist, his hand on my shoulder. Leaning back to press against his torso and chest, I lifted his wrist and pressed a kiss to the inside.

His eyes went molten. I'd meant the kiss to be a chaste, reassuring one, but somehow it lit another fire in his blood. His hands found my terrycloth-covered hips. He twisted me around and lifted me onto the counter, unwrapping the towel till my naked body was exposed to him.

His cock was fully hard. I had to suck in a breath every time I looked on that lovely appendage of his. Goddess help me, he was the perfect length and girth and shape. If his looks didn't appeal, all a girl had to do was get one look of his dick, and she'd be his. But even while I pondered how absolutely exquisite his cock looked and felt inside me, there would be more pain than pleasure if we had sex again this morning.

He'd woken me twice last night. Not counting the broken window incident. Once in the middle of the night, he'd pulled me on top of him and had me ride him till we both came. That was when I'd gotten the love bite on my breast. The second, he'd simply been spooned around me. He woke me with caresses of my breast, pinching my nipple. The moment I sighed and arched my back, pressing my ass into him, he slid inside me and fucked me again, nice and slow.

"I hate to even say this, Ruben, but I need a reprieve."

"I'm not going to fuck you," he said, eyes glinting silver as he dropped to his knees. "But I'm still hungry."

"Oh boy," I murmured, knowing I could never, ever turn away his mouth.

That man knew what he was doing with his head between my thighs. Already, my clit pulsed and moisture pooled in anticipation. He grinned, seeing the proof of how quickly my body reacted to him.

Leaning back till my head and shoulders hit the mirror, I lifted my legs, placed the soles of my feet on his shoulders, and let my knees fall wide. His jaw hardened at my easy compliance. I knew what turned Ruben on, and nothing got him harder than when I submitted to him. Especially since I wasn't a submissive person.

"Always ready for me, eh, darling?" He held my gaze as he circled the tip of his tongue around my clit.

"Yes, Ruben." My voice was smoky and laced with lust. I reached down and cupped his jaw, feeling the muscles working as he licked me. "I've missed you," I admitted with heady emotion.

His metallic gaze shot to mine. I couldn't say aloud how deeply I felt for him. I knew I was falling for real this time, not into a frenzied, manic obsession, but into a strong, powerful connection.

To be truthful, I'd been falling for him all this time. Especially in the last few years when we seemed to constantly be working together. I fought against my own heart, but he'd been seducing me slowly back into his arms. His steadfast dedication to our supernatural community, his constant search for justice for the innocent victims, but most of all, his unbroken loyalty to me, always allowing me the right that was my due as head of coven. Whether he'd known it or not, and whether I'd wanted it or not, I'd been falling in love with him while we were apart.

I'd never seen it coming. But it was real and true and deep, more so than ever before. I could see clearly now. The time apart had hurt, an acute kind of torture, but it had also given me clarity on what I wanted. On *whom* I wanted.

"When you told me at the wedding that my time was up," I said, a little breathless while he continued his slow torment of my clit, "I was both terrified and relieved."

He didn't stop what he was doing, but his eyes were intent on mine.

"My fear didn't stem from the same place as it did twelve years ago."

He lifted his hand, never removing his tongue and lips from my pussy. Placing a palm under my left cheek, he massaged his thumb around my entrance, barely breaching with teasing thrusts. His other hand was at his cock, stroking slowly. I couldn't see, but it was obvious from the movements of his other arm down below.

On a soft cry, I lifted my hands to my breasts, lightly pinching my taut nipples. His eyes were mostly black from his blown pupils, circled only with thin rings of silver.

"I know myself better now. And I know what I want. Who I want."

I moaned when he slid his mouth down to my entrance and thrust his tongue inside me, then eased his thumb in deeper. The warmth of his mouth and gentle probing lessened any soreness there.

"What terrified me at the wedding," I told him, mounding my breasts, feeling my climax quickening, "was . . ." But I couldn't say it, couldn't admit it yet. Because I knew if I lost him this time, it would kill me.

Ruben's eyes blazed as he stood to his feet, his thumb still stroking inside me. He said not a word as he towered over me, his potent dominance overpowering my senses. He stroked his cock with a tight fist, and the sight of him working himself, muscles bunched, catapulted me toward climax.

I reached down and circled my clit with the tip of one finger the way he'd done with his tongue as he continued to fuck me with his thumb, not going too deep, but just enough to send me spiraling faster. He grunted as he watched me touching myself, moaning louder now, no longer able to talk.

"I'm coming," I told him right before I did, hips jerking.

He growled and thrust his thumb inside, then held, jerking himself faster, mouth falling open and revealing the tips of his canines. Pressing his thighs to the backs of mine to spread them wider, he came on a barrel-deep groan, jetting ropes of cum on my pussy, belly, and breasts.

He shivered as he slid his thumb free of me, then smeared his cum all over my slit, pressing some back inside me, his gaze fixed on where he spread his seed.

Both of us panting, he spread the cum on my stomach all over my skin and my breasts. He took a dry towel to wipe some of the excess, leaving behind a thin, sticky sheen.

"I'll need another shower," I said, still catching my breath.

"No you fucking won't."

He gently pulled me into a sitting position, his eyes burning into mine, then he cupped my face. One thumb brushed my cheek while the other that had been busy being my dildo a few minutes ago, he brushed along my bottom lip.

"You're going to let it dry on your skin, then go get dressed."

He slanted his mouth over mine, humming with pleasure as he stroked his tongue inside. His kiss was more intense than last night, consuming me with strokes of his tongue and nips of his lips and tender adoration.

When he pressed his forehead to mine, his eyes were closed, and I could feel the overwhelming emotion radiating outward. I wondered if I had a little of Clara's magic because his emotion was a tangible, palpable thing. It swirled and cocooned us and tightened with a frantic, clinging hold. I bit my lip so I wouldn't cry.

"I need them all to know," he said, voice cracking.

I cupped his neck, letting my fingers brush into the edges of his soft hair. "I think they'll know it regardless, Ruben. You don't have to be worried about any of that."

He laughed, but it was a desperate sort of sound. He lifted away, still cupping my face with tenderness.

"One thing you don't understand about most vampires, darling, is that we are more animalistic than even the werewolves. Trust me when I tell you that I need you to do this. Wear my scent, and I might not maim or kill one of my own men when they get too close to you today."

I'd never recognized this level of possessiveness when Isadora and Devraj started dating, but she'd also fallen fairly fast into his arms. I was sure this level of Ruben's dominance I was seeing was because of our long separation and his desperation to keep me. He didn't have to worry about me going anywhere this time, but I also wanted to give him what he wanted. What he needed to feel secure in this.

"Okay," I agreed. "I never noticed that before about vampires."

He clamped his jaw tight before finally saying, "There were a few things you didn't know before."

"Like what?"

He pressed a soft kiss to my lips. "Later. When we have more time. We're leaving in thirty minutes, so we better get moving."

"Oh, crap!"

He gripped me around the waist and helped me down, then slapped my butt before I could get the towel back around me.

"Hey!" I rubbed my bum as he laughed and walked toward the shower.

Rolling my eyes, I tightened my towel and headed for the bedroom. "You can wash off, but I can't?"

"Don't worry," he called back, flashing a salacious grin before stepping into the shower and turning on the water. "I'll have your cum on my face again before dinnertime, so it's all well and good."

"Ruben!" Even as I fussed at him, my belly clenched with arousal. This was ridiculous!

"Mmmm." He poked his head out of the shower, hair adorably wet, grinning like a demon. "From the smell of it, she likes that idea."

I marched from the room to the sound of his laughter, hating yet again how good vampire senses were. But I smiled from ear to ear the entire time I got dressed and packed for London.

*

"London has the best vampire dens in the world." Sal and Roland were sitting in the two bucket seats across from me on the plane. Sal nudged Roland with his elbow. "Right, Roland?"

"Germany had some pretty kickass dens," agreed Roland. "And what about Paris?"

Sal rolled his eyes. "London beats them all. Trust me, Jules."

"I don't think she'll be interested in going to any vampire dens," Roland added.

Sal looked at me, a frown puckering his brow, as if he suddenly remembered I was not, in fact, a vampire. "Oh yeah. Maybe not."

I simply grinned, having been completely entertained by Sal's nonstop chatter since the plane took off, as he tried to convince me why London was the coolest city in the world. Roland had been rolling his eyes and giving me sheepish apologetic looks for the last half hour. Especially when Sal retold a story of when the two of them had gotten into a fight with six local vampires and, according to Sal, had kicked their asses with just the two of them.

Roland was a mountainous behemoth of a vampire, the scariest of Ruben's men, especially with his clean-shaven head, giant, squared jaw, and the neck tattoos. But he was actually the most approachable and kindest of the three of them. A gentle giant once you got to know him.

"But I will add this," interjected Roland. "They do have the best human pubs in the world."

"Ah yes. What's the name of that one we like to go to? Where they sing all the old songs?"

"The Bird and Whistle."

Sal's eyes lit up. "Ah yes! That's the one. We're taking you there." He gave me a wink right as Ruben sat down. Sal straightened, his eyes widening a little in fear.

Ruben took my hand and laced our fingers on his lap. "Where do you think you're taking my girl?"

His girl? I grinned at him like a damn schoolgirl, all while a flush of heat filled my cheeks. He glanced my way, giving me a swift wink.

"The Bird and Whistle," said Sal, rubbing his palms on his pants legs like they were sweaty, "but only if you both want to go, of course."

"It's up to her." Ruben's devastating gaze fell on me. My stomach flip-flopped at his sudden weighty attention.

"I'd love to go," I told Sal, giving him and Roland a smile.

They both grinned. "See, Roland. I told you she'd want to go."

"When did you tell me that?"

"I was just telling you on the way here that she was cool and would want to hang with us. You said she wouldn't."

Roland flinched. "That was *Gabriel.* Not me!"

Gabriel didn't even spare us a look from his seat toward the back of the jet where he was tapping away on a laptop and where Ruben had just been meeting with him. But he did say quite clearly and loudly, "I said that she wouldn't have time for whatever nonsense you two dreamed up."

Sal snorted and leaned conspiratorially toward me, but then glanced at Ruben and pulled away a little. I frowned at Ruben, wondering what he'd done to scare the bejeezus out of Sal.

"It's not nonsense. It's a hell of a lot of fun. As a woman of New Orleans, I bet you'll like the people and atmosphere there."

"I'm sure I will, Sal. I can pretty much bet you two have the pulse of where to find the fun in London."

Sal leaned back and crossed his arms, nodding at Roland. "Smart girl, our Jules."

A growl rumbled in Ruben's chest. "Don't you two have some work to do?"

"Oh. Yeah." Sal nudged Roland, who then stood up rather quickly. "We've got to check on security with Perry Baxter's people."

"Make sure they're aware we'll only be staying a couple of nights before we head to Northumberland," commanded Ruben.

"Got it, sire," said Roland.

"Nice chatting with you, Jules." Sal gave me his charming smile, which seemed to come natural to him, before he glanced again at Ruben, then cleared his throat and hurried away.

"You too," I told Sal as he and Roland made their way to the back with Gabriel. I turned to Ruben and whispered, "Is he always that fidgety around you?"

"No." Ruben lifted our entwined hands and nibbled on my knuckle with blunt teeth, his canines not extended at the moment.

"What did you do to poor Sal?" I watched his mouth and teeth coasting to my other knuckle.

"Nothing." His tongue trailed where he'd bitten.

"Liar."

His deep blue eyes flared with mischief. "I would never lie to you."

"Well, you're lying about this. I've seen Sal around you a million times, and he's never checked himself like he's afraid you're going to rip out his throat every other second."

He laughed, his breath huffing against the skin on the back of my hand. "I might've warned him a little too roughly to watch his flirting with you."

I let my head fall to the headrest and smirked at him. "Ruben. Seriously. What? You think after last night—"

"And this morning," he added with the devil in his eyes.

"And this morning," I repeated, feeling the heat crawl up my neck, "that I'm going to suddenly change my mind and run off with Sal?"

"Of course not."

"Then why terrify your own man about flirting with me?"

"I can't help it, darling." He angled toward me and sandwiched our clasped hands between the headrest and his cheek, the back of my hand now resting against his skin. "I'm insanely jealous and possessive where you're concerned, and now that I'm permitted to show it to the world, I'm not holding my feelings back anymore."

He looked like a little boy, nuzzling his cheek against the back of my hand with that glint in his eye. A sweet, naughty little boy. Smiling, I basked in the luxurious pleasure of being the center of Ruben's affection for a moment, then I got back to business.

"Why did you tell Sal we were heading to Northumberland after a few days in London?"

"Gabriel's family castle is there. His brother is head of coven of basically everything north of London."

My brows shot up. "Castle? Like with a moat?"

Ruben's expression softened, his eyes warming, his mouth spreading into an amused smile. "Like with a moat. Gargoyles. Drafty towers. The whole shebang."

"Say *shebang* again," I teased.

"Why?"

"Because it sounds ridiculous coming from you."

"Does it?" He reached over with his other hand and dug his fingers into my rib cage, tickling.

"Stop it!" I squealed with laughter and squirmed to get away, trying to yank my hand free of his.

"Oh no you don't." He easily managed to scoop me up and plant me on his lap, continuing to tickle me.

Dammit! He knew how ticklish I was and right where to tickle me.

"*Ruben,*" I gasped, trying to catch my breath. "Stooop."

He finally eased up but didn't let me wiggle off his lap like I was trying to do. "Stop, they'll see," I hissed as I craned my neck over the seats to see absolutely no one sitting in the back rows. "Where'd they go?" I asked, panting and bewildered, wiping a tear of laughter from the corner of my eye.

He wrapped his arms more firmly around my waist and thighs, settling me comfortably on his lap, looking at me like a moonstruck schoolboy. "I told them to use the conference room for a while."

"There's a conference room?"

"And an office and a bedroom."

"Oh."

206

"Oh." His eyes glittered.

"Ruben Archibald Dubois, you may *not* seduce me on this plane."

He curled his lip in disgust. "Archibald? Now you're pulling out my middle name?"

"That's what southern women do when they mean business. Especially with misbehaving children."

Rather than appear chastised, remorseful, or even a smidge offended, since he was obviously *not* a child, he grinned wider and hugged me tighter. I cuddled into his chest, my knees up. We were quiet a minute while I refastened the button on his shirt that had come loose in our tickle fest.

He grazed my forehead with his nose. "You smell divine, sweetheart."

I shot him a glare. "I can't believe I did what you told me to do this morning."

"I can't either."

I hit him on the shoulder, which only made him laugh. "You didn't mean for me to?"

"I absolutely *wanted* you to. I wanted my scent all over you. I just didn't think you'd agree to it."

"I didn't so much agree to it as not fight you on it."

"Good thing you did since you won't let me seduce you right now on the plane."

"Speaking of . . . this."

"This?"

"Seduction," I clarified haughtily. "It's a damn good thing I'm on the pill after all the *seduction* that took place last night."

"I wouldn't have endangered you in any way, Juliana," he said, a tad more seriously. "I knew we were safe since you're on the pill and neither of us has an STD."

"Excuse me? And how do you know I have none?"

"I have my sources."

"I'll bet it happens to be a certain grim."

He shrugged, which had me snapping back.

"And how do I know that you don't—?"

Then I remembered. After all these years of thinking he'd been plowing through the beautiful women of New Orleans, he hadn't been.

His expression sobered, but not in a sad way, as he inched his head lower to mine. "The last woman I was with was you, so I know I don't have anything."

My fingers curled reflexively into the collar of his shirt, like there was some chance he might get away. We had been broken up when I was with Carter, but it had felt wrong even then.

"I'm sorry, Ruben." My voice was rusty with the emotion climbing up my throat, the apology sounding pathetic and not near enough.

He didn't say it was all right or give me platitudes like it didn't matter. Because it had mattered. Being with another man had sickened me, shamed me. So much so that I never even tried with anyone else.

Ruben didn't speak, but held me, watched me. So I went on and confessed a little more of my shame.

"I didn't have a connection with Carter. Not really. He was nice. Compatible. But he wasn't . . . you."

Ruben's arms flexed and tightened around me, but he kept still and silent.

"It was only once," I explained, like that made it better. A tear slipped free. "And it made me sick. Physically sick. I'd tried to *be* with Carter to forget about you." I licked my dry lips. "But it didn't work. It only made me realize how lost I was. How ruined I was."

He wrapped a hand around the back of my skull and tucked my head under his chin. "You weren't ruined, but yes, you were lost. Of course, you became ill."

"What do you mean *of course?*" I asked bitterly. "People break up all the time and move on and have relationships with other people."

"They do," he agreed in that quiet, steady, controlled voice of his. "But they aren't soul mates."

I pushed away so I could look at him. "Are you referring to the human definition of soul mate?"

Because that meant a person was ideally suited to a romantic partner. It wasn't the same for supernaturals. Not at all.

"No, Juliana. I mean true mates."

Werewolves and vampires—and actually grims, too, now that Livvy had told me of their ancestry—knew their mates by scent. For vampires, it was the scent of blood. Ruben had never drank my blood, but I knew as well as he did that he could smell it without actually tasting me. A mate in the supernatural world meant two halves of the same whole.

If this was true, that Ruben was mine, then yes, I'd become sick. It was like cutting a piece of myself away by laying with another person.

I held his calm gaze, wondering if this horrific, hollowed still-ness I felt inside was shock. "How long have you known?"

He clamped his jaw and tucked a strand of hair behind my ear. "I suspected when we were dating. But I wasn't sure until after you broke up with me."

"How long afterward?"

"Six months."

I made a choked sort of sound in my throat. My pulse pounded wildly. "What changed to make you realize it?"

"I tried to date again. Like you did with Carter."

A stabbing sensation ripped me from the inside out as I clutched my hands into his shoulders. "I don't want to hear." I closed my eyes.

"Sweetheart." He cupped my cheeks gently. "Look at me."

I opened my eyes.

"Trust me when I tell you it never got past a brief, tongue-less kiss before I ended the date. I dropped the woman off at her home and never attempted to date again. The devastating level of betrayal I'd felt, even when nothing had really happened, was enough to burn the truth into me."

"I wish I'd gotten that sort of sign."

"You did. With Carter."

When a sob erupted from my throat, he pulled my head back to his chest. I cried with shaking, racking sobs. I'd never cried like this before. I'd never even let my emotions take hold of me like this before.

"I'm so sorry, Ruben." I curled my fingers into his shirt while I soaked the expensive fabric with my tears. "I'm so fuck-ing sorry." I hiccuped like a child.

"It's all right, darling." He rubbed his big palm up and down my spine, pressing me close, kissing my temple. "Shhh. It's all right."

The sweeter he was, the more I cried, blubbering a string of half-coherent sentences. "I should've known. I'm so sorry. You must've hated me."

"Never," he growled into the crown of my head. "I could never hate you."

He eased me back, having somehow procured a handkerchief from somewhere. Only Ruben. I laughed and sobbed at the same time as he wiped my face until I was finally cried out, making those little hiccup sounds like my niece, Celine, did when she cried herself to sleep. I took the handkerchief and finished wiping my face clean.

"Why didn't you tell me?" I asked, almost accusingly.

"You weren't ready. You were still trying to take control of your new leadership. Figuring things out for yourself. It wasn't the right time. And later, I wasn't sure when the right time would be. To be honest . . . I was afraid."

"Afraid?" I finally looked up at him, his ocean-blue eyes swimming with uncertainty. "Of what?"

"That maybe it wouldn't matter if I'd told you I knew you were my mate. Perhaps you'd decided I wasn't worth the trouble regardless."

"Oh, Ruben."

"So I bided my time and watched you become a strong, confident coven leader, waiting for destiny to give me a sign. When we started working together when Mateo was cursed with that hex and with that vampire blood-trafficking ring and you didn't seem repulsed by my presence, I thought"—he shrugged, his brow pinching with sorrow—"*maybe* I still had a chance."

"But you still didn't pursue me."

He swallowed hard, his Adam's apple working as he glanced away, then back to me. "It wasn't until Devraj and Isadora's wedding. That moment in the driveaway when I'd decided it was time and I'd told you as much and the way you looked at me. That's when I finally started to hope."

"How did I look at you?"

"Like you'd been waiting for me too. Like you were afraid and excited and hopeful all at the same time. Like I was."

"I was . . . all of those things."

"For a vampire of my years, it didn't seem like that much time. But also, it felt like an eternity. I never thought I'd hold you again like I am right now."

"I didn't either." I smiled as I curled my fingers around his nape, digging into the softness of his hair with my other hand.

He still cupped my face, his thumbs sweeping over my cheek-bones, his expression open and honest. Wrapping my arms around his neck, I basked in his warmth as he held me tight, soothing me with long strokes of his palm up and down my back. As I started to drift off, I felt him shift toward the aisle, then drape a blanket over both of us and ease the seat back. There had been a blanket folded on the empty seat across the aisle.

Cocooned in his arms next to his body, I did something I hadn't done in years, perhaps in my whole adult life. I let someone else carry the burden of caring for me and keeping me safe and secure and warm. I'd always been the one to do those things for my sisters. My family. Even my own parents at times. It was my instinct to be maternal. Overbearingly so sometimes. It wasn't as if my sisters didn't want to support me or help me. I've always been extremely private, preferring to bear my burdens on my own.

I never knew how lovely it could feel to set all my worries aside and let someone else carry the weight for a little while. I'd actually experienced this in small degrees when we had dated. But I'd been too preoccupied, worrying and planning my transition as coven leader. Even then, I couldn't let go of the reins long enough to simply enjoy being cared for. Being adored and, most importantly, loved.

As Ruben coasted a soothing palm over my head and hair, I cherished this blooming bond. So lovely and sweet. I didn't have the old feelings of insecurity about my place in the world to stop me.

I wanted a partner. An equal. I wanted my soul mate. My deep, true love. And I wanted him at my side, always, from this day forward.

Sighing contentedly, I pressed my lips to his neck, inhaling the most enticing scent in all the world—Ruben.

The growl that rolled from inside his chest was more purr than anything else. He pressed a kiss to my temple again. The bittersweetness of the moment—grief for the loss, the mistakes on both our parts, and the joy of rekindling what we had, what could be a great deal more—sank into me.

"You remember the day we broke up, and you told me you hoped I'd feel the regret, that I'd feel half the pain you did."

He clung to me tighter and didn't say anything.

"Well, I do. And it hurts a lot, Ruben."

His lips coasted against my temple and his soothing hand continued to caress me, his arms holding me so close. "Sleep, darling. We've found each other again. It's all right. Rest now."

Sighing, I nuzzled into his neck and fell into a contented sleep in my vampire's arms.

CHAPTER 15

~RUBEN~

"WAKE UP, BEAUTIFUL."

Jules roused when I pressed a kiss to the crown of her head. My men had already deboarded.

"How'd I sleep that whole flight?" she asked, stretching and straightening till the blanket fell off her torso.

She looked like a sleepy kitten, and I wished like hell we weren't disembarking to deal with people and work and... people. I wanted her all to myself. I finally had her, but now we'd be emmeshed for the next few weeks in inner-guild politics and shady vampires making power plays.

I knew our biggest obstacle would be my own brethren. I'd been gone from England a long time, but I continued to keep my finger on the pulse of the political arena here in the UK. As it had for over a millennium, vampires still ruled here.

I handed over her flats that she'd kicked off the second she'd boarded back in Massachusetts. "I'm glad you slept. You needed it. We'll be busy for a while now. No more leisurely jaunts to bed-and-breakfasts."

The worry lines that always seemed to furrow her brow were nowhere in sight. She appeared rested and content.

"That's too bad." With a tilted smile, she slipped on her shoes. "Now I wish we could go back to the Willow's tantric sex workshop."

I clamped my jaw tight, shaking my head at her. She laughed when she saw my face, and the ball of irritation in my chest eased.

"Don't worry, my darling. I've got plenty of tricks of my own I'll be trying."

A pink blush heated her cheeks as she picked up her laptop bag.

"Wait, slip this on," I added, holding up her midnight-blue peacoat that I'd pulled out of her luggage before Roland brought it down. "It's cold."

"Not like a November in Louisiana, I take it?" she asked lightly while slipping her arms into the sleeves.

"Not at all."

I turned her to face me and buttoned up the front. She tied the sash, her endearing smile fraying my sharp edges one thread at a time.

"I grew accustomed to managing the serious, distant Jules for so long, I don't know what to do with this soft, smiling Juliana."

She cupped my jaw in her delicate hands and pulled me down to her. "Well, you better get used to the soft, smiling one because I'm not going anywhere." Then she pressed a kiss to my lips, slipping the tip of her tongue inside my mouth.

Groaning, I lifted her off her feet and took over the kiss, meeting her tongue with the same fierce desire. I didn't want anything more than this at the moment, my girl secure in my arms, making up for lost time with deep, pleasurable kisses. After a too-long embrace that had her heart racing, and mine, I set her back on her feet and then pulled my gray wool coat on before taking hold of her hand.

I guided her out into the chilly London air, noting the tall, slender woman on the tarmac with dark blonde hair twisted into a neat knot on her head. In a stylish coat, scarf, and gloves, she waited for us to make our way down the ladder and across the tarmac.

We were expecting Perry Baxter's assistant, so this must be her. She chatted with Sal before he joined Gabriel and Roland in the first black SUV awaiting us on the tarmac.

"That must be Eleanor Young," she said beside me.

"Must be."

The young witch smiled as we drew closer, her Aura personality beaming brightly.

"Hello, there. I'm Eleanor Young, Perry's executive assistant. Welcome to London," she greeted kindly, shaking Jules's hand, then mine.

"Hi. Thank you. I'm Jules Savoie, and this is Ruben Dubois."

It was a formality since she obviously already knew that.

"Pleasure to meet you both," she said in a melodic voice with a pleasant, rolling English accent. "Why don't we get out of this cold and get you all settled at Perry's residence, which also serves as his headquarters. He likes keeping things informal." She laughed. "Though his house isn't exactly informal."

"Oh, really? Where is his residence?"

"It's the penthouse apartment at the top of one of our capital's most revered Gothic buildings, St. Pancras Renaissance Hotel. I've got a two-bedroom suite reserved for you in the hotel."

Jules leaned closer to me with a mischievous glint in her eyes. "Two bedrooms finally when we only need one."

"We can make use of both," I teased with a smile as I held open the door for her.

We loaded into the second black SUV, Eleanor in the front seat with the driver, Jules and I in the back.

"Jules and Ruben, this is Daniel. He'll be your driver while here in London."

"Hallo." He nodded with a quick glance in the rearview mirror. He was a burly warlock, giving off Influencer vibes. By his looks and watchful observation, he doubled as a guard, not just a driver. That was a good sign.

"Hi, Daniel. Thank you for toting us around," Jules said politely.

"My pleasure," he said gruffly, following the other SUV toward the gate out of the small private airport and into the city.

"So, Eleanor, when will we be meeting with Mr. Baxter?" Jules asked.

"You may call him Perry. He'll insist upon it," she said with a smile, giving us her profile as she spoke. "He's in other meetings today, but he would like to talk over drinks and dinner tonight."

Damn.

"Eleanor," I interrupted, "can we change that to drinks and appetizers, perhaps? I've made plans for me and Jules tonight."

And they were unbreakable.

"Oh, of course. Not a problem. I should've checked with you first. I'll let the chef know." She sent a quick text on her phone.

Jules turned to me and arched a brow. I wasn't going to tell her a word. Not yet anyway. Still, the thought of my plans for the night sent a thread of nervous tension through my body.

"My second-in-command, Gabriel's brother, is also in London," I told Eleanor before turning to Jules. "I was going to tell you, but you were resting on the plane."

"Do you mean Edmund Stonebridge?" asked Eleanor.

"Yes," I replied, catching the downward lilt of her voice.

She turned fully to face us from the front seat. "Do you know him well?"

"Not well. We've met a few times years ago, but now I only know him through Gabriel. I know that he controls a large portion of guilds in England."

Eleanor turned back toward the front but kept her profile to us as she spoke. "That's putting it lightly."

"Why don't you like him?" asked Jules, catching on just as quickly as I did.

"It's not that I don't like him. It's that he holds a tremendous deal of power here in the UK. Not only does he lead a large population in northern England, but his influence reaches here to the south as well."

I glanced at Jules. She returned my curious expression.

"Is that a problem?" I asked.

"That all depends," answered Eleanor.

"On what?" asked Jules.

"On what side he's on."

"Do you know if he and his brother are of the same mind?" I asked. "Gabriel intimated that they were close, but I haven't gotten a read on his political leanings."

"That may be, but it doesn't mean that Edmund will simply fall in line. We'll get an idea tonight anyway."

"Why's that?" Jules asked.

"Edmund sent an email this morning that he's currently in town and would like to greet the two of you personally at Baxter Hall."

Gabriel hadn't mentioned it. I wondered if his brother kept him out of the loop for a purpose. I'd hoped since Gabriel was my second that his brother might be persuaded more easily to our side, but Eleanor seemed to have some idea that he wasn't all that malleable. No matter how close he was with Gabriel.

"Is there something wrong with that?" asked Jules, obviously reading the tightness of Eleanor's voice.

She turned from the front seat, smiling. "It's not very polite. Perry likes to stick to the old etiquette where you're invited first, rather than invite yourself."

"I see." Jules nodded. "Southerners kind of feel the same as Perry in America."

We made our way through the busy traffic, passing near King's Cross Station.

"Perry's residence sounds interesting," said Jules. "Can you tell me more about it?"

"Of course." Eleanor turned toward us again. "It's the penthouse apartment, as I mentioned, on top of St. Pancras Renaissance Hotel, which was built in 1873. The penthouse has been renovated and has a stunning view of King's Cross Station and the neighborhood. But I think Perry enjoys the security of his place and the building."

"Does he have lots of trouble with supernaturals?" I asked.

"Not since he bought the penthouse," she answered with a cheeky smile.

Perhaps things were more unsettled here than I'd been told. Jules gave me another knowing look.

Once Daniel pulled up to the St. Pancras Renaissance Hotel, Jules looked out the window and up. "Wow. That's beautiful."

"Thank you, yes. It's a beautiful building."

The Gothic style was complemented by the dark red brick and the arched windows in cream-colored stone.

I took my suitcase, and Daniel carried Jules's bag as we followed Eleanor into the hotel. Gabriel, Sal, and Roland were already waiting for us at the door.

"Hi, again," Eleanor said to them. "You're all on the same floor, if you'll follow me."

My men fell in behind and in front of us, two in the back with Gabriel alongside Daniel in the front. We walked through the ornate and light-filled lobby and straight to the bank of elevators. Eleanor turned to us and handed us each a key card, including my men.

"You're all on the fifth floor of the hotel, but you'll have to take a separate set of elevators to the penthouse. Can I get your phone numbers, Jules and Ruben, and I can text you the information for cocktail hour?"

"Sure." Jules pulled her phone out of her bag.

We exchanged numbers with Eleanor as the elevator dinged and opened.

"I've got that," I told Daniel, taking Jules's bag.

"Great," said Eleanor, "then we'll see you at five for cocktails."

"Us too?" asked Sal, winking at her.

"You too. You wouldn't be very good security if you weren't in the same building, now would you?" She arched a brow at Sal as the elevator doors closed.

"She's sassy. I like her."

"You like all women," said Roland.

"And why shouldn't I?"

"Can you two shut it?" Gabriel asserted as the elevator door opened and he led the way down the hall.

"Gabe, are you going to loosen up while we're back in your hometown?"

"If you call me Gabe again, I'm going to loosen your jaw. And this isn't my hometown. I wasn't born in London. I was born in Northumberland where my family estate is."

"Where's that?" asked Jules.

Gabriel slowed his pace to walk alongside Jules while speaking to her. The walls were decorated in elegant wallpaper with peacocks and gold and green filigree, the rugs plush and stylish.

"Wulfric Tower, Miss Savoie. I'll be delighted to show you my home while we're here."

"I'll be happy to see it. Please call me Jules, Gabriel."

"Of course . . . Jules."

"You'll have to forgive Gabriel," said Sal from behind us. "He was born with a stick up his ass and hasn't been able to wiggle it free yet."

Gabriel growled, his dark eyes flaring silver at Sal.

"Enough, Sal." I caught Jules' attention. "Gabriel prefers for-mality and polite manners. Something a few of my other men don't follow."

"Hey!" argued Roland. "Why am I always roped in with Sal? I'm a polite guy."

"This is us," said Gabriel. "You two take this room. I'll take the one across from Ruben and Miss Sa—I mean, Jules."

I guided Jules toward our door a little farther up.

"Why do you get the solo room?" whined Sal.

"So I don't have to listen to you snore all night," Gabriel called back.

Jules laughed as she opened the door and held it open since I had both bags.

"Gabriel does have a sense of humor, if a little dry," she said after she'd closed the door.

"He does," I agreed.

"This is so beautiful. I've never stayed in a five-star hotel," she admitted shyly, looking around the room.

We were in an exquisite living area decorated monochro-matically in tans and mahogany, the sage-green curtains and an oval-shaped white marble coffee table the only other color in the room. Two bedroom doors led off the suite.

I walked up behind her, set the luggage down, and wrapped my arms around her chest. "You should only stay in five-star hotels." And if I had anything to do about it, I'd make sure that happened.

"Why do I deserve it?" she teased, gripping my forearms where they rested crisscrossing her collarbone.

"Because you work so hard all the time for everyone else," I said against her temple. I pressed a light kiss there, inhaling her lovely scent. "And you should be treated like the queen that you are whenever you have to leave home."

"I don't deserve special treatment because I work hard."

"That's your opinion."

"You're a bit biased, aren't you?"

"Possibly. But if you let me, I'll never let you forget how special you are, Juliana."

A shiver passed through her. I trailed my lips behind her ear and down to her neck.

"I think I'd like that." She tilted her head to the side to give me better access.

"I know that I would."

Since Salem and her breakdown on the plane where we both faced our mistakes, what had hurt us most in the past, and what had separated us, a peaceful thread of calm had spread between us. That didn't mean my raging lust for her had subsided, but I felt more content simply standing here and holding her now.

In Salem, all I'd wanted and needed was to stamp my name all over her body in every possible way that I could. It was almost shocking how I'd nearly lost control of my senses that night. But also expected since it was our first night together after all the time apart. Now, I felt calmer and more tranquil. Perhaps that was because she felt more like mine than ever before.

"Where are you taking me to dinner, Mr. Mysterious?" she asked, tugging out of my arms and picking up her bag.

And suddenly, my tranquility vanished. "You'll find out later."

"I'm taking a shower now." She walked toward her suit-case and arched a brow at me over her shoulder. "If that's okay with you."

The fact that she was wearing my scent all day and smelled like sex had been comforting to my beast. But I wasn't a complete Neanderthal. I had to let her shower sometime.

"Fine by me." I watched her grab some things out of her suit-case and head for the bathroom. "I might join you."

She let out a low laugh and kept walking. My heart was so content, simply having her at my side and within arm's reach, knowing I could embrace her whenever I wanted. And she'd return the affection.

Yet, there was so much to do—meet Perry Baxter and his associates to discuss our cause, devise a plan for the High Guild vote here in the UK, meet Edmund Stonebridge to discover whose side he was on, and find out from Gabriel if he had any real influence on his brother. All of this played a huge part in whether or not Jules and I would win this campaign. Not only did the vote here in the UK determine what Declan's coven and likely many others in the US would do, but the UK held the biggest influence over most European covens as well.

This was a big deal. And yet, all I could think about was the dinner, party of four, that would take place after the big meeting tonight. I wondered what Jules would think when I took her to a certain house in Bloomsbury.

CHAPTER 16

~JULES~

"EDMUND STONEBRIDGE. IT'S A PLEASURE TO MEET YOU." THE VAMPIRE shook my hand, giving me a light squeeze. He held it a little longer than was proper, then let his index finger slide over my pulse as he released me.

I'd dressed conservatively—another little black dress that Violet had insisted I'd need—and yet Edmund devoured me with his gaze like I was nearly naked.

I dismissed Edmund's behavior. Vampires were flirty by nature, but this guy didn't quite understand the level of possessiveness Ruben had for me. If looks could kill, Edmund would currently be decapitated and dismembered into tiny little pieces on the floor of Perry Baxter's very expensive penthouse living room carpet.

"Pleasure to meet you too," I responded in my formal voice.

I'd slipped back into the role of Enforcer once outside our hotel suite. It was easy to relax when it was just me and Ruben and his men. But Edmund Stonebridge put me immediately on alert. He had the dark good looks of his brother Gabriel but was entirely different in his demeanor. I needed my stoic Siphon garb to put me at ease around him and his second-in-command, Aaron.

Aaron stood behind him at the door next to Gabriel. But while Gabriel's typical grave expression gave him the look of a man who means business, Aaron's lascivious smirk while boldly checking me out—and either finding me wanting or determining I'd make a decent fuck toy—wasn't simply unprofessional. It was brazenly disrespectful. In the place of hierarchy, I was farther up the ranks than Aaron. But his attitude told me he didn't really care.

Thankfully, Ruben's raging gaze was on Edmund and not on his subordinate behind him. In the past five minutes, I'd been able to see quite clearly that we had a serious hill to climb with our cause here in the UK if this was the man with all of the influence.

"Very powerful signature," commented Edmund as he finally let my hand go.

"Does that surprise you?" I asked.

"A little."

"You thought an American coven leader would be weaker than me? Or you simply thought because I'm a witch, I'd be weaker?"

His eyes glinted with merry mischief. "I'm not sure what I expected actually, but I've never met a witch with your level of power before."

That was rather insulting to say aloud when there were three other witches present, including Perry Baxter—warlock to be precise—who was a Siphon like me and ran all of England. Edmund had summarily told them all that I was the most powerful of my kind standing in the room.

"Please, let's have a seat, shall we?" suggested Perry, irritation in his voice.

That could've been because of the obvious insult about his prowess or the fact that Edmund had arrived unexpectedly early. We'd just made our own introductions and Perry had mentioned wanting a few minutes alone before Edmund arrived when the elevator to the penthouse buzzed. It was Edmund, of course, interrupting our tête-à-tête before we'd even gotten started.

"Thank you for having me at your beautiful place," crooned Edmund in his sensual voice.

It was stunning, which I'd already remarked upon. Above the square of red velvet sofas were dark wooden beams crisscrossing in Gothic fashion all the way to the high vaulted ceilings. There was a giant window on one wall with a magnificent view of the city. Now that it was dark, the city lights sparkled beautifully below us.

"May I get you something to drink?" asked Eleanor, who had just delivered a glass of red wine to me and a Scotch whiskey to Ruben.

"O negative, piping hot," replied Edmund.

Ruben stiffened where he'd sat next to me, while Eleanor had frozen and stared, blinking in surprise. It was more than rude to request a glass of blood in a witch's or warlock's home. We'd never have that on hand.

Edmund laughed. "Only jesting."

"Not really fucking funny," Ruben said in a low voice.

"Ruben." I elbowed him.

Even if this guy was a rude asshat, we had to play nice, but Ruben wasn't really having it.

"No, you're right. Bourbon on ice, Eleanor." He took a seat on the sofa across from us next to Perry and another warlock I'd just met, Russell.

"You know my ambassador, Russell," Perry snapped and gestured to the thin, cerebral-looking Psychic sitting in the leather club chair perpendicular to the sofas.

"Yes, good to see you again." Edmund nodded and sat down, smoothing his gray tie against his charcoal shirt.

Like most vampires in power, he dressed impeccably. He still didn't look nearly as handsome as Ruben, but I might be biased.

"So how do you like London, Jules?" asked Edmund casually.

"I haven't seen much of it just yet, but it's a beautiful city."

"We'll have to rectify that tonight."

"We have plans." Ruben's cold rebuttal was a bit too harsh.

"That's too bad. I thought we'd all go find some entertainment tonight. I was hoping to spend time with my brother." He glanced over at Gabriel, whose expression remained blank as usual.

"Gabriel will be off duty tonight. He can go. But Juliana and I have plans."

"Shall we get to the matter at hand?" suggested Russell in a sober, businesslike voice.

"Yes. True enough, Russell. Thank you, Eleanor," said Perry, taking his drink and setting it on the crystal coaster on the coffee table.

Eleanor took a seat on the sofa next to me, her white wine in hand. Though her face was blank, there was a glint of wariness as she watched Edmund.

"We could hold the presentation and vote of Ms. Savoie and Mr. Dubois's proposal here in London in a week's time. That would give the covens in the north enough time to travel."

"True," agreed Edmund. "We could, and it would. However, I should remind you that some of my coven leaders won't travel south to London. Some prefer not to leave the safety of the north."

"Safety?" I asked. "Why wouldn't they be safe?"

"The Great Fire of London still haunts many of them."

Ruben shifted forward. "The Great Fire of 1666?" he asked incredulously and a heavy dose of sarcasm.

"That's the one." Edmund sipped his drink.

I laughed. "Wasn't that a bit long ago for them to still be afraid?"

"For a witch as young as yourself, I'm sure that would be true. You seem rather fearless anyway," he teased, then went on more seriously, "but the coven leaders of the north are all elders, you see. They have long memories. They also remember how the fire got started, which might put a damper on your proposal, Juliana."

A deep growl rumbled in Ruben's chest. No one ever called me that but him. Edmund was playing games. And enjoying himself.

"How did it get started?" I asked.

"A werewolf brawl that tipped over a lantern in an alcohol-soaked pub, according to one of my coven leaders."

"Not true," Perry defended. "It was started in a bakery."

"According to human historical records," added Edmund. "But I have my own records as well as an eyewitness. My guild coven leader of Manchester was there."

Perry bristled. "Tobias is a crotchety, sour, embittered vampire who is still angry he didn't get control of London when I did."

"True," agreed Edmund, "but it doesn't make his eyewitness account untrue."

"Even so," I interjected, "even if the Great Fire that was almost *four* hundred years ago was started by werewolves, it doesn't mean they're to blame for the injustices done to them today. That could've happened just as easily with a vampire brawl, if we're to be completely honest. Vampires have the ability to be just as violent as werewolves. They are simply better at hiding their inner beasts."

The room went silent as my accusation, or rather truth-bomb, landed. I could feel the stares from both Gabriel and Aaron. Even the extremely unruffled Russell arched a surprised brow at me. Ruben smirked with what seemed to be admiration.

Edmund smiled at me in a respectful manner this time rather than a flirty one. I preferred this much better.

"You Americans are so bold." He laughed and shook his head. "I like it. And you're entirely correct."

"I suppose the real question is," I added, "are the elder coven leaders so fixed in their ancient prejudices that they're unwilling to support justice in the modern age we live in?"

Perry coughed, and Eleanor smiled into her glass of wine.

Edmund maintained that same transfixed expression. "Right again. That is the question, though you might want to compose it in a less aggressive manner."

"Why?" I asked coolly. "So that the elders aren't confronted with the reality of their backward ways of thinking?"

Then Edmund let out a bark of laughter. "This is going to be the most fun I've had in ages," he pronounced, glancing at his watch. "But I do have a dinner engagement."

Which was weird to hear since he'd insinuated he wanted to have dinner with us earlier.

"Ruben, if you don't mind, I'll take Gabriel with us now."

"As I said, he's free for the night. I have Sal and Roland." Ruben had stated it with a push of magical dominance, as if Edmund were a threat. I suppose the way he'd been ogling and flirting with me since we walked in was reason enough to set Ruben off. But I also wondered why Edmund was behaving this way. Was he just the type who liked playing with people in general?

"So what day will be best to gather your coven leaders?" asked Perry. "Mine have already been made aware of Ms. Savoie's visit and are prepared to attend at any time."

"How about one week from today." He stood, and Ruben and Perry stood with him. "Ruben, I'd like your party to come up sooner." He reached into his pocket and pulled out a black envelope with gold embossed writing on the front. "I'll be having a ball at Wulfric Tower in honor of such illustrious guests."

He aimed his sultry smile at me again. Ruben reached over and accepted the envelope, then wrapped an arm around my waist.

I dipped my head to hide my own smile. "We'd be happy to."

"Wonderful." Edmund smiled more congenially now. "We'll see you in a few days in Northumberland then."

Ruben nodded. Edmund buttoned his jacket and headed for the door. He stopped and whispered something to Gabriel, who then left his post and walked over to us.

"Are you sure you don't need me for the rest of the night?" he asked.

"It's fine. Let Sal and Roland know on your way out that we'll be down shortly." They were currently guarding the elevator entrance downstairs.

"Yes, sire." Gabriel dipped his head in deference to me, then followed his brother and Aaron toward the winding staircase that led down to the main floor with the elevator.

"Ruben, if you and Jules will wait a moment," Perry whispered after the vampires and the witch disappeared out of view. "I wanted to—"

Ruben held up a hand to stop Perry from speaking and gave a shake of his head. He was listening to their exit downstairs. After another long moment, Ruben sat back down beside me. Perry sat as well.

"They're gone," said Ruben.

"I don't like him," said Eleanor.

"That makes two of us." Perry leaned back against the sofa.

"He is annoying and conceited," I admitted, "but is there something more we don't know?"

Perry nodded. "Edmund has been slowly controlling more and more of the north, gaining supporters with bribes and promises and gifts."

"What kinds of gifts?" I wasn't sure I wanted to know.

"Cars, pieces of property his family has owned for ages, blood-hosts, you name it."

"So he's corrupt," I added.

"Yes and no." Eleanor sat forward, her elbows on her knees as she held her glass of wine between both hands. "No gifts he's given correlate directly with a vote of any kind. He's already the leader of the largest coven in the UK. But he seems to be amassing allies for some reason."

"Or he simply likes having people owe him favors," Russell murmured with disgust.

"That's probably true," agreed Ruben. "I don't know him like I know Gabriel, but he's always been an arrogant son of a bitch."

"True enough." Perry rubbed his chin thoughtfully. "I suppose it goes without saying that Edmund is warning you both that you're outnumbered in passing this vote, but I wanted to tell you that he's wrong."

Ruben sat forward. "What do you know?"

"First, Edmund is right that there are dozens of guild members who are of the old faction and have no intention of changing their archaic ways. But there are far more than he realizes who will vote against him when the right argument is put forward. They're not all in his pocket. Not yet."

"Agreed," said Russell, "and from the portfolio you sent ahead of time and what Perry's daughter Clarissa told us about your proposal in Houston, we know that we have quite a few on our side."

Russell was a serious, no-nonsense guy with a very English way of comporting himself. I liked him.

"That's good to hear." I nodded to Russell. "We have something else."

"What's that?" asked Perry.

"Well, at least I think we will anyway. We met a coven leader in Salem, a vampire named Zuri, and she happens to have werewolf blood in her family. It goes back quite a ways, but apparently one of her distant cousins lives here with a pack in the Scottish Highlands and may be able to help."

Perry frowned, then glanced over at Eleanor. "You think it's his pack?"

"Has to be," said Eleanor. "They're the only one in Scotland."

"What are you talking about?" Ruben asked.

Eleanor sat down beside Perry, quite close actually. "One thing you should know is that most werewolves have left lands in northern England altogether, preferring life in the Scottish Highlands. There are lone wolves everywhere and a few packs here in London. But none are as organized—"

"Or who show as little violence," added Perry.

"Yes. Or who have the fewest violent crimes assigned to them as the Highland pack. They call themselves the Sutherlands."

"Like the clan," said Ruben.

"Yes. It's their leader's clan. His name is Magnus Sutherland."

"What do you know of him?" I asked.

"Very little," answered Eleanor. "All we know is that once he started gathering werewolves into his pack about twenty years ago, the violent crimes involving werewolves diminished.

The problem is that we've tried to contact him before, but he's extremely private. He won't even respond to our query. Very protective."

"A werewolf trait," added Russell.

I huffed out a short laugh. "Don't know what things are like on this side of the pond, but vampires, grims, *and* were-wolves are all pretty damn protective where I come from. Not just werewolves."

Perry raised his brows. "Perhaps so. He may be paranoid too."

I set my wine down on the coffee table. "Possibly both. I can tell you that the werewolves in America have experienced the same kind of discrimination," I admitted guiltily. "Even from myself. I mean that, until recently, we've followed the same old code of excluding werewolves for a long time, and I was reluctant to let my sister Evie, a hex-breaker, get involved with a were-wolf who needed our help with a hex. But after meeting him, I realized how wrong I was to shun his kind simply because our ancestor had been hunted by his forefather. What a ridiculous cycle of revenge and injustice."

Ruben placed his hand on my knee and squeezed comfortingly.

Everyone knew that the prejudice by witches and warlocks against werewolves began from the fact that their forefather had relentlessly hunted and burned witches. It was my own kind who'd perpetuated this centuries-old feud into unjustly dismissing the werewolves. That was one reason I felt so strongly in leading this campaign to undo the wrong done to wolfkind.

"What happened with this werewolf?" asked Eleanor. "Did your sister help him?"

"Yes, she did." I smiled, thinking of Evie, Mateo, and their children. "Then she married him and had triplets with him."

"Oh!" Eleanor laughed. "How wonderful."

"It is," admitted Ruben, giving my knee another squeeze. "The Savoie family is a beacon of what supernaturals should be to one another, showing compassion, kindness, and love, no matter their origins."

I placed my hand on top of Ruben's and laced my fingers through his. "I'll message Zuri and see if her cousin can arrange a meeting for us with him." I looked at Ruben. "I just don't know if we'd be able to squeeze in a meeting before we have to be in Northumberland."

"Fortunately, Wulfric Tower is very close to the Scottish border." Ruben glanced at his watch and stood, still holding my hand. "We should be able to get away a day while we're there, I should think."

They all stood with us.

"Good. Since you have plans tonight," said Perry, "let's plan to have dinner together tomorrow night. Hopefully, you'll have some news by then."

"And let me know if there's anything you need." Eleanor shook my hand and smiled sweetly, giving me that peaceful Aura mojo with a simple handshake.

"Thank you," I told her.

We headed down to the elevator while Russell remained chatting with Perry about something. My mind was already reeling. I needed to get that business card from my purse downstairs so I could text Zuri right away.

The elevator dinged and opened, then we stepped inside.

"Can we pop back into our room on our way down before we head out? I'd like to contact Zuri as soon as possible."

"Of course." Ruben had opened the black envelope and was frowning down at its contents.

"What is it?"

"It's not a ball." He heaved a sigh. "It's a vampire masquerade."

"Oh. What's the difference?" He'd handed the envelope over, and I skimmed the details.

Nothing struck me as unusual. Time, place, date. Formal attire required. "I don't understand the problem."

"That's because you aren't a vampire." He laced his fingers with my hand again.

"Are you going to keep being cryptic or are you going to reveal the big, shocking surprise?"

"*Shocking* is a good word for it."

The elevator dinged and opened. Sal and Roland were standing there waiting.

"How was the cocktail party?" asked Sal as they followed us to the separate elevator for the hotel floors.

"Riveting," answered Ruben.

"Enlightening," I said more lightly.

"Terrific. So where are we off to?" Sal asked as we all stepped into the hotel elevator.

"That's a good question." I raised a brow at Ruben, but I was more curious about something else. "Sal, what's so special about a vampire masquerade?"

Sal laughed and clapped his hands together, shouldering Roland, who frowned, even while the tips of his ears turned pink.

"We're going to a masquerade?" He snatched the invitation out of my hand. "Holy shit! It's at Wulfric Tower? *Sweet.*"

Ruben sighed with heavy frustration.

"Sal? What's so special?"

"Well, let's just say that vampires have zero inhibitions when it comes to voyeurism."

Ruben squeezed my hand, seemingly involuntarily. "The vampire masquerade is an old custom. Similar to the era where the masquerade and wearing of masks allowed social classes to intermingle and behave in a way outside their station, vampire masquerades took the idea a step further. The masks give them permission to surrender to their desires in the middle of a crowded room."

"Are you saying we've been invited to an orgy?" My heart raced ahead at the idea of Ruben cornering me in a crowded ballroom.

"Yeah, basically." Sal laughed.

His thumb brushed my pulse, drawing my attention up to his heated gaze. "Not always," Ruben amended. "But yes, they can be . . . salacious."

"And it would be rude of us not to go," I added.

"Why wouldn't you want to go?" asked Sal.

"Because not everyone is a horndog like you, Sal," growled Roland.

While they bickered, Ruben pulled me closer and pressed his lips to the back of my hand. "If you don't want to go, we don't have to."

"And insult our host, who has a big sway on the vote of my campaign? No, thank you. We'll go. I'm not worried about a bunch of lusty vampires."

"Why's that?"

"Because I've got a badass one of my own who will protect me."

His grin against the back of my hand was the wickedest I'd ever seen. "You've got that fucking right, darling." Then he nicked my knuckle with a fang without breaking the skin, soothing it right after with a flick of his warm tongue.

And, suddenly, I had zero interest in going out on our mystery dinner date.

CHAPTER 17

~RUBEN~

"What a beautiful neighborhood." Jules stared out the window at a row of white Georgian Terrace houses. "Are you finally going to tell me where we're going for dinner? Because I don't see a restaurant nearby."

Our driver, Daniel, pulled up to the address I'd given him when we left. I pointed to a forest-green door with a brass knocker. "We're going there."

She turned her quizzical gray eyes on me. "And who's in there?"

"We'll be done in about two hours," I told Daniel.

"I'll be right here."

I exited on my side, then traced to the other side and opened her car door before she could.

"Ruben." She smiled up at me. "Who are we having dinner with?"

I couldn't put it off any longer. "My parents."

Her eyes widened in something close to fear. *"What?"*

The old panic and fear of rejection reared its ugly head. Keeping my expression as passive as possible, I asked, "Is that all right?"

She stood there, mouth agape, and all the while dread sank like a leaden ball into the pit of my stomach.

Clearing my throat, I gestured toward the car. "If you'd rather not, we can go somewhere else. I can call them from the car and tell them business came up."

Finally, she snapped out of her stupor. "Are you crazy? And stand up your parents?"

My pulse hammered hard against my rib cage, but I kept myself calm and steady. "Then you don't mind?"

"Of course I don't mind meeting your parents." She immediately looked down at her dress even though it was currently covered by her coat. "But why didn't you tell me? I would've worn something nicer."

A nervous laugh slipped from my lips before I took her hand. "You look divine. Come on."

I nodded over her shoulder to Roland and Sal with a second driver that Perry's team provided, then surveyed the street and Bedford Square Gardens across from us. Jules had thought I was being overly protective about her safety. I'd rather be overprepared than not guarded enough. Though my men and I hadn't sensed any threats since we'd arrived in London, I was taking no chances with her.

I guided her to my parents' front door, then looked down at her. "Ready?"

"No, dammit." She lightly punched me on the arm, then whisper-yelled, "You should've given me warning so I could prepare myself."

Smiling, I opened my parents' door and led inside the only girl I'd ever wanted to bring home.

"There they are," I heard my mother say excitedly and then the soft pad of her flats and Father behind her.

They met us right as we walked through the archway into the large living room. My mother was in her typical casual pants and cardigan sweater, her long white-blonde hair twisted into a bun. My father, towering over her, wore his khakis and casual button-down. I wondered what Jules thought. They appeared more like a simple couple rather than posh Londoners one might expect of a five-hundred-year-old vampire couple.

"Ruben!" My mother beamed as she launched into my arms.

"Hi, Mum." I pulled close her much smaller body and hugged her tight. "Missed you."

"Because you never come home, darling." Her voice and accent were as lovely as she was.

She pushed out of my arms and popped me lightly on the shoulder, very much like Jules had done on the doorstep. Then she cupped my cheeks like always and admired me the way mothers do. Yes, I was nearly four hundred years old, but to my mum, I was still her little boy.

"Let him be, Catherine. We've got a guest as well."

"Oh, where are my manners?" She reached out with both arms and pulled Jules into a hug. "I'm so happy to finally meet you, Jules."

The wide-eyed shock and awe and joy that flitted across Jules's face had me exhaling a relieved breath.

Her cheeks and ears flushed bright pink. "I'm so pleased to meet you too."

"You are most welcome to our home." Mum was pouring it on thick, but that was likely because I'd told her I'd found my mate and would be bringing her home.

"My turn, Catherine. Go and get the wine, dear."

Mum hurried away toward the kitchen while my father moved in.

I'd kept my parents in the dark about my relationship with Jules because it was complicated, to say the least. Yes, we'd fallen deeply in burning lust and were venturing toward love when she'd broken up with me. I was furious at her for a while because she was right. I didn't understand what it was like for her and why that meant we couldn't be together.

Over time, as I watched from a distance and as she came into her full power and control over the New Orleans coven, I finally did understand. Then, not long ago, I began to truly hope. It wasn't until last month when I knew we'd be taking this trip that I finally admitted to my parents I'd be traveling home on this business trip with my mate—a witch—and would bring her home to meet them.

I realized it was bordering on rude not telling Jules ahead of time, but for the life of me, I couldn't force the words out of my mouth. If she'd decided not to meet them for any reason, I feared it would be a sign that she still wasn't ready. That she still didn't want this. Want me.

Strange to hinge so much on a simple meeting with my parents, but the current look of utter joy on her face as my father took her hand in both of his and welcomed her to their home pulled loose the last thread that held all my doubts and fears.

"Bloody hell, Ruben. You told me she was pretty, but not *this* pretty."

"*Father.*" I barely stifled a laugh while Jules turned a deeper shade of pink.

"Here we are." Mum carried in a glass of merlot for both me and Jules.

"Thank you so much." Jules took the glass from Mum. "My favorite."

"Yes, we know," Mum teased. "I asked Ruben a hundred questions when he told me he was bringing you to meet us."

"A hundred and one," I corrected.

"Whatever you're cooking, Mrs. Dubois, it smells divine."

"Oh, please call me Catherine, dear. Actually, I wonder if you wouldn't mind testing it for me. You're the chef, of course."

"I'm always happy to taste test. What's the dish?"

"Chicken Tikka Masala. I just want to be sure the sauce isn't too spicy." Mum started leading her into the kitchen. "Though I hear you like spicy foods in Louisiana where you're from."

"Yes, ma'am." Jules smiled sweetly over her shoulder as she followed my mother into the kitchen, and I could've died a happy man on the spot.

"She's lovely, son."

"Thank you, Father."

He gestured for me to have a seat in their cozy living room. He picked up his glass of Macallan. While my parents might not show their wealth in their appearance, or even in fancy cars, my father did in that he only drank Macallan 25 Year Sherry Oak.

"Would you like one instead of the wine?" he asked me.

"I'm fine." I set my glass down, not really wanting to drink tonight. "But I'd like to peek in at the women for a moment."

He seemed to understand my need to be near her, to watch her. He simply said, "I'll be right here."

My obsessive tendencies where Jules was concerned might be considered overzealous by many. But Father understood the compulsion of the newly mated vampire. Besides, I wanted to see her standing in my parents' kitchen.

I slipped in through the back entrance from my father's den to see Jules at the stove stirring the pot, while my mum watched in earnest.

"I double the amount of butter in my recipe and the cream." Jules poured more cream into the saucepan. "You can never have too much butter or cream."

Mum smiled. "I always stick hard to the recipe. Afraid I'll muck it up otherwise."

"That's the one thing about cooking I love so much. If you have the right ingredients, it's hard to muck it up. You simply follow your instincts and add what you love. Or what the ones you're cooking for love." Jules reached for a spice and sprinkled some more into the sauce. "I make this for my brother-in-law Devraj sometimes, and he likes it heavy on cumin and coriander."

"Oh yes. We know Devraj. Our son's dear friend. I'll have to remember that when he comes to visit. Hopefully with your sister, his new bride." My mum's face lit up with wide-eyed hope. "It would be lovely if you came for a long visit, and your family would be most welcome here. Any time you ever want to come see us. You don't even have to ask."

I held my breath as Jules turned her head and smiled sweetly. "I'd really love that."

Mum wrapped an arm around her waist and gave her a side hug. "Wonderful. Now, show me the best way to garnish the sauce when we're done."

My heart squeezed at the loveliness taking place in my parents' kitchen. A sight I never thought I'd see. Slipping away, I returned to the den and took a seat, smiling to myself.

Father seemed to mirror my expression with a knowing glint in his eye, but he didn't remark on it. "So how long will you both be in town?"

"We'll be leaving London the day after tomorrow, but I'd like to return and stay a little longer after the vote in Northumberland."

Dad scowled, and I was reminded that he once was a formidable vampire overlord himself. He'd run London for over a century from the 1800s to the 1920s. When he retired, wanting a quieter life with Mum, and Perry Baxter took the position, I headed to America, drawn by the Roaring Twenties and the exciting idea of living in New York. Little did I know that was the first step toward finding Juliana.

"Your mother and I would love for you to stay a little longer when you're done in Northumberland. Can't say I'm happy about you two going up there at all."

"Why not?"

He gave me that steady, steely look, the one I'd learned how to use directly from him.

"It's not balanced. Too many vampires."

I smiled. "A little harsh on your own kind, Father?"

"Not at all. One thing I've learned is that when a supernatural gains too much territory, villainy follows."

"How do you mean?"

My father was five hundred years old and had seen far more than I had. "Our kind, those with magical gifts, are all tethered together, whether some like to believe it or not. We're bound by the Goddess herself and the Creator, whoever you view that as. Beings created with humanity and with magic. There must be harmony and balance among our kind in order to use our magic for the betterment of society."

I loved that my father was an idealist, but he was also right 99 percent of the time. "What you're saying is that when our populations vary, it off-balances the Goddess's intentions?"

"Indeed, and her desires. Her wishes for us to be whole are directly related to the balance of power. When one supernatural race takes over a territory, it offsets the balance of magic and opens up the possibility for darker powers to emerge."

I considered what he was saying. "Has this ever happened before in our history? Where one supernatural kind offset the balance?"

"Yes, son. It was called the Dark Ages for a reason."

"Hmm. And then the Enlightenment."

I was born after the Renaissance and that glorious age of discovery led by men like DaVinci, a rather ingenious warlock himself.

My father sighed. "That was a good age. Though I still prefer the modern age of plumbing."

I laughed before sobering again. "You're not saying we're headed for that kind of imbalance, are you, Father?"

"No, no." He scratched his clean-shaven jaw. "I don't sense we're in that sort of peril. But the vampires, Ruben . . . If any supernatural kind had the ability to offset the balance, it would be us. And that's what worries me about the north."

"I learned that the werewolves are mostly gone."

"They are. Most witches and warlocks have even left the lands up north. And the grims who are there?" He raised both brows. "They're not the kind you'd want to be near. You wouldn't want vampires who indulged their darker urges near those grims either."

Spoken by anyone else, and I'd suspect prejudice of some kind. But my father wasn't speaking of disassociating from a race; he was warning against being in proximity to evil. Grims who'd let their inner darkness overwhelm them could be dangerous and even lethal to other supernaturals, especially ravenous vampires who let their appetites lead them. Those vampires who disregarded their own humanity to the beast inside them that craved sustenance. Blood.

"I see," was all I managed to say, worrying even more about this trip to the north. About taking Juliana there.

"Who do you have going with you?" he asked me.

"Gabriel, Sal, and Roland. My best men."

"Mmm. No one else?"

"Perry and his allies will be coming up a few days after us." I leaned forward, the hair on the back of my neck standing on end at the thought of my father's doubts. "Do you really believe it's that dangerous?"

"It's not a belief, son, so much as I'm watching the signs of the time. The imbalance. The dark stories that come out of the north."

"Like what?"

"Rituals, chanting in the woodlands, werewolves evacuating. Some disappearing altogether. Signs of dark magic being practiced." He sipped his Macallan.

"Disappearing? Where did you hear that?"

"My friend Abrams. You remember him?"

"Yes, I remember."

"He still lives in Derbyshire. He'd said two of his nephews and a werewolf friend of theirs took a backpacking trip to Yorkshire. One night, they stopped in a pub in a small village. Their werewolf friend left for a smoke outside and never returned."

"Strange," I admitted. "And their friend wasn't the type to simply disappear, I take it."

"Never. They'd been friends since primary school and had been planning this adventure together for a year."

"It could be a coincidence alongside the other stories."

"Could be," he agreed. "And might not." He sipped his drink. "That's one thing I can tell you about the werewolves, son. If they've had the good sense to leave, then something's going on. The wolves are instinctual supernaturals and more in harmony with their beasts than most vampires, truth be told. You're staying at Wulfric Tower?"

"Yes."

"Mmm. You'll be protected by Edmund Stonebridge then."

I bristled at the name. I hated the way that fucker had eyed Juliana like a fresh piece of meat he'd like to sink his teeth into. I couldn't blame him, but I sure as hell would knock his teeth out if he tried.

"You don't think there's anything to worry about where he's concerned, do you?"

"You don't trust him?"

"Not really."

"But isn't his brother your second?"

"Yes, but Gabriel doesn't ogle my mate the way Edmund does."

My father burst out laughing, a hearty, deep sound that made me smile.

"I don't blame you for hating him then," he finally said, still chuckling. "The Stonebridge family has a very long legacy. He might encourage vampiric expansion, but I can't see him doing anything that would jeopardize his place as vampire king of the north."

I huffed out a disgusted breath. "Fancies himself king, does he?"

"He's a vain creature." He took another sip of his Macallan, becoming especially pensive. "All the same, son, you keep your lovely girl close while up there. Yes, there are strange, dark stories coming out of the northlands, but where there are rumors and stories, there is always some truth."

His words resonated with a cold tremble down to my bones. "Don't worry, Father. I'll not let anything happen to Juliana."

CHAPTER 18

~JULES~

"You promise you'll come spend a few days after you return from Northumberland?" Ruben's mother whispered intimately to me as she hugged me goodbye.

"Yes, definitely. I would love to get to know you both better."

"You are a dear."

She pulled back, her hands still holding my arms. I realized then we were seeing eye to eye. She was as short as I was. A delicately framed, beautiful woman.

For some reason, I'd always imagined Ruben's parents would be dour and grave and extremely formal. They were the exact opposite. I mean, there was an air of gentility to them, but they were personable and made me feel right at home. And though I wouldn't admit it to Ruben, his dad was a pure silver fox. I was quite pleased to see this mature version of Ruben, smiling at the thought of the son taking after the father in old age. Hoping, of course, that Ruben and I would be spending our old age together.

"You'll take care of him, won't you?" she whispered, even though I knew Ruben could hear from the doorway where he spoke to his father.

"Of course I will," I assured her, and I meant it.

I wanted to take care of Ruben. Like I wanted him to take care of me. I looked over my shoulder, catching his fleeting glimpse while listening to his father.

"Oh! Ruben," his mother suddenly said, hurrying off into a small den right off the foyer entrance. "You forgot something when you were here last holiday."

I joined Ruben and shook his father's hand while Mrs. Dubois was fetching whatever it was.

"An absolute delight to meet you, Jules." He grasped my hand in both of his in a kind, familiar way but not uncomfortably so since we'd only met a few hours ago.

"And you. I've promised Mrs. Dubois that we'll spend a few days when we return."

"Wonderful."

"I told you, Jules dear, to call me Catherine." She beamed as she handed over what appeared to be a book wrapped in parcel paper.

"Thank you for not shipping," said Ruben, not even opening the package.

"Well, you told me not to. So there you are."

He reached over and wrapped his mother into a one-armed embrace. "Good to see you, Mum." Then he kissed her on the crown of her white-blonde head, and my heart melted a little.

A man who loved his mother was a good man indeed.

"Father." He hugged him as well.

"Take care, son. We'll see you in a week or so, I suppose."

Then we turned and headed for the door. I looped my arm through his and leaned in close. "Your parents are wonderful."

The smile he shot me was nothing but radiant. "I'm so pleased you think so."

"And I find it adorable how your English accent has returned since we came here."

His mouth quirked into a lopsided smile. "I hadn't noticed, but I suppose it does when I return."

"What's in the wrapping paper?"

"Just a book I left when I was last here." He looked up the street, then took my hand to cross to Daniel, who was starting up the SUV.

"Ah, one of your precious books," I teased. "Didn't trust your mom to mail it?"

"Not this one," he said rather seriously.

"What is it?"

"Hey!" yelled Sal with a big grin from the open window of their vehicle parked three cars behind ours. "Let's all head to the Bird and Whistle."

Ruben shook his head on a laugh and looked down at me. "You want to go?"

"Come on, Jules!" called Sal. "It's the best pub in London."

"It's not a vampire den?" I aimed my question at Sal.

He rolled his eyes. "Hell, no. Human pub. Come on!"

"Fine, Sal. Just for you," I teased, which had him grinning and giving a little whoop of excitement.

"I think you just made his whole week," said Ruben.

"I'm glad you're not mad at him for being, you know, friendly with me."

Ruben opened the door for me, and I slid in. "I'm a little more content than I was then."

"Me too."

Ruben was silent and pensive on the ride over to the Bird and Whistle.

I was the same, ruminating about the night. Content. That was a good word for how I was feeling. Dinner had been delicious and the conversation was easy and enjoyable. "Your mother is an exceptional cook."

He squeezed my knee where his hand was resting. "That's quite a compliment coming from you."

Of course, regular food didn't feed their magic. Only blood did. His parents only drank wine and water with dinner, no goblets of blood like in Salem. Ruben had never consumed blood in front of me. That had me wondering something that had been troubling me for some time. What did vampire couples do for blood?

"Who do your parents use for blood-hosts?"

That got his full attention. He turned and looked at me, the streetlights and darkness of the car cutting his intense features into even sharper angles. A shiver raced down my spine.

His voice rumbled low and intimate. That feeling of contentment vanished, a slow burn of heat melting into my limbs.

"They use each other," he answered with deliberate slowness.

"Only each other?"

His eyes rolled silver in the dark of the cab. "Only each other."

"I didn't realize you could. From one person only."

He was so still, speaking in a perfectly level tone. Yet, there was a new sensation weaving into the thread between us. We didn't talk about this. We never had really, because the one or two times it came up when we were together before, I had become angry. It always angered me because I couldn't be that person for him. For some reason, I always assumed that vampires had several blood-hosts to drink from.

"Doesn't that hurt them?" I finally asked.

"As you know, older vampires can go long periods of time without drinking to replenish their magic. They alternate. Just like humans, their body replenishes the blood loss in plenty of time for when their partner needs to drink again."

"So"—I licked my lips, mouth suddenly dry—"most vampire couples rely only on each other? This is common?"

"It is expected with monogamous partners. Blood-drinking is intimate, as you know."

"Right." I dropped my gaze to my lap.

Ruben lifted my chin gently with the tip of one finger. "I will continue to drink from Damon. This won't come between us again."

Pressing my lips together, I nodded.

He slid his palm to cup my jaw, fingers sliding into my hair. "You know that, don't you?" he asked softly.

"Of course I do. I trust you in that. It's just—"

"What is it?"

I shrugged. "I don't know exactly."

I didn't like that we couldn't share that pleasure. A vampire's nature was to give and receive pleasure to his or her partner through blood and toxins. It was as intimate an exchange as sex. Yet, he would forgo this primal part of himself forever and get his blood through the platonic exchange with Damon or through a vampire blood bank service in order to be with me. It just wasn't fucking fair. To either one of us.

He seemed to recognize where my thoughts had gone. "Come here." Then he hauled me close so that I rested my head on his shoulder.

We remained quiet after that. The pub wasn't far away, thankfully. I needed to get my mind off things we couldn't have.

The Bird and Whistle was packed. We could hear the singing before we opened the door.

"Wow. How old is this place?" I asked Ruben as he pointed to the booth in the back where four people were just standing to leave.

"About two hundred years old or so."

Roland had barreled ahead of us to grab the table before anyone else did, pushing past people milling and standing about, holding their tankards of beer, some of them singing along with the musicians.

"It's loud," I called up to Ruben.

He smiled and nodded, keeping a firm grip on my hand.

On a small stage, which was really just a dais one foot off the ground in the farthest corner, sat three musicians. One played a fiddle, one an accordion, and another a flute of some kind. The fiddler was leading the sing-along. It was a lively song about a sailor at sea who didn't want to come home to his wife and seven kids.

I laughed as I caught the gist of the narrative that each time the sailor came home, he impregnated his wife again, then happily shipped off to avoid domestic bliss.

"What'll ya have?" asked a red-cheeked waitress.

"Four Newcastle Browns, please," answered Sal, and then she was off.

"But I don't drink beer," I told Sal.

"You do here, Jules. No fancy wine or whatever."

I pointed to a lady two tables over with a glass of white wine in her hand. "What about her?"

Sal rolled his eyes. "Do you want the full London pub experience or don't you?"

"Fine, fine." I laughed, knowing I'd never get more than a few sips down.

I truly wasn't a beer girl. I'd tasted Newcastle Brown Ale once before when JJ started stocking it for locals at the Cauldron. Way too stout for me. But I wasn't going to spoil Sal's fun. For me to be out having fun and not handling the Cauldron or Enforcer business at all was a rarity. I hardly recognized my happy-go-lucky self. Ruben beamed down at me, seeming to like what he saw in my expression.

"Oh, now this is a good one." Sal stood, clapping with the crowd as another rowdy song began. More people started toward a cleared-out space in front of the stage to dance. "Ruben, may I please dance with your lady?"

Ruben smiled rather than looked as if he wanted to rip Sal's head off per usual. "Of course. If she wants to dance with you."

"I'm not much of a dancer," I told him as I let him haul me out of the booth and lead me to the floor. "And I have no idea what they're doing."

"It's just a jig. I'll show you."

"But how do you do it?" I shouted, watching a tipsy woman leaning on her partner, who was jostling her around.

"Just bounce up and down and shuffle your feet every once in a while."

"I can't believe I'm doing this," I muttered more to myself as Sal gripped me by the waist and hand and we danced. Sort of.

"You're doing great!" he yelled, beaming down at me.

"I am not!" I screamed back.

He tossed his head back and laughed, then whirled me in circles. Sal was a terrific dancer, and I was a mediocre, but at least enthusiastic, partner. I stepped on his toes once and bumped into the tipsy lady twice. But Sal just smiled and encouraged me. "You're doing fantastic!"

"You're such a liar, Sal."

The circling jig and my constant laughter had me breathless by the time the song came to an end with a flourish of the fiddle and flute.

"Well done," said Sal, nodding back to our table.

I was surprised to see Gabriel standing next to the booth, leaning against the wall, talking down to Ruben, who listened intently. He moved over at my approach to let me slide into the booth.

"Hi, Gabriel. I didn't expect you."

"Hello." He smiled tightly. "I was able to get away early." He didn't expound on that, and Ruben didn't either.

"How'd you find us?"

Sal waved his phone screen at me. "We've all got a phone tracker app. For safety reasons."

Of course. That would make sense. I took a sip of my beer, needing something to drink after that dance. Roland had finished his mug already. He swiped the foam off his lip with the back of his hand, then shoved on Sal to get out of the booth as another spirited tune started to play, luring more onto the dance floor.

"My turn," said Roland. "Now let me show you how to really dance, Jules."

Grinning at Ruben, I took another brave sip of my beer, somehow finding that it tasted much better in this atmosphere, then followed big Roland to the dance floor.

"So you're the better dancer?" I called up to him. He was at least six and a half feet tall and beefier than Ruben.

"If we're going to be honest, Jules, I'm the better everything when it comes to Sal. Except perhaps storyteller."

I laughed as he whirled me into a graceful loop, easily bypassing the other dancers.

"You're a great dancer."

"You say that as if it's unexpected."

"Well, you're kind of . . . big and all."

He laughed, a deep rumbling sound. "I am. But my mum was Irish, and she could outdance and outsing any woman in the village. She made sure all her children could do the same."

"Even the boys?"

"Especially the boys. How were we going to woo a pretty lady otherwise?"

I don't think I'd laughed as much as tonight in ages. The dinner with Ruben's parents was so amazing. His parents, especially his mother, made me feel like they'd known me my whole life, like they simply knew Ruben and I were a done deal.

Glancing back at the table, he was watching us while listening to Gabriel, but his smile was entirely for me, a sweet, sentimental expression. I grinned wider, then had to pay attention because Roland, even though he was a giant, was light on his feet and was putting me to shame.

When the song came to another flourishing end, he twirled and twirled me till the fiddler zipped his bow off the strings in a high chord. We all turned and clapped, then the fiddler started playing a slower tune by himself. As I turned to follow Roland back to the table, Gabriel stepped in front of me.

"One more, please, Jules?" He held out his hand. "I don't want to be left out."

"Of course."

Gabriel took my hand in his and placed his other high on my back. Respectful placement, which was good since Ruben was still watching me with keen interest.

"Did you have a nice dinner with your brother?" I asked, the violin lilting in a sorrowful tune.

"Nice isn't what I'd call it, but I did enjoy seeing my brother again."

"Oh." I didn't know what to say to that.

"That is," he continued, his brow pinching, "I love my brother. Of course, I was happy to spend time with him, but he can be a bit . . ."

"Overbearing?" I offered when he seemed to be having trouble finding the right word.

"That fits. Among other things." He glanced over my head. "Enough about him. And please don't take offense at this question."

This didn't sound good.

"Are you truly sincere this time? With our sire?"

"Sincere?" I asked, unsure what he meant.

"I realize this may come across as forward, but I hold Ruben in the highest regard."

I could feel his heavy devotion in the thickness of his voice and the intensity of his dark-eyed gaze on me.

"But do you truly care for him now?"

The implication was that I didn't care for him when we were together before. I had to cool my instant reaction, which was nothing but red-hot anger.

"I cared for him before," I clarified steadily, holding his gaze.

He clenched his jaw. "Perhaps you did," he conceded, as if I didn't know my own mind. "It's only that, I saw what became of Ruben afterward. He recovered eventually, but apparently . . ." He looked away again, over at the stage, the song about a changeling fairy being lost and unloved. "He never truly had. He just hid his emotions well."

He seemed rather aggravated that Ruben had never gotten over me. I couldn't understand what he was actually upset about, whether I truly wanted Ruben this time or the fact that I was back in his life at all.

I had to remember that this vampire was Ruben's second-in-command and was completely devoted to his sire. Vampires took their hierarchy and allegiance to their overlords very seriously. More so than witches and warlocks. It was almost obsessive, it seemed. Or at least, it did right now because Gabriel had obviously taken personal offense to me ending our relationship and breaking Ruben's heart the first time. When, in truth, it had been a mutual breaking of hearts. I was forced to let him go. I'd never wanted to. But that was also none of Gabriel's damn business.

"Trust me when I tell you, Gabriel, that Ruben means everything to me. And I don't plan on leaving him again. Not ever."

He flinched, maybe at the tone of my voice, or the depth of what I said to him, or perhaps even the zing of magic that flared outward when I made that vow. I hadn't even told Ruben as much yet, but I wasn't going to stand here and let Gabriel think anything different.

"I see."

Interesting response.

"I am glad to hear it," he finally said, his hold tightening on me, then loosening at once.

I wasn't sure if he was glad to hear it, but I didn't care either. I was relieved when the song ended, and we could return to the booth.

Sal and Roland were recounting a story of when they wooed two trapeze artists from a circus in the 1800s and ended up being the elephant caretakers for three months. Ruben kept his arm around my shoulders as we all listened and laughed at their antics.

Finally, Ruben nudged me. "Ready to go?"

"Mm-hmm. Long day."

Without another word, he took my hand and guided me out of the booth and through the pub. Sal, Roland, and Gabriel flanked us from the front and behind, watching the street carefully as we got back into the vehicle. They piled into the other SUV, and we made our way back to the hotel.

On the ride up the elevator, Sal was the only one talking, chattering away about wanting a shepherd's pie and wondering if they had it on the room service menu in our fancy hotel. I leaned against Ruben, who practically held me up, then we all meandered to our rooms.

I sighed heavily once we were finally alone and in our bedroom.

"Tired?" he asked, setting the paper-wrapped book on the bed before he removed his jacket.

"Yes. But it was a good night, Ruben. Meeting your parents was best of all."

He smiled tenderly, somewhat subdued, and went about undressing, hanging up his jacket and taking off his shoes.

As I kicked off my heels and tossed my coat on a chair near the window, my gaze shifted to the bed. Walking over, I picked up the book and unwrapped the brown paper. "*The Great Gatsby?*" I murmured as I gently flipped open the obviously well-used volume. "I remember you saying you loved this one."

It wasn't by accident that Ruben owned a rare-books store. He truly appreciated and loved old books. He'd once mentioned his fondness for Fitzgerald's classic.

The book fell open in my palms to a bookmarked page. There was also a highlighted passage. Funny, I thought as I started to read, I never thought Ruben would— My thoughts scattered suddenly. A startling and heartrending realization dawned at what I was reading. The highlighted quote described Gatsby standing on his lawn in the middle of the night, stretching out his trembling hand and reaching through the darkness toward the green light on the other side of the harbor. It was the green light at the end of the dock where Daisy lived, the woman he loved and longed for so desperately.

"The Green Light," I whispered to myself, voice shaking.

I jerked my head up to find Ruben standing on the other side of the bed, shirtless but still in his pants. His arms were at his sides, his body taut, chest heaving in deep, slow breaths.

"You," I began, swallowing hard at the lump in my throat, "you renamed your club the Green Light . . . for me?" I could barely get the words out of my mouth.

His expression—aching and adoring and severe—belied the calm tenor of his voice when he said, "I've been bleeding inwardly for over a decade."

A sharp breath mingled with a sob escaped my throat. I bit my lip and then closed the book in my shaky hands, holding it tightly against my chest.

"Ruben," I whispered, a spark of magic igniting between us.

That magical thread wove tighter, stretching the very air between us.

He didn't move but went on in that melodic, steady voice of his, even while tension continued to build. "When we broke up, I knew that I couldn't simply let you go. There was something tying me to you that went beyond words or explanation. But I also knew that I hadn't given you what you deserved. I set out to earn your trust. And hopefully one day, your love."

I hugged the book tighter against my chest.

He glanced at it, then went on quietly, softly, "I sank myself into the club, into business, hoping I could lose myself in work. But at the same time, I wanted a reminder of you. I renamed it the Green Light so that my longing had a tangible place in my life. So that it could be a constant reminder of what I lost and what I still wanted. And when I realized that you were more than an obsession to me, that you were the only one I was ever meant to be with, I watched and waited and yearned for this day when I could tell you."

Tears slipped silently down my face at his heartbreaking confession. The quaking in my body didn't match the calm words and quiet of the room. His expression broke into a mixture of both tenderness and despair.

"Since the day I realized you were my whole heart, I've never stopped loving you. Not for one painfully paralyzing minute."

He swallowed hard and remained unmoving, his fists balled at his sides. I unclenched my fingers and forced myself to set the book on the table behind me. Walking unsteadily around the bed, I swiped at the tears with my fingers, wiping it all away so that I could look up at him with clear eyes.

"The longing between us has become a beast of its own," I said gently, placing my palm on the left side of his chest. He flexed beneath my hand but remained unmoving, his eyes molten pools of silver. "While you suffered, knowing we were meant for each other, I suffered, believing fate wouldn't ever let me have you."

In a whoosh, the ball of tension in the room burst into nothing. A tingle of magic hummed along my skin, sinking into my chest as I held his gaze. "I love you, Ruben."

His chest caved beneath my hand with a shuddering breath. "More than that, I trust you."

My magic warmed inside my chest. Goddess was telling me something. My gaze fell to his parted mouth, fangs long and sharp as he covered my hand with this own, holding my hand to his heart. "Ruben, I want your bite."

He flinched, eyes flaring wide for a second. "What?"

"You're right. You're my mate, and I'm yours. The Goddess wouldn't have paired us together if we couldn't join in every way."

Even as I said the words, they sank into my consciousness like truth stones. Sparks of brightness filled me with warmth and overwhelming assurance. I could never have found this certainty before now, before I knew myself and the reality of the amazing man and vampire overlord standing before me.

"What about the possibility of mania?" he asked, brow pinching together in disbelief, finally cracking his cool facade.

"I won't get that from you. Not my mate."

"How do you know?"

I wanted to laugh. It was as if he were trying to talk me out of something I know he desired as much as I did.

"Because I know. Goddess tells me so." Spirit sang sweetly to me, humming joy. Like one of Clara's happy spells, but it was generated by me, by my discovery and faith in what I knew must be right and true.

"What about me gaining your power as a Siphon?" he argued still.

He couldn't believe this moment any more than I could. I couldn't imagine feeling this way the first time we were together. It was a knowing that I could hardly put into words.

"Ruben, I trust you. I have faith in you. I believe in *us*." My voice broke at the end.

He still didn't move, apparently frozen in fright or disbelief or both. I stepped back and unzipped my dress, letting it slide down my body and pool at my bare feet. He watched as I unfastened my bra and let it fall to the floor, leaving me in red lace panties. Taking his hand, I tugged him backward toward the bed.

Laying down on my back, I pulled him, and he came, hovering over me, his forearms holding his weight. I opened my legs and he settled between them, his hard cock making me whimper.

"This is right," I whispered to my powerful vampire, who remained rigid and frozen on top of me. Almost like he couldn't force himself to take that step he believed for so long was forbidden.

His eyes were swallowed by black, dilated with desire and heightened awareness of my own arousal. I trailed my fingertip along his lower lip, then slipped it inside, tracing one long, sharp canine to the tip. I slid the pad of my finger to the point and pressed until it stung and a droplet of blood pooled.

His eyes slid closed, nostrils flaring, his chest heaving faster as a single drop of toxin poured into my bloodstream. I moaned at the ecstasy that sizzled through me, my hips pressing up with want. Trailing my bloody finger over his bottom lip, I coaxed my vampire out to play.

I'd never been the seductive one. That had always been his role, but I gladly took the reins to prove to him I was telling the truth. That this was meant to be. That *we* were meant to be, in every way, shape, and form of that definition.

"Taste me," I whispered, rocking my lace-covered pussy against his hard cock.

On an agonizing groan, he closed his mouth over the tip of my finger and sucked, eyes opening, a single silver ring surrounding the black.

"Yes." I rocked my hips again, clenching my hand in the back of his hair. "More . . . *please* more."

On a rattling growl that vibrated from his chest to mine, peaking my nipples to tight points against his warm skin, he grabbed my wrist and pulled my finger from his mouth. Within a second, he had both wrists pinned above my head in one hand, bearing his fangs with primal hunger sharpening his features.

"No going back once we cross this line," he rumbled, voice hard and rough. "Be fucking sure."

He was terrifying in his intensity, a feral shift in his gaze that told me I was looking at the beast inside him. All signs of the sophisticated overlord were gone, replaced by a wild, ravenous predator.

"Taste me, Ruben. Take all of me."

With lightning speed, he sank his fangs into my throat, and the world disappeared. Sharp pain paralyzed me, swiftly followed by unimaginable pleasure. I arched my spine, pressing my breasts against him, crying out and moaning with agonizing ecstasy. Magic, his and mine, pulsed and tangled together with a vicious surge, binding around us.

He groaned as his lips and tongue and teeth worked, sucking my blood and pouring more of his toxin into my veins.

"Oh God!" I screamed. "I'm—" Then I was sucking in breath, unable to form another word, my mind mindless, my body boneless. I was nothing but pure, maddening ecstasy.

The lamp rattled on the coffee table. The legs of the desk at the window knocked against the carpeted floor as it wobbled.

My telekinesis had slipped free, seeking something to thrash as overwhelming emotion poured through me.

His violent growl vibrated against the skin of my throat as he reached down with his free hand, jerked his pants and zipper open, yanked my panties to the side, then plunged inside me.

"Ahh!" The pleasure was too much. My orgasm was fierce, my sex squeezing as he drove inside me with deep, pounding thrusts.

When the pulsing ebbed, he eased, stroking slower, before he let go of my wrists to cup one of my breasts. Holding himself up on one forearm, he thumbed my nipple and stared down at me. His hunger had not abated, but he seemed slightly more in control. I was not. I lost myself entirely, and it was wonderful.

I kept my arms over my head, gripping the pillow and soaking in the brain-hazing pleasure coursing through me. I wasn't aware of the soft whimpering moans I was making till he leaned down and trailed his tongue along my lip, still fucking me slowly.

"I love these sounds you make for me." He nipped my lip, the sting of breaking flesh pulling another eager moan from my throat. He licked the hurt. "But your blood." A flash of silver in the dark. "Your blood is a siren song to my heart."

I gasped as he pulled his cock out of me, still thick and hard. Leaning closer, he placed a kiss to my throat where the bite was tender and raw. I could feel it even under the toxin's tranquilizing effects.

"This bite is for everyone to see."

He trailed down my body, tonguing one nipple, then continuing down. He stripped my panties off and his pants and briefs in a blink, then settled between my open legs, nuzzling my inner thigh.

"But this one"—his voice was silk and velvet, his eyes locking on mine—"this one is only for me."

Then he opened wide and sank his canines into my thigh.

~RUBEN~

HER SOFT FLESH YIELDED BENEATH MY FANGS, MY LIPS PRESSING TO her silken skin. The rush of her sweet blood sent me into a semi-conscious state, body-shaking pleasure rippling through me. I never thought to taste heaven. But now it filled me, flaming through my veins with euphoric rapture.

She clawed at my hair, nails digging in. The small pain was a fierce whip of pleasure, adding to the onslaught of divine sensation taking hold of me. I groaned, still sucking the sweetness from her, hands clamped on both her thighs to keep her still while I took what I needed. What she sweetly, willingly gave to me.

"Goddess help me," she cried out, seemingly as lost in ecstasy as I was, rocking her hips.

Her telekinesis started acting up again. Vaguely, I heard the sound of cracking and splintering wood. Something thudded on the ground, but I didn't care. My body and brain was pure sensation and solely hers.

The first bite had been a punch of blinding pleasure. The second bite seemed to milk wave after wave from me with ruthless ferocity.

"I can't—I can't—" She thrashed her head on the pillow, hips coming off the bed.

A crash of glass sounded to my left, but I didn't even look.

On a purring rumble, I unlatched from her thigh and licked the wound to help heal it. I hadn't done the same to the bite on her throat. On purpose. I wanted every motherfucker on the planet to see my mark on her, to know she was mine and mine alone.

Then I latched my mouth onto her sweet pussy.

"No, I can't take it," she begged, clenching her fingers into my hair.

"Yes, you can. And you will," I whispered against her clit before I pricked it with my fang.

Her hips shot off the bed with another cry as I opened my mouth over her clit and sucked. While my toxin shot to her throbbing core, I sucked her blood and cum into my mouth, nostrils flaring at the sheer bliss of it. My cock was so hard, I was afraid I wouldn't make it inside her before I came.

"Fuck, Ruben. Oh God."

She moaned and squirmed and cried, literal tears streaming to the pillow. "Please, please, I need you."

"Where do you need me?" I whispered, flicking her clit with my tongue, which made her flinch on a gasp.

"Inside me, Ruben. *Please.*"

The desperation in her raspy voice sent me into action. I was on my knees. I hauled her legs up, clasping them together and against my right shoulder. I pressed a kiss to the top of one foot as I lined up my dick and slid inside her tight sheath.

Biting her lip, she clawed both hands into the coverlet to hold on.

"No, Juliana. Let me hear you," I emphasized with a deep thrust.

Her mouth fell open, and those lovely wanton sounds poured from her throat.

"That's my beautiful girl."

I clutched both arms tighter around her thighs and really started fucking her. With the high from her blood still singing through my veins, I groaned and nipped her ankle without drawing any more blood. I just needed my mouth and tongue on her.

"Feels so good, baby," I murmured, slipping one hand to her pussy and sliding my thumb to her clit, stroking in swift circles.

"Ruben!"

"Fuck, yes," I growled, holding myself deep and grinding, feeling her fluttering orgasm start. "Give it to me again, Juliana."

With a near savage scream, she climaxed, throwing her head back and arching her neck. The sight of her vulnerable throat and my bite mark right where it was supposed to fucking be sent me over the edge. I came on a guttural groan.

She went limp as I continued to pump inside her, my long, deep moan echoing off the high ceilings. I thrust till I was fully seated again and then massaged my hips in slow circles, my cock still pulsing inside her. I couldn't get enough. I wanted to stay inside this sweet haven forever.

Finally, I finished, but I still wasn't ready to leave her body. Holding her just where I was, her legs still stretched up my chest and draped over one shoulder, I reached down and stroked my thumb lightly over the bite mark.

"Hurt?" I asked, worried.

"Not in the least," she replied, her smile a sweet balm to my fears.

We simply stared at each other, smiling, when there was a knock at the door.

Frowning, I pulled out of her, stood from the bed, and slid on my pants. She crawled under the covers.

"Stay in here," I ordered before closing the door behind me.

I opened the outer door of the suite to find the maître d', an employee I recognized seeing downstairs earlier.

"May I help you?" I asked.

He took in my half-dressed state, blinking and becoming flustered when he said, "Forgive me for the intrusion, sir, but we've had a complaint from a guest on this floor. There were . . . screams heard coming from your room. And breaking furniture. Is everything okay with you and your partner, Miss Savoie."

My partner. I smiled, liking the sound of that. Though wife would sound even better. One day.

"I apologize for the noise, but we are both well. We will pay for any damages to the furniture."

Sal then stepped out into the hallway, approaching us with a scowl on his face.

The maître d' glanced his way, then back to me nervously. "Thank you, however, I must insist on seeing that Miss Savoie is safe."

I couldn't help smiling at what he thought had happened. "Miss Savoie wasn't screaming from pain, but from pleasure."

The maître d's eyes widened, his face flushing a deep rosy-pink.

"I—I—"

Sal huffed, then set the man straight with a few words that had me outright laughing. I quickly cast glamour over the maître d', who seemed about to faint. His expression went blank, then turned pleasant.

"Thank you, sir. Have a good evening." And he went on his way.

"And thank you, Sal. Good night."

He winked at me. "I'd tell you the same but seems you're already having a good night."

I slammed the door as he laughed and returned to the bedroom, then glanced around at the wreckage. Her TK had broken the legs off the desk, shattered the lamp, splintered then flipped the dresser on its side.

"What?" she asked, pretending she hadn't destroyed the room like a drunken rock star.

No spoiled celebrities throwing a rager here. Just my telekinetic witch under the influence of orgasmic euphoria that I was responsible for. I laughed as I shoved off my pants, enjoying how her gaze dropped, enjoying everything about this moment.

After I crawled under the covers with her and pulled her into my arms to drape over my chest, I finally said, "It seems we had a complaint called on us."

"Who?" She pushed up with a hand on my chest.

"Apparently, someone down the hall heard a woman screaming like she was being murdered and the sound of furniture being broken like there was a struggle taking place."

"Was I that loud?" A lovely blush washed up her neck as she glanced at the lamp in shattered pieces on the floor. "Sorry about the furniture. I'll pay for it."

"No. I'll gladly pay it. I might even buy some breakables for my bedroom back home just to hear them destroyed as I make you lose your mind."

"Stop." She bit her lip to keep from laughing. "Who was at the door about the complaint?"

"The maître d' on duty." I couldn't hold back my grin. "I had to confirm with him that all was well and that the screams were from ecstasy, not murder."

She slapped me on the abdomen. "You didn't."

"What else was I supposed to tell him?"

"I thought I heard Sal."

"You did. He came out of his room when he heard someone at my door. When the maître d' wanted to speak with you to be sure you weren't, in fact, in pieces in the bedroom, Sal told him, and I quote, 'If my sire says he fucked his woman to screaming orgasms, then he did, so sod off.'"

"Stop it, Ruben. He didn't say that."

"He did indeed. When the maître d' was still hesitant, I cast a glamour spell so he'd think all was well and he went on his merry way."

She lay back down, her head on my shoulder. "How unbelievably embarrassing. If Sal heard, then so did Roland and Gabriel."

"For someone so small, you've got a good set of lungs."

"Stop teasing me."

I rolled over on top of her and pressed a soft kiss to her lips, coaxing them apart gently. She melted into our sizzling kiss that was mostly lips. When she moaned and pressed up, wanting more, I pulled away and threaded both hands into her hair, cradling her face. "I love you, Juliana."

She smiled, sincerity and deep affection shining on her face. "I've always wanted to hear you say that."

"It's true, darling," I promised her.

"You know I love you too."

I looked down at her throat, brushing lightly beneath it with the pad of my thumb, marveling at bonding with her in this most intimate way for vampires. Something I'd resolved to never have from her, yet she gave it so easily and freely.

"For so long I didn't." I held her gaze and dipped down to press a soft kiss to her pretty mouth. "But I do now."

CHAPTER 19

~JULES~

"That one's pretty." Perry's assistant, Eleanor, tilted her head from the boutique dressing room waiting area, giving my dress the once-over. She'd become a fast friend the past few days.

"Just pretty?" I asked, looking at the coral-colored gown in my reflection.

"I think you can do better. Try on that gold one next."

I returned back behind the curtain and started changing into the one she'd suggested. "When are you and Perry and his entourage coming up?"

"We're two days behind you. Edmund made it plainly clear that we were not invited to his masquerade, so we'll be up the following morning. If all goes well, we can have a vote that very afternoon. Lord knows most of his cronies will already be at his castle for the masquerade."

"I hope that's true." I pulled up the spaghetti-strapped dress with a deep vee that hit my sternum and made my breasts look fantastic. "Honestly, I'm hoping to get this over with as soon as possible." Which came as a surprise, quite frankly.

"Really? What's the hurry?"

"I don't know," I called through the curtain, turning to look at the elegant cut of the backless dress. I'd never worn anything this sexy in my life. "I think I'm simply homesick, to be honest."

"I can understand that," she said as I stepped out of the curtain. "Oh my!" She grinned. "That's the one. It'll look perfect with the mask we found in the last shop."

We'd actually found a black mask with beautiful filigree around the edges and a sprinkle of gold glitter dust. I stared at the cut and details of the dress, knowing Ruben would love this one.

"But stay close to Ruben in that dress," added Eleanor, "or you'll become another vampire's dinner."

Laughing, I stared at my reflection in the full-length mirror, remembering the extraordinary pleasure I'd experienced with Ruben last night. Giving myself to him had felt so easy and normal, it was borderline absurd. I knew that what I'd done wasn't something to decide on a whim, and quite frankly, I hadn't.

The thought of being Ruben's blood-host had haunted me for years and years. That feeling of forever not being what he needed in a partner. But when it hit me, it hit so fucking hard I couldn't ignore the truth of it.

I was meant for Ruben, like he was meant for me. Soul mates, or blood-mates, as vampires often called them. Whatever the name, it didn't matter. All I knew was that Spirit whispered to accept him, to let him take me in every way. I had to have faith in my instincts and trust in Ruben.

I was right. No mania had taken hold of me. Though that first orgasm had me wondering for a moment or two since it felt like an out-of-body experience. And I was absolutely positive now that Ruben would never abuse my love and take advantage of the power we now shared.

Interestingly, my magic had responded to his toxin, absorbing his power and strength as well. I couldn't trace like a vampire, but I felt the amplification of my own magic by giving him some of mine. It was a bond that I couldn't even imagine twelve years ago. I suppose there was a time for everything. And mine and Ruben's time started now.

"Well, well, well. I'd say someone has been treated right by a certain vampire lord," teased Eleanor.

"You'd be correct," I told her. "And I'm buying this dress to knock his socks off."

"You'll be knocking more than that off him, I can assure you."

After I changed and we went out toward the cashier, Eleanor whispered, "Be careful while you're up there in Northumberland."

"Don't worry. We've been warned. Ruben told me this morning over breakfast that his father said there have been strange stories coming out of the north lately."

"Here you are," said the cashier, handing over the receipt and the dress in a plastic bag.

"Strange indeed," agreed Eleanor.

"What have you heard?"

We walked out onto Bond Street and nodded to Sal and Roland leaning against the SUV where Daniel was waiting behind the wheel. Ruben and Gabriel were working with Perry and his men on the details of transportation and security while at Wulfric Tower. And Eleanor had explained that if I was going to a masquerade, I needed a formal gown. None of my little black dresses would do.

"Let's get in, and I'll tell you."

Roland opened the door for us. Eleanor slid into the back first, then me. Roland took a seat on my right.

Sal hopped in the front. "Got what you needed?"

"Yep. Ready for my first vampire masquerade."

He laughed. "I doubt that." He gave me a wink over his shoulder as Daniel pulled out into traffic.

"Go on," I told Eleanor. "Tell me your story."

"Ooh, I love stories." Sal twisted from the front seat to look back. "What's this one about?"

"I was about to tell Jules why she should be careful while up north. And why you guys better keep a close eye on her."

"Don't worry," said Roland next to me. "We'll guard our Enforcer with our lives."

A sudden burst of warmth filled my chest. I'd expected him to say he'd protect me because I was Ruben's mate and he was their sire, but his allegiance to me as their leader meant more than he could possibly know.

"Thank you, Roland," I said softly.

"It's the truth." He nodded solemnly.

"What kind of stories?" persisted Sal. "Now you've got me all worked up, I want to know what's going on up there."

"The thing is, no one exactly knows what's going on. Only that the werewolves have moved out and most of the witches. My cousin Jessica, an Aura like me, shared a flat with another witch, a hex-breaker in Nottingham, until about nine months ago."

Roland, Sal, and I were riveted by Eleanor as she told her story.

"Jessica's flatmate Cori would leave for days at a time, telling her she was heading to Yorkshire to see family. Jessica found some receipts while cleaning up the flat for a restaurant in Boroughbridge, a small town in Yorkshire. The bizarre part was that Jessica's flatmate didn't have family up north."

"What about her job?" I asked.

Eleanor huffed lightly. "Cori was a bartender for a pub in Nottingham. She didn't have business or kin up in Yorkshire. And when Jessica asked her what all her trips were about, she'd tell her that it was none of her business. Then one night, Jessica heard her come in late and she was talking to someone. She overheard them talking about the Devil Arrows. Cori said something was disgusting, which Jessica didn't hear. Then the guy who'd come home with her said it made someone chuffed to bits, and he laughed. Jessica couldn't hear the person's name he was speaking about. She only knew that they were happy about the disgusting thing at the Devil Arrows."

"What happened at Devil Arrows?" asked Sal.

"Daniel can say a little to that, but wait, listen. When Jessica walked out into the kitchen, they immediately stopped talking. The guy with her was a grim. She said he was dripping with dark, creepy vibes. Jessica asked her the next day who the guy was. Cori said a friend from Yorkshire. And when Jessica started interrogating her about what she was doing up there and warned her that her aura was changing colors to a darker shade, Cori said it was nothing to worry about. The next day, Cori had packed up all her stuff and abandoned the flat without a word."

"That is some crazy shit," murmured Sal. "Daniel, you know anything about all that?"

"Only a little more than Eleanor. But Mr. Baxter did have a team of us check out the Devil Arrows in Yorkshire."

"They're standing stones, ruins, I'm assuming?" I asked Daniel.

"Yeah. They're a tourist site. When we went, there were coppers all over the place. They had it blocked off from tourists. My mate Rick was an Influencer so he used persuasion to get some answers as to what had happened. The coppers said some sort of satanic ritual took place on the Devil Arrows."

Sal frowned. "Satanic?"

"Yeah. Said they found a pig carcass and some chalked demonic signs."

"But it wasn't demonic signs," added Eleanor. "It was witch sign."

"Not satanic rituals then," I corrected. "It was black magic spells."

"Indeed." Eleanor sighed. "Perry has spoken with Edmund about not having a handle on some wild coven practicing the dark arts up there. Edmund said he's got all his men in search of these witches but hasn't found any sign of them."

"Aye," agreed Daniel. "But the stories keep coming. Teenagers going missing. The coppers say it's runaways. Could be true. But the runaways might be a prime target for these nutters casting black spells with blood magic, whoever they are."

We were quiet for the rest of the ride back to the hotel, the mood more serious and somber than before. I'd have to fill Ruben in on all of this. Seemed that there was a lot more going on up north than discrimination against werewolves.

As if conjured by magic, and maybe it was, my phone buzzed with a text from Zuri.

"What is it?" asked Eleanor.

"My contact in the States has a time and meeting place for us with this Magnus Sutherland."

"Where?"

"At Castle Inn in a town called Bamburgh? The day before the masquerade."

"Perfect," she added. "We should arrive the morning after that."

"And the proposal presentation that afternoon. Everything seems to be falling into place."

But for some reason, a nervous energy had found its way into my body and my mind. I couldn't understand how Edmund could ignore the reports of black magic. It was something that would need to be addressed, but only after we got past the proposal and the vote. One problem at a time.

After Sal and Roland made sure I got into my hotel room safely, I locked the door and found the suite empty. Ruben must still be with Perry and his team. I packed my dress since we were leaving in the morning and then pulled out some comfortable pants and a sweater to travel in and laid them out on the chair.

Feeling homesick and a bit troubled from the stories Eleanor had told, I opened my laptop on the table near the window of the suite and texted Evie.

Three minutes later, I was receiving an incoming video call. I instantly answered, my heart leaping with complete joy at the three smiling faces on the screen.

"Hey, Jules!" yelled Evie.

Oh, four faces. She hiked Celine farther up in her arms. My baby niece had a lock of her mother's auburn hair in a fist and was stuffing the hair and her fist in her mouth.

"Hey, sis!" called Violet.

"How is London?" asked Clara. "Did you ride on the London Eye yet?"

They were all talking at once, and my heart soared at this little bit of chaos of home and family.

"Hey, y'all." I laughed a little as my voice broke with emotion. I hadn't realized how much I'd missed them. "No, Clara. We haven't had time to sightsee. But we plan to stay a week or so after the vote of the guild in Northumberland. Then we're going to go do some touristy things."

"Weeee?" Violet waggled her eyebrows. "Pray tell, who is *we*?"

I couldn't even suppress the laughter or the heated blush flushing my cheeks. "Ruben and I."

"Oooooo!" Evie grinned like a fiend. "*Ruben and I.* Did you hear that, Violet?"

"I did. So it seems to me . . . by the near-purple color of your face and that glassy, googly-eyed look you're wearing that you and Ruben are officially back together."

After a slight pregnant pause where their eyes rounded in anticipation, I answered, "We are."

Clara squealed like a banshee and clapped her hands.

"Holy fuck, Clara." Violet backed her head away from her twin. "You're going to break my damn eardrums."

"Oh, Jules." Evie's wide green eyes pooled with tears, then she burst out crying. "I'm so happy for you."

"Yeah, she can totally see how happy you are," snarked Violet with a snort.

"Who is it?" called Livvy from the background as she walked toward the screen, carrying my sweet nephew Joaquin.

"It's Jules!" Violet turned her head. "And she's fucking Ruben Dubois!"

"Whaaaat?!" Livvy ran over excitedly.

Joaquin stared wide-eyed into the screen, and then his mouth tipped up into a smile when he recognized me. That one was an old soul, for sure. He already wore the expression of an old grandpa.

"Oh my God, y'all. I've missed you all so much."

"Yes, yes. But tell me more." Livvy's blue eyes narrowed with fiendish glee. "Is it as good as you remember?"

"What are you talking about?" I snapped back. "I never told y'all we were sleeping together before."

Violet and Livvy rolled their eyes. Violet leaned in after putting her hands over Celine's ears. "But seriously, was it? I bet that vampire can fuck like there's no tomorrow."

"What about Joaquin's ears?" I gestured.

Violet scoffed. "He already knows everything."

"What do you mean?" Evie was still wiping her face. "He's just a baby."

"Ha! That"—she pointed to the straight-faced Joaquin currently examining Violet closely with those wizened eyes—"right there is a fifty-year-old man in the body of a three-month-old werewolf/warlock baby. I'm a Seer. I'm telling you. He's not offended by sex talk. Are you, Joaquin?"

The infant in question blinked, then turned his face back to me and put his tiny hand on the laptop screen, which of course made his hand disappear from view. He might be an old soul, but he didn't understand technology enough to know that the screen wasn't the camera.

I leaned in closer and smiled at him. "I miss you, too, little one. I'll be home soon."

Livvy sighed sweetly. "Jules, I'm so happy for you."

That was when Celine decided to vomit up a stream of milk that hit her mother, Violet, and Livvy all at once. Then Celine giggled.

"Holy hell, chick, you're like Mount Vesuvius." Violet pulled her soiled shirt away from her body.

"Language, Vi. Stop cursing around the babies," fussed Evie, then they all hopped up and moved off-screen.

I could hear the faucet in the kitchen running and all of them fussing and Celine laughing. It was utterly delightful.

Clara, completely unscathed by the milk catastrophe, leaned in and smiled sweetly. "Jules, your aura," she whispered and shook her head, blinking quickly with glassy eyes, "it's so stunningly beautiful."

"Really?"

Clara was always gentle and kind, giving us the emotional boost we always needed. I never had appreciated her more than I did in that moment. My spirits had been doused by the dark and strange happenings in the north of England, and even though Clara wasn't in the same room casting a spell on me, just hearing her sweet voice buoyed me up.

"It's a radiant gold, deep orange at the core," she went on. "You're filled with joy, aren't you?"

Thinking of Ruben, I most definitely was.

"Oh my." Clara's blue eyes widened as she leaned closer to the screen. "Is that what I think it is?"

I'd worn a scarf while out shopping to cover the bite even though Ruben hadn't wanted me to. Eleanor had seen it, of course, when I was trying on dresses. She hadn't said a word, but did give me a cheeky grin when I walked out in the first dress. I'd left the scarf on the bed after I returned from shopping. I touched my fingers lightly to the bite, relishing the memory of last night.

"Yes."

"That's wonderful." Clara beamed right back. "I'm so happy you finally trust him. That you truly love him."

Of course, Clara would know before I'd even said a word about love. She wasn't a Seer like her twin, but in some ways her intuition and ability as an Aura to read people made her even better at knowing the hearts of people. Her approval of the step I'd taken last night only solidified my belief that what I'd done was right.

Not that I needed it. Spirit had kept me floating on a high long after I fell asleep last night and well into the morning. Eleanor had asked if I'd had too much coffee because I wouldn't stop grinning and laughing like a loon at the smallest things while out shopping.

"Thank you, Clara. And how is everything at home? Other than Celine overeating and spitting it back up."

Celine had always been a greedy little thing, rivaling Diego for crying for her bottle in the middle of the night.

"Everything is fine. It's wonderful to have Mom and Dad here, but we miss you, of course."

"Is that why you look so sad all of a sudden?"

"Oh no." She pulled her long, gold-blonde hair over one shoulder, a nervous habit of hers. "That's because I don't understand why Henry doesn't just admit that he likes me."

"Henry . . . Blackwater?" I'd seen the way Gareth's cousin had been staring at my youngest sister for some time now. It wasn't a secret among us sisters that he enjoyed working outside Ruben's vampire den so that he could watch the comings and goings at Mystic Maybelle's. Specifically the comings and goings of my kindhearted sister.

"Who else would I mean?"

"Clara, I believe he very much does like you."

"I know he does." Her smile faltered, like she was unsure. "I think he does. But he doesn't want to act on it, and I keep waiting for him to figure out we're supposed to be together. I mean, most men like to take the initiative, don't they?"

"Yes, they do. That's true."

"So I've been giving him a chance. I thought for sure at the wedding, especially after he agreed to wear a rose-pink-and-gold sherwani so that he could match me at the altar, that he realized it was time to stop ignoring fate and take the next step."

"To ask you out, you mean."

"Of course. We have to date first before we get married and have our seven babies Travis predicted we'd have."

"Wait." I laughed and blinked a minute. "What? Travis predicted you'd marry Henry and have seven babies?"

Travis was the warlock who lived with our cousins Drew and Cole in Lafayette. They ran their own microbrewery and often came to visit when they could. Travis was a Seer like Violet.

"He did. Henry and I are going to have six boys and one girl. But not if he doesn't ask me out."

I bit my lip to keep from laughing. Clara was never frustrated, but right now her face was flushed with pink, tipping the tops of her cheekbones. There was an angry vee between her brows. It was so unlike her.

"Maybe he's shy," I suggested.

"Henry?" She tilted her head in thought, ruminating over that. "Maybe."

"Perhaps you should be the one to ask him out, Clara."

"Hmm." She thought a second, then smiled. "Maybe you're right, Jules."

It was getting late, and I wanted to get my shower before Ruben returned. "I'd better go. Tell the girls I'll call again soon after my trip north."

"I'll tell them." She blew me a kiss. "Take care, and we love you."

"I love all of you too. Talk soon."

"Say bye to Jules, everyone!"

There was a sudden barrage of *goodbyes* and *love-yous* from off-screen. I waved and laughed, then ended the call. Feeling monumentally better, I got up and finished packing, ready for our trek up north and whatever awaited us there.

CHAPTER 20

~RUBEN~

W E DROVE THROUGH THE WINDING HILLS TOWARD WULFRIC TOWER.
A mist rolled thicker as we drove closer, climbing an incline
toward a rocky hill and Gothic castle. There was even a draw-
bridge still in place that was lowered, allowing us through the
castle walls and up to a curved drive in front of the dark gray
fortress. Even gargoyles protruded from the top cornices. One
central tower rose on the north side, but there were battlements
in a giant square around the rest of the castle.

"Are we trying to win a prize for most vampire-like?" Jules
whispered teasingly.

I squeezed her hand, glad she was in a lighthearted mood. I
hadn't been from the second we'd entered Edmund's territory.
It was oppressive with his dominant magic as though he spent
time warding the place heavily.

"I believe he is," I answered her as the car, driven by one of
Stonebridge's men, came to a stop.

There were warding spells that kept humans away with a kind of persuasion charm. Though they never realized why they didn't want to go, humans would automatically stay away from his boundaries. Even supernaturals would feel the weight of the charm and wouldn't want to go near it unbidden. Edmund was a strange one, and Gabriel's constant assurances that his brother was merely eccentric weren't sitting well with me. I couldn't wait for this fucking vote to be over and done with.

"And there he is," I added.

Edmund stood on the wide stone steps in front of the iron double doors.

"If he was wearing a tunic, trousers, and fur-trimmed cloak, he might look exactly like one of his royal ancestors."

Jules pressed her lips together to keep from laughing. The driver was, after all, in Edmund's employ. He wasn't very friendly either. When the car stopped, I didn't wait but hopped out, traced to the other side, and opened the door for Jules.

"There you are!" called Edmund in his dress shirt and slacks. "I was beginning to wonder if you'd make it before nightfall."

The sun had just set, but it was hard to tell behind the gray clouds and the mist rolling in.

"We're not afraid of the dark," I told him, guiding Jules by the hand up the steps.

"Of course not." His mouth slid into a smirk that sent a shiver up my spine.

His man Aaron, who made me want to punch him in the teeth every time I looked at him, stood behind him in the door-way, smirking like an arrogant ass.

"Brother, glad you all made it," said Edmund over my shoulder. Gabriel, Sal, and Roland were walking up behind us. "I've had dinner guests brought in for all of you. If you'd like to follow me to the dining room."

Jules stiffened at my side. I knew exactly what he had planned, a vampire feast of blood *from* the dinner guests.

"Forgive me, Edmund," Jules said sweetly, stepping forward to offer her hand. "I'm so tired that I'd rather go straight to bed."

He took her hand as if to shake it but didn't let it go, and somehow I managed not to rip his throat out. It was a miracle, to be honest.

"But I have human food for you as well, Juliana. You don't think that I'd forget about you."

I froze at his use of her full name. He was goading me, and he fucking knew it. Yet his eyes were solely on her, his thumb rubbing over the back of her hand. I was truly trying not to murder him on his doorstep because that wouldn't be good etiquette, but he was making it very difficult for me to maintain control.

"I appreciate that, but I'm just exhausted."

His eyes tightened around the corners. He was aggravated that she didn't want to lay around and watch everyone suck and fuck in his parlor. We'd have to endure enough of that at the masquerade unless we stood him up for that too. Jules was intent on playing his game until we didn't have to, keep the peace till the vote, but I wasn't sure that I could.

Fucking finally, he brushed a kiss over the back of her hand and released it. "Come this way, and my housekeeper, Hazel, will show you to your rooms."

"Ruben and I only need one room," she stated loud and clear.

My chest puffed with pride. I couldn't fucking help it. Edmund's gaze dropped to her throat. Today, she'd dispensed with the scarf, and though the mark was healing, it was prominent enough for vampires to see it peeking from the top of her sweater.

"Of course," he said silkily.

This fucker. I wasn't sure what his game was, but if he thought he was going to make a play for Jules, he was sadly mistaken.

He led us inside. The castle looked just like how it must have looked like for hundreds of years. Wall tapestries and giant oil canvases displaying medieval battles and shields and swords decorated the walls. Like Edmund still wanted the world to know this was a place of bloody triumph over its enemies.

"Hazel, this is Juliana Savoie and Ruben Dubois. And his men, Sal and Roland. Please escort them to their rooms. Gabriel can stay in his own room, of course."

"Yes, sire," said the meek vampire.

She wore a bite mark herself on her forearm. She didn't appear afraid of Edmund but definitely was subservient to him. I imagine that was the only kind of servant he allowed in his home.

As she led the others up the stairs, I turned to Edmund. "A word, if you don't mind." I wasn't fucking asking.

"Of course, Ruben. Right this way."

He led me down a corridor beyond the stairs, through an archway into a great hall, then finally to a door at the end that led into what must be his study. Aaron followed on our heels, but when he tried to enter behind me, I spun and flattened a palm on his sternum.

"Ah, ah, ah." I shook my head. "This is big boy talk. You stay out here."

His eyes narrowed into slits, and I actually thought this fool was going to challenge me, which would've been a terrible mistake on his part. He'd lose a limb if he dared.

"Go help his men get settled, Aaron," called Edmund tersely.

He huffed, and I slammed the door in his face before he managed to even turn around.

As expected, Edmund's study was decorated in nothing but rich, crimson-covered fabrics. Besides a wall of books there were crisscrossing swords on the opposite wall as well as portraits of past Stonebridge kings in royal regalia. And yet again, there was an Anglo-Saxon battle depicted in another painting, but in this one, the marauding victors had distinctive silver eyes.

"Someone seems mired in the past, Stonebridge."

"Nothing wrong with honoring our ancestry."

I stared again at the barbaric painting where one of the invaders had a helpless peasant woman in his arms and was obviously drinking blood from her throat.

"There is when you're honoring your marauding, pillaging, and raping ancestors."

His eyes flashed, his expression losing its insipid, indifferent facade. Now it was tight with simmering anger.

That's more like it.

"What is it you want to speak to me about?"

"Juliana."

A wicked smile cut through his momentary rage. "What about her?"

"If it wasn't clear enough, I'm telling you vampire to vampire"—because that was a distinct difference from man to man—"that she is my mate."

That gave him some pause, his repulsive smile slipping. "Is she?"

"Truly. So if you have any nefarious plans about seduction, let me explain quite clearly that I will eviscerate you if you try." Because he was certainly the type to try to use his glamour on her unlawfully to get her attention. "If any harm comes to her at all."

"I have no intention of harming the most powerful Enforcer I've ever met, especially one in such a pretty package."

I clenched my fists, which only had Stonebridge smiling again. I wasn't going to attack him for saying asinine things to bait me into a fight.

"I know a vampire on the hunt when I smell one." My voice had dropped low and lethal. "So I'm warning you. Change your course now while you can. Use glamour on her, touch her, or in any way try to harm her, and you're a dead man. I don't give a flying fuck how many lofty ancestors bloody your walls with their triumphs. I'll hang your head in the foyer on your great-grandfather's sword."

He'd gone motionless. All I knew was his stillness reflected the severity and the genuineness behind my promise. Because it wasn't a threat; it was a fucking *promise*.

"Are we understood?" I asked in a more civil tone.

"I have a lovely, powerful woman of my own, Dubois," he replied in that repellent, silky voice. "What would I want with yours?"

I didn't bother answering. I left swiftly and followed Juliana's scent up the stairwell and down a corridor on the third floor to a room facing the east. She was standing at an open window, looking out over the rolling hills, the moon now coming up.

Satisfied Stonebridge now clearly understood my position, I wrapped my arms around her from behind.

She wrapped her fingers loosely around my forearms. "It's quite lovely here."

"It is. You're not cold?" The air was biting.

"A little, but it feels refreshing after being cooped up in the plane and a car all day."

"Mm."

"What did you talk to Stonebridge about?"

"Nothing to worry about. Just had to get some things settled between us."

"Is this one of those man things I don't need to bother my delicate sensibilities about?" Her voice was light and teasing, but I didn't want her to think I was trying to take the upper hand.

"It had nothing to do with the vote."

"What was it about?"

"You."

She gave a little laugh and peered up at me, her head leaning to one side. "That's not something I should be worried about?"

I leaned my head down and brushed a kiss across her lips. "I simply had to warn him that I'd be forced to murder him if he decided to try to seduce you."

"You did not."

"I did."

She laughed. "A man flirting with me doesn't mean—"

"Juliana." I nipped her bottom lip, my canines not out at the moment, but it got her attention. "Please trust me when I tell you that I know vampires, and he had plans. Or was making them. But I've put a stop to them."

And if he didn't stop them, he knew the consequences.

"All right," she said softly, pressing a kiss to my still lowered lips. "I trust you."

And that phrase had so much meaning now, so much faith and loyalty lodged behind it that I couldn't help but ravage her mouth, cupping her jaw with one hand. She whimpered softly and teased her tongue inside my mouth. Right when I took the kiss deeper, an eerie, distant howl rose over the hills and through the open window.

We broke away and looked out. Three seconds went by, then another howl.

"But there's no full moon," she whispered. "It's just over half full."

"You're right."

"Then why are they shifting?"

There were no natural wolves in England. Those could only be the howls of shifting werewolves.

"That's a very good question. Especially since we've been told by everyone that the werewolves have moved out of this territory."

"Maybe Magnus will know."

"Maybe so," I agreed, though I felt unsettled.

And though we were on the third floor behind a castle wall, the thought of wandering werewolves—perhaps rogue ones, essentially feral beasts—had me closing and locking the windows.

"Let's go to bed, darling. A few more days, and we can return to London."

"That will be so amazing, Ruben." She smiled tenderly as she went to her open suitcase. "And then sightseeing and dinners with your parents. Clara said I have to take a ride on the London Eye."

"Then I will take you, my love. Don't you worry."

I injected all the lightness in my voice that I could manage, but my predatory instincts were on high alert. It wasn't just Edmund's obvious infatuation with my mate that had my nerves fraying at the ends. It was the oppressive atmosphere of this place and now the possibility of rogue werewolves roaming the moors.

"I'm going to take a shower," said Jules, wandering into the connecting bathroom to our bedroom.

My phone buzzed.

"Go right ahead. I'll join you in a minute."

It was a text.

Roland: Did you hear the werewolves?

Me: Couldn't miss them. Tell Sal to keep your interior doors locked.

Roland: You think the werewolves might get into the castle?

> Me: I don't know what the fuck is going on up here, but I'm not taking chances. I don't trust Stonebridge. Keep that between you and Sal.

I didn't have to say, *Don't tell Gabriel.*

Roland: Got it.

> Me: Meet me downstairs at 6 a.m. Tell Sal to keep close to Jules if she leaves her room.

Roland. Yes, sire.

> Me: Roland and I could do a little investigation in the morning into these wolves. I'd like to see how close to the castle they were.

I walked across the room to lock the door, then I pulled a wardrobe in front of it. Of course, a strong werewolf or vampire could still get through that, but it would slow them down long enough for me to be ready to rip their throats out should they try to come through that door.

Gabriel had been my right-hand man for a century. Ever since I'd left England, he'd been at my side. I trusted him with my life, but I sure as fuck didn't trust his brother. I didn't want Gabriel knowing I suspected something was going on around here or there was some sort of neglect that was his brother's fault. I trusted Gabriel's allegiance, but I also understood the ties of blood, and I wouldn't take that chance. Not with my men's life, not with my own, and certainly not with that of my mate.

"Are you coming?" called my sweet siren.

"No, my love," I called back, stripping off my shirt. "But I will be soon."

Her laughter was the balm to my soul, shaving away the layer of old hurt a little at a time. So I went in search of the comfort only she could provide. Tomorrow, we'd deal with whatever devilry was amiss in the north.

CHAPTER 21

~JULES~

"Thank you, Hazel."

"Can I get you anything else?"

"No. Thank you. This is more than enough. I won't be able to eat even half of this."

I stared down at the breakfast feast on the table on the veranda overlooking the back gardens. The table was laden with sausage, bacon, scrambled eggs, spicy breakfast potatoes, biscuits, toast, and jams and jellies of every flavor. There was also a full pot of coffee and hot tea. I'd eaten a small pile of bacon and eggs and was already nearly full.

"Our cook is excited to have someone to cook for. He knows Americans like coffee, but he also wanted to send up a pot of his best tea."

"I appreciate that very much. Is Edmund not here quite a bit?"

"Mr. Stonebridge? Why do you ask?"

"You said Bernard was glad to have someone to cook for, so I assumed he wasn't at residence often."

"Oh." Her brow pinched together, and she replied hesitantly, "He is at home, most of the time, but he . . . dines out. And often prefers a liquid diet, if you catch my meaning."

"Yes. I do."

Hazel seemed nervous all of a sudden. Perhaps she wasn't supposed to share that. I'd have to mention to Ruben when he came down for breakfast.

"You have a beautiful garden here." Though it was approaching winter and there were no flowers, there was a pretty, well-manicured hedge that ran the periphery of the garden. There was also a hedge maze beyond beds of flowers that weren't currently in bloom.

"Yes, Miss Savoie. But please don't go wandering too far."

That got my attention. I looked up at her with my coffee cup halfway to my mouth. "Why's that?"

"What I mean to say is, feel free to go as far as the fountain there, but don't go into the hedges." She made a nervous sort of laugh. The fountain was several yards beyond the veranda in front of the hedge entrance. "We've had guests get completely lost in there, and it's so cold now, you'd catch your death."

"Hazel," came the crooning voice of Edmund behind us at the open doorway. "It's time for you to get back to work and not rattle Miss Savoie's ear off."

"Yes, sire." She actually dipped a curtsy, then hurried back into the castle.

Suddenly, I'd lost my appetite.

"Don't mind her," he told me. "You know how humans spook so easily."

"Why would she be spooked? She knows about the existence of supernaturals." Her bite marks were evidence enough that she knew vampires existed, and likely knew about the rest of us.

"Yes, but these small-town villagers like to tell ghost stories and nonsense to entertain themselves."

I sipped my coffee and pushed my plate away, ready to change the subject. "I imagine your garden is lovely in the spring."

"It is. That's the original fountain, which was installed by my great-great-grandfather. It dates back to the Middle Ages."

I hadn't taken much notice of the fountain, situated prettily at the opening of the hedge maze. I tried to see what the old sculpture depicted, but it was difficult from this angle. The side facing us seemed to be a tree with leafy branches.

"Would you like to see it?"

I glanced to the right of the veranda where Sal stood guard in the corner. Ruben had tried to put me at ease last night and this morning, but I knew he was concerned about this place when he told Sal to guard me over breakfast. He left this morning at daybreak while I was still in bed and said he wouldn't be long.

When I stood and stepped down the wide steps, Edmund followed.

"So your ancestors were some of the first to arrive here in England?" I asked casually, like it was perfectly normal to have two bodyguards follow me around.

"They were," he replied, pride in his voice. "The first wave of Saxon conquerors bore the first Stonebridge who would one day build this castle."

He might've said something else, but my mind drifted as I took in the scene displayed in marble, the clear water trickling with an ironic sound of tranquility. The statue was of a large man, a vampire actually, with subtle canines peeking from his mouth. Brandishing his sword, he wore a tunic and had his foot upon the chest of his fallen foe. The enemy he was celebrating victory over was a giant wolf, misshapen just enough to give hints of a human physique beneath the fur.

"My ancestors were also the first to rid the lands of the wolves that terrorized villagers so long ago."

He couldn't be serious. This wasn't a depiction of ridding the land of natural wolves.

"Wulfric Tower," I ruminated. "Your castle is named after wolves. Or rather the ones you conquered."

"Indeed. Clever woman."

His superior gaze told me everything I needed to know. I couldn't tiptoe around it anymore. I needed to know where he stood. "So I take it you're against opening a seat for the werewolves at our guild table. You're against our proposal."

His mouth quirked, giving him a boyish look with his handsome features, but there wasn't anything boyish about this vampire.

"I admire you, you know." He stepped closer, but not into my personal space thankfully. "Leading such a campaign that is bound to lose. Only a powerful woman such as yourself could take something like this on."

Patronizing prick.

"I disagree. It isn't bound to lose. And it has nothing to do with how powerful my magic is that leads me to do this. It's what is right."

He scoffed. "You can't remove the monster from the man in werewolves. The curse is in their blood."

"As it is in yours."

Rather than get angry, he only smiled wider. "But vampires aren't beholden to our beast, our cravings. For example, your blood smells sweeter than anything I've scented in a century. The temptation to taste you is unbearable. But still . . . I won't bite you."

"If you tried, I'd fry you where you stand," I replied just as pleasantly, without a hint of anger. Because I wasn't. I was simply annoyed by his unbelievable arrogance. "You'd be a bag of magicless bones before you could blink."

He laughed, his canines sharp. "I like you."

A whoosh of wind, and suddenly Ruben was standing at my side, vibrating with fury. I quickly grabbed his hand and squeezed it. Though he was as hard and rigid as the marble fountain in front of us, he turned his gaze down to me. At once, he seemed to read my expression. I didn't want violence. It would only ruin our entire mission here. Maybe that's what Edmund had wanted.

"Let's go, darling. Our appointment awaits." He tugged me, and we walked briskly away from Edmund.

"What appointment is that, Dubois?" asked Edmund.

"None of your fucking business, Stonebridge. Oh, and we're taking one of your cars."

"Are you taking Gabriel?" he called after us, but Ruben didn't answer.

By the time we'd made our way through the castle corridor and out the double doors, Sal and Roland were in the front seat of a sleek sedan similar to the one we'd ridden in here from Ruben's jet at the private airport. When we were belted in the car and rolling away, Ruben sat back, fuming.

I couldn't help but smile, not at his aggravation but at the protectiveness behind it. "You know, I could've thrown him over the hedges if I needed to. My telekinesis is strong."

"I know. But my inner caveman is shrieking for me to just club you over the head and drag you all the way back to my cave. In New Orleans."

I wrapped my arms around one of his and pressed my chin to his biceps, looking up at him. "You don't have a cave."

"I'm going to get one."

"Is this a vampire thing? Bats and all?"

He huffed out a breath, finally looking down at me, the fury having abated somewhat. "Stop being this way."

"What way?"

"Flippant. Dismissive. Comical."

"You think I'm comical?" I grinned with wide eyes. "You must have me confused with one of my sisters. Violet, probably. Or Livvy. I'm the serious one."

"You're the impossible one." He unlatched my seatbelt and pulled me onto his lap. "The one who's going to turn my hair gray early."

"Well, if you look anything like your father when you're gray, then by all means, age away."

"Oh really?" He arched a brow, and his fingers curled slowly at my ribs, his other hand just above my knee.

"Don't you dare."

He tickled me anyway, which had me laughing and kicking and wiggling in complete and total embarrassment. And while I was a little mortified being seen losing all composure in front of Roland

and Sal, I was glad it had removed the feral look from Ruben's face. It wouldn't do to meet the wolf pack leader of the Highlands in that state, and we were about to in less than an hour.

When he finally put me back in my seat, then belted me in, I asked, "Where were you and Roland this morning?"

His hand on my knee tightened. "Remember those werewolves we heard last night?"

"Yes."

"Roland and I found their tracks. I wanted to see how close they were coming to the property."

"What did you find?" I asked eagerly.

"They're actually on the property, running a perimeter it seems, about a half a mile out. Wouldn't you say, Roland?"

"Yes, sire. I found one set of tracks slightly closer."

"But if they're inside the property then they're inside the wards Edmund has erected, aren't they? Why would he cast spells that allow rogue werewolves so close to his home? After the conversation I just had with him, he obviously hates werewolves."

"I'd love to know, darling."

"Perhaps Magnus has some answers," added Sal.

"Perhaps," said Ruben.

Then we rode the rest of the way in silence, all of us pensive about what in the world was actually going on at Wulfric Tower.

~RUBEN~

THE VILLAGE OF BAMBURGH WAS A QUAINT LITTLE TOWN, AND THE pub at the Castle Inn was perfect to meet in a quiet corner uninterrupted. The village seemed used to tourists and travelers wandering through, so we didn't even receive that many odd or questioning looks.

But the behemoth of a werewolf who marched in with two other werewolves similar in his size did draw attention. The auburn-haired giant strode straight toward us. He motioned for his two men to sit with Sal and Roland at a table nearby, easily sniffing out the vampires in the room, and folded his body into the bench opposite us.

"I'm Ruben Dubois. This is Jules Savoie."

"I know who ye are." His Scottish brogue was thick. His amber-gold gaze flicked between us. He radiated strength and power, a man who was accustomed to giving orders. "Magnus Sutherland, though I imagine ye dinnae need an introduction either."

He was brusque and to the point. Rather refreshing.

"Zuri told you about our proposal to the guilds?" Jules asked.

"Aye. I imagine ye want to know how our violent crimes have lessened the past few decades."

Straight down to business. Also refreshing.

"We do," I confirmed.

He waved a big paw toward Jules. "You'd know more than anyone. Your sister, the witch doing the tattoos."

"Violet."

"We've got one of our own like her."

Jules and I shared a surprised look.

"My man Collin there." He pointed to the dark-haired werewolf watching us from the table with Sal and Roland. "His mate's a witch, descended from a druid who knew the same tattoo magic that we hear your sister is spreading in America."

"That's wonderful." Jules leaned forward, her hands clasped on the table. "My sister Violet has been apprenticing with witches in Europe as well."

"Good thing she's doing. That's why I took this meeting with ye."

"Let me ask you this, Magnus," I said. "You know that we plan to put forward our proposal to the High Guild in a few days?"

"High Guild?" His wide brow furrowed. "Ye mean the Witch Guild?"

"No," said Jules, straightening with pride. "We've renamed it the High Guild. At least in parts of America we have as of recently. It's time we removed Witch from the title if it's to include everyone." She paused, assessing Magnus's unreadable stare. "At least, that's what I think. And why I proposed changing it."

His blank face broadened with a grin. "I like ye, witch."

Bristling slightly, because I couldn't fucking help myself when another man found my mate beguiling, I said, "Back to the proposal. Zuri told you we'll be pitching it here in a few days?"

"Aye."

"How do you feel about taking the first seat for the werewolf clans on the High Coven Guild of the UK?"

Jules and I had discussed this last night. If anyone could handle his own as the first werewolf coven guild leader in one of the most powerful countries in the world, it was Magnus Sutherland.

"I'd rather dip my arse in a bucket o' crabs." He heaved a sigh and glanced to the side before returning a darker look on me, his eyes rolling wolf-gold. "But someone's gotta step up and do the work now, eh? I'd love to sit across the table from that bawbag, Stonebridge."

"What have you heard about him?" I asked quickly.

"Not what I heard. It's what I know."

"And what's that?" asked Jules.

"There's supernaturals going missing. Mostly teenagers. Wolf-kind, but also witches and others alike."

"We heard something similar from Perry Baxter," I told him. "You think it's Stonebridge?"

"I dinnae ken if it's him, but there's nothing good around his castle and his lands. The place reeks of something foul going on. Why's he got all that heavy glamour and spells around the castle?"

"I felt them too," I added.

"If yer staying there, yer aff yer heid. Werewolves can smell the foulness about it. Won't go too near. That's one reason so many have left the lands altogether."

"As to that," I added, "you may be wrong."

"Come again?"

"My man Roland and I"—I pointed to him at the table with the others—"heard rogues howling last night around the castle. We weren't sure how close they'd come or why, so we inspected their tracks this morning. They were running a perimeter of the castle. Like they were guarding it."

"I don't believe it. No werewolves I know of would go near that place."

"But they are," added Jules. "Have you heard about the practicing of black magic in other places up north?"

"Aye. Tis known. Some witchy shite going on. No offense."

"None taken," she said.

"Tomorrow afternoon will be the proposal and the vote." I leaned back against the booth. "Will you come to the vote? It'll be at Wulfric Tower. We could use your support."

A sly, devilish grin spread the hard man's expression for the first time since he'd sat down. "Aye."

"The proposal meeting begins at five in the afternoon."

"Aye. I'll be there. You can guarantee."

CHAPTER 22

~RUBEN~

"There it is again," said Roland, staring out the third-floor window near the staircase landing.

"I know." I was now even more convinced that there were rogue werewolves surrounding and protecting Edmund's property. For what reason, I had no idea, but rogues weren't just dangerous. They were lethal.

The strings of the orchestra carried up to the third-floor corridor where I waited for Jules. Guests had started arriving about a half hour ago. Murmuring conversation, laughter, and the tinkling of glasses—the sounds of any formal cocktail party—filled the downstairs ballroom. But knowing that it wasn't a regular party at all had me on edge.

I'd tried to convince Jules that we should simply lock ourselves in the bedroom for the night and forget about the masquerade, but she'd pointed out that it was a great opportunity to feel out some of the coven leaders who'd be here tonight.

Find out who were our allies and who weren't. After all, the vote would be tomorrow night with these very people, in addition to those not invited to the party.

When I'd pointed out to her that Edmund had most certainly stacked tonight's guests with all his sycophants and allies, she'd argued again that it was the perfect reason we needed to show our faces, play the game, and try to persuade those who would be swayed to reason.

"Magnus's man said they'd likely stay the night in Bamburgh and come straight here early tomorrow," said Sal at my side.

"I think the highlander would be more than happy to play a part in the High Guild here in the UK."

Sal chuckled. "I believe so."

"More wolves arrived in Bamburgh than when we'd gotten there." Roland crossed his arms, his black Venetian mask not hiding his identity at all. "I saw them gathered in the corner of the inn when we left."

"I saw them too," I told him. "But I'd wonder about Magnus's intelligence if he'd come back here without a number of guards."

"He doesn't like Stonebridge much," said Sal.

"Don't blame him. I—"

The air left my lungs as I caught the vision stepping from our bedroom. All three of us froze and watched as Jules walked toward us in the most stunning—and revealing—dress I'd ever seen her in.

Standing a few inches taller in stilettos, which she never wore, she was draped in a shimmery gold gown with spaghetti straps. The material dipped into a deep vee past her breasts, where it clung lovingly. I knew that once she turned around, I'd see the same shape in the back. When she walked, the floor-length dress revealed a peek at her shapely legs as the fabric was fringed into tassels from mid-thigh down. Her short, dark auburn hair was slicked back and curled around her ears. It struck me that she'd mimicked the twenties fashion, looking somewhat Gatsby-esque. The ornate black mask, dusted with gold, that curved around her blue-gray eyes only enhanced her ensemble and beauty.

I swallowed, finding that I had no saliva at all left in my mouth. Then Sal wolf-whistled and shocked me back into reality.

"Sal," I grumbled as I strode forward to meet her.

"I can't help it, sire. Jules, you look smokin'."

Roland cleared his throat, then said something under his breath. I ignored their bickering and pulled her closer, my hands at her waist, shaping my palms along the silky fabric while I looked my fill.

"Goddess save me, darling. Are you trying to kill me?"

"You like?" she asked, her full, red lips curling sensuously.

"I'm not sure I can allow you to be in a room full of depraved vampires in this dress." I kept gliding my hands back and forth along her waist, wanting to slide my palms to her ass but Sal and Roland were right behind us.

"I'd hoped you'd like this dress."

"It's for me, isn't it?"

"Of course it is. I thought"—she shrugged an elegant, pale shoulder, drawing my eye to her neckline again—"you might like it . . . since you got your Daisy."

My gaze lifted back to hers, heart pumping hard at the reminder that she was mine. I'd never get tired or take for granted this woman in my arms. I dipped my head close to her ear. "I love you, Juliana."

"And I love you," she replied easily. Naturally.

It was like manna from heaven.

I held out my arm, and she took it, then we followed Sal and Roland down the stairs. Gabriel was waiting at the foot in his tuxedo and a white mask.

"Sire." He nodded to me, then to Jules. "You look lovely, Miss Savoie."

"Thank you, Gabriel." He walked before us through the giant archway into the ballroom, completely transformed from the vast, vacant hall when we'd arrived.

"Oh my," whispered Jules.

"I hope you find it satisfactory," added Gabriel to her wide-eyed astonishment.

"Satisfactory? Gabriel, this is lovelier than a Mardi Gras ball back home."

Truly, it was magnificent. There were giant gold-and-crystal chandeliers, which had been lowered from the high ceiling to offer more reflective splendor and an elegant canopy. The lighting was a soft glow from the chandeliers and the gilded wall sconces.

The walls were draped in swaths of crimson silk. Black chaises, sofas, and chairs—all covered in the exact luxurious velvet brocade design—were spread around the room. Some in small groupings in corners, others facing the dance floor to watch the party. Sporadically around the room, there were gold vases overflowing with dozens upon dozens of blooming roses of the deepest scarlet. He must've paid a pretty penny to some hothouse to have so many delivered if he'd managed to get anyone to deliver to the house at all with the wards around this place.

Kudos to Edmund that there was a giant bar to one side, serving actual liquor and wine rather than simply blood. And the large orchestra sat on a dais at the front of the hall along a full wall of mirrors that reflected the dancers swirling in their beautiful finery. The hall was dripping with extravagance and splendor, all made more intriguing with the guests in masquerade masks. In between those guests, liveried servers carried platters of hors d'oeuvres and long-stemmed glasses of champagne.

"Would you like a drink, my love?" I asked Jules.

"Please."

I led her through the crowd, all vampires and a few warlocks and witches I didn't know. I sensed a grim or two among the throng as well, but no recognizable faces yet. Though they all wore masks, I'd know friends or foes from their magical signatures. I still knew some of the coven leaders of England through my parents, but none seemed to be here.

When we arrived at the bar, I noticed several guests hovering to one end.

"Is that absinthe?" asked Jules.

There were several absinthe bars in New Orleans. I'd even wanted to take Jules to the one in Pirate's Alley someday, knowing her love of licorice. But she wasn't going to drink this.

I stood behind her, hands on her shoulders, and whispered down, "That's not the kind of absinthe you want."

"Why not?"

The ornate glass canisters were oversize crystal decanters with silver spouts. A bartender had three spouts running on all sides, each dripping green liqueur. Beneath the spouts were tumbler glasses with a silver strainer set on the rim and a sugar cube on top of the strainer. The green absinthe dripped over the cube and down into the glass.

"They lace absinthe with vampire toxin at these things."

Her eyes widened behind her mask. "Why? I thought . . ."

She stopped herself, glancing around nervously. I pulled her a little to the side and out of hearing. Though I'm sure some could hear us, the orchestra was loud, and everyone seemed distracted and entertained by ogling each other.

"What did you think?"

She tiptoed up and cupped her mouth close to my ear. "I thought the fun of it was getting the toxin from your lover's bite."

My whole body went rock hard. I had to inhale and exhale a deep breath to keep from carrying her behind one of the velvet screens that had been hung for semiprivate trysts and blood-drinking for partygoers who preferred to not have an audience. All that did was drag in an intoxicating whiff of my woman's scent. I could feel her pulse humming in the air, near enough to taste.

"For me," I whispered softly against her ear, my canines sharp, "it is the only way I ever want to exchange blood for toxin."

"You know, Ruben. You won't need Damon anymore. Or anyone else."

I pulled back enough to peer closely at her. The sincerity shining in those lovely eyes nearly broke me. Once upon a time, I'd only hoped that she'd take me back and give us another chance, and I swore I'd never even mention the possibility of drinking her blood. I'd never take the chance of losing her again.

Never in my wildest imagination did I dream she'd offer it to me freely, even hopefully. It was staggering, the level of trust and devotion she had proven she had for me in that one small act of offering me her blood.

"I have no words for such an offer," I finally said.

That only made her smile brighter.

"Ruben," came a distantly familiar voice behind me. "Is that you?"

Turning, I was relieved to find my father's friend who was the coven leader of Derbyshire, the one he'd mentioned to me a few days ago. Mr. Abrams was easy to recognize as he was thin and elegant and had black hair with a stylish wave of gray in the front that some might think he paid for in a salon. But he did not. He was quite charming and debonair. Even at his age, all the young men flocked to him in the hope that they would be his next blood-host and paramour.

"Mr. Abrams." I shook his hand. "It's so good to see you."

"And you, my boy. I haven't seen you since the turn-of-the-century gala your parents put on in London."

"Indeed. I've been busy in America."

His gaze swiveled to Jules. "I see that. And who might this lovely lady be?"

"Mr. Abrams, please meet Miss Savoie. She is leading the proposal you'll be voting on tomorrow evening."

"Is she now?" He took her hand and patted it like he would a grandchild. Of course, his great-nephews and nieces were all around two hundred years old. "And what's the subject matter of this proposal, young lady?"

"Pleasure to meet you, Mr. Abrams. I'm campaigning for the equality of all supernaturals."

"Are you now? Quite right about that. But what, pray tell, does that mean?"

She laughed softly. "Specifically, I'm proposing that we offer a seat on the High Guilds to our supernatural brethren, the werewolves."

His brows drew together, but he looked pensive, not offended. "And how will we do that with so much violence they reap everywhere? I can't sit down with my secretary without hearing about some other incident from Stonebridge's reports."

Jules and I shared a look, then I added, "We have data and research that proves those numbers are actually on a sharp decline. Jules, tell him about your sister."

She relayed briefly what Violet had discovered and had been doing the better part of this year to help the werewolves control their inner beasts.

Mr. Abrams rocked back on his heels, his champagne glass seemingly forgotten in one hand. "This is all quite revealing news to me, Ruben. I've never heard the like. Nor have my compatriots in Lincolnshire or Norfolk."

Jules practically beamed up at me before looking back at Mr. Abrams. "We plan to present all the data and bring this good news out into the open tomorrow afternoon."

"Can't wait to hear it."

"Mr. Abrams, so good to see you." Edmund cut into our small party. I instinctively wrapped a hand around Jules's waist and stepped back.

"Let me introduce you to someone I think you might like. He's Welsh and has a home in Derbyshire."

I didn't miss the scathing glare Edmund shot me over Abrams' shoulder as he steered him away. I was annoyed, too, because I'd hoped to ask him more about the missing werewolf from Derbyshire.

"Guess Edmund heard that conversation." Jules glanced up at me.

"He most definitely did."

At that moment, the orchestra died down and a svelte black-haired woman stepped up to a microphone on the dais. She was draped in a skin-hugging red silk gown that perfectly matched the decor of the room and the deep scarlet of the roses.

The few dancing couples who'd been whirling to the music paused as the witch began to sing. And did she ever sing.

A haunting melody carried into the room along with the plucking of a harp as the witch sang "A Lullaby of Woe." The cellos and violins joined her voice and the mystical lyrics that warned all creatures of the Witcher out to get them. How he'll slice and dice the monsters in the dark. It was a song from the television show, but something about her words resonated in the air, prickling me uneasily.

As she sang the melancholy tune, her milk-pale arms at her sides, her dark eyes whispered over the room until they landed on me. I felt her warning—menacing and cold—down to my soul. The room was entranced, completely hypnotized, by the scintillating magic tingling against my skin, raising the hair on the back of my neck. I didn't fucking like it.

There was something wrong about this witch. She was using glamour with her siren-like voice, swaying sensually, her hands caressing slowly up to her hips, then back down to her sides. Dancers began again, whirling in flowing, ghostly circles. In the wings, other guests began to sway to the melody, the conspicuous fondling of blood-hosts having already begun.

I squeezed my hand tighter around Jules's waist, pressing my lips to her temple. "She's a Warper witch," I whispered.

"Like Livvy."

"Not just like Livvy. There's something deceptive about her."

"I don't sense that, but I can feel the weight of her glamour."

"I think it's instinctual." My fangs had descended without me even realizing. My inner beast had reacted to the witch, sensing a threat. That bothered me.

Jules placed her hand over mine that splayed over her hip. "Her magic is strong." There was a thread of trepidation in her voice.

"Are you all right?" I asked.

"You don't feel the heaviness of her magic?"

"I do."

Her gaze fixed on mine, her pupils dilated. Not with stress but with another emotion I knew too well. Her eyes dropped to my mouth.

"Juliana—"

"Ruben, let me introduce you to someone," Edmund interrupted me.

When we both turned, it was to find the Warper witch standing at Edmund's side. I hadn't even heard her stop singing. Her magical melody was indeed powerful. The strangest thing of all was that she radiated a similar signature as a grim. Not the same as a grim, but similar enough that her nearness had me instantly thinking of sinking my fangs into Jules and fucking her against the wall. It was disturbing since, in my right mind, I'd never expose her in that way.

"This is my consort, Tatiana."

I stiffened. *Consort?* That was a term vampire kings used a millennia ago for their chosen partner, their favored concubine. Yet again evidence that Edmund considered himself much grander than he was. He needed to be knocked down a peg.

"Hello." Her voice was husky velvet and oozed sex. When she held out her soft, long-fingered hand with black-tipped nails to shake Juliana's, I squeezed her hip to warn her not to touch the woman. She didn't.

Tatiana grinned and dropped her hand, murmuring against Edmund's jaw. "I'm not sure they like me, love."

He had one arm around her waist, pulling her against his side, and the other hand rested on her rib cage. The one on her ribs skated up to loosely cup her breast as he turned his head to kiss her, tongue and all.

Now it was Juliana's turn to stiffen at my side.

"But I like you," he whispered against her lips before turning back to us.

"Where are you from?" I asked the witch abruptly.

"Oh, here and there. Everywhere." She shrugged a shoulder, her skinny strap falling off. She didn't bother lifting it as the bodice of her dress sagged, revealing half her left breast.

It wasn't her wardrobe malfunction that had me so disturbed; it was that grim essence pricking like needles at the shield I kept up against such influences.

"Tatiana is a worldly, powerful woman," said Edmund. His hand trailed from the covered breast to the other one, sliding the red silk down the last inch so that he could expose and fondle her dusky nipple. "Those have always been my favorite kinds." His gaze slid to Jules.

His open fondling would've appeared rude if I hadn't expected it of him. Or if half the party hadn't already descended into open exhibitionism while the rest danced and drank and watched. This type of display was expected at vampire masquerades.

Just as my temper spiked and I was contemplating how Edmund could no longer cast his lecherous stare at Jules if he was headless, my mate grabbed my hand and tugged.

"Come, Ruben. Dance with me."

CHAPTER 23

~JULES~

Sweat had broken out over my entire body. It wasn't the lack of cool air, which was blowing in from one side of the ballroom where the french doors had been opened, gossamer white curtains billowing. It was the thickness of sex dripping everywhere in this room—in the decor, the music, the dresses, the masks, but most importantly, the magic.

It draped the room with a hedonistic urge to fuck. Ruben held me close in waltz fashion, twirling me in rhythmic circles around the dance floor. While I tried to take this moment to cool my blood, everywhere I looked caused my senses to reel and my blood to race, and the steady thrum between my legs only grew.

Ruben whirled me one way where I saw a shirtless man, still wearing his mask, on his knees between his vampire's legs, bobbing his head vigorously. His lover had his head tilted back on the chaise, his mouth agape, fangs exposed.

Ruben turned me again, and I saw two male vampires with a woman braced over a large ottoman. One vampire was on his knees fully naked but for his mask, fucking her mouth. The other man covered her from behind, her black gown up to her waist. He pounded her with ruthless thrusts, while drinking from her throat.

A fresh wave of sweat broke out all over me. Then my gaze landed on the worst.

Edmund sprawled wide-legged on a wing chair. Tatiana was facing him, riding him, her gown up to her waist. Edmund's hands were curled into her ass, guiding her up and down. But his silver eyes sparked brightly as they held mine when he sank his fangs into her throat.

"Look at me," commanded Ruben, his fangs so long and sharp they had altered his speech.

He cupped my cheek and tilted my head upward. "Fucking hell, darling. Your eyes are black."

I imagined they were. The song ended and another began. Strangely, an accordion accompanied this piece. The dancers whirled around us—one vampire drinking from his lover's wrist as they circled—while Ruben cupped my face, worryingly examining me.

"We're leaving." He took my hand, but I pulled him back.

"Wait." I looked toward the orchestra dais.

The mummer playing the accordion was dressed in a harlequin suit, like one might see in an 1800s circus. His face was fully covered by a mask, his head bobbing back and forth to the music. The music . . .

"I know this song."

"What?" Ruben had my body pressed to his so the spinning dancers wouldn't hit me.

"From a vision, Ruben."

Then the accordion player and three female violinists matched their voices to the eerie rhythm of the melody.

"What vision?"

The music seeped into me, and I remembered. "Goddess gave me a vision."

"Come, Jules." He tugged me harder, not stopping this time.

As we wove through the party, I was awarded the view of a vampire masquerade in full debauchery. More couples had paired off on other pieces of furniture, on the wall, another threesome on the rug. I'd even caught sight of Sal with a pretty blonde, taking her on the balcony banister. Right before Ruben pulled me from the room, I noticed Gabriel propping up a wall with no one at all, watching the entire depraved throng, the moans growing as loud as the music. Yet, he stood alone.

Once in the hallway, Ruben swung me up into his arms, cradling me against his chest, which was likely a mistake. My arousal was unbearable, my clit throbbing with need. I opened my mouth on his neck and licked the salty sweat from his skin. He was also suffering like me.

"Fuck," he cursed, shoving open the door of a room on the opposite side of the ballroom. "I can't wait."

I mewled at the feral sound of his voice, squirming against him, sucking on his neck.

Suddenly, I was on my back on a desk, Ruben was between my legs, and my gown was ripped up to my navel.

"Yes, yes, yes," I pleaded, spreading my legs wider for him.

He gripped my thighs and pushed me farther up the large black marble desk. I clutched my nails into his scalp as he sank his teeth into my inner thigh.

"God, yes!" I cried out, my vision hazing with the toxin.

I reached down and slid my panties aside so I could rub my clit, the wetness already slick and dripping.

Ruben growled, pulling one more long, hard draught from my vein, then he unhooked his fangs and licked the wound, spreading his toxin to help it heal. All the while, he whispered adorations and naughty curses.

"I want to suck you and fuck you all night long. So fucking beautiful, aren't you? Destroying me, little by little." He shoved my fingers aside and sucked my clit, sliding three fingers through my embarrassing wetness before pumping inside me.

I gripped his head harder and held him down, thrusting up and rocking against his mouth. But my desire became a beast of her own, wanting to dominate him. Suddenly, I shoved his head away from between my thighs, then waved my hand, pushing him with TK back to the shelf of books. He stared, wild and ravenous and aroused, probably because I'd overpowered him to take control. I wanted to do something I hadn't done in far too long. I pushed myself up into a sitting position, then slid off the desk and onto my knees.

"Oh, darling." He braced a hand against the bookcase to his right as I went for the buckle of his belt. "It's been a long time."

"Too long," I breathed as I worked his zipper.

His finger came beneath my chin and tilted my face up. He stared down with that flinty, molten gaze. "Too long is right," he murmured as I managed to get his cock free and wrap my hand around the base.

He hissed, still holding his fingers gently under my chin. "Open wide, darling. Perfect."

Then he eased inside. I latched my lips around his crown and sucked till I hollowed out my cheeks, holding his gaze. His eyes slid to slivers of silver as he grunted and thrusted forward.

"Yes, just like that. Take me deeper," he growled, his hand sliding to my nape to hold me still while he fucked my mouth and tapped the back of my throat.

I tried to pump my hand at the base where I couldn't fit him all the way in, but he wanted control. He wanted to do the fucking, so I let go and placed both hands on his thighs, peering up from my mask.

"Fucking hell, yes." He widened his stance, cradling his other hand behind my head and slid deeper.

I gagged. He pulled back so I could breathe through it, saliva trailing out, my eyes watering.

"Beautiful," he murmured before deep-throating me again.

I eased one hand underneath, mounding his sac before sliding a finger along his taint to his back hole.

"Goddamn, Juliana." He was all growl and beast, no velvet and silk left in his voice as he fucked my face. And I loved every second of it, a pulse throbbing between my legs.

When I slid my middle finger inside him, he grunted and cursed, then jerked free of my mouth. He gripped me under my arms and hauled me up against the wall of books. Instantly, I wrapped my legs around his waist, moaning as he ripped the crotch of my panties and slid inside me.

He ripped both our masks off. Then his mouth was on mine, his cock buried deep as he clutched me tight and fucked me slow

and deep. He swallowed my moans, then broke his mouth away
to kiss down my jaw to my throat.

"So beautiful, my love," he whispered reverently before delicately sinking his fangs into my throat.

That now familiar sweet ecstasy of his toxin filling my veins
as his body glided inside me pushed me to climax. I screamed up to
the ceiling as he groaned against my throat, lifting gently away and
licking the wound.

"Look at me, Juliana."

I did, seeing all the love and longing and unending loyalty
shining from his eyes, my blood on his lips. Holding my gaze,
he pumped inside me, spreading my thighs wide so he could go
deep. Then he was coming. His face contorted into a grimace of
pain and pleasure, his mouth agape, fangs sharp.

He was so beautiful. And he was so mine.

His groan was long and deep, his grip tightening on my thighs,
fingers curling into flesh. When he finally opened his eyes, he
kissed me deeply. Sweetly.

"I like this position," I teased, breathless.

"I remember," he teased back.

We laughed and kissed a little more with soft pecks and little
tastes. When he finally set my feet back on the ground, we were
both panting as he pressed his forehead to mine.

"I'd wanted to make it to our bedroom, but I just couldn't."

"There was a heady concoction of magic in there."

"At least I managed to get you out of the room."

I laughed, combing one hand into the hair at his nape. "There
is that."

Then something caught my eye. The thin, golden spine of a book over his shoulder.

"Ruben," I whispered in a hush. "My vision . . ."

"What?" He turned to look at whatever I was seeing.

"We had a witch's round right before we left on this trip. And I had a vision. I thought it was Spirit feeding me nonsense or symbolic images. I hadn't even thought about the masquerade until I heard that song by the orchestra. The same one from my vision. And this book was definitely in it."

I reached out and pulled at the book. It tilted out but didn't come away in my hands, then there was a sudden click and whir behind the bookshelf. Ruben lifted me off my feet and traced backward to the other side of the room. Nothing nefarious happened, except that the bookshelf popped open.

Raising my brows, I looked at Ruben. "Edmund has a secret passageway."

"But of course he does. And Spirit led you straight to it."

He took my hand and guided me through the dark opening. It was pitch black. I paused because I couldn't see one step in front of me.

"Ruben, I can't see."

"I can. Just keep hold of my hand. I'll guide you through."

So I edged forward, one shuffling step at a time.

"The corridor is growing a little wider up ahead, but there's some uneven flooring in about three steps."

He slowed for me to manage walking over the lopsided bit. I gasped when my heel slipped, but Ruben caught me quickly and steadied me.

"There's a sharp left up ahead. Grab on to my coat."

I moved directly behind him and clung to his coat, the sound of my breaths coming quickly and too loud in this closed space. Distant and muffled, we could hear the orchestra still entertaining the guests at the ball. Orgy, rather.

Ruben paused, seeming to peer around the corner for any danger.

"All clear. It stops at another door."

I heard him turning a knob. "Is it locked?"

There was a click and the slight creak of a door opening. "No. He wouldn't expect anyone to find his entrance back in the study."

Ruben led me into a room that felt fairly small compared to the study and other parts of the castle.

"Hang on. I see a candle. There's a light on the door but I don't want to turn it on in case it will somehow alert Stonebridge."

"Good thinking."

He lit a three-tiered candelabra. At first glance, it looked like a philosopher's study with more books on one wall, but there were also jars and bottles stacked on a table against another wall.

"Here," said Ruben. "I don't need it."

I took the candelabra as we walked on opposite sides of a large rectangular table at the center of the room. I startled at something tall gleaming in the corner. Horror dawned on me as I walked closer and recognized the upright metal coffin-like cabinet of an iron maiden. When I stepped even closer, candlelight flickering on the favorite torture device of the Middle Ages, I recognized the dark stains on the four-inch spikes lining the interior of the human-shaped torture device. Or rather, kill device.

"Ruben," I whispered.

He was at my side in a few steps.

"Is it a real one? From the ages of the Spanish Inquisition?"

"It is," he answered gravely, then he froze. "Goddess in heaven." He eased closer to take a whiff. "That blood isn't centuries old. I'd say a month maybe."

"Are you saying that Edmund has been murdering people with his iron maiden?"

Ruben clenched his jaw. "There's no doubt he's been torturing and experimenting on them."

My eye caught on some sort of harness on a shelf to my right. I picked it up. "What's this?"

Ruben took it from me and opened the leather straps. The steel cage at the end confounded me.

"It's a muzzle. For a werewolf."

"No." My stomach turned.

"We've heard of the werewolves going missing," he added tightly. "My father mentioned a friend of Abrams' nephew was one of them. There's something else. Come see."

He guided me around the center table to the far wall. "These books, Jules. This one in particular." He pointed to one sitting out on the center table.

I leaned over. There was no title on the front, merely witch sign etched in gold. Signs I didn't want to see. I swallowed hard. "This is black magic."

"I thought so. I don't know witch sign like you do, but there's a bad essence surrounding these books. My skin is prickling with the stench of it."

I flipped open the book to a page that had been marked with a piece of parchment. My gut clenched, wanting to expel whatever was in my stomach.

"I've seen this before. Once." Shaking my head, I could pick out bits of the old tongue, but not much.

"What's that language?"

"It's ancient witch tongue. It isn't used anymore."

"Why not?"

"It was written and created by one of the first covens, thousands of years ago. It's a secret language, a dead one now. It tied words with the Goddess's magic. It was a good language until one witch used it for evil, then it became tainted. She conjured and bound the Goddess's magic with unearthly powers. She wrote dark spells. When she stitched them with witch sign and bound them with sacrificial blood, even the Goddess couldn't thwart the evil she'd awakened." I flipped to another spell, my fingers shaking. "So the language was banned, but as in all wicked things, some survive and live on."

I shut the book and closed my eyes, chest heaving with terror. "You may know one of the spells that survived. It was cast by the witch Esmeralda with her dying breath, which created and cursed the first werewolf. But there have been even worse hexes whispered over time, stories passed down from witch to witch. Like some using spells to try to raise the dead, to create their own army. But the worst"—I backed away from the book and pointed to it—"are the ones not yet created but can be."

"What do you mean?" Ruben gripped me by the upper arms, concern etched in his brow.

"There are some spells of creation." I licked my lips. "Meaning creation of anything, of any kind of spell a witch can dream up. You only needed two things."

Fear shook me to the core at what was dawning on me. Edmund, and most undoubtedly his Warper in the ballroom, were involved in something very dark. Unfathomably vile.

"What do you need?"

"The witch sign and ancient tongue of creation in that book." I nodded to the tome, fearing that even pointing to it now might somehow tie its contents to my soul. "And the fresh blood of a sacrifice."

"A willing sacrifice?"

I shook my head. "Evil doesn't demand the blood be offered. Only that it's taken and used."

We both swept the room, catching sight of other instruments—scalpels, saws, binding cuffs, chains attached to handcuffs. Neither of us needed any imagination on what they might be used for. There were other dark stains on the center table I hadn't noticed until I'd set the candelabra atop it. And I could only imagine what poisons were in the jars on the wall. In one swift glance, I recognized the toxic leaves and petals of foxglove, oleander, larkspur, black hellebore, and the ironically pretty yellow blooms of the paralyzing woodbine.

I thought of Isadora and how her beautiful spells could amplify the medicinal effects of purple pansies into powerful pain-relieving potions. Similarly, the powerful dark spells like those in that book on the table, combined with the contents of the jars on the wall, could kill a small village.

"Ruben, his glamour is so thick here. It's because he's hiding the aura hovering around this place."

"You're right." He snatched the book and put it in the pocket of his inside jacket. "I've felt the ward spells but wasn't sure why he was using them. Now I know. He's disguising the aura he's created over Wulfric Tower. To hide what he's doing with his Warper witch. Come here."

He pulled me into his arms, guided me out of the room, and closed the door before he traced back out and into the study. Still dark and no one there. He closed the secret entrance, then picked me up again.

"Close your eyes."

Right as I did, he traced lightning fast up the stairs, the orchestra music growing closer, then fading away as he stopped inside our bedroom and slammed the door closed.

"Get changed. Comfortable clothes."

He locked the door and started undressing right away. He removed the book and set it on the nightstand. I hurried to the small dresser on my side of the bed where I'd stored my clothes and quickly changed into jeans and a sweater.

Sitting on the trunk at the end of the bed, I pulled on socks and shoes. I asked, "What's the plan?" Because I knew he had a plan.

When he glanced up after pulling on a black cable-knit sweater with his expensive dark jeans, he looked concerned. He shoved on some lace-up boots, then stood straight. "Do you mind if I take the lead on this?"

I snorted a cynical laugh. "Don't even ask that. This isn't the case of a hex gone bad or a political maneuver. We're in serious danger, and I trust you, as my partner, to lead the way."

He stepped closer and cupped my face, his thumbs tracing my cheekbones, his expression adoring and tender.

"Whatever you decide," I whispered, wrapping my fingers around his thick wrists, "whatever you tell me, I'll do. You're my partner. My mate. We're in this together."

His throat worked as he swallowed hard, but then the affection vanished behind the facade of all-business Ruben.

"I'm going to find Roland and Sal first. Then we're going to get the fuck out of here. Use your TK to push that wardrobe in front of the door, and the trunk too. Don't open the door for anyone but me."

"Got it."

He pressed a swift kiss to my lips, lingering for only a brief few seconds, then traced out of the room. As soon as he was out the door, I locked it. I pulled my magic forward and then shoved the wardrobe and the heavy trunk from the foot of the bed in front of the door.

I paced past my small barricade, holding a letter opener I'd found in a writing desk. I could use my TK to weaponize any object against an enemy, but there was something about having a sharp object at the ready that made me feel safer.

After only about eight minutes, I heard the shush of soft steps. A pause, then a knock at the door.

"Jules? It's Gabriel. Are you okay?"

Why wouldn't I be okay, Gabriel?

Immediately, I was suspicious. After all, this castle was his family's, and Edmund, the deranged, lunatic host, was his brother.

"I'm fine, Gabriel."

I frowned at my answer. What else was I supposed to say?

He wiggled the doorknob. I stepped closer, holding my letter opener tighter. I could launch this through the air if he tried to push his way in.

"Won't you let me in?"

"No, Gabriel. I won't."

"Why not? Ruben sent me up here to check on you."

My heart plummeted because now I knew he had betrayed his overlord. Ruben wouldn't send him up for me. Ruben said not to open the door for anyone, and I wasn't a fucking idiot.

I was about to answer when there was suddenly a barrage of crashing noises on the other side of the door, and I could hear Gabriel making grunts and sounds of anguish. I couldn't make out whoever else was there, but the crashing sounds continued as objects hit the wall, making all kinds of noise.

"Ruben! Is that—? Ow!"

I dropped the letter opener and stared down at my arm where I'd felt a sharp sting. I couldn't see through the fabric of the sweater what had bitten me, what had caused this ripple of pain through my limbs.

"What . . . ?"

My vision grew hazy. The pain receded, a dull numbness sweeping through me. I couldn't feel anything. The only thing I could do was suck air in and out of my lungs.

"Sorry, sweetheart."

I spun to find Aaron standing behind me, a syringe in his hand, still in his tuxedo from the party but no mask. His malicious grin told me he wasn't apologetic at all.

"No," was all I could manage to eke out of my quickly numbing lips.

His grin disappeared as he bared his fangs and lunged for me. Even as I stumbled sideways and caught myself on the bedpost, I swatted my other hand in the air, sending Aaron flying across the room, where he hit the wall with a heavy thud and a crack of wood before falling to the floor. I'd sent him flying so hard, he'd left a rough imprint in the now splintered wall, paint and plaster flaking to the floor, exposing the thick timber that comprised the walls of the castle. He now lay on his side, eyes lifeless, a pool of blood pouring from his head.

Another wave of numbness bled through me. My knees buckled, and I fell to the floor. I rolled to my back, unable to feel anything at all now. Dizziness blurred my vision.

"What's happening?" I murmured to myself.

While I realized I'd been drugged with some sort of paralyzing potion, the sound of soft footsteps on carpet alerted me someone else had entered the room. I still didn't know how or where they'd come in. Then Gabriel was standing over me. He knelt at my head and brushed the lock of hair from off my face that had fallen there.

"Just relax."

I trembled, my voice quivering, lips numb, as I asked, "Why?"

He simply smiled down at me. "I need you out of the way. It's nothing personal, Jules." He glanced across the room where Aaron had fallen. "Glad I ordered him to do the hard part. Looks like you shattered the back of his skull. Thought that might happen."

I felt no remorse for Aaron, but Gabriel's indifferent manner about his death flooded my body with cold. Or maybe that was just the spelled drug.

"You are quite the powerful witch," he admitted.

He moved around to my side, pulling something from his jacket. Another syringe. I flicked my fingers but nothing happened. My TK was gone. When I tried to pool my Siphon power, I felt nothing at all.

I whimpered as he stuck my arm with the needle. "Shhh," he whispered, like one might to calm a child. "Best you go to sleep for a while."

I tried to protest, but I couldn't even form the words. Against my will, my eyes slid closed as Gabriel lifted me into his arms.

CHAPTER 24

~RUBEN~

"Where the fuck is Sal?" I asked as Roland and I rushed back upstairs to the third floor.

I hadn't seen Gabriel either, but my focus was on getting my men upstairs so we could escort Jules to some safe place and then deal with Stonebridge. Sal had likely gone off somewhere with that blonde he'd been with on the balcony as we left the ball. But I couldn't put out a fucking search party or let on that I was gathering my men to get the hell out of here.

I didn't mention to Jules that I'd heard the howling werewolves again before the party. And after finding that harness in the mad scientist's workshop downstairs, I could only imagine what had made those werewolves go rogue and why they were circling his property.

I might've managed to trace her to safety if we'd gone straight from the study, but there was also a chance I could've been attacked by a feral rogue, hopped up on whatever-the-fuck potion Edmund's witch had injected him with. Werewolves were eight-to-ten-foot monsters with five-inch claws and razor-sharp teeth and jaws that could crush a skull like a walnut. Whether we traced or took a car, a werewolf could still stop us either way.

If I'd been injured or worse by a rogue, Jules didn't have the capacity to trace away. She'd never outrun a werewolf. Especially one that had been magically altered with blood spells. The thought turned my veins ice cold. No, I had to get my men to help me in case one of us fell while trying to flee this fucked-up place. But now, it looked like it was just Roland and I because I couldn't fucking wait another second. My instincts were urging me to get out *now*.

I was also sure why Tatiana reeked of darkness. It was a symptom, or consequence rather, of practicing black magic. Once we got Jules safely away to Bamburgh, for I felt that was the closest and definitely the safest place to leave her with the Highland clan, I'd come back for Sal and deal with Edmund.

"Sorry, sire."

"Don't be. It was my fault. I knew what vampire masquerades were like. I didn't suspect Edmund would have a bloody Warper witch who could cast dark spells on him, though."

I'd managed to give Roland the shortened story of what we'd found and now suspected.

"We'll get Jules out of here, then come back, sire. Perhaps with a few Highland werewolves to help us."

"Now you're talking."

The thought of having a pack of strong werewolves at my back when I confronted Edmund and his men sent a wave of relief through me. Then I rounded the corner of the landing onto our hallway and froze in place.

"What the fuck—" wondered Roland.

"Jules!" I shouted, tracing to our bedroom door, kicking away the broken chair, table, and vase, all furniture that had been neatly displayed at the end of the hallway the whole time we'd been here. "Jules!" I bellowed again, banging on the door.

Not a sound on the other side. No breath of air from her lungs. No birdlike heartbeat fluttering nearby.

"No, no, no," I muttered as I battered the door with my shoulder.

On the third hit, I cracked and splintered the center of the door, then Roland was right there with me, battering with his bulk.

"Juliana!" I yelled again, knowing full well that I heard no sounds of life on the other side.

How could they have gotten to her?

The door was still intact, the wardrobe piled against the door, that was until, with a final push, Roland and I splintered the door from the hinges and pushed the entire wardrobe out of the way.

"*Stop*," I told him suddenly. "She might be unconscious on the other side."

When we'd managed to get over the broken door and around the wardrobe, she was nowhere, but Aaron was crumpled against the far wall beside the window. Dead.

"She killed him with TK," said Roland.

I traced to the bathroom and jerked open the shower, hoping she was safe and hidden. "Jules!"

Nothing.

"Sire. Your pulse."

I was aware that it was racing at a dangerous speed, but how was I to calm myself when my mate—my love—was suddenly missing in this godforsaken place.

"How did they get in?" I sniffed, finding another scent in the room I recognized. A growl rumbled in my belly as I followed the scent to my side of the bed and to the corner of the wall.

"Sire?" Roland asked, obviously confused why I was now smelling the wallpaper.

"I smell him." I trailed my fingertips along the wall, knocking softly, disbelief and rage washing through my frame. "That traitor was in my room with her."

"Who, sire?"

Then I felt it, the barest difference in sound. Rather than look for the hidden mechanism, I simply kicked in the wall. My foot went straight through and not into another room. With another battering of my shoulder, I knocked through a hidden door and found yet another secret passageway.

I closed my eyes and clenched my fists. I had been so trusting that Edmund was just an arrogant asshole and not a true threat that I hadn't searched our bedroom for security issues. Like secret fucking passages directly into the place where we slept at night.

Roland stood with me, staring down the dark corridor. "I found this on the floor, sire. It has her scent."

I took the silver letter opener gently, sniffing the handle where her scent was indeed strong, then I took off down the corridor with Roland behind me. The passageway led to a set of stairs that wound in circular fashion like a tower stairwell. Finally at the bottom, there was another door. Unlocked.

When I opened it, a blast of cool night air rushed in. We hurried out, looking in every direction. Nothing but the moonlit night.

"This is how he took her out," I mumbled more to myself as Roland and I were already searching the ground for traces of them.

There were no signs of struggle, but their scents were strong. We walked farther out, then both stopped several yards away from the castle wall and knelt where a patch of grass was crushed down.

"She was laying here," said Roland. "And look, tire tracks. They loaded her up and drove back toward the road."

I reached down with my hand, pulled a clump of grass, and then raised it to my nose, inhaling deep. An agonizing revelation cut me off at the knees. I must've made a sound because Roland snapped his head to me.

"What is it, sire?"

I held out my hand with the clump of grass. "The traitor."

He smelled, his eyes rolling white-silver. "Gabriel."

"He'll die for it, Roland."

"Yes, sire. As treason of this kind deserves."

I stood and looked out into the night just as a werewolf howl erupted over the hills. I had a bad feeling about those rogues now that we'd found Edmund's little lab.

"If she's hurt, I'll kill them all. Every last one."

"They could be anywhere, sire. How will we find her?"

I pulled my phone from my pocket and checked the phone tracking app. Of course, Gabriel had turned it off. I dialed a number I'd been given this morning, misdialing once because my hands were shaking so badly. When the werewolf answered, I could barely keep the quaver from my voice.

"I need your help. I need it now and fast. It will likely end in the killing of many vampires. Possibly some werewolves. Are you in?"

CHAPTER 25

~JULES~

I AWOKE TO THE FEELING OF SOMETHING HARD AT MY BACK. THOUGH I couldn't move my neck to see, I was sitting up on the cold ground and leaning against a tree, facing a clearing in some sort of woodland. This wasn't close to the castle because all we could see for miles from Wulfric Tower were rolling empty hills.

I was fully dressed except my socks and shoes were gone, which struck me as odd. But more so was the fact that I couldn't move my goddamn body.

My vision was blurry at first, but then I could make out a torch at the center of the clearing in front of me. No, a campfire of some sort. On an iron tripod, dangling above the fire, was a giant black cauldron, steam rising in snaking tendrils.

"What the hell?" I murmured.

"Glad you're awake." Edmund squatted down in front of me and tucked a lock of my hair behind my ear.

I flinched and instantly summoned my magic to null him but . . .
nothing happened. Just like before I fell unconscious earlier.

"I feel sick." I sucked in a deep breath, unsure whether the nausea was from the desolation of not feeling my power or whether it
was from the poison they'd injected into me.

"That will wear off. And by then you'll feel no pain at all."

"What have you done to me?" I could feel everything, the cold
night air and fear that had me trembling, but I couldn't lift my arms
or legs. I could barely manage to turn my head.

"Nothing that can't be undone. Just a little paralysis charm
that Tatiana cooked up in the lab that you and Ruben were pok-
ing around in."

He seemed calm—too calm—for someone who'd been outed
for practicing spells that were punishable by permanent magical
nullification, at the very least. Depending on what their spells
had done to others, the consequences could be much worse than
that. It could mean execution.

"Are you planning to kill me?"

He laughed and cupped my face, his palm cold against my cheek.
I was furious but could barely muster the energy to focus on what
was happening to me.

"No, sweet dove. Why would I want to kill you?"

"I have no idea. But I also have no idea why you drugged me
and dragged me out here in the middle of nowhere." Then a new
horror washed through me. Perhaps he wanted my powers. "Did
you *drink* from me?"

"What would be the fun of it while you're unconscious?
Besides, we have some business to attend to first."

Some figures milled around in the dark near the cauldron and fire pit. A cloud moved off the moon, illuminating standing stones around a stone altar at the center of the clearing. A flash of moonlight revealed that Tatiana was naked, but then she moved into the shadows on the far side of the stones.

Stones are old, stones are cold, but blood is colder.

Violet's nonsensical words from the witch's round flitted back to me. Now, they made much more sense. All of it had to do with blood spells and ancient standing stones. My own vision about the cauldron, about the vines and feeling smothered. It was about this moment.

A shadow emerged from the woods off to the left. Gabriel carried a body slung over his shoulders. My heart lurched as I tried to see who it was, but I could barely make out the shape of a tall man's body as Gabriel lay it beside the steaming cauldron. My chest squeezed with anguish, knowing the pain Ruben would feel when he realized Gabriel had betrayed him so horribly.

"Edmund." I focused on my captor's cool facade. "Whatever this is you're planning, you have to know it will all end badly for you. For all of you."

"Doubtful. Once Tatiana casts a very special blood spell that I've requested especially for you, then everything will be as it should be."

Suddenly, Tatiana was standing in front of me, her beautiful nude form illuminated by the moon.

"It's time, my king." She twirled her fingers into the locks at the base of his neck.

He continued to observe me but captured her hand gently and turned his mouth to press a kiss to her wrist. "Thank you, Tatiana. We're coming."

She sauntered back toward the altar and her cauldron, her unbound hair brushing her bare hips.

"What spell, Edmund? What do you plan to do to me?"

He planted one knee beside me and scooped me into his arms, then lifted me off the ground. When my head fell back, he shifted and jostled me so that my head rested on the crook of his shoulder, my arms dangling uselessly. Not only was my power paralyzed, I couldn't even defend myself with my body. Not that I could overpower him, but I'd die trying.

"Mmm, you smell so good."

Fighting the rising panic, I repeated, "What spell are you going to do to me?"

"One that will make you my queen, little dove." He gazed down at me as if he truly cared for me. "My perfectly adoring, devoted queen." Then his smile turned sinister in a blink.

No longer able to control the panic, my pulse hammered faster, a feverish cold sweat breaking out over my skin. "How?"

"Well, first we have to get rid of your erroneous notion to put the werewolves on the Coven Guild." His menacing glare remained steady while his words were laced with honey. "They're not our equals, Juliana. They're monsters. I'm surprised someone with your pure and powerful bloodline should think to let them into your own family." He scoffed. "It's repulsive."

Voice shaking, I snapped, "And you're not? Doing ungodly experiments on them? Torturing them? *You're* the monster." I injected all the venom I could since the rest of me, my magic and my body, was completely impotent.

"They don't seem to mind." He shrugged, still carrying me slowly across the clearing, like we were on a moonlit stroll. "As a matter of fact, those experiments helped us find the right combination of ingredients for your spell."

"What spell, Edmund? Tell me." There was no hiding the horror now creeping into my voice.

He stopped within the standing stones, the altar in front of us. Looking down at me, he said very coolly, "The one that will make you forget your devotion to anyone else but me. You'll forget your need of home, your sisters, your family, the werewolves. But best of all, you'll forget all about Ruben. You'll want *only* me."

Trembling, my cold breath exhaling in white puffs, I whispered, "You're mad. I'll never forget them. Never."

He laughed, his canines long and razor-sharp. "So naive, my pet. You don't know the power of blood spells." He lay my body down on the cold stone.

Stones are old, stones are cold.

"If you want my power, just bite me and get it over with. Take it!" I screamed. "I don't fucking care! Just don't take my will away. *Please*. Don't take my family, my—"

Ruben. Dear Goddess. Don't take him away from me.

Behind him, Tatiana stood near the cauldron, murmuring words of ancient witch tongue, undulating her hands over the bubbling brew, now glowing as green as her skin.

"Settle down." He placed a hand right beneath my throat on my chest. "When we're done, you won't feel any of this. I don't want your power, Juliana. Not in that way. I want you by my side. The most powerful Siphon witch on record in America. You should be mine. My bloodline is the oldest of the vampire overlords in the United Kingdom. With you by my side, I'll finally be what I should be. A vampire king."

"*No.*"

The word was small and paltry and didn't convey the deep-rooted terror coursing through my shaking body, but it was all I could manage to say. I tried again to summon my magic, but the lock they'd put on it was iron-tight. It felt as if my magic were behind a steel door too thick for me to break.

"Vampire mania?" I breathed out hoarsely.

"My clever queen. Yes. A permanent form of vampire toxin psychosis."

I stared in utter horror, breaths coming faster in the cold night air. A blood spell that would cast me into that hellish psychosis I'd always feared. He'd strip me of everyone that mattered to me: my parents, my sisters, my family, my friends. He'd take Ruben away, and in all of their places would be only Edmund. I wouldn't just *want* him. I'd die and kill to have him, to keep him.

Bile churned in my gut.

"*No.*" A tear slipped from one eye and into my hair.

He leaned closer and trailed a finger across my forehead and down my nose. "There now, sweetheart. Calm yourself. Soon enough, the suffering will be over, and all you'll want is me, and everything will be perfect and right as rain."

He stepped to the foot of the altar and gripped my bare feet, massaging his thumbs softly into my arch like a lover would.

By now, Tatiana's murmuring of the witch tongue had subsided, yet her body glowed with the green light, her magic pulsing under her skin.

"Hold this," she told Gabriel, handing him a golden goblet.

He'd been standing by her side, and there were also others standing nearby. The men I'd seen around the castle the past few days, all of them standing guard, watching whatever hellish ceremony that was taking place.

Then there were others milling on all fours in between the trees, circling the standing stones in a wide arc. Their yellow eyes and specific magical signature told me they were werewolves. And they weren't on my side. That's when I realized the howling werewolves we'd been hearing were those he'd experimented on, creating his own small army of werewolves by infecting them with his vampire toxin psychosis.

Tatiana bent on the ground with a dagger in her hand. I could actually turn my head enough now to see the person on the ground whose arm she'd lifted.

"Sal," I gasped.

Gabriel glanced at me, but my focus was on Tatiana.

"Don't hurt him."

"That's inevitable, I'm afraid," said Edmund, still massaging my feet like he had the right to touch me.

"Please, don't!" I cried out to the witch.

She didn't even bother to look as she slit his wrist vertically. Gabriel leaned over and caught the streaming blood into the goblet. After a few seconds of filling the cup, he dropped Sal's arm, where he would undoubtedly bleed out if left like that.

"How can you, Gabriel? He'll die! He's your brother!"

Edmund clenched my feet painfully. "*I'm* his brother."

I couldn't take my eyes off Gabriel. "Ruben trusted you," I accused.

"And he still will after this. Tatiana knows a deep memory implantation spell now. Ruben won't remember what happened here at the castle. Except that you chose another man over him. And this time, he won't forgive you."

The gutting picture he portrayed in a few casually placed words sliced me in half. They planned to twist my mind with this fucking blood spell, then use the pain I'd caused Ruben in the past to convince him I'd fallen for another. Whatever foul blood spell that Tatiana knew would supplant our true memories with false ones. And the fact that I'd be utterly obsessed with Edmund after this spell . . . He'd be convinced it was all true and I'd chosen another over him, my own mate.

"It will kill him, Gabriel." My voice trembled.

"I will keep him from going under." Gabriel took a step closer. "I can always call Beverly back to console him."

"Why?" The pain of his easy betrayal was crushing. "Why would you do this to him?"

"To him? I'm saving him from himself. He doesn't understand the importance of lineage, the power of his own birth. He never has. He should've been in charge in New Orleans. We vampires were always meant to rule."

Glimpses of the past twelve years came to me in a blink. Gabriel blocking me from seeing Ruben when he was allegedly too busy. Gabriel sending me back to Ruben's office so that I'd catch Beverly with him. Gabriel often being friendly with Beverly.

"I'll bet you encouraged him to stay away from me all these years."

"For a time, he wanted to go back, but I convinced him it was best to leave you alone. Then he seemed to give up. Unfortunately, when that fucking werewolf Mateo got a hex, you and he started working closely again."

I cringed at the deep loathing in his voice when he spoke of my dear brother-in-law whom I loved as much as my own blood and family.

"And one night," I added, "you decided to take a picture of him feeding from a beautiful woman and text it to me."

For the first time ever, Gabriel's straight mouth tipped up into a smile. "That seemed to help keep you away. For a while." He stepped closer, bracing a hand on the stone by my head. "But you always kept fucking coming back and giving him hope."

The horror of what I was hearing formed an aching chasm at the center of my chest.

"And so," I said softly, peering into his hate-filled eyes, "I'm good enough for your brother, but not for Ruben."

He glanced at Edmund, who seemed content to eavesdrop and massage my goddamn feet like a psycho. "Edmund will keep you in line with Tatiana's many, many concoctions. Perhaps he'll even let me have a taste." When his gaze dropped to my throat, I truly wanted to vomit. "You won't usurp Edmund's throne the way you did Ruben. And finally, Ruben will take his rightful place as the head of the New Orleans coven. From there, we will go much higher."

"Enough," snapped Edmund. "It's time. Back away, Gabriel."

Tatiana dipped a ladle into the boiling cauldron and then poured some of it into the goblet to mix with Sal's blood. She continued to chant the words of the spell in witch tongue. The power swirling within the standing stones began to pulse and build.

Though I could only move my head enough to look down at the altar, I noticed there was no witch sign chalked there. A sliver of hope bloomed in my chest. I saw nothing on the grass or on the stones either. The spell wouldn't take without witch sign to channel into the host, which was me.

As Tatiana sauntered closer, her knowing smile was on me. "I haven't forgotten the witch sign, Siphon. I've cast more spells than you can count," she said sweetly, now standing over me.

Dipping her thumb into the goblet, I realized she'd be putting the witch sign directly on me.

"No!"

"Hush now. It will be easier if you don't resist." She glanced at Gabriel as I thrashed my head. My shoulder and arm flinched for the first time with feeling coming back into them. "Hold her."

Gabriel and Edmund were there on both sides of me, holding my arms. Gabriel gripped a handful of my hair to hold my head still.

Tatiana chanted again, writing a witch sign in blood and brew onto my forehead. The searing pain felt like a spike piercing through my skull. I screamed, my cry echoing into the night.

The werewolves howled, seeming to remember the pain coursing through me.

Tatiana continued with her ritual, adding witch sign to the middle of my throat and to my wrists. She lifted my sweater and added a blood-tainted sign onto my stomach and then finally to the tops of my bare feet.

All the while, the agony increased until I could scream no more. Mouth open wide, the pain was too intense to even breathe as I gazed up at the near-full moon high above us. For what felt like forever, I was only pain and nothing more. It burned as if dissolving my flesh into my bones, and I wondered how my heart could keep beating beyond this torture.

As it started to ebb, Edmund stood over me. He brushed my hair away from my forehead with a gentle touch, his silver eyes full of adoration that sickened me.

"Almost over, little dove. Just one more part."

He opened his mouth and lowered his head to my neck. I had no voice left as my mouth opened in a soundless scream. I could do nothing at all, tears slipping down my cheeks as Edmund sank his fangs into my throat and drank. All the while, Tatiana whispered her incantation. Whispering, hissing voices rose from the cauldron, or from the netherworld or some other plane that was not here. Witches who'd been expelled and condemned for practicing the forbidden arts, for hurting others willfully, now chanted with Tatiana in the circle of stones. The werewolves howled a lament, and that was when my soul started to tear apart.

My concern for my community was cut away first as if with a sharpened blade. I felt it being severed. The loss was acute but not as blinding as the next. The separation of my love for my friends was sliced cleanly. JJ, Charlie, Belinda, Sam, Mitch, and sweet, smiling Finnie. They were there, standing in the Cauldron, looking at me with affection and kindness. Then they were gone. The bar empty, vacant. A void.

I couldn't remember what that sudden aching pain was for when my mother and father appeared in my mind, my little nephews, my laughing niece, my sisters' partners—tall and strong—all smiling at me from our family living room at home. A quick slice, and they vanished. I couldn't . . . what was I trying to remember? Who was here a moment ago? It hurt, it hurt!

"Ahhhh!" my voice came back but was a ghostly cry up into the starry sky.

I trembled and shook, an iron door appearing before me, replacing the moon high above. Was I hallucinating? Then I remembered. My magic was there, right behind that thick door. If I could only—

My sisters appeared: Livvy, Violet, Isadora, Evie, and Clara. They smiled from our witch's round in our secret garden. Clara waved, calling me over to take my seat at the wheel. Then my chest caved in with an agonizing slash, like someone had actually cut out my heart.

"Nooooo!" I screamed. I cried. I begged. "*No.*" A gust of breath left me with excruciating anguish.

Not my sisters. Dear Goddess, save me.

"Please, no," I whispered.

The battering ram against that iron door vibrated through my frame. My magic? Was it near? Yes. She was calling to me. Bellowing.

"Please don't go, my sweet sisters."

They were smiling at me, then they vanished like spirits in the mist, nothing but vapor and air in our secret garden. In my mind, I clawed at the invisible hands reaching inside my soul and taking them away. I clawed and tore but they evaded me, taking those best parts of me. The ones who mattered most. All of them.

Suddenly, I felt bereft, but I wasn't quite sure what for. There was something missing, something wrong. Terribly wrong. But it was just out of reach. I should *know*.

What was I missing? Why did I feel like a hole had been punched through my chest?

"Ruben," I called, the only one I could think who could help me find what I'd lost.

But no one answered. Only the whispering chants of witches long dead and gone and Tatiana answered my desperate cry.

Ruben appeared in my mind, stunningly handsome and so beautiful my heart ached. He gave me that tender smile and soulful look that made me love him even more. Why was he here and why was he so sad?

Then I knew. The monster wanted to take him away from me. The witchy whispers grew louder. The wind stirred and whipped through the circle of stones.

"You can't have him," I promised, curling my nails into my fists until I felt the stickiness of blood in my palms. And when I did, I gouged my nails deeper until I felt it drip off my fist onto the stone altar beneath me. "No one will take him from me."

The battering at the steel door grew louder in my mind, entwining with the monster yelling at the beautiful, chanting witch.

"Hush, Edmund!" she yelled, rushing to my side and putting her bloodstained thumb on my skin—my hands, my chest, my cheeks.

When she looked down at me, her eyes glowing green, I trembled at the pain still rocketing through my body. But I managed to speak what was left of my broken heart. "You will not take him from me. I'll die first."

"So be it." She chanted louder, her bloody palm on my forehead and a hand on my chest, the agony piercing me to the stone.

I couldn't breathe. I wouldn't survive.

That iron door creaked and broke from its hinges, magic flowing lavalike through my veins as the invisible hands encircled my throat and bound my hands and tried to tear and grasp with claw-tipped nails the very heart of me. My mate. My sweet love.

Ruben began to vanish, becoming as ethereal as the ghosts haunting this glen who were stealing him away from me. Their power was so great, so oppressive, so sinister, it wanted the blood spell to work. It needed it to work, the darkness wanting sway in this world. But I wouldn't give up. I was far more powerful than they understood. They would soon know.

I squeezed my fists even tighter, my own blood dripping onto the stones.

A banshee-like cry ripped from my throat as if it wasn't my own. My back bowed, and my spine and neck arched with intense, bone-breaking pain. Magic collided inside me. I could see the witch spirits encircling Ruben in my mind, tearing at him, trying to pull him apart and out of my soul where he belonged.

The monsters desperately wanted to take him away from me, but I couldn't let that happen. I'd never let that happen again. They didn't understand. No one would take him away from me. He was mine, and I was his, and nothing could sever us again.

"Never again." My words were puffs of white air, hardly breath at all.

Then I screamed and screamed, the altar seeming to float upward, the moon drawing closer. No, it didn't *seem* that way. We *were* floating away. My magic throbbed and rippled, vibrating the stone beneath me, lifting us away.

The claws turned from Ruben onto me, ripping and ripping, tearing my skin and my soul to shreds. But I only smiled, my limbs and body falling lifeless to the cold stone.

Stones are cold, but blood is colder.

I petted the stone beneath me, watching the moon draw closer as if the Goddess was indeed watching over me, taking me into the cradle of her comforting arms. They wouldn't take Ruben from me. Not him. I'd go to the Goddess first.

The hissing chants and whipping wind continued. There were howls in the night, new ones I hadn't heard before. Then . . . a distant voice I knew that sang to my soul.

"Juliana!"

See? You can't take him away from me, I told the witches even as their claws sank deeper, trying so hard to tear my will and my heart from me, but I kept it close and floated farther and farther away on magic's wings where they could never reach me.

CHAPTER 26

~RUBEN~

I'D NEVER KNOWN TRUE HORROR UNTIL I'D HEARD JULIANA'S AGONIZING
screams through the woods as we traced toward the clearing.
Magnus's man Collin was from these parts and knew where the
closest standing stones were—a deserted set of ruins on private
property. Once we were within a few miles, we left the vehicles
and traced closer, scenting our prey. We knew we were right the
closer we came.

And the closer we came, the greater my fear grew. But it
didn't compare to the reality I saw when we entered the clearing. I didn't stop at vampire speed until I stood at the edge of
the wood so that I could find my enemy and ensure Jules was
safe. She wasn't. She was lying on a stone floating thirty feet off
the ground. That fucking witch stood naked, her arms above
her, screaming a chant, the voices of ghosts rising with her own,
raising the hair on the back of my neck.

"I've got Gabriel," said Roland at my side. "You get Edmund."

In under a second, we were there inside the standing stones. That's when I saw Sal lying on the ground, blood pooled around him, body lifeless. Edmund stood inside the circle, his head tilted upward toward Jules like everyone else, until Magnus and his werewolves tore into the circle, cracking the necks of eight men and shaking their heads loose from their bodies before Edmund had even turned to see what was happening.

I was on him, pinning him to the ground, my claws out and in his throat on either side of the carotid artery.

"Oh, Edmund," I grated with trembling rage, "you have no idea what you've done trying to take her away from me."

His eyes widened as it finally dawned on him who had him on his back with claws inside his neck, inches from severing his carotid. The next step would be pulling his head from his spine.

He laughed, the maniacal fool. "You're too late. Can't you see?" He pointed toward the sky. "It's working. My toxin is in her blood. She's already mine."

"You *bit* her?" My timbre had deepened, my vision hazing, my very being falling to that feral place where only the beast inside me lived.

"How else can I make her my queen?"

I'd wanted to make this painfully slow. I'd wanted to draw out his agony to satisfy my carnal need to hear his pain, but it was too much.

I dug my claws in deeper. The roar of rage filled me so completely, it sucked away all thoughts but death. My voice came out a trembling whisper. "Too much, Edmund."

Before I could gouge out his artery, he traced from beneath me, leaving a chunk of his neck in my hand. Unfortunately, he hadn't sliced through his own artery in getting away.

Without a thought, I reached out with my hand. It was instinctual, a subconscious action driven by something more powerful deep inside me.

"Stop," I commanded with cold finality.

A whistle of magic pulsed through my body and shot like an arrow toward Edmund. He was a blur, tracing fast, and getting away. Suddenly, he stopped and stumbled on an agonizing scream. For a split second, I stared at my hand, processing what I'd just done.

It was Juliana's magic coursing through me. Her power that had helped me stop the murdering, kidnapping villain from getting away. I'd just siphoned all of his magic from me. He could no longer trace, and he'd lost all of his vampire gifts. I could've simply used telekinesis, for I felt the power of it inside me as well, but I wanted to end him with my own hands.

The thought that even now Juliana was with me, aiding me, her pure, scintillating magic a bright flame in my blood, filled me with strength and resolve.

He was at the edge of a clearing, leaning against a tree, holding on to his bleeding throat, no doubt wondering how he'd just lost all of his magic in a blink. A new surge of fury coaxed me forward. I stalked across the open clearing in long, unhurried strides.

"You can't get away from me," I promised him.

All the while, there were snarls and howls and cries filling the night, feeding my beast's need for blood and carnage and savage punishment.

His head snapped in my direction, his eyes glowing silver. He bared his fangs, but it was all for naught. He was already bleeding out.

"Now, now, Edmund." My voice was a sharpened blade. "You're going to ruin all my fun if you die from blood loss."

He hissed, but he couldn't walk but a few feet before he stumbled and fell again. He was already faint and weakened, leaving a trickling trail of his rank blood behind him. He clutched the knotty roots of an oak, his gaze shifting sideways right as I was knocked to the ground by a growling, slobbering werewolf.

I had both hands on his throat, keeping his snapping jaws away from my face. He was barely taller than me in wolf form, which meant he was likely a boy just past puberty. One of the teenagers Edmund had kidnapped and injected his fang mania spell upon.

His eyes were fully dilated with a tiny ring of gold around the irises. His heart rate sped at a dangerous pace, like he was intoxicated—or fang-spelled.

Edmund gurgled with laughter. "Like my pet?"

Furious that he'd made werewolves into nothing but his crazed watchdogs and knowing it wasn't their fault, I refused to hurt the pup. It might even be Abrams' nephew's friend. He was someone's child who'd been abused and tortured and twisted to do Edmund's will.

I shoved the beast several feet away. Before he could spin and snap at me again, I traced through a thicket, keeping my speed slow so the werewolf pup could keep up. I quickly found what I needed, grabbed it, and then leaped up onto the branch of a tree.

When the gangly werewolf loped beneath me, I leaped down with the stone, hitting him precisely in the head where I knew it would knock him out. It did.

Leaving the unconscious werewolf behind, I returned to the grove where I'd left Edmund, fear gripping me hard that he'd somehow gotten away. But he was still there, fading, his eyes on the circle of stones. The platform with Juliana still floated high above.

My concern for her urged me to be done with this motherfucker. I strode with quicker steps to the foot of the tree where he still clung to the roots, his entire white tuxedo shirt that he'd left on from the masquerade soaked through with crimson. I pressed a foot to his chest and stared down at him. His glazed eyes finally shifted away from the circle of stones and up at me.

"I warned you, Stonebridge. If you touched her, I'd rip your head off. And I meant it."

His mouth slid into a gruesome smile, blood trailing from one corner. "It was worth it. My reign would've been—"

I sliced his throat, cleanly severing the artery this time. I refused to listen to any more of his insanity.

"You weren't a king and never would be," I told him as his eyes grew glassy with death. "But she *is* my queen. And no one will take her from me." I grabbed hold of his head, then twisted and pulled till it came loose, dropping it with the lack of reverence he deserved.

Instantly, I rushed back to the circle of stones to find Roland at Sal's side, his wrist to Sal's mouth. I could hear the faint thump of Sal's pulse from here. Gabriel was dead on his other side. A twinge of pain twisted my heart at his betrayal, but not his death.

The witch was cowering on the ground against a standing stone with a growling Magnus keeping her cornered. I could vaguely hear his men handling the others in the woods, but my attention was above me.

She was too far away, floating on that slab of stone. My heart twisted with fear.

"Juliana!"

The witchy whispers still filled the circle of stones, weaving in and out and around. I stormed over to Tatiana, took her by the arm, and lifted her roughly.

"Make them stop! Those fucking witches. Make them stop!"

The arrogance was long gone from her pale face, seeing her protector decapitated in the distance.

"Make it stop or I'll feed you to the wolves who you tortured and scarred for life," I ground out with a lethal promise.

"Turn the cauldron over," she said shakily.

Magnus, in his ten-foot werewolf form, loped over to the cauldron and sent it flying with a swipe of his giant paw. It overturned and landed topside down. Tatiana chanted something I didn't understand three times.

The wind died. The witch's howls stopped. The air grew frighteningly silent. Then the slab of stone with Juliana on top of it fell from the sky.

My heart lurched. I flew toward the falling stone. Magnus and Collin were there first, catching it halfway down. Roland and I braced the sides as it lowered.

"Heaven save us," murmured Roland.

Magnus huffed. Collin rumbled a growl. For a moment, I froze, barely able to breathe, stricken with horror.

There was blood all over her—her own blood by the scent saturating the air—soaking through her sweater and jeans.

"Sire?" Roland's voice was a hoarse hush.

I knelt and pulled her into my arms. Her birdlike pulse thrummed swiftly, like a hunted animal who's found a hiding spot from her predator.

"I've got you, love," I murmured as I gently lifted her into my arms, her deadweight both unsubstantial and too heavy.

"It's all right now, darling," I whispered against her temple as I stood. "I've got you."

"Magnus," said Roland, "can you take care of this? We have to get Juliana and Sal to healers at once."

I vaguely heard a growl. He must've agreed with a nod or something. I wouldn't know, because I was standing there with my entire world in my arms, bleeding and unconscious.

"Sire. Let's go."

Roland had Sal over his shoulder. His calm presence got me moving. We traced away from that nightmare. But some part of me whispered that my nightmare might have just begun.

CHAPTER 27

~RUBEN~

"It is my love that keeps mine eye awake. Mine own true love that doth my rest defeat, to play the watchman ever for thy sake. For thee watch I whilst thou dost wake elsewhere. From me far off, with others all too near."

I closed the book of Shakespeare's sonnets and set it on the nightstand. "How long do you want me to play your watchman, my love?"

I held her delicate hand in mine and stroked my other hand down her arm to wrap around her wrist so I could feel her pulse. It comforted me to feel the strong beat. "I'll play watchman forever if you like. But I'd rather have you here."

I trailed my fingers up her arms and over the raised marks that we'd found covering her entire body that were quickly healing. Except for the slightly raised flesh in the shape of nail scratches all over her, she seemed well. But she would not wake.

I clasped her hand in both of mine and pressed it to my mouth. "I miss you," I confessed for the thousandth time. "So desperately. And I need you to come back to me." The hollow helplessness expanded. "Please don't leave me alone any longer."

Bowing my head, I pressed her hand to my forehead and prayed for her to return to me. I'm not sure how long I was like that when I heard three people coming upstairs and my mum's soft voice.

"He won't leave the room. Won't sleep. It's been three days. I can't even get him to drink a glass of water."

A growl reverberated in my chest at the smell of a virile male vampire, but I instantly snuffed it, recognizing my best friend's scent and his mate.

I stood as the door opened. Isadora stepped inside first, and instantly closed the space between us and enveloped me in a tight embrace.

I went rigid and unresponsive, then she said, "She's okay, Ruben. Violet has seen it."

I crumbled, my body bowing, arms going around her. I squeezed my eyes shut as her healing magic bled into my body, soothing the empty, dark place that ached for solace, for comfort. Tears sprang to my eyes. I tried to swallow them down, but I'd been holding it all in for so long—my fear of her never returning, of leaving me all alone forever.

"She won't wake up," I whispered, allowing Isadora's healing balm to seep into me further, a welcome respite from being so afraid since the moment I stepped into our bedroom at the castle and found her gone.

After a moment, I pulled away and wiped my eyes with my sleeve, clearing my throat and turning to look at Jules.

"She's completely unresponsive. She seems at rest, but not even a flicker of movement other than her breathing steadily."

I'd already told her this once when I called them after getting her back to London and Eleanor had sent in a healer. The healer didn't know what had happened to her when she was under the spell, and neither did Isadora. But when I'd told her that Jules had cut her own palms and let her blood fall onto the stone altar during the spell, she said that was her way of fighting what was happening to her. It was a good thing. At least, that's what we'd thought.

Isadora had a hand on my arm. She gave me a squeeze and looked up at me. "Go with Devraj. You need to rest."

"I can't." I shook my head. "If she wakes even for a second, I need to be here."

"Ruben," she said sweetly, "I promise that if she wakes for even a second, I will come and find you."

"Come with me, brother," said Devraj with a hand on my shoulder. "Let's get some fresh air for a minute."

Staring at Jules, I gulped hard, unwilling to admit my irrational fear that, if I left, she might disappear from me altogether.

"I'm going to sit with her and give her my healing spells," Isadora said softly and reassuringly. "If there's any change at all, if even a finger twitches, I'll call you."

Devraj urged me toward the door, and this time I let him guide me out into the hallway. We'd put her in the bedroom I kept as my own when at my parents'.

"How about a drink, brother?" asked Devraj as we made our way downstairs.

"That sounds divine."

"I'm sure it does."

It was late afternoon. Mum was in the kitchen, cooking potato soup, one of my favorites from when I was a child. She was trying everything to tempt me from Juliana's bedside. I felt a little guilty for refusing her at every turn.

"Your father has a nice bar set up in the den."

"He does," I agreed, following him into the small den where my father liked to make himself a Scotch and watch the sun set on a small patio overlooking a park of trees to the west.

Devraj made us both a drink, and we sat on Father's patio. The cool air at dusk actually did soothe me. I closed my eyes for a moment, drink on my knee, wishing yet again that I'd never taken her to the north. Because of my arrogance, I'd convinced myself that I could protect her from anything. But I had been wrong.

"Stop it," said Devraj.

I opened my eyes. "What?"

"Beating yourself up. That's enough of that. You look like hell."

I sipped my drink. "You look quite well."

As he should, recently married to his mate and having spent several weeks loving her daily, nightly, in the south of France.

"It wasn't your fault, Ruben," he tried to assure me.

But it did no good. The guilt wouldn't leave me with a few paltry words. "If it had been Isadora, you'd be flagellating yourself hourly."

"Look, Ruben, how do you think I feel that Gabriel had been betraying you all along? And I, a Stygorn, had never detected his deceit. It's my job to sniff out traitors and villains, and I never even considered that he could be in league with his brother's delusions of grandeur of returning to the days of vampire rule."

Gabriel's betrayal cut deeply. He'd been a trusted friend and he'd been at my side so long. But he'd fallen into the trap that bloodlines and legacy were more important than compassion, humanity, and equality for all.

Interesting that it was Jules who'd taught me this lesson more than anyone. When she'd broken up with me twelve years ago, I'd still been the arrogant know-it-all I'd always been. I hadn't seen that I'd trampled on her authority at all. It took the gutting slap in the face of her rejecting me because she couldn't trust me with her vulnerability and her power. It was her belief that I might abuse my position as her partner to overstep her that finally made me take a good long look at myself.

Hindsight is a vicious bitch, but an excellent teacher. It took losing Jules to see that I'd been wrong, that I hadn't respected her as I should've, and Gabriel had been the one urging me to let her go. I remembered all the times he stepped in with subtle words of being better off without a witch who didn't understand vampire ways. I didn't mourn his loss, but I grieved that he'd been led astray by his brother and by an archaic way of thinking that had no place in a world where we should all respect the equality of others.

"Any news from your father?" asked Devraj.

"Last night, he said there would be a hearing in London under Perry Baxter's supervision."

In the past few days, the supernatural world had been turned upside down. My father went to Perry Baxter, stepping in for me to tell my side of the story. I'd been told not to leave the country and was essentially on house arrest since I'd admittedly murdered the High Coven Guild leader of the north.

Perry Baxter and his warlocks, witches, and vampires on staff had been investigating everything that had been going on up north, quickly finding any allies that Edmund had and who had been using his witch Tatiana to spread her dominant evil through blood spells. Magnus and his men had returned to Scotland but had been in open communication with Perry, telling all that they knew of what had happened the night of the vampire masquerade as well as the kidnappings and disappearances of young werewolves and other supernaturals used in Tatiana's experiments the months before.

Thankfully, Magnus and his men had managed to subdue the rogue werewolves who'd been under the witch's fang mania spell without killing any of them. Healers and hex-breakers were working around the clock to try to remove the spells and bring them back to themselves. Now that Edmund was no longer alive, it seemed to be easier and was working. And yet, Jules hadn't come back to me yet.

"Fortunately," I told Devraj, "the witch Tatiana was all too eager to name all the coven leaders she'd performed blood spells for."

"She wasn't ready for a summary execution then."

"No. Apparently, she did have some self-preservation. Now that her *king* was dead. Though they've already had her trial, and Perry nulled her magical powers for good."

Dev sat back, staring out at the golden sunset. "Insane, Ruben. How could Stonebridge think he'd be able to get away with it?"

"How do all megalomaniacs believe they will succeed in their plans? They believe it until they're caught. Well, I caught him."

A growl rumbled in my chest as I sipped my drink, savoring that memory of pulling his head from his body.

"Don't go there, Ruben," Devraj said gently. "You've tortured yourself enough. You need to let go of some of the hatred."

"But she won't return to me, Dev." My voice shook again with the emotion I'd been holding back for so many days. I set my drink down on the patio table, placed my elbows on my knees, and combed my fingers through my hair. "What if she never comes back to me?"

"She will. I promise. Violet scried with all her sisters back in New Orleans. She promises that Jules is safe. That she is okay where she is."

The Savoie sisters and family had already been working on plane tickets when I'd called with news of Jules. Violet had scried to discover if she would be okay and, apparently, that was all it took to calm them from vacating New Orleans and descending on London. That and the fact that Isadora and Devraj were already on their way. Isadora had convinced them to wait and let her do her healing spells first before they rushed over.

"If she's well, why won't she come back to me?"

That, Devraj couldn't answer. We watched the sun slip behind the trees in silence. His presence was comforting, more than I could put into words. Yet my heart still yearned to go to her.

"Take a shower before you go back to her. At least try to look presentable for when she wakes."

Devraj's smile and assurance that she *would* wake made my heart leap with hope. I smiled. "Thank you, Dev. For coming. For being here."

He reached over and gripped my forearm in a warm gesture. "Of course, Ruben. That's what family is for." Though we weren't blood-related, we were close as brothers could be. "She'll be all right. She'll come back to you."

Swallowing the constant fear that she would not, I nodded, stood, and returned to my watch.

~JULES~

"IT'S LOVELY HERE, ISN'T IT?"

Ribbons of gold, pink, and orange glowed on the horizon of the water. I sank my bare toes into the sand, cradling Ruben's heart in my palms as I had been since I'd gotten here. It had beat gently, steadily, and true since I'd carried it away from that storm. Those witches couldn't get him here. Or me. We were safe.

It was so pleasant here. White-sand beach as far as I could see, a gentle breeze in the palm trees, the waves lapping gently at my toes. The bungalow just above the dune where I rested had open doors to the perfect balmy weather.

We often sat there on a lounge chair to watch the sun rise. Interestingly, the sun never rose too high or got too hot. It always seemed to be perfectly temperate in this place. It buzzed with magic.

When I had awoken here, I was curled on the sand with Ruben's heart clutched to my chest. I hurt so much that first day. I didn't move from my soft place on the sand. The breeze caressed me like a mother's hand with soothing sweeps until I felt my magic hum beneath my skin. It was a slow, tender awakening.

On the second day, I'd walked the beach till I was tired, keeping my lover's heart cradled close to mine. We sat and watched the waves roll in, the rhythm the same tempo of the beating organ in my palms.

No one disturbed us. No one could find or hurt us here.

There was something missing, but I wasn't quite sure what it was. Still, I knew that it would come for me whenever it was time. For the past days—I wasn't sure how many—we simply existed, breathed, rested, and healed.

"Ruben," I whispered, "I think someone's coming."

Down the beach, I could see movement. Someone was coming, walking slowly closer.

Rather than fear that someone had invaded our sacred space, I welcomed the stranger, knowing it would be someone important. Spirit assured me this person was good.

It was a woman, beautiful, with long blonde hair, wearing a yellow summer dress that billowed around her knees as she came closer. I stood, holding my heart with a protective arm around him.

The woman smiled at me sweetly, complete joy in her eyes. It was contagious. I couldn't help but smile back.

"Hi," I told her as she drew within a few feet of us, then stopped.

"Hey, Jules."

She knew me, but . . . "Do I know you?"

"Yes. You do." She held out her hand. "Let me show you."

I hesitated, glancing down at the healthy heart in my arms.

"I won't hurt you," she promised.

"Or him either?"

Her brow furrowed as she looked into my arms, then understanding seemed to light her face. "I won't hurt him either."

"They tried to take him away from me," I explained.

She swallowed, her pretty green eyes glassy with emotion. "I know they did, but they failed. You were stronger than them. You protected both of you from them. Just as you've always protected us, Jules. I'm here to take you home."

I glanced up at the bungalow, then at the rolling waves. "But we like it here. It's safe."

"It is. And the Goddess has protected you here, but we need you at home now."

"Home?" I took a step closer, observing her face, the familiar slope of her nose and chin reminding me of someone. A memory flitted across my mind. A greenhouse. Making a candle. Gentle laughter. A rooster? "I do know you."

"You do." She licked her lips, blinking swiftly.

"Are you sad?"

"It's only that we miss you, and we're all worried about you. You're in a magical sleep."

"I am?" I looked up into the sky, which shimmered with gold. "Yes, I am. I knew that. Who put me here?"

"You did. I'm sitting beside you right now in the waking world. I've never been able to do this before."

"Visit someone in a magical sleep, you mean?"

"That's right. But I believe that, because my husband, Devraj, and your mate, Ruben, are so close and we've both ingested their toxin, I was able to find you here."

"Devraj?" I smiled, a flash again of this pretty blonde with a dark, handsome man. "He's a good dancer, isn't he?"

"He is!" She laughed, but a tear slipped down her cheek.

"I do like it here, but I've been missing something."

"Yes, you have. For one, the man who owns that heart in your hands. He's aching for you to come home."

I looked down into my hands where I cradled my softly beating purpose, the entire reason I came here to this place.

"You're waiting for me," I whispered.

"Please take my hand," she begged again, still holding hers out to me. "I'm your sister, Jules. And I'm here to take care of you for once. Come home with me."

A rush of wind whirled around us, stirring some of the sand around my ankles. A knowing and assurance filled me, heart and soul. I reached out my hand and wrapped it around the pretty woman's.

A pulse of magic buckled my knees, and I gasped. She caught me before I fell.

"Isadora?"

She burst into tears while laughing. "Yes, Jules. Come home with me now."

A flood of pictures played across my mind. My sisters, my mom and dad, my niece and nephews, JJ, Charlie, my friends at the Cauldron.

"Ruben." My voice trembled.

"Come. He's waiting."

She wrapped an arm around me and walked me down the beach.

❧

My fingers twitched. Someone said my name. A familiar voice that spread warmth through me, humming along my skin like a magical spell. It was Ruben. His voice was so deep and heavy it scraped right across my soul.

My eyelids fluttered, and I opened them. He was there at my bedside, his expression etched with pain and fatigue, dark circles under his eyes from lack of sleep. He looked terrible, not like the Ruben I knew.

"Ruben."

He sucked in a breath, but he didn't move, simply stared at me with that look of anguish, then he breathed out my name with quiet despair. "Juliana."

My head hurt with a dull throb like I'd stayed up reading too long. My entire body ached with a lingering pain I couldn't identify, but the prickling throb over all of my skin told me it was an aftereffect of magic. Black magic. A flicker of stones and chanting and a bubbling cauldron came to mind, then it vanished, like my psyche was trying to protect me from my own memories. That was fine. I could remember later. I only wanted to look at Ruben.

I heard the door close with someone leaving, and I somehow knew it was Isadora. Her healing signature filled the room.

When I lifted a hand, trying to reach for him, Ruben finally moved, jolting forward. Pulling my torso into his lap, he cradled my head with shaking hands, his long fingers a delicate cage around my skull. His sapphire eyes bright with love and relief. He drank me in, perusing my face like he hadn't seen me in years.

"Thank the heavens," he murmured softly.

But my thoughts were jumbled. They bounced between reality and the safe place I'd been.

"I was lost in another place and so confused," I told him, voice rough with disuse. "But I had your heart, Ruben. I held it close to make sure no one could hurt it. I wouldn't let anyone take it away from me, no matter how hard they tried."

"Oh, Juliana." He pressed his forehead to mine. "My darling. My love." His voice broke with emotion, his whispered words raw with heartbreaking intensity. "You've had my heart in your hands from the very start. You always have."

Pausing, I cherished this closeness. "I have, haven't I?"

"Yes. Always."

"I suppose that's only fair."

"What do you mean?"

"Since you captured my body and soul so many years ago. I suppose it was an even trade."

He pulled his forehead from mine, our faces still inches apart as he looked at me with the deepest love. "How about we keep all parts of each other safe and sound from now on?"

On a thankful breath, I smiled. "I'd like that very much."

Then he pressed my body against his, our hearts beating against one another just as they should. Still weak, I wrapped my arms around his neck and exhaled a heavy sigh. He did the same, rocking me gently, neither of us saying a word as we simply held one another to our hearts' and souls' content.

EPILOGUE

~JULES~

"You're not peeking, are you?" Ruben asked.

"I'm not peeking. I promise."

I laughed because he was being silly about this surprise. I was just glad to get out of the house finally. For the past two weeks, he would barely let me leave the bedroom without carrying me himself. His mom and I had conspired to get him to go to the grocery store for us so we could walk across to Bedford Square Park and enjoy the sunshine without the mother hen pecking around us.

"I'm so happy Ruben has you," his mom had told me that day.

"And I'm happy to have him. I promise, I'm not letting him go this time."

She took my hand and held it tight. "A mother always worries, you know."

"I know." I'd smiled a little sadly. "I've always felt like a mother to my sisters. But also, I want to be a mother as well one day."

Then his mother broke down into happy tears and pulled me into a hug. "You'll be sure and let us know when the wedding will be."

"Of course I will."

There was no doubt there was going to be another wedding in our future. All Ruben and I talked about since I woke up was how soon I would move into his house, how soon we could arrange the wedding. We weren't even engaged, but it was obviously a foregone conclusion. We would never separate again.

"Watch your step," said Ruben, holding me around the waist and guiding me across concrete ground.

It was nighttime, and yet I could see light through my eyelids. "Now?"

"Yes, open your eyes."

I opened them to see a giant Ferris wheel in front of us, lit up brightly with golden lights. Then I smiled. "The London Eye!"

"Our own private ride. I've bought it out for the next hour. All to ourselves."

"That was a waste of money, Ruben. We need to talk about the frivolous way you use your money."

"Come on. In you go."

A man was there to help us into the car.

We sat down, Ruben glued to my hip and an arm around my shoulders as the worker closed the door. A minute later, it gently rose backward, lifting us high above London where it then stopped.

"Look at the Thames." The city lights flickered like fractured glass. "It's so pretty. Clara was right."

"It is." But his gaze was on me, not on the river.

I looked out, soaking in the stunning night view. "So peaceful."

Clara had wanted me to ride the London Eye. I missed my sisters so much. I promised them I'd be home soon, but Ruben had wanted a parade of healers to all sign off on my traveling first. And I'd also wanted to spend more time with his parents before we returned to New Orleans, knowing it might be some time before we could return.

We laced fingers and looked out together, quiet for a moment.

"So Magnus is happy he took the position?"

After all the trials were over and Ruben, Roland, Magnus, and his crew had been exonerated for the executions of Edmund, Gabriel, and those who'd kidnapped me, Magnus had been voted into the first seat of the werewolf clan on the High Coven Guild for the UK. I'd been exonerated first for the self-defense killing of Aaron. We were worried for a time that some of the covens would put Ruben on full trial, but that was until Mr. Abrams came forward and vouched for what had been going on. He had done some investigation of his own after the night of the masquerade and discovered how Edmund had been not only manipulating the coven leaders but also was responsible for the disappearances of two werewolves in his own province.

"I'm not sure that Scottish werewolf will be happy about anything, but he's eager to serve. He'll be the firm hand and strong voice the werewolves need here."

"Clarissa wants us present when they vote for our region in the US. She thinks the others will follow suit. She's already gotten the votes in the Midwest and northwest regions."

"And Declan fell into line as well."

"He did?" I smiled. "I texted Zuri yesterday to tell her thank you for getting us the interview with Magnus."

"I did better than that. I sent her a ridiculously expensive crate of Montrachet wine."

"Ruben." I turned away from the scenery and glared at him. "That was a bit ostentatious. I'm sure a simple bottle would've been enough."

"Well, I hope you don't find this too ostentatious."

Then he lowered to one knee in front of me. My heart tripped faster, and he grinned with that devilish smile because he heard the beat, of course.

He pulled a blue velvet box from his pocket and opened it, revealing an elegant, square-cut yellow diamond in a white gold band, ringed in white diamonds. I knew instantly that I'd never wear it while cooking, but I'd never take it off outside the kitchen either.

"As you know, I'm impatient for you to be mine in every way. I hope you'll consent to be my wife and make me the happiest vampire in the world."

"Yes," I answered without a second's hesitation and held out my shaking hand. "You'll make me the happiest witch in the world."

He slipped the ring on my finger with trembling hands. Then he cradled my face and pressed a sweet, lingering kiss to my lips.

It wasn't enough for me, so I scooped my fingers into his hair and held him while I coaxed his mouth open wider and slid my tongue along his. On a moan, he kissed me back, leaning farther between my open knees.

Then the Ferris wheel started moving again.

I broke the kiss, laughing. "Is our hour up already?"

He rose to his feet with a secretive smile and hauled me up, holding me close and pressing tender, soft kisses to my lips. This time, I was content just to feel him against me, his sweet mouth pressed against mine. Then the wheel stopped, and the door opened.

Still in Ruben's arms, I turned to look out and gasped in surprise.

All my sisters were standing outside, side by side. Livvy, Violet, Clara, Evie, and Isadora beamed at me. Without saying a word, Ruben ushered me out, helping me step down, and then I was running and in their arms.

"You came," I cried, bawling my eyes out as we clustered in a giant group hug like we used to do on Christmas mornings when we were little.

"Of course we came," said Violet. "Ruben said he'd fly us in his private jet, and I wanted a look at what kind of crazy-ass engagement ring he'd buy for you."

"We should probably ask if she said yes," chimed in Livvy.

"Of course she said yes," snorted Evie.

"She did," said Clara, beaming with pink cheeks, weaving us in one of her happy spells that none of us needed at the moment.

"I love y'all so much," I said, crying like a baby.

"We love you too, sis," said Violet, serious for once. "And no one deserves happiness as much as you do."

We hugged and laughed and cried for another minute until finally Livvy pulled away.

"Okay, fine, but I want to see this ring now!" Violet demanded excitedly. "Ruben said he had it designed at some fancy-schmancy London jeweler."

I lifted my hand and smiled again as they ooed and ahhed over the ring. I glanced around, finding Ruben standing next to Devraj, Nico, Mateo, and Gareth, the latter three holding my niece and nephews. Gasping, I tore away from my sisters and rushed over to them.

Celine giggled, Diego gurgled, and Joaquin held out his arms for me. I took him and held him close. "You sweet angels, I missed you so much." I inhaled the sweet newborn scent I'd come to love so much since they'd been born. Then I looked at Mateo. "But I can't believe you flew them all the way over here."

Evie was there with an arm around my shoulders, brushing a hand over Joaquin's brown curls. "It's not so hard in a private jet. Now, if we'd flown coach, I might not have made it."

My sisters were now clustered back around, close to their men. Except Clara. My heart squeezed. I wondered if she'd taken my advice about Henry. I'd have to ask her when we had a private minute together.

"Ruben begged us all to come," said Violet, now pressed against Nico's chest, his arms around her.

"Like he had to ask twice to get you on that plane," Nico added.

"No, I was packed ten minutes after the phone call, but I want it known that Ruben Dubois actually begged us. He's not the begging type."

I looked over at Ruben, whose gaze was solely on me. "Thank you," I said softly.

He walked over and took Joaquin from my arms, who went easily. He looked up at Ruben and placed a palm to his cheek.

"My goodness," I said. "Seems you have a fan. He fusses when most people other than me or his parents or Mom try to hold him."

"He likes me too," argued Violet.

"He is picky, though," agreed Clara.

"Sounds like a Savoie trait," said Ruben. "Now, why don't we all head home. My mum has a small feast planned for all of us. And my father is anxious to meet all of you."

"*Mum*," echoed Violet. "That's so cute."

That reminded me and made me a little sad. "Mom and Dad didn't come?"

"They most certainly did," said Ruben. "Didn't you wonder why my mother has been sneaking out every afternoon the past three days? They've been planning our wedding."

"But I just got engaged!"

"I think your parents want more grandchildren. And mine want any at all." His heated gaze was heavy and intent on me as he looked absolutely magnificent holding Joaquin in his arms.

"You know?" I whispered up to him over Joaquin. "I didn't realize this, but seeing you with a baby is quite the aphrodisiac."

"We can hear you," said Devraj several yards away. Every man there was staring at us with sheepish looks.

"Let's go," said Livvy. "What are we waiting for?"

We all headed toward the several cars idling at the curb for us. Roland and Sal stood beside one, smiling at me. I ran forward and wrapped them in a hug, which was quite the feat since they were so much bigger than me.

"Congratulations, Jules," said Roland, patting me on the back.

Sal squeezed me tight. "Glad you two finally made it official."

"Thanks, guys."

Then we were all piling into cars. Evie took Joaquin since their car had the car seats. I scooted in the back seat with Sal and Roland in the front, happy to feel this familiar feeling of safety. And I was so thankful that Sal had survived that terrible night, but none of us talked about it anymore. We were putting it behind us, slowly but surely. I only spoke to Ruben about it when the bad dreams would come.

I'd never been one to share my feelings with anyone else. I was the kind who liked to keep my burdens to myself. But now I had a partner. An equal. My soul mate. And to keep these things from him felt wrong. He was as much a part of me as I was him. We leaned on each other, and neither of us ever had to carry a burden alone again.

He laced his fingers with mine, raising my left hand to see the ring sparkle in the streetlights we passed.

"I love you," I told him easily, naturally, gratefully.

"I love you too, Juliana." He pressed a kiss to the back of my hand and clutched it against his heart as we rode home together to celebrate and simply be with *our* family.

About the Author

JULIETTE CROSS is a multi-published author of paranormal and fantasy romance and the co-host of the podcast *Smart Women Read Romance*. She is a native of Louisiana, living in the heart of Cajun land with her husband, four kids, her dogs, Kona and Jeaux, and kitty, Betty. When she isn't working on her next project, she enjoys binge-watching her favorite shows with her husband and a glass (or two) of red wine.